Unforgettal

Few writers capture
Jack Ballas. With startli
Ballas's tales are a panorama of the raw beauty and savage glory that is the Old West of a young America.

GRANGER'S CLAIM

Colt Granger defends justice and his Montana claim against the murderous outlaws who are terrorizing settlers in the West—and have their own personal vendetta for Colt. . . .

BANDIDO CABALLERO

Once a Confederate spy, Tom Fallon has found a new career stealing gold from the French and giving it to Mexican rebels. He's becoming a legend on both sides of the border as the mysterious gunslinger Bandido Caballero. . . .

THE HARD LAND

Though Jess Sanford left Simon Bauman for dead, the man is still alive. And there's one thing more relentless than the law: a shamed son with all the wealth of the Bauman family behind him. . . .

THE RUGGED TRAIL

Ex–Confederate soldier Hawken McClure watched as the carpetbaggers took away everything he fought for—and now the ex-soldier for the South is ready to give them a whole new war. . . .

TRAIL BROTHERS

Cattleman Quint Cantrell is about as tough as they come. He's settled down to a solid job and a beautiful wife—but when his adopted family is in trouble, he's ready to risk it all to help them. . . .

WEST OF THE RIVER

U.S. Marshal Roan Malloy, also known as The Gunfighter, is on the trail of a gang of kidnappers smuggling women across the Mexican border to be sold into prostitution. . . .

Titles by Jack Ballas

HANGING VALLEY
WEST OF THE RIVER
TRAIL BROTHERS
THE RUGGED TRAIL
GRANGER'S CLAIM
BANDIDO CABALLERO
THE HARD LAND
IRON HORSE WARRIOR
MONTANA BREED
MAVERICK GUNS
DURANGO GUNFIGHT
TOMAHAWK CANYON
ANGEL FIRE
POWDER RIVER
GUN BOSS
APACHE BLANCO

HANGING VALLEY

JACK BALLAS

BERKLEY BOOKS, NEW YORK

HANGING VALLEY

A Berkley Book / published by arrangement with
the author

PRINTING HISTORY
Berkley edition / March 2002

For information address: The Berkley Publishing Group,
a division of Penguin Putnam Inc.,
375 Hudson Street, New York, New York 10014.

Visit our website at
www.penguinputnam.com

ISBN: 0-425-18410-2

BERKLEY®
Berkley Books are published by The Berkley Publishing Group,
a division of Penguin Putnam Inc.,
375 Hudson Street, New York, New York 10014.
BERKLEY and the "B" design
are trademarks belonging to Penguin Putnam Inc.

PRINTED IN THE UNITED STATES OF AMERICA

10 9 8 7 6 5 4 3 2 1

In Memorial:
To My Love, My Wife—Harriette

1

LINGO BARNES GLANCED at the pile of boulders a couple of hundred yards ahead, looked from them to the copse of pines up the hill above them, and reined his horse toward the trees. Although it was late summer, this Colorado country could heat up pretty quick on a clear day and get cold enough at night to freeze the horn off an anvil.

In the shade of the pines, he pulled his pipe from his shirt pocket and packed its blackened bowl. About to strike a lucifer, he paused, his gaze locked on the trail below. Four men coming from the direction of Durango dismounted, pulled their horses and what looked like a packhorse behind the pile of boulders. Then, two on each side of the trail took up positions in the rocks.

Barnes studied them a moment. Everything they'd done bespoke of a holdup. He shook his head. It was about time for the Chama to Durango stage—but coming from Chama it would carry no gold shipment, and they'd apparently brought a pack horse to carry whatever they intended to take.

Still pondering that thought, the rattle of trace chains and the crack of a whip cut into his thinking. He hooked a leg around the saddle horn, stuck his packed, unlit pipe back in his pocket. Then waited to see what would happen.

The stage rounded a curve, and the team—not yet in the all-out run the driver would whip them into when only a few hundred yards outside of town—slowed of their own accord; two of the men Barnes had seen go into the boulders stood in the trail. One of them held up his hand, palm outward. The driver pulled the team to a standstill. The men now had bandanas tied over their faces.

"What you gents want? I ain't carryin' nothin' but one passenger—no gold comin' from this direction." Barnes heard the driver as clearly as though standing next to him.

"Shut up and hold them horses steady." The bandit who'd held his hand to signal the driver to stop stayed where he was, the barrel of a shotgun pointed at the driver. He looked at the other bandit. "Git the girl outta there an' let's git outta here."

Lingo glanced at what he'd thought to be a pack saddle and from what he could see of it, partially hidden behind the boulders, decided it was a sidesaddle. Then one of the bandits pulled the horse to the side of the stage, opened the door, and pulled a petite, brown-haired girl from it. She swung her reticule to the side of the outlaw's head. He moved his head aside, grabbed the slight figure by the hair, jerked her head down, and snatched the reticule from her hand.

Blood surged up behind Barnes's eyes. He stiffened his legs to dig spurs into his horse and ride down the hill. He stopped barely in time. Hell, he'd get himself and the stage driver killed; maybe the girl, too. He settled into his saddle. He'd wait and see what happened.

The bandit who'd taken the reticule picked the slight form up and threw her into the saddle. "We wuz sent out here to take you off'n that there stage. We done it. Now you be good an' we ain't gonna hurt you, yet."

That "yet" tightened Barnes's neck and chest muscles. It was clear that none of what the bandits had in store for the girl was good, but Lingo figured he'd best be patient.

The bandit who'd stopped the stage, a short wiry man, tilted the shotgun, pulled the trigger, and the driver slumped into the boot. Barnes had no doubt the man was dead. Then, one of the bandits climbed to the boot and made sure the straps were tied securely to the brake. He apparently wanted the horses to stay where they were until someone came along, thus giving the four, and the girl, time to get as far as possible from the scene.

The riders toed their stirrups and, leading the girl's horse, headed up the side of the mountain across the trail from where Lingo sat his horse. Before leaving, a big rawboned rider edged alongside the stage and pulled a valise from its top. Barnes assumed it held the girl's belongings. He stayed in the pines until the five disappeared around a bend into some jumbled rocks. Not until then did he ride from under the trees. The acrid smell of gunsmoke still hung in the air.

He glanced in the direction of Durango, checked the driver, and as he'd thought, the man was dead. He loosened the straps from the brake and popped the whip over the horses backs. They headed for Durango.

He sighed for want of seeing the sights he'd not seen for two months, worked his tongue around his teeth imagining he could taste and smell the whisky, and at the same time wished for a water glass full of the strong liquid. He reined his horse in the direction the bandits had taken. There would be time for the bright lights after he had the girl safely back to wherever she'd been heading.

At the jumble of rocks he dismounted, walked to the shoulder of the farthest one, and peered in the direction in which he thought the outlaws might go. They'd first put distance between them and Durango, then if they had a cabin, or hideout of any kind they'd cover their tracks as well as they could and head for it.

He studied the country ahead. A steady climb showed itself. He pulled the knots from a couple of pigging strings behind his saddle and draped his sheepskin across the saddlehorn. It would not take long for the higher elevations to push the heat aside, although the warmth had been welcome down along the trail.

An hour later, he shrugged into his coat. The bandits had shown no fear of being followed and at first he had no trouble following them; then the going got rougher. In most places smooth rock covered the trail. The only clue as to which way they'd gone was an occasional scrape mark on the smooth surface, then their hoofprints in soft soil would prove he'd taken the right course. The hoofprints dug deeply into the underfooting that had washed from the sides of the mountain; then again they'd ride across rock.

Purple shadows pushed their way from under trees. Lingo glanced at the sky. It would show a clear blue long after dark settled in here, far below the peaks. Should he try riding after dark and risk losing the gang, or should he take the chance that they'd leave the girl alone until they got where they were going? After studying on the kind of men he trailed, he decided to keep going. They'd sit around a fire, and eventually they'd decide the girl could give them that for which they hungered.

He followed until darkness blotted the tracks from sight, but he noticed the bandits followed the easiest path alongside the mountain. They obviously let their horses pick their way. He did the same, but ever so often he stopped his horse to listen, then he'd test the air for the smell of wood smoke.

Finally, his sense of smell and hearing were rewarded at about the same time. The scent of smoke, and loud, boisterous laughter broke the silence. He had ridden too close, but had been riding on one of the stretches of soft soil and had made no noise. The down-slope wind carried the smoke to him, but would also carry the scent of the bandit's horses. He reached around and held his hand over his horse's nose. When he removed his hand, he felt certain his horse would not announce their coming.

Lingo climbed from his saddle, picked his way back along the trail, found a place to tether his horse, then headed back toward the campsite. He'd been in situations like this before and had felt fear pull at his neck muscles. Tonight was no different.

About ten feet from where he'd first stopped, he planted his feet again, firelight shimmered and danced along the top of a huge boulder. If he could see the reflection on that rock, the fire had to be between him and the rock. He found a crack between two boulders and peered between them. He could almost touch the back of one of the outlaws who sat leaning against one of the rocks he looked between. He moved his gaze out into the small clearing. The other three sat, legs crossed, warming their outstretched hands by the fire. Where was the girl?

He searched the area twice before his eyes settled on what at first he'd thought a small pile of rocks. He moved his gaze away, then back. Now he was cetain he looked upon the huddled form of the young woman. Her legs were pulled up tight against her stomach, her hands tied behind her, her feet lashed together. Her head rested on what he took to be her valise. Her eyes blazed between tendrils of tangled brown, almost auburn hair. She lay in plain sight of the bandits. Lingo memorized every inch of the campsite: where each man sat, where their saddles and blankets lay, where they'd stashed their rifles. Each wore a sidegun. At the girl's back, bare ground about four-feet wide stretched. Barnes sighed. He saw no way to free her without being seen. Then he'd probably get them both shot.

The horses. He had to find them—and move them, if he could do so without alarming them and the outlaws. Then he'd worry about getting the young woman out of their grasp.

He slipped back down the trail they'd come in on for a few feet; then began circling the camp. About halfway around, the form of one horse loomed out of the dark, then he spotted the other four, all standing in a circle, their noses almost touching.

Horses were social animals, so he wasn't surprised to find them like that. He left them like he found them, went back to his own horse, gathered the reins in his left hand, and tested every inch of soil in front of him, making sure his pony's shoes wouldn't ring against stone.

Coming in on the downwind side of the five horses, he stroked each powerful neck to quiet them, then placed his own horse among them. When he left he looked for a place, not too far from where they were, but far enough to cause the outlaws confusion when not finding their horses where they'd left them.

About fifty yards from where the bandits had staked them out, he found a small clearing, checked that he'd have a clear path of escape, then went back to where the six horses were tethered.

When he stood in the middle of them, he pondered how to move them without being heard. If he moved all six at once they'd make too much noise. If he moved them one at a time it would take too much time. He decided to take two and make three trips.

He gathered the tethers of two horses when they all seemed to take notice of him. They blew, then moved enough to stamp their hooves.

Standing in the middle of them, holding tether ropes with his left hand, he squatted and drew his Colt .44. Sure enough, one of those in the camp took notice of the noise and came to check.

Before reaching them he bellowed, "What the hell's botherin' you jugheads? Ain't nothin' out heah gonna bother you. Now settle down."

Barnes watched while the man walked to the nearest horse, patted him on the neck, and turned back toward the fire. Lingo willed his tight-drawn muscles to relax. He breathed deeply a couple of times and thanked every deity he'd ever heard of that the man had not counted the horses.

The outlaw, apparently now at the fire, said, "Wan't nothin'. Them bangtails mighta got spooked out yonder alone. They know we're in country where they's many a big cat huntin'." He chuckled. "Reckon they don't wantta make a meal fer one o' them cats."

While he talked, Barnes led two horses from the small bunch, then went back for two more. He left his horse until he led the last two from where the bandits had tethered them.

Then, he worked his way back to the edge of the clear area behind the girl and studied long on what to do next. Not so much what to do, but how to do it. Getting close enough to free the young woman of her bindings without being seen wasn't even a consideration; they'd see him before he got two feet into the area.

He smelled the rich aroma of coffee before one of the outlaws stood, went to the fire, poured himself a cupful, then hung the coffeepot back on a hook hanging from a green bough spanning the distance between two forked sticks on either side of the fire. Blood surged through Lingo's head, his muscles tightened, his lips thinned. He knew how he'd cause them to react—hopefully before they put thought to their actions. Now, should he try to get the girl's attention to let her know to expect something, or would it be best to set hell to breaking loose without warning her? He decided that to try to get her attention would be too risky—then impulse took over.

He pulled his Colt in one smooth motion. Fired into the

coffeepot. It jumped and bounced from the hook; threw scalding coffee on at least two of the bandits and most of the fire. He thumbed another shot into the fire. Hot coals scattered among the outlaws, and the light furnished by the fire dimmed to a dull glow. The bandits all had their handguns in action. Blinded by the sudden darkness after staring into the fire, they threw shots in every direction.

Barnes holstered his .44, sprinted to the small, huddled shape, scooped her and the valise into his arms, and ran like Satan had tied a can to his tail. Every muscle in his body braced against the stunning impact of a bullet. The numbing pain he expected didn't happen. He reached the horses.

Not waiting to free the girl of her lashings, he held her with one arm, grabbed the horn with his free hand and lifted her to the horse. She lay facedown across the horse's neck in front of him. He slipped out of his sheepskin, placed it over her slight body, then gathered the tether ropes of the other horses and went from the small clearing at a run letting his horse pick the way. The girl had not uttered a sound. Lingo marveled at that. Most women would have been screaming and raising all sorts of hell.

He slowed the horses, figuring the bandits would stumble around in the dark not knowing what hit them, then by the time they had it figured out, he and the young woman would be beyond their reach; until they could get horses.

After about a half hour, he reined in, turned the extra horses loose, swung his leg over his horse's rump, and pulled the girl off. He then cut her bindings and looked down at her. Even in the dark, he saw that she was petite, and an uncommonly pretty young woman. "Sorry I had to treat you like a bag o' grain, young lady, but I had no choice."

In a soft, husky voice, she said, "I know. You did what had to be done." Then almost so soft he had trouble hearing, "Thank God. The horrible things they talked of doing to me were things I had only heard whispered by those who survived the war."

"Ma'am, I listened to them make their brags. I'll assure you nothing like those things're gonna happen to you. We'll ride awhile, then I'll set us up a camp. We'll talk then."

He looked from her to his horse. One saddle, his saddle, no sidesaddle. "Ma'am, didn't have time to get that sidesaddle. I'll ride behind an' hold you in front of me."

She nodded, toed the stirrup, and swung to his saddle sitting sideways. He swung up behind her, and led them from the clearing.

Careful to make sure he did nothing she might misconstrue as trying to get familiar, he held her caged between his arms while holding the reins. They rode for another two hours, then rounding a bend, Lingo moved into a jumble of large boulders and climbed down. He held his arms up and helped her slide to the ground. He had no doubt that she was tired to the bone, but he'd not heard one whimper from her.

"Ma'am, know you're worn out, you just sit over there by that rock while I get a fire started an' put on a pot o' coffee. Those who took you won't be close until they find horses. I figure they'll walk back to Durango before they find any."

"Durango is where I was going. My father was to meet me. Is there no chance we could make it there tonight? He'll be worried sick."

"We'll talk about that after I get you comfortable."

Barnes worked at collecting broken branches, bark, and pieces of sturdier wood. He started the fire while she talked, then he set about pouring water from his canteen into his coffeepot, which he'd untied from the cantle of his saddle. He took the old blackened pot with him even if going to town.

Finally, the fire burning to his satisfaction, he glanced at the girl. "Ma'am, come close to the fire, I know you must be chilled."

She smiled. "Hardly, sir, you're the one who must be cold. I'm wearing your coat." She nodded toward the valise Barnes had dropped at the side of the horse. "I have a coat in that bag. If you'll hand it to me, I'll give you back your own."

It took only a moment for them to shrug into their own coats.

He went to his bedroll, took his cup from it, and poured a cup of coffee for her. The handle of the tin cup burned his hand. He wrapped his bandana around the handle and handed the coffee to her. "Drink this, it'll warm you from the inside." She took the cup from him.

Barnes stared at her a moment. "Ma'am, I'm gonna have to know your father's name, and your name. Right now I don't think it'll be safe for you to go into town. Those men who stole you can't afford to let you tell your story and identify any of them. They'd be hung from the nearest tree without a trial. Let's talk. You tell me your story and we'll decide what to do from there."

She stared into the fire a few moments, then raised her eyes, the bluest he'd ever seen, to meet his. "Of course. I'm Emily Lou Colter; my father is Miles Colter. He has a mine somewhere outside of Durango. I've not seen him in two years.

"About six months ago, my brother, Rush, left to come out here after father wrote that he'd struck a rich vein of gold. I stayed in Baltimore waiting for them to send for me. Word didn't come. The longer I waited, the more I worried—so I packed and came west. I wrote my father and mailed the letter the same day I left." She shrugged. "That's about it, except, as far as I know, Papa is the only one who knows of my coming, and my brother, if he ever got here."

Lingo dug in his pocket for his pipe, looked questioningly toward the girl. She nodded, so before answering, he lighted the tobacco he'd packed into it back alongside the trail. "Well, Miss Colter, I'm Lingo Barnes. Call me Lingo. I've a cabin and a few head of Texas longhorns in my hanging valley a few miles from here." He took a drag on his pipe, blew out the smoke, and glanced at the fire. "If you trust me, ma'am, I want to take you to the cabin, then I'll go to town and see what I can find out." Then, in case she misjudged his meaning, he hurriedly explained, "Ma'am, there's another girl stayin' there, a girl my partner, Wesley Higgins, pulled outta a mess over in Taos, New Mexico Territory. She has her own room. You can stay in there with her." He took the cup from her hands, filled it, and handed it back. "I want you to understand: I figure you won't be safe in town until I corner those men who took you off the stage—an' I think I'd better try to find your father, tell 'im what happened, and that you're well and safe. Apparently he's not the only one who knew of your coming."

"You make it sound so ominous, sir. Why would anyone want to harm me?"

He shook his head. "I don't know the answer to that question, ma'am, but we know for sure *someone* wants to do you harm."

She nodded, then handed him the cup. "You'd best drink some of that devil's brew to warm your insides. I know you must be cold."

"Tell you somethin', ma'am, I been a lot colder." He pinned her with a gaze. "Well, what do you think, young lady? Is it my hangin' valley, or try to get into town unseen?"

She studied him a moment. He couldn't be much older than herself, yet he seemed so confident he could take care of her troubles. He was handsome in a rugged sort of way, tall, maybe six feet, and well built: wide shoulders, slim waist. But most of all, he was willing to go along with her decision. Too, she felt that something must be terribly wrong with her father, or those men would not have known she would be on that stage. "Let's go to your valley, Mr. Barnes. There must be something wrong in town, and I think we'd best know what we're getting into before we expose our hand." Her face turned warm. "That's a poker term my father used to use. He taught me to play the game from the time I could hold a deck of cards. Of course, I only played at home. Father, my brother, and I whiled away evenings playing for pennies."

"I recognize the term, young lady. Wes, the girl he brought home, and I often do the same thing." He stood, unsaddled his horse, rubbed him down with dried brush, and spread his ground sheet, then his blankets. "You'll sleep there, ma'am. I'll curl up in some of this pine straw."

She opened her mouth to protest, but he cut her off. "Don't want any argument. You'll use my bedding, an' we'll get going before daylight in the morning." His face warmed. "Uh, ma'am, my bedding's clean. I scrub it every time I use it on the trail." He tossed the remains of the coffee on the fire, walked to a tree, and raked straw into a pile.

Before going to sleep, she asked what a "hanging" valley was. "Well, ma'am, it's a valley, much higher than what you'd expect, an' mostly surrounded by mountains higher than those at lower elevations." His explanation seemed to satisfy her. They curled up and went to sleep.

True to his word, Barnes roused her long before daylight and set them on the trail after a hurriedly prepared breakfast of beans, bacon, and coffee.

They wound around the side of a mountain, crossed several meadows, then climbed again to cross a saddlelike pass between two peaks. Every so often he glanced behind. Although he thought it might take a while for the bandits to get horses, he didn't let down his guard.

Emily Lou glanced at him several times, then her curiosity got the better of her. "You know your way around these mountains like you've been born and raised in this country."

Lingo shook his head. "No, ma'am. I grew up on a ranch, Pa's ranch, west of Fort Worth. I don't profess to know these mountains at all, but when you've spent most of your life outdoors you develop a sense of direction." He grinned. "That's what I'm usin' now, but I'll bet you a nickle we'll be in my valley before sundown."

His grin had sent a ray of sunshine across his face, made him look boyish. Emily Lou took that look, as well as the disappearance of the stern businesslike look he had carried since rescuing her as comforting, that she'd done the right thing in putting her trust in him. "Mr. Barnes, I'll not call that bet. If you think we'll be there, so be it."

"Ma'am, I'd surely be pleased if you'd call me Lingo. Every time someone says 'Mr. Barnes' I want to look around to see if Pa's anywhere around."

"All right, Lingo, but if we do that, you must call me Emily Lou, or Emily."

He flashed her that grin again. "How 'bout 'Em'?"

She smiled. "I'd like that. Papa used to call me 'Em.' "

They rode another hour before Barnes reined the horses in alongside a steep granite bluff; the trail upon which they rode spread only wide enough for a wagon before the off-side fell away a thousand feet or so. Lingo nodded in the direction they were riding. "My valley's just beyond where this pass opens out. I'll signal Wes we're comin' in." He pulled his 1873 Winchester from the saddle scabbard, fired into the air, jacked another shell into the chamber, fired again, and then did the same thing again. He worried that the shots might be heard if the bandits had managed to get horses—but Wes had to be warned to expect him. There were too many out here who took what they could get away with. Wes was much like him in protecting what was theirs. Neither of them figured to give up any of what was Lingo's without a fight.

The echo of his last shot had not died away before he urged the horse ahead to a small depression in the cliff. At one time or other he and Wes had spent many hours standing or sitting in the rocky alcove guarding it so that no one came into their valley. He dismounted and held his arms up for Em.

They waited there several minutes while Barnes looked in the direction from which they'd come. Then, from the valley direction, the ring of shod hooves sounded on the rocky trail. In only a moment the rider rode into sight. He was young, but only four or five years younger than she judged Lingo to be, and good-looking. Em thought she'd never seen so handsome a man; then she compared the rider with Lingo. Smiled to herself. Two handsome men. The women back home would be flat-out jealous. Then Barnes broke into her thoughts with introductions.

Wes glanced at both of them, and returned his look to Emily. "Ma'am, you sure picked a cantankerous old mossy horn to go ridin' with—or, I figger they's a bunch of trouble ridin' your backtrail."

Lingo nodded. "Your second guess is right. We have at least four men who'll sooner or later be comin' this way."

Wes grinned. "An' I reckon you picked me to sit here an' give 'em a good old Texas welcome."

Barnes stared at his partner a moment, his face hard. "Wes, I'm tellin' you right now, don't just shoot to scare 'em away. Empty their saddles. They stole this little lady off the stage, so they aren't worth wasting 'scare shots' on. I hear you firin', I'll be up here in a hurry. I want to get Em settled in, an' for her to meet Kelly. I reckon they're gonna like each other."

Wes glanced down the trail. "Knowed it had to be somethin' bad for you to give up a couple nights in town. Go on down to the cabin. Ain't nobody gonna get by me." He nodded, and tipped his hat to Emily. "Mighty proud to have met you, Miss Emily. Now y'all git on down there."

Lingo again lifted Emily to the saddle and climbed up behind her. After a few minutes of riding, they passed through a narrow defile, bluffs on both sides, then the trail widened and opened out into a small valley, its floor lush with tender mountain grass. Occasional clumps of spruce and fir dotted the land, and farther up the slopes the trees thickened to give the slopes a dark, almost black look in the clear air. Em gasped. "Why it's beautiful, and so peaceful." She pulled a deep breath into her lungs. "And the air is so pure and clean, one can almost taste its sweetness."

Lingo nodded. "That it is, ma'am, my valley, that is. An' for some reason, it's sheltered such that winter snows are light. Those longhorns I brought in have no trouble pawing their way to food in the winter." He smiled. "As for bein' peaceful? Well let's say that's the way it is most o' the time. Don't want to scare you, ma'am, but once in a while we have visitors from the outlaw trail. They're usually right peaceful, so don't you worry your pretty head about them."

She frowned. "The Outlaw Trail? I've heard about it back East, but I thought it was only a figment of one of our writer's, Ned Buntline's, imagination. There really is an Outlaw Trail?"

"Yes'm, but most of those boys are right nice. For the most part they took the wrong fork in the trail back along their past. There aren't many like the four men who stole you—an' if they're of that stripe, I figure I can take care of them."

At that moment they rounded a bend in the trail, circled a copse of trees, and the cabin came into sight. Em gasped. "Why an artist couldn't have painted a picture more like heaven on Earth." She twisted to look at him. "You must have studied every inch of your valley before selecting that spot for sheer beauty."

He grinned. "I'd like to take credit for that, but I picked that spot because it was sheltered from wind and snow, and gave us a good field of fire if anyone tried to approach with intent to harm us."

They rode to the front of the cabin. A woman stood in the doorway, a young woman, about twenty years old by

Emily's guess. She was pretty: blonde, fair-skinned, green-eyed, and with a figure to make a man drool. Em felt a twinge of jealousy, although she couldn't imagine why.

Lingo was in the middle of introducing the two when rifle shots sounded from the pass. He handed the reins to Kelly, said to make Emily at home, handed her from the saddle, and headed back in the direction from which he'd come. Every muscle in his body tight, he worried about Wes.

He reined in his horse short of the alcove, dropped from the saddle and sprinted to Wes. "How many?"

"All four, an' I got a hunch they's more behind 'em."

"You get any with those two shots?"

Wes only nodded toward the backtrail. About a hundred yards down the rocky surface two bodies lay stretched out; one lying still, the other trying to crawl to some rocks at the side of the trail.

Lingo jacked a shell into the chamber, eased around the raw, rocky edge of the depression in which he and Wes stood, and squeezed off a shot toward the crawling man. At the same time the whine of a bullet chipped splinters from the side of the cliff. He ducked back behind cover, then looked at his partner. "They might be the scum of the earth, my friend, but at least one of them can handle a rifle."

"We gotta figure all o' them can." Wes shrugged and grinned. "You can bet your prize pony *I'm* gonna treat 'em all like they got a bead on me all the time." He ran his cupped hand down the barrel of his rifle, then cradled the Winchester in the crook of his arm. "Tell you what, Lingo, you mighta taught me too good 'bout cows, guns, knives, but mostly 'bout bein' careful if they's any chance my hide's in danger." He nodded. "Danged tootin' I ain't gonna sell any o' that bunch short on nothin' 'cept bein' decent folks."

While Wes talked, Barnes squinted down the trail. There was only a few feet he had to keep his eyes on, due to the narrowness of the road he and Wes had picked and shoveled out of the mountainside.

A hat brim edged around the side of the cliff. Lingo waited. He'd seen men use that trick before, and most of the time the hat didn't have a head inside it. This time, though, the hat had an ugly face under it. Barnes squeezed off a shot. "Damn! Missed."

Another shot from downtrail and more rock splinters showered the rocky alcove. Lingo looked Wes in the eye. "Looks like we got a Mexican standoff here. Don't figure it's gonna take both of us to keep 'em outta our valley. Go on back to the cabin. One o' us is gonna have to be here around the clock 'til we convince 'em to leave."

Higgins peeked around the edge of rock. "That'n what was crawlin' away made it. He ain't in sight." He looked back at Lingo. "Tell you what. I'll go back now, an' when I get there I'll set them two girls to makin' torches outta rags an' pine tar. We gonna need to keep that section o' trail 'tween us and them bandits lit up like day come nightfall." He toed the stirrup, swung into the saddle and left.

As soon as Wes left him alone, Barnes set about studying the area between him and the bandits, trying to think of some way to sneak up on them and end this standoff. Finally, he shook his head. When he and Wes built that road, they'd done much of it with the idea of one man being able to keep an army out if he had to. They'd done a good job. Lingo let a grim smile crack his lips. Emily called his valley beautiful. He now thought of it as a trap; attackers couldn't get in, but those inside couldn't get out. There were many times he thought of it as Trap Valley.

After roaming every inch of the bowl in which they'd built, he'd found one other way out—but if he used it, he'd be on the opposite side of the mountains than the one he wished to be on to get to Durango. He nodded to himself. "Yep, it's a neat little trap." His muttered words did nothing to make him feel better, and now he and Wes had two women to worry about.

He kept his eyes and ears peeled for sight or sound from down the trail, and after about an hour the smell of food cooking assailed his nostrils from two directions. Kelly was cooking supper, and so were the bandits. His stomach growled.

All afternoon he waited, watched, and once in a while fired a shot at the bluff around which the trail curved.

The sun dropped below the high peaks although only midafternoon. Lingo shivered, and thanked God Emily had not taken his coat to the cabin with her. It was going to be a cold night.

He squirmed, shuffled his feet, and wondered if he could set out running and get to the bandits hiding place before they saw him. He put that thought to rest almost as soon as the idea came to him. He'd learned patience growing up as a boy. Raised in Comanche country you developed the ability to wait.

Shadows had long since melded into a soft semidarkness folded between the snow-capped rocky peaks around him. The sound of a horse's hooves on the trail sharpened Lingo's senses even though coming from the direction of the ranch. He pressed his back against the rocky wall and waited. Then, Wes whispered from the semidark, "Wes here. Got the torches. Them women took to makin' 'em like they wuz raised down Texas way."

He came into the alcove, his arms folded around a bundle of sticks each with rags tied to the ends. He dropped them at Lingo's feet. "You know what? Them womenfolk done took to each other like sisters. Man, it wuz sure good to see Kelly so happy. Don't reckon I been payin' it much mind, but thinking back on it I can see that Kelly's been in need o' seein' other women. Sure made me feel good to know that girl wuz feelin' good 'bout bein' with someone to talk woman talk to."

"Hell, Wes, men need the same thing. We, once in a while, need to get in the middle of a bunch o' men so we can tell lies, drink a little whisky, an' even fight a little."

In a sober voice, Wes chided, "That bein' the case, Lingo, you gonna be one lonesome ranny one o' these days. Most men done heard 'bout your fists and gun quick. Soon ain't gonna be nobody left who'll fight you."

"That's strange. I haven't felt like anybody's been avoidin' me lately."

Wes chuckled. "Buddy, that's 'cause you ain't been nowhere to meet people much. Course there's me, an' I done got to know you ain't gonna hurt me."

Just then Lingo heard movement in the direction of the outlaws.

2

Abruptly, Lingo grabbed Higgins's arm. "Shhhh. Here, take my rifle." Silence settled around them, then a soft scraping from down the trail. Barnes placed his mouth close to Wes's ear. "Gonna light one of those torches you brought an' toss it on the trail. Be ready to fire." Wes nodded.

This had to be fast and fluid as a quick draw. Lingo pulled a lucifer from his hatband, raked it across the seat of his jeans, and stuck it to the pine pitch–soaked end of the torch.

The torch flared. Lingo ducked around the edge of their shelter and tossed it as far down the trail as he could. The area came into sharp, fire-golden brightness.

Before the torch landed on the rock surface, Wes stood at Barnes's shoulder, firing and jacking shells into his rifle. The outlaw closest to him staggered, tried to catch himself, and stumbled toward the edge of the trail. Then he fell over its edge. A shrill scream trailed off as the outlaw fell into the dark void below.

As soon as the bandit staggered, Wes pulled trigger on

the second man, who ran back the way he'd come. Higgins missed. The man had turned, staggered to the side trying to catch his balance, and lucked out. That stagger caused Wes to miss. Before he could get off another shot the bandit disappeared around the bend in the trail.

Higgins turned and ducked behind the edge of the alcove, but not before rock slivers sprinkled his shoulder and face. "That ranny we shot earlier, the one who dragged himself away, wuz waitin' fer me soon's I stepped out where he could see me."

Lingo grabbed him and pulled him deeper into the rocky depression, then twisted him to the now dull torchlight to look at his shoulder and face. "You're danged lucky, young'un. That man got in such a hurry he didn't make sure of his shot. Bet money he wasn't from Texas."

Finally, making certain the rocky splinters had done nothing more than draw a little blood, he pushed Wes from him. "Smelled food cooking awhile ago. Go on back to the cabin an' let Kelly clean the rock outta your face an' shoulder, then eat. I'll hold down things here until you get back."

"Et fore I come with them torches, Lingo. Ain't hurt enough to bother Kelly. You git on down yonder and feed yourself. 'Sides that, Miss Emily's gonna be wonderin' 'bout all the shootin'. You can make her know it wasn't much."

Barnes stepped toward his horse, then stopped when Higgins asked, "Why you always call me a young'un, Lingo? Hell, I'm almost old as you are, lackin' 'bout five years."

Barnes chuckled. "Those five years were the ones I used to go up the trail twice while you were growin' up."

"Yeah, but then you took me on trail drives twice, an' the second time made me trail boss of the herd follerin' the one you wuz bossing. We wuz about a day behind you all the way."

This was an old subject between them, and try as he

might, Lingo still thought of Wes as the kid his pa had raised. "Aw, hell, Wes, reckon I look on you like my kid brother. Know you can handle guns, knives, cattle, but I like to feel like I can stand between you and harm."

"Them two years your pa sent you back East to school, I growed up plenty."

Lingo nodded. " 'Cause you stepped in an' took my place while I was gone. Pa put a lot on you in those two years." He peered around the edge of the rocky alcove. "Don't know whether all that smoke hangin' in layers out there is from the torch, or the powder we burned gettin' rid o' those skunks. Smells like both."

"Don't make no difference, they done ducked for cover. Now you go on an' git some victuals under your belt."

Lingo swung into the saddle, held up his hand in farewell, and said, "Take care, young'un."

He thought he heard Wes snort, and say, "Young'un, hell."

Lingo rode to the front of the cabin, looped the reins over the hitch rack, and stepped toward the door. Before he'd covered ten feet, Kelly came out the door on the run. "Wes—where's Wes? He ain't hurt, is he?"

Barnes grabbed her by the shoulders. " 'Course he's not hurt. I left him up there to keep those varmints outta our valley while I get a bite to eat." He sniffed. "What's that that smells so good?"

Kelly glanced toward the pass. Her eyes still showed worry, then absentmindedly she mumbled, "Venison steaks."

"Where's Em?"

"She's in yonder tendin' your steak. She seen you comin' an' took over at the stove right then. Said she could tell you was hongry soon's you come in sight."

Lingo chuckled. "She was sure right about that." He draped his arm across Kelly's shoulders and pulled her toward the door.

Emily Lou put a still sizzling steak on his plate, raked

him from head to toe with a searching look, then apparently satisfied he was all right, dished up vegetables and took bread from the oven. "Didn't take them long to find us, did it, Lingo?"

He shook his head. "Might as well be now as later. Don't like to sit around and wait for things to happen."

"Is there another way into your valley?"

He nodded. "Yep, but only one, an' they'd have to know a lot more about this country than I think they do in order to find it. Now you stop worryin'. Soon's we take care of those up there at the pass I'm gonna head for town an' see what's happened to your pa."

She stood by the table, looked from his plate to him, and shook her head. "The way you're putting that food away looks like you're gonna want another steak."

Lingo shook his head, wiped his mouth on a frayed dish towel and stood. "Nope. Gonna get back up there and send Wes down for Kelly to clean up his face and baby him a little."

Kelly stiffened. "He's hurt?"

"Nope, just got some rock slivers sprayed on his face. Not enough to hurt his good looks even." He grinned. "'Course I don't think you care a whit how he looks."

Kelly's face turned a bright red. "Now you stop teasin' me, Lingo Barnes. You know I just feel beholden to him for savin' me from them men in Taos an' don't want nothin' happenin' to him."

Lingo's grin widened. "'Course not, little one. I never figured it any other way." He chuckled again. "'Course, you bein' a pretty blonde little spitfire, and stickin' to him like a south Texas cocklebur, don't mean nothin'."

"Ain't no pretty blonde, just a faded dishwater blonde. Ain't no man gonna look at me right serious."

Emily smiled. "You believe what you want, Kelly, but you're a very pretty young lady." She nodded. "And if you ask me, Wes has already taken note of that." Her smile widened. "I have a hunch you have taken more than a hard look at him, too. He's so handsome as to be almost pretty—if it wasn't for that hard look his face takes on when he thinks Lingo's in trouble."

Barnes seeing that the two women had settled into a comfortable relationship, clamped his hat to his head, waved good-bye, and went out the door.

As soon as he disappeared, Kelly looked at Emily Lou. "Want you to know, I ain't lookin' at Wes all cow-eyed. He saved me from a downright terrible life, an' I'm gonna be whatever he wants me to be whenever he wants me to be it."

Emily poured them each a cup of coffee and pulled Kelly to a chair at the table. "From the short while I saw Wes, I believe that whatever he wants you to be will be honorable. Tell me how you met."

Kelly shrugged. "Ain't much to tell. My folks an' me wuz headin' for the gold fields over yonder at Durango. We wuz with a wagon train when they died of pneumonia. Nobody in the train wanted to take on another mouth to feed; I wuz only fifteen at the time an' the womenfolk were used to doin' their own work, so when we reached Taos I went lookin' for a job.

"They wuz some men in that town tried to pull me into a saloon full o' soiled doves an' make me work there. Wes stepped in; braced four of 'em an' took me away from there on the run. Lingo stayed behind to keep 'em from followin' us." She pulled her shoulders up around her neck as though to ward off the thought of falling into the hands of the likes of men like that. "That wuz over five years ago; I took care o' them as much as they'd let me. I growed to be a woman in that five years an' I need a man to take care of." She pinned Emily with a look sharp as a dagger. "Want you to know, ain't neither one o' them ever made an improper move toward me. They ain't said nothin' bad to me either."

Emily dropped her look to stare into her cup, then again looked into Kelly's eyes. "Kelly, from what little I've seen of them, you couldn't have fallen into the hands of two finer men. After we find my father, I want us to keep in touch."

Kelly stood and gathered the dishes to wash them. "From the way I seen Lingo tryin' to keep you from harm, I reckon you can bank on it that we'll see a whole lot of you." She cocked her head as though listening. "A couple more shots from up there on the mountain." She stared toward the door. "Hope them menfolk are all right."

Lingo stood, his back pressed against the granite wall of the alcove. "Well, reckon we know they're still hidin' around that bend. No use in both of us wastin' time here. I can hold 'em. You go on down to the cabin and let Kelly clean up your face."

Wes stared at him a moment. "You sure you'll be all right?"

Lingo, although not wanting to be alone against the outlaws, grinned. " 'Course I'll be all right. You ever seen three or four men buffalo me?"

"Done seen times they should have—if you had any sense in that hard head o' yours." He pulled his hat tight on his head and toed the stirrup. "Be back up here soon as Kelly gits through with me."

Lingo shook his head. "Nope, you stay down there 'til I signal I want you up here; get a little sleep. This may be a long wait for them to get enough."

"Promise you ain't gonna pull any damn fool stunt like tryin' to rush 'em all by yourself."

Lingo shoved another couple of cartridges into the loading gate of his rifle. "Ma didn't raise a total damn fool. I'll hold fast 'til I see you again."

Wes cast him a look as though he didn't believe a word of it, reined his horse down the trail, and soon disappeared around a bend.

Lingo lighted another torch, reached around the edge of

the alcove, and tossed it onto the trail. It had not touched the roadbed before shots rang out. The torch jumped, sputtered, but continued burning. Then the idea hit Lingo square between his ears.

He took his boots off, though not liking the idea of running up the trail in sock feet. But if he had this girl-stealing trash figured right, they'd stay there until that one who had dragged himself back around the bend bled to death.

He waited. The reflected glow of the torch grew dimmer. Lingo shuffled his feet, then rubbed them up and down against each other, trying to get some warmth in them. He sucked in a deep breath, trying to ease the fear that threatened to grip his nerves. Then a flare, and the flame died.

With the last sputtering ember, Lingo launched himself around the edge of the alcove. His sock-clad feet made no sound. He ran toward the bend around which the bandits hid. He held his rifle in his left hand, and while running flipped the thong from the hammer of his Colt, thumbed back the hammer, and came face-to-face with the outlaw he'd heard called "Slim" back where he'd freed Emily. He slipped the hammer and thumbed it back again. His two shots sounded almost as one to his ears.

Slim staggered and lurched toward the edge of the cliff—but pulled the trigger on his rifle while stumbling. A streak of fire burned along Lingo's side, and at the same time knocked the wind from his lungs. He thumbed off another shot. That shot knocked the dark shape of Slim over the edge of the cliff. He didn't yell, scream, nothing. Barnes figured he died before starting the long descent.

Lingo choked on a heavy cloud of powder smoke, but never slowed as he went around the bend in the trail. Two horses raced for the next curve. The dim light showed one with a rider, the other with a smaller shape leaning over the saddlehorn. Lingo holstered his Colt and brought his Winchester to his shoulder. He fired twice, but doubted he hit either of the bandits. Then the pain grabbed him. The slug in his side bent him double. Then hoofbeats from the valley side of the trail came to him.

Lingo raised his head enough to see Wes coming off the side of his horse at a dead run. His bootheels dug against the rocky surface and he skidded to a halt beside him.

"Damn you, Lingo, you said you wouldn't try anything dumb. Now you went an' done it." While berating his friend, Wes gently pushed him to the ground and looked him over from head to foot, then he ripped Lingo's shirt to the side so he could look at the bloody gash in his side. "Crease, nasty-lookin' crease." He ran his fingers along Barnes's ribs. "Didn't splinter none of 'em, but I figure at least one's cracked. Gotta git you down to the cabin. You feel like ridin'?"

"Hell no, but reckon I got it to do." He rolled to his side. Despite his trying to hold it back, a moan pushed through his tightly compressed lips.

Wes put his hands under Lingo's armpits and pulled him to his feet. "Hold on, old friend, gotta git you on your hoss: Gonna hurt like hell, but it's gotta be done."

They struggled a few moments, Wes trying to hold Lingo upright, and Barnes gritting his teeth and trying to stand without falling. Wes finally got his partner to the granite bluff and leaned him against it. "See if you can stand there long 'nuff for me to get your horse."

While Wes went for his horse, Lingo tried to suck in a deep breath. It caught in his throat. He wouldn't try that again. From the pain that caught his chest in a vice grip, he nodded; Wes was right. He had at least one broken rib.

Higgins came around the bend leading Lingo's horse. "This ain't gonna be easy, partner, but we gotta do it. You grab the horn while I try to get your toe in the stirrup."

It took the better part of a half hour to get Lingo in the saddle, and another equal amount of time to get down to the cabin.

Emily beat Kelly to Lingo's side. She reached up her

arms to help him from the saddle, apparently not thinking that his two hundred pounds would take them both to the ground, then Wes shouldered his way between her and the horse. "I got 'im, little one. You an' Kelly go in and rip one o' them sheets into strips 'bout six-inches wide. I'll git 'im in the cabin."

Without argument they did as they were told. Lingo clamped his teeth tight and didn't utter a sound while Wes wrestled him off his horse and to his bedside—then he passed out.

He must have been out for only a few seconds because when he swam out of the darkness Wes was ranting and raving. "Knowed soon's I left 'im up yonder he'd pull some fool stunt." He nodded. "Yep, knowed it, an' that's 'zackly what he done. He charged them three what wuz left all by hisself."

Lingo took a shallow breath and mumbled, "Got one of 'em, too. The other two left right fast."

"Pull him to sit so I can get these bandages pulled tight around his chest." Emily held the end of one of the sheet strips tight against his ribs while she talked. When Kelly and Wes had him upright, she wrapped the strip of cloth around and around his chest. Finally, she stood back. "I felt along each of your ribs and could detect only one broken. That wrapping will keep you from breathing deeply while holding the cracked rib together. Now you lie still while we take care of you."

Lingo forced a grin. "Not much danger of me tryin' to get up right now. Where you learn to take care of things like this?"

She smiled. "I volunteered to help doctor beat up, cut up, shot up sailors at a place called 'Sailors' Rest' before leaving Baltimore. They seem to think it's a lot of fun to come ashore and fight—along with the other things they do while off their ship."

Wes chuckled. "Sounds like a bunch o' cowpunchers at the end of the trail."

Lingo sniffed. "If that's coffee I smell, I sure could use a cup."

Emily beat Kelly to the pot, poured a cupful, and went back to Lingo's bunk. She wouldn't let him try to hold the cup, instead she held it to his lips while he sipped the hot liquid. Barnes noticed the sly grin Wes cast Kelly. If he wasn't careful, they'd try to get him and Em interested in each other. He looked over the rim of the cup Emily held to his lips. She *was* one danged good-looking female, and she took to trouble like one of these Western women. He liked her.

Emily made him stay in bed, or at least in the cabin doing nothing, for two days, then he pronounced himself well enough to be at work. At breakfast that morning, he looked at Wes. "Know what, young'un, we're not through with that bunch who stole Em. If they'd take 'er off a stagecoach, they want 'er pretty bad. They'll be back." He took a forkful of pancake, chewed it, and swallowed. "Back there at the fire that night, I heard 'em call the big beefy one Bull, an' the one I heard called Shorty was the one hunched over his saddlehorn. He's the one who dragged himself back around the bend." He took another bite. "I figure they've gone back to Durango to get Shorty doctored, then they'll gather up a few more o' their kind an' come back to finish the job."

Emily stared at her now empty plate a moment, then swept them with a glance. "I've brought a whole bunch of trouble down on you folks. I'm terribly sorry."

Wes chuckled. "Miss Emily, if you hadn't come along, I reckon me an' Lingo would've gone crazier'n a rabid skunk. We wuz gittin' flat-out bored with babyin' them cows o' Lingo's." He nodded. "Yep, you saved us from havin' to go to the nuthouse."

Wide eyed, Emily looked at them, then centered her glance on Lingo since they all seemed to look to him for leadership. "What do you think to do now, Lingo?"

He frowned, took a bite of venison steak, chewed a while, then having made up his mind, gave a jerky nod. "I figure to go into Durango, none of that bunch knows me, it was dark when I took you outta their camp, and I'll try to find what has happened to your pa." He forced a tight smile. "Too, I might luck out and run into some o' that bunch who took you. I figure to see 'em either in town or on the trail."

Emily carefully placed her fork beside her plate, clenched her fists, and leaned across the table. "And, sir, if you run into them as you so succinctly stated it, what do you think to do then, fight them all by yourself?"

Wes let out a belly laugh. "Damn, Lingo, Miss Emily's done got you figgered right down to a nubbin'." He cut the laugh off short, and looked Emily in the eye. "Yes'm. Reckon you done nailed that horseshoe on tight. That's 'zackly what he figgers to do." He took a swallow of coffee and a slow grin spread across his boyish, handsome face. "An' you know what, Miss Emily? He'd win. I been with 'im when I seen 'im out-Comanche a Comanche. Ain't many who figure themselves as gunfighters who would on purpose face Lingo." He shook his head. "No, ma'am. I know he's been on his best behavior here with you, an' he's really what most would call a gentleman, but when he goes against men, he's a ring-tailed, foot-stompin' piece o' hell."

Lingo's face heated until he thought it would catch fire. He gave Wes a hard look, then looked at Emily. "Ma'am, you gotta understand that Higgins, with that kind of talk, has kept me in hot water most of the time I been tryin' to raise 'im to be a man." He shrugged. "Most o' the time I think I made a miserable failure of that job."

Two days later, Lingo had briefed each of them on what they were to do if any of the gang got by him and made it to the valley. He toed the stirrup, swung into the saddle, and again looked at Wes. "Don't forget, young'un, stay up there at that cutout place in the cliff. The women'll bring you your meals. *And*, be sure and take several sticks of that dynamite up there with you. I'll see y'all soon's I can find out anything." He swung his horse as though to leave when Emily caught his bridle.

"Lingo Barnes, you won't let me go with you 'cause there're those in town who would recognize me, but I'm tellin' you right now, you be careful. I don't want you to get hurt on my account." And then so soft Lingo barely heard her, she said, "Don't want you gettin' hurt on any account. Don't think I could stand it."

When he rode off, he puzzled over her words. If she'd said what he thought, he couldn't understand why she'd care so much—but the thought made him feel all warm inside.

3

LINGO RODE INTO the muddy main street of Durango. It had rained on him all but about a mile of his ride to town. He swept the row of saloons and false-fronted stores with a searching glance. The town had grown. The last time he came to town most of those who owned businesses in Animas City were in a frenzy to find spots in the new railroad town of Durango, only a couple of miles down the trail. Now, it looked as though most had found what they were after and were putting up buildings that had an air of permanence to them. He nodded in approval. This was where he'd be doing much of his business.

He wondered what to do first: try to find Miles Colter, get a room, or have a drink. He shivered. The drink won that argument hands-down.

He reined in at the nearest saloon, The Golden Eagle. He'd drank there before. It was owned by Faye Barret Hardester, although she never used the name Hardester since leaving her husband, and she stood by the reputation of running a place with straight games, and women who served nothing but drinks and a few dances to her customers. They didn't go upstairs with anyone.

Faye apparently saw him come through the batwings. She walked to the end of the bar to serve him. "Hello, Lingo, what brings you to town?"

Barnes grinned. "Figure a man deserves to wet his whistle at least once a month. It's been almost two since I was here last."

"Two months? You missed all the fun. Quinton Cantrell braced the remains of the Hardester brothers. Pretty good gunfight." She smiled. "I even took a bullet in the fight, but I'm almost over it."

Barnes grinned. "I don't mind missin' that kind o' fun, but I sure do miss that good whisky o' yours." He nodded. "Pour me a glassful."

Faye had already reached under the countertop and poured him a drink of what Lingo knew to be her best whisky. He took a swallow into his mouth and swished it around a couple of times. The flavor flowed over his taste buds. "Ummm, Faye, you'll spoil me for any other kind of whisky." He stood there sipping his drink.

Faye went to wait on other thirsty men. He wondered if he should ask her if she knew Miles Colter, and decided to wait awhile, check other sources, maybe the new newspaper, *The Durango Herald.* The sign over the door told him it had been established in 1881. This was 1881. He knocked back the rest of his drink, stood, and told Faye he'd be back in a few minutes, that he'd pay her then.

He went to the newspaper office, bought a paper, and went back to the Golden Eagle where he had another couple of drinks, and then went to the hotel for a bath, dry clothes, and to read the *Herald.*

After his bath, he read every word in the paper and found nothing that would give him a clue about Miles Colter and his finding a rich vein, but there was almost a page given over to somebody named Randall Bartow who'd made a good strike. The more he read the tighter he drew his neck muscles. He had a bad feeling about Emily's father, a feeling that something may have happened to him. True, he had nothing that would warrant his concern, but he'd learned long ago not to ignore such feelings.

He'd been lying on his bed reading, but now he swung his legs over the side and decided to get something to eat, the smells of food cooking in the cafe down the street wafted all the way to his front second-floor room and made him hungry.

After eating, he figured to check the saloons where the rough crowd hung out. He might spot Bull or Shorty. They wouldn't know he was the man who'd taken Emily from them, and he wanted to get a feeling for what he faced.

While eating, Marshal Nolan came in, pulled back the chair across from Lingo, and sat. "Want company, Barnes?"

Lingo let a slight smile crinkle the corners of his lips and eyes. "Looks like I got it whether I want it or not." He reached across the table to shake hands. "Howdy, old timer, good to see you."

"You, too, Lingo. How're things goin' up yonder in your valley?"

Barnes thought to tell Nolan about the trouble he'd had, then decided to let it go for the time being. "Goin' good, Marshal. Cows dropped a good number o' calves. Grass is good, so is the water. Can't complain."

"How's that young hellion you mother like a baby chick?"

"Wes? Aw hell, he's doin' good. Long's I keep 'im outta town he can't get in too much trouble."

Nolan's face softened. "You think an awful lot o' that kid, don't you?"

Barnes nodded, flinched, and bent into his side a little.

Abruptly, Nolan's face hardened. He closed his eyes to squint at Lingo. "You hurt, boy? What's the matter?"

"Horse threw me a couple days ago. Still sore, probably cracked a rib."

"Seen a doctor?"

Barnes shook his head. "Nope." He almost said Emily took care of it, but changed it to Kelly. No one knew about Emily Colter yet, and he didn't want anyone to until he was ready for a good fight. He needed a lot more information; at that time he'd count on the marshal as an ally.

Their meals came and they ate in silence as hungry men will do everywhere. Finally, when he'd finished eating, Barnes stood. "Got a couple people I want to see 'fore I settle in for a couple good drinks. I'll give a yell, an' buy you a drink; maybe by the time you finish your last round of the night."

"Look forward to it, son. See you then."

When Lingo walked from the cafe, he felt Nolan's eyes studying him. He'd not fooled the old lawman one whit. Nolan always separated the chaff from the wheat, and got to the bare bones of trouble quicker than any lawman he'd ever known, and he'd known some mighty good ones in the Rangers down Texas way.

Barnes went directly to the Magic Shovel, looked the patrons over, didn't see either Bull or Shorty, then went to the saloon only fifty feet or so down the street. There, the first man he looked at glanced his way when he swung the batwings open, then turned his eyes back to the cards he held in his hand. Shorty. Pale, probably from loss of blood out there at the pass, but getting around enough to play poker. His eyes hadn't shown recognition when they looked at Barnes. If Shorty was here, Lingo figured Bull would also be in the room.

Barnes walked to the end of the bar, ordered a drink of "good" whisky, and studied the people in the room. His first sweep of the room didn't reveal Bull. He swung his glance around the room again, then looked at a massive man coming from one of the tables at the back of the room;

a tired-looking girl with brown hair trailed him. She looked as though she'd left her bloom of young womanhood long ago in the trail towns to the east. The big man was the one he'd heard called Bull.

As soon as the two reached the dance floor, Bull left her standing alone. She had apparently thought he would dance with her. She stood there. He walked to the table at which Shorty sat, pulled out a chair, then glanced around the room. His eyes passed Lingo, hesitated then came back to him.

Barnes went quiet inside, his back muscles tightened. There was no way the big brute of a man could recognize him, but he flipped the thong off the hammer of his Colt without thinking.

Bull came to stand a few feet in front of him. "You ain't no miner. What you doin' in here? This here's miner territory."

Lingo placed his drink softly on the bar. It was pretty good whisky and he didn't want to spill any of it. He stared into the mean, reddish eyes of the man. "Didn't figure I had to ask anybody's permission to drink here, or anywhere else. I told my mama I was a big boy when I left home."

"You ain't a big 'nuff boy to whip me."

Lingo nodded. "Yeah, I'm big enough to whip you, but I don't feel like havin' to do it tonight." One blow of Bull's big fists to his ribs would put him out of action, maybe kill him if the sharp end of his broken rib punctured a lung. His .44 slipped into his hand. He'd not tried to make a fast draw, but for him a fast draw came naturally. "You'll notice, big man, I got a Colt .44 pointed at your gut. You make one swing at me an' you gonna die right sudden. I ain't in no mood to fight."

Bull glanced at the big revolver in Barnes's hand. His face went from whisky-flush to bedsheet white, but he apparently wasn't ready to let it go; he had to bluster enough to save face. "You put that gun away an' I'll whip your butt all over this here floor."

Slowlike, Barnes swung his head from side to side. "Not tonight. Next time I see you, I'll shuck this gun if that's the way you want it, an' I'll do the whippin'—but not tonight." His voice hardened. "Now get on back to that chair you pulled out and sit the hell down."

Bull stared at him a long moment, shook his head, and said, "This here ain't over yet. Don't nobody pull a gun on Bull Mayben an' git away with it." He took a step toward the seat Lingo told him to take, then stopped. "I figger you for yellow right down to your toes. If you ain't, next time I see you, come a' swingin'."

Shorty stood by his chair and he was packing a handgun. He looked toward Bull, who only now reached for the back of his chair to pull it out. "Gonna see if that cowboy's got guts enough to use that gun he pulled on you." He stood there until Bull took his seat then walked in careful, measured steps toward the bar. He walked to within about six feet of Lingo. "You jest pulled iron on my partner. He ain't packin' no gun. I am. Let's see can you use that'n you jest stuck back in your holster."

Lingo had found what he wanted. The two thugs hung out in this saloon. Now he wanted a chance to find who they worked for and where they put in their time. He stared at Shorty a moment. "Don't want to have to kill you, shortstuff. Go on back to your seat and let it be."

Shorty dropped his hand closer to his handgun. "I heered Bull paint you as yellow. Figger he wuz right, but you ain't gonna git outta this here fight 'cause I'm gonna force you to stand still while I blow your damned head off."

Lingo had seen a few small, fast men in his time, this might be one of them. His neck and back muscles tightened. He forced himself to relax. Tenseness would slow his draw, and affect his aim. "All right, little man, cut loose your wolf."

While he talked, Shorty's hand swept for his side. Barnes, without thinking, drew, fired, then thumbed off a shot into the small one's leg. Shorty's legs went from under him. Before he could get over the shock of having taken lead, Lingo stepped two steps through the acrid smelling gunsmoke toward him and kicked his revolver from his hand. "Now, little man, you need a doctor. Maybe your partner'll find one for you." Then, on the off chance he could luck up on some information, he said, "Like to know who you work for so next time I can tell 'im I killed you."

"Ain't none o' your damned business who I work for. 'Sides that, I'll be tellin' your boss 'bout you not bein' fast nuff to beat me."

Lingo smiled, forcing it from between stiff lips. "Think 'bout it, little man, or boy, you only now failed to beat me."

He moved to the bar, and using his left hand, picked up his drink, knocked it back, and looked at the short man lying in the sawdust on the floor gasping in pain. "Hitting you in the leg was no accident. Next time, I'll kill you." He holstered his Colt, looked the crowd over, and not seeing anyone who appeared to want to take the fight on their shoulders, nodded and stepped toward the door.

Before he could get to the batwings Marshal Nolan looked over the doors, then pushed them open. While they still swung in and out, Nolan glanced at Shorty, then at the crowd. "Who done it?"

Lingo said from the marshal's side. "It was my doin', Marshal. They brought it to me an' I settled it without a killin'—this time."

Nolan swept the room with a hard look. "Anybody here see it happen different?"

A burly miner stepped forward. "I seen it, an' it happened like the stranger yonder said. Looked like he come in here for a peaceable drink, an' Bull over yonder tried to force him into a fight. The stranger didn't want to fight right then and sent Bull back to his seat, then Shorty tried to make it into gunplay, an' he didn't carry a big enough gun to get the job done."

Nolan nodded. "Good enough for me." He pinned Barnes with a "don't-argue-'bout-it" look, and said, "Come over to my office. I wantta talk."

A hard smile forced its way to Lingo's lips; the old lawman would now hit him with the lie he'd told about his injured ribs. He held his glass toward the bartender. "Two. One for me an' one for the marshal."

They knocked back their drinks and left. Outside, Nolan glanced at Lingo. "You're lucky them miners don't like Bull Mayben an' Shorty Gates or they'd have made dog meat outta you by now." They took another couple of steps before the marshal said, "Now we gonna go sit down in my office, an' you gonna tell me how you really hurt your side."

Lingo cast the old man a sour grin. "Knew when I told you a horse did it that you didn't buy my story." He shrugged. "All right, I'll tell you what's a fact—but you gotta promise to let me handle it until I find out what's going on. I'll keep you knowing what's goin' on; then I'll probably yell for help."

In Nolan's office, Barnes made a fresh pot of coffee, and while it boiled, he and the marshal packed and smoked their pipes. Then Lingo told Nolan the story, and about Emily Lou Colter being out at his ranch, and particularly her worry for fear something had happened to her father. "Don't know, Nolan, but before I let on I'm in the game, I want to find out where her pa is, what he's doin', who works for him, where her brother went if he didn't show up here—oh hell, I need a whole passel o' answers before I can make a move."

The old man frowned, then gave a jerky nod. "Good, I'll stay outta your way 'til you holler for help." He took a swallow of his coffee, ran his finger down a deep scratch in his desk, and shook his head. "Makes me mindful I ain't seen hide nor hair of Miles Colter in several months. Wonder if he's sick, or been hurt out yonder at his mine."

"Why don't you go to wherever it is an' check on 'im?"

"If I did that, it'd have to be purely not official. I ain't got no authority outside of town."

Barnes stood, walked around the room, then asked, "Couldn't you do the askin' as a friend?"

Nolan shook his head. "Me an' Colter never was that close. I liked 'im, an' he seemed to like me, but him bein' out yonder at his mine, an' me bein' tied down here in town, we never had a chance to get to know each other well."

Barnes went back to his chair and sat. "Well, I reckon I better take another day or two, find what I can in that time, then get back to the valley and let 'em know what I've found. Then I'll come back in town, figuring on stayin' 'til I can bring Em in to stay."

"Tell me 'bout Emily Lou. She a pretty girl, smart, what?"

"Tell you, Marshal, I didn't think there was a woman around any prettier than Kelly, but I gotta say that Em will stack up with any woman I ever met; both with looks and brains." He took two powerful puffs on his pipe. "Reckon she's a woman to ride the trail with."

Nolan choked back an explosive laugh, then let it out. Then, wiping tears from his eyes, he shook his head. "Boy, you better be mighty careful, that woman's already got you to thinkin' higher of her than I ever thought. I figgered all along they wouldn't be nothin' you ever thought much about more'n you do that ranch o' yours."

Lingo's face caught fire. "Naw now, Nolan, don't you go an' try bein' a matchmaker, wh-why hell, I hardly know the girl."

Through a grin around his pipe, the marshal nodded. "All right. Now you take some time an' get to know her."

They finished another cup of coffee and Lingo went to

his room. He hung his gunbelt close to hand on the headboard, and lay back on the bed, his hands behind his head. Where should he start? Where was Colter's mine located? Should he try to get out there and take a look at it and the people who worked for him, or go back to the valley?

He thought on that for a few moments and decided to go to the mine, but try to remain unseen while studying it. If Colter had made a good strike, Lingo wanted to know why he'd not been in town to sell some of the nuggets he must have collected. Maybe he didn't need the money right now, or maybe he couldn't come to town. Maybe something, or someone kept him from having that freedom. Lingo swung his legs off the bed, buckled his gunbelt around him, and headed for the land office.

In the land office, the agent placed a map on the table, traced his finger from Durango up toward Sunlight Peak, over fourteen-thousand feet, then he tapped his finger the other side of the peak, between it and Silverton. "Right here the other side of Sunlight, you're gonna have to start lookin' on your own." He stuck a pin in the map where he told Lingo the Emily Lou mine was located. "Tell you right now, son, it's a whole lot easier for me to stick this pin in a piece of paper than it'll be for you to find that mine, but right where I stuck that pin is where it is."

Barnes thanked the agent, shook hands, and left. Back at his hotel, he pondered whether to head out for the mine, or go to his ranch and make them aware of what he figured to do. The ranch won the argument. He wouldn't leave them there to wonder what was taking him so long. He thought it might take as much as a week to find the mine, see what he wanted to see, and get back to Durango, or his valley. He packed his gear, bought four bottles of whisky, and headed for home.

Emily Lou looked across the table at Wes. "Do you suppose Lingo will be careful? He charged into the camp where those men held me without seeming to care a thing about his own safety."

"Ma'am, gotta tell you, I've seen Lingo in a mighty lot o' tight spots, but them wuz spots he put 'imself into knowin' what the gamble wuz. I guarantee you, 'fore he went into that camp where them men had you, he knew eggzactly what the chances wuz o' gettin' you outta there without gittin' you or him hurt."

Emily let a faint smile break the corners of her lips. "Wes, you're worse than Lingo. You talked all around giving me a straight answer. Now answer me, will he take unnecessary chances?"

His face sober, Wes nodded. "Yes'm, reckon he will, if he thinks it'll git 'im what he wants."

Emily sighed. "I was afraid of that." She pinned him with a look that went through him like an arrow. "You—either of you—don't seem to fear anything."

Wes grinned. "Miss Emily, don't reckon you looked at us close enough. Tell you what's a fact, Lingo an' me's been in places where we both sweat gallons o' sweat we didn't have to spare. Yes'm we git scared, mighty scared, but we both know what we gotta do, an' do it despite bein' scared outta our boots."

Emily stared at her now empty plate a moment, then raised her eyes to look into his. "That's what I think real bravery is: smart enough to know the danger, feeling the fear from it, and then going ahead and doing what has to be done."

Kelly had sat there, not adding anything to the conversation; now she cut in. "Tell you somethin', Em." She'd taken to calling Emily *Em* when she heard Lingo call her that. "Tell you, when the man up above made real men, he practiced up on all the rest an' then made Wes an' Lingo. They ain't no man, nowhere, can stack up with the two men we got with us."

Emily smiled. "That's as good an endorsement as I can

imagine any man getting. Thank you, Kelly. You've put my mind at ease." But her words belied her true feelings. She cast a look at the door, wishing Lingo would come through it.

Wes finished eating and made as though to help with the dishes. Kelly placed her hands on her well-rounded hips. "Shoo now, Wesley Higgins, know you gonna go back up the side o' that mountain to keep us safe. Git your rifle, some dynamite, an' git goin'. Me an' Em's gonna take care o' this end o' things."

He grinned and did as he was told. When the sound of his horse's hooves died in the distance, Emily poured herself and Kelly a cup of coffee and sat, wanting to talk some more before getting busy with chores. She looked at Kelly. "That man ever said anything about loving you?"

Kelly stared at her, eyes wide. "Em, don't reckon the thought ever entered his head. He's got that head o' his full of cows, grass, water, guns, an' mostly tryin' to measure up to what Lingo thinks o' him. Lordy day, he cain't see that Lingo loves him like a big brother would. He says Lingo's done taught him everything he knows 'bout them things. He thinks he's workin' here for nothin' so's he can repay him for takin' 'im under his wing, but I happen to know Lingo counts Wes as a full partner in this here ranch."

She stood and refilled their cups. "One day while I was cleanin' up I seen a piece o' paper—didn't mean to, but there it lay, so I looked. It wuz the title to this here valley, an' both Lingo's an' Wes's names wuz on it. I ain't never said a word to Wes 'bout seein' it; ain't gonna neither. Lingo'll tell 'im when he figgers the time's right."

For a reason she didn't understand, Emily's throat swelled, her chest warmed. "Sounds like you think Lingo's about the best man you ever met, uh, of course that's excepting Wes."

Kelly sipped her coffee, then looking down at the table she said, her words soft, "Em, I love both o' them men, but in a different way. Reckon I think of Lingo as someone above all other men. Ain't nobody gonna tame him." She stood. "Reckon we better red these here dishes up so's we can wash 'em."

Emily tried to ignore the words *Ain't nobody gonna tame him*, then she wondered why anyone would want to tame a man like him, and at the same time she wondered that she was beginning to think of him as did Kelly—well, not exactly as did Kelly. For some reason her face warmed.

The next afternoon, Wes and Lingo came down from the pass together. Wes wanted to stay on watch while Lingo went to the cabin for supper, but Lingo squashed the idea. In his mind, Bull and Shorty would stay in Durango until Shorty got so he could walk after being shot in each leg, and then they'd probably go to whatever mine they worked. And he wondered what interest the owner of that mine had in keeping Emily from going to her father. He intended to find those answers.

Before they got to the door, Wes yelled, "Supper ready yet? I'm starved."

From the doorway, Kelly stared at him and shook her head. "Wes Higgins, don't reckon I ever seen you when you wasn't starved. Yep, supper's ready. Git washed up an' come on in."

When Lingo came through the door a few steps behind Wes, Em stood bent over the oven, her face flushed from the heat. She pulled beautifully browned biscuits from the hot interior. Lingo looked at her and admired the pretty picture she made. "Em, don't reckon there's anything prettier than a girl carrying a pot o' fresh brewed coffee or a plate of hot, browned biscuits."

She glanced over her shoulder at him. "Lingo, those words won't get you even one extra biscuit. Now get to the table while everything's still hot."

He pulled out a chair and held it for her to sit. "Gonna try something on y'all, but we'll talk 'bout it after supper."

4

LINGO LOOKED AT Emily. He frowned. "Ma'am, I figure somethin's wrong up yonder at your father's mine."

Her eyes widened, and showed fear.

"No now, little miss, don't get upset 'til I do what I'm gonna propose." He took the plate of buttered carrots Wes handed him and helped himself to a couple spoonfuls, then again looked at Emily. "There might not be anything wrong, but I aim to find out who's workin' for 'im, how much time they're puttin' in at the shaft, where your pa is," he sat back and shrugged. "I reckon what I'm sayin' is, I'm gonna figure out if everything's all right. If it is, I'll take you to him." He chewed a bite of steak, swallowed, then took a swallow of coffee while thinking how to get her to stay here in the valley until he could do the things he knew must be done. It turned out not to be a problem.

"Em, we'll take good care of you; won't let nothin' happen to you, an' I b'lieve you've figured out by now Wes an' me'll be gentlemen."

While he talked, Emily's eyes never left his, then her

face turned a pretty pink. "Lingo, I never had a doubt about your and Wes's behavior." She stared into her cup a moment. "I know I want to see Father in the worst way, but I know if I try to tag along I'll probably get in the way at the most inappropriate time." She nodded. "I'll stay here with Kelly and Wes 'til you find what you need."

Lingo stared at her a moment. She was the most level-headed woman he'd met. Most women would insist on having their way, or cry at the thought of something being wrong at the mine, but not Emily. She might be torn up inside with worry and desire to go with him—but she sat there quietly and accepted his idea.

After a couple more cups of coffee, Lingo stood. "Y'all go on an' finish eatin'. I'm gonna get my trail gear ready to put on a packhorse come daylight." He smiled. "Then, reckon you'll see me when you see me. Don't know how long it'll take me to cut through the mountains an' find the right hole." He stepped toward the door. "I'll sleep in the stable tonight so as not to waken y'all when I leave."

Before anyone could say anything, Emily stood, placed hands firmly on her hips, and looked Lingo in the eye. "Lingo Barnes, you'll do no such. You'll leave here with a full stomach, and a hug from each of us. We want you back safe."

While she talked, Kelly looked at her with a slight smile crinkling the corners of her eyes and lips.

Bull Mayben had watched Lingo leave the saloon with Marshal Nolan. Now he sat at the bar, his face flushed, eyes red, veins sticking out on his forehead. He looked at Shorty Gates. "Gimme your gun. Gonna go after that bastard and kill him."

Gates shook his head. "Naw, find me a doctor. Gotta git my laigs patched up. Don't figger I got any bones broke, don't figger it's gonna take me long to git 'em well.

"Too, reckon I'm better with a handgun than most. Sure

figger I can beat that there cowboy, but we ain't gonna do nothin' 'til we see the boss, tell 'im we messed up gittin' the girl." He grimaced, held his left hand tight against his thigh and took a long pull on the beer he held in his hand, then sat it back in front of him. "Tell you what, I ain't in no hurry to tell the boss what happened. He's gonna be madder'n a skunk-sprayed hound-dawg. But these holes I got in my laigs gonna give us a good reason to stay away from him a few days. Maybe by then we can figger how to git in that valley."

"When you figger we oughtta git goin'?"

Gates took another swallow of beer. "We better git some trail supplies first. Then a couple days for my laigs to git healed some, then we gonna see what we can do."

Bull stared at him a moment, sat back, took a couple of deep breaths, felt his anger grow to a cold knot in his stomach, and then decided Shorty had it figured right. "All right. We gonna do it your way; first 'cause we gonna have to face the boss sooner or later; second 'cause I figger to be packin' iron, my own gun next time I see that ranny." He knocked back his drink and stood. "I'll git the doc to look at your legs, then I'll git some supplies. Finish your beer, the doc'll be here 'fore you can finish it."

Bull left. Shorty figured he had given in only because his anger pulled on him less than the fear he had of the boss and the boss's sleeve gun. Gates thought of himself as one of the fastest draws he'd seen—but a sleeve gun was only inches from a man's hand, and ready to fire as soon as his fingers curled around it. A tinge of fear at the thought of facing that kind of gun ran chills up his spine, yet he might have to do it. The boss had a temper that flared up seemingly for no reason.

He sipped on his beer. A pain stabbed him where Barnes's bullet had burned through him. He flinched, and told the girl to bring him a water glass full of whisky, knocked it back, and tried to stand. He made it on his third try. Then limping on both legs, he went to find Bull. To hell with the doctor; if he could stagger along, he didn't need a doctor.

Two hours later, the two renegades wound their way along a deeply pine-forested, rocky trail. Bull looked over his shoulder at Gates. "What we gonna tell the boss?"

Shorty thought a moment. "Reckon we gonna tell 'im 'zackly what happened, only in the dark we couldn't tell how many they wuz what jumped us; but they wuz a whole bunch. We didn't have a chance."

Bull nodded. "Sounds good. Think maybe he'll figger we done all we could do. He'll most likely give us a few more men an' send us after her agin."

"Yeah, maybe, but if'n we'd of had a hunert men we couldn't of got any farther along that there pinched-in pass."

Bull urged his horse up a steep incline, then muttered, "Ain't gonna tell the boss that."

They made camp that night alongside a snow-melt stream that tumbled down the side of the mountain. Berry bushes flourished along its banks and onto the small flat that bordered it. Bull sniffed. "Don't like this place, Shorty. Smells like big cat, or bear country to me."

"Aw hell, Bull, this whole country's full o' them mountain lions an' grizzly bears. If we rode on into the night, we'd still be in their territory."

"Yeah, reckon we better stay where we are." He shook his massive head. "Sometimes I wisht we'd of stayed in Texas."

Shorty nodded. "Yeah, all we had down there wuz Comanches, Comancheros, and a bright new rope waitin' fer our neck to fit into. . . ." He shrugged. "I'll take my chances with them wild animals we wuz talkin' 'bout."

"Yeah, but this here minin's hard work."

Shorty laughed. "Yeah, hard work, but no harder'n rustlin' cows, an' hell, Bull, you an' me ain't done one day's work since we come to work for the boss. He jest wants my gun, an' your muscle."

They talked while the coffee boiled, then ate beans and bacon, and crawled into their blankets. Soon Bull snored loud enough to shake tree limbs above him; Shorty followed suit.

Restless, Gates stirred, turned to his side, then to his back, came partially out of the fog of sleep, then sniffed. A foul odor permeated the camp—bear smell. He froze, then eased his hand from under his blanket to touch his Winchester. His fingers closed over the barrel. He dragged it inch by inch under the blanket with him, wishing with every breath that Bull would wake up, then knew it was better if Mayben stayed asleep; he'd do some damn fool thing to arouse the bear and get them both killed.

Shorty cut his eyes toward the sounds the bear made tearing into their provisions. He couldn't see him, but the noises he made pulled Gates's nerves to the breaking point. He wanted to jump from his blankets and put space behind him. He squashed that thought. The bear could catch him in seconds—even if he hadn't had hurt legs.

Maybe if he lay still, didn't make any noise, the monster would leave. But Bull still snored too loud for the bear to ignore. To hell with him. If the bear picked the source of that noise against which to make his attack so be it. He, Shorty Gates, would survive. He breathed only enough to keep living.

After what seemed hours of tearing, grunting, slavering, and smacking, the bear reared to his hind feet, looked about the camp, and lumbered into the woods at the side of the trail. Not moving anything but his eyes, Gates drew deeper and deeper breaths into his lungs. He still didn't move until the sound of crashing and breaking brush faded from hearing. He wished then that Bull had wakened so he could have suffered the same fear with which he'd been paralyzed.

He wanted to crawl from his blankets, throw brush on the embers, and fix a pot of coffee, but feared he'd again attract the bear to their camp. He lay there in a pool of sweat, fear sweat, now chilled by the mountain night, cold, afraid to move, exhausted, and he finally fell into a deep, troubled, pain-filled sleep.

When he wakened, light filtered through the trees. Groggy, he felt as though he'd only fallen asleep a few moments before, but the coming daylight told him different. He rolled from his blankets, looked at Bull still snoring, then glanced about the camp. Their provisions lay scattered about the camp; saddles and saddle blankets shredded. Then he thought of the horses. He stumbled to where they'd picketed them the night before. Picket stakes, ropes, horses, all were gone. In their fear the horses had bolted. Shorty stood there cursing for a good five minutes.

Bull's voice came through the trees. "What you raisin' so much hell about? Ain't through sleepin' yet."

Shorty sucked in a tremulous, anger-ridden breath. "Yeah, you through sleepin'. Look around the camp. Wish to hell you'd of woke up, maybe the bear would've got you." Then Mayben's curses cut off anything else he might have said.

When Bull stopped, apparently to catch his breath, Gates said, "Pack what gear you got left; we got a long walk ahead of us—if I can make it. My laigs're hurtin' bad 'nuff to put me to bed. The horses run off." Bull again commenced his tirade.

Two days later, the two stumbled to the mine entrance. Colter had built his living quarters in the first thirty or forty feet of the mine shaft—not the usual place to live while mining.

Before Shorty could pull open the door, it slammed open against his outstretched hand. Their boss, Randall Bartow, came out, his face red. "Where the hell have you two been? I figured you'd have taken care of that business I sent you on and been back here long before now." He raked them with a look that took in their disheveled appearance: dirty, clothes ripped and torn, several days' growth of beard, and Shorty's pants soaked with old, dried and blackened blood. His face reddened even more. "You botched the job, didn't you?" Without waiting for an answer, he straightened his right arm toward them, and as if by magic a pepperbox slipped from his sleeve into his hand. It held four shots. "I oughtta blow your damned dumb brains out right now." He struggled a few moments to get control of his temper, swallowed a couple of times, then jerked the door open, almost tearing it from its hinges. "Get inside. Tell me what happened, then I'll decide what to do with you."

Shorty skittered in ahead of Bull, and edged into a corner as though he would be safer there. Bull pushed up beside him.

Bartow, still holding the sleeve gun on them, waved to chairs at the table. "Sit, tell me about it, and it damned sure better be good."

Bull looked at Shorty, apparently waiting for him to tell the story.

First, Shorty told about the bear, apparently trying to put off telling Bartow about the girl.

"I don't give a damn about a bear in your camp. I wantta know what happened to the girl. You kill 'er, dump her body where it won't be found? Anybody see what happened? What did you do with the stage driver?"

Shorty shook his head. "Boss, you ain't gonna b'lieve what happened."

"Try me—an' it better be good."

Gates started with the stage holdup, embellishing it all the way. ". . . an' when they broke into our camp, don't know how many they wuz—five or six at least—me an' Bull killed three of 'em 'fore they got away with the girl. Then we went for our horses an' they wuz gone. We walked to Durango, got more horses an' tracked 'em down.

Had a gunfight. I got hit. Bull took me back to Durango to see a doctor, then we saddled up an' come here."

Bartow nodded, holding a tight rein on his fear and temper. "So you don't know where the girl is now."

"Naw, we never got past that pinched-in pass over the mountain. I figgered you might give us a couple o' men, an' we could go back there an' pick up their trail."

Bartow thought a moment. He'd kept the stealing of the girl down to four men in the beginning because the fewer who knew what happened the better chance no one else would ever know. The two who'd gotten killed at the pass saved him from having to rid himself of them later. He planned to get rid of Shorty and Bull also, but now he'd have to wait until they found the girl, or until she showed up here at the mine. Damn! Nothing was going right. The old man wouldn't tell where the rich vein was located, these bumbling idiots messed up everything they touched, and he wasn't ready to make an appearance in Durango with the news he'd bought the mine owned by old man Miles Colter. He'd already announced that he'd struck a rich vein, but no one knew it was on Colter's claim—or that he still had to find where the old man had found the vein.

He gave his two cohorts a look he hoped would throw the fear of God into them. "We'll not try to find her at this time. She'll show up out here, and when she does, I'll take care of her personally."

By now, his anger had cooled, and he began to think clearly. "You didn't see any of the men who attacked you and took the girl?" They shook their heads simultaneously. He said, "All right, we'll have to play the cards dealt us. Sooner or later someone will bring her out here. We get rid of whoever that turns out to be, then we'll use the girl to try to make the old man tell where the rich vein is." He sighed. "I'm tired of messing with him, but we can't do anything until we get the story out of him."

He stood, went to a cabinet, took a bottle from it, pulled three glasses out of a drawer, and poured them each a drink. He knocked back his drink, looked into the bottom of the empty glass, pushed the pepperbox back up his sleeve, then pinned them with a look. "I don't want either o' you goin' anywhere without your gun and holster 'til I tell you it's all right to put them aside—understand?"

They nodded, and apparently having waited until he put his gun away, knocked back their drinks. He poured another, then changed his mind about looking for the girl. "We'll wait a week; if she doesn't show up here by then, we'll go looking for her. Now stick around outside and make sure no one comes poking about."

When the door closed behind them, he stood and went to the back room. Colter lay there on a dirty mattress. He was as dirty as the mattress, and had a month's growth of beard. "Old man, I want to know where that last strike of yours is located. Soon's I know, you're gonna sign over this mine to me, an' once that's done I'll cut those ropes and you can go anywhere you damned well please."

Colter gave a dry, pain-filled chuckle. "You take me for a fool? I no sooner tell you what you want to know, then you kill me. I'll wait you out. When Emily gets here, she'll start a search for me. You kill me before that and neither you nor that woman you brought here will ever find that rich vein."

Hot blood surged to Bartow's face. He backhanded Colter and stomped from the room. He'd already tried torture; burned Colter's feet, starved him, deprived him of water; everything short of killing him. That he wouldn't do until he got what he wanted.

He walked past the table, noticed the bottle still sitting there, poured himself another drink, and sat. He stared into the amber fluid. He didn't like the idea of Emily Colter running around loose in this country. She might talk to anyone, raise suspicions, start a manhunt, hell, anything; and those two dumb bastards he'd sent after her? He relished the idea of blowing them into the next world. He rubbed his hand across the little hideout gun in his shirt sleeve. And that woman he'd brought here, Maddie Brice, he'd keep her as long as she satisfied his needs; then when he could afford a first-class woman, he'd get rid of her, too.

Lingo threaded his way across meadows, up the rocky sides of mountains, forded streams, and every time he came into a clearing took note of the sun, and picked another landmark to home in on. He chuckled to himself. Most people would think him slam out of his mind, roaming around these mountains with very little idea of the exact location of one mine shaft; perhaps only a small hole in the ground. He shrugged. He'd found things in miles upon miles of open prairie; he'd find Emily's father's mine, and he prayed he'd find her father at the same time.

He bedded down the first night in a wind- and rain-cut hollow in the side of a mountain: no stream, no trees, only the protection of the cavelike hollow above the tree line.

Hoping for a place like this, he'd collected enough firewood when in the trees below, and tied it to his packhorse to keep him warm during the night. And, when he found his place to camp, he'd put his horses into the hollow first. Again he glanced at the sky. A storm was building over the closer peaks. He could survive the rain, but lightning in these elevations was another story. All the while he worked, his mind kept going back to the small bundle of beautiful woman he'd rescued. She had more spunk than most men. She faced up to whatever the situation was and acted accordingly.

Cold penetrated his sheepskin. He shivered, then again pushed his horses as far back in the cave as they could go and still stand. Then he unloaded the bundle of wood, stared at it a few moments, and finally nodded; it should last most of the night; the storm should pass, and he'd get himself and the horses back down below tree line. He went about building a fire, filled his coffeepot and put grounds in it, then glanced at the sky again. With his look, a blinding flash of lightning speared the mountainside. Thunder crashed, bounced, and rumbled around him. His neck tingled as though his hair stood on end. He swallowed the brassy taste of fear deep in his throat.

He stood by the horses, his arms around their necks to soothe them. They trembled under his touch, then quieted. That lightning bolt was not the last he'd see this night. Then another spear tore at the mountain; then one after another they crashed about him, and with the noise and blinding light came rain. Rain like he'd seen on the Texas plains—in sheets, blocking out all around him. His visibility penetrated only a yard or so in front of the hollow; enough to see that the runoff was a fast-moving stream down the mountainside. At least one thing broke his way: His camp wouldn't wash away. He picked up the bundle of wood and held it on his shoulder. If it got wet, he'd spend a much more miserable night than already seemed his fate.

Lightning continued to burst about him and the sulphurous smells of brimstone burned his nostrils and throat—then the storm's sounds drew on across the peaks, growing fainter by the minute. Rain slowed to a steady downpour slackened to a steady, gentle falling, and then stopped. He walked to the edge of his camp and looked down the mountainside. Even though the lightning had drawn away it continued to light the mountains and forests about him as though day had dawned. Far below, a ribbon of smoke pushed its way from the trees. Then an orange flare grew from the now increasing plume of smoke, and the orange light spread.

Forest fire! A shiver ran up his spine. Thank God he wasn't among the trees. He'd known fear many times, but never like that he'd felt once in a West Texas prairie fire.

In the next flash of lightning he glanced down below. He was about a thousand feet above all vegetation. Surrounding him was only the slick, wet sides of cliffs, blackened from the water which had deepened their usual gray. Fear washed from him. He went about starting his fire, thankful that he could control it to his needs.

While his supper cooked, he rubbed down the horses, thus quieting them even more; then he ate and crawled into his blankets. Throughout the night he wakened and put a little more wood on his fire. Occasionally he stepped to the front of his shelter and glanced at the valley below. The fire raged on.

The dim light of morning pushed its way into the hollow, the horses snorted and nuzzled him from his blankets. He stepped to the front of the shelter and looked down upon desolation. What had only yesterday been a beautiful, green forest, now shoved blackened, denuded spikes of wood toward the sky. Still farther down the mountain a pall of smoke hung over all below it. Lingo mentally pictured the look of the entire valley below the smoke blanket. He wondered if Colter's mine had been in the line of the fire. If so, he hoped he'd not find charred bodies among the ashes.

About midmorning, thinking the fire had burned itself out in the valley upon which he looked, he packed his gear, saddled, and toed the stirrup. When he came upon the first of the scorched ground, he stepped from the saddle and with his bare hand tested the ground to see if it would burn the frog of his horse's hooves. He gave a slight nod. He'd ride, but ever so often he'd test the ground again. He snorted, tried to clear his nostrils of the strong smell of burned wood, and shook his head. The smell would be in the air for months.

From where he sat his horse, he studied the mountainsides and the valley below, looking for landmarks that only yesterday had stood out prominently. Most were gone, even the colors of rocks were hidden under scorched, blackened surfaces. The things he'd learned at the land office were now next to useless.

He thought to head for Durango and see if he couldn't get an idea about where Colter's mine might be if he headed straight out of town toward it. He shook his head. He'd try to find it from here; then if he couldn't find the right hole in the mountain, he'd go to town and start from there. Silverton should be around the shoulder of the mountain in front of him.

The sun shone red through the pall of smoke when he finally looked at the lights of Silverton, but the town was too far away to try to get there by dark.

The fire had stayed the other side of the ridges from the town, but heavy smoke lay over it like a blanket. Barnes stopped and made camp by a stream that, unmindful of the fire, still gurgled and sang its way toward some larger stream. Lingo knelt, cupped his hands and tasted. The water was cold, fresh off snowmelt in the mountains. His horses wouldn't eat but they could drink their fill. He'd buy them grain when he reached town the next day.

In his blankets that night, he studied long on how to go about finding a mine that he would be hesitant to ask about by its name or its owner's name. He'd found out in town that Miles Colter had named the mine for his daughter: "The Emily Lou." Lingo studied on that awhile and decided that to ask for it by name wouldn't arouse suspicion. Tired of pondering the problem, he pulled his blanket to his chin and went to sleep.

The next morning, he cooked bacon, beans, and fixed a pot of coffee. Em had packed him several biscuits. He ate them with his breakfast. While drinking his last cup of coffee, he studied the stream. A bath would be something he needed. He'd try to get the smoke smell off his face and body. When he took his last swallow, he shook his head. He'd wait until he could have bath water warmed at the hotel.

That evening, walking to the hotel after taking his horse to the livery, he took a good look at the men standing about on the boardwalks on each side of the street. He didn't see a person dressed as he was—a cowboy. These men were miners. Their heavy workboots, scuffed and worn, loose-fitting trousers and shirts, even their hats marked them as different from him. Most of the men he looked upon wore caps with earflaps.

After his bath and shave, he tore the sheet from his bed in strips, dressed his wound, and wrapped his side as tight as he could, even though his rib felt much better.

He ate supper, then went to the saloon closest to his hotel. Standing at the bar, alongside a brawny redhead, a miner by his dress, Barnes knocked back his drink, held his glass for another, then looked at the redhead. "Any of these mines needin' workers?"

Before answering, the miner swept Lingo's tall frame with a searching gaze, smiled, and shook his head. "Mister, you ain't no miner, you're a cowboy. What you want to go down in one o' them pits for?"

Barnes grinned. "Tell you how it is: When a man gets near broke, an' sometimes hungry, he can't afford to be choosy." He knocked back his drink and looked at the miner. "Man over in Durango said as how there was a mine over here might be lookin' for workers; said the owner was a right nice man to work for." He scratched his head. "Can't remember the name of the man who owns it, but the name of the mine is The Emily Lou."

The redhead nodded and stuck out his hand. "Name's Slagle, Sam Slagle. Yeah, that'd be a pretty good place to work but," he shook his head, "I ain't seen Miles Colter around here in a couple months—maybe more. Don't know what happened to 'im."

Lingo ordered them both a drink, and when the bartender placed it on the bar in front of him, he picked it up, stared into the amber liquid a moment, then twisted to again look at Slagle. "You reckon when it gets daylight you could point me in the right direction to find it?" He shook his head and grimaced. "All these holes in the ground look the same to me."

Slagle grinned, then laughed. "Hell, I'll go you one better'n that. I just set off a charge o' dynamite in my mine an' I ain't anxious to go in there to start clearin' it out. Them dynamite fumes give me one helluva headache. I'll walk up there with you. We'll see can we roust Colter outta his hole."

"I'll sure be obliged to you. Meet me at the cafe; I'll buy breakfast, then we'll head up there." He looked at Slagle's drink, but the miner shook his head.

"Naw, now, if you're might nigh broke you got no business buyin' me drinks—or breakfast. I'll buy the breakfast, then we can head up that way."

They tossed their drinks down, shook hands, and when they parted at the door, Slagle said over his shoulder, " 'Bout five o'clock at that there cafe 'cross the street." Lingo nodded.

In his room, Barnes thought about Sam Slagle: a friendly sort, and big and brawny as he was he'd be a mean one to tangle with, but he'd shown only the desire to make a friend. Lingo decided he liked him, but he'd hold back trusting him enough to tell him what he was here for.

The next morning, Barnes sipped his second cup of coffee when Slagle came in. "Howdy, Sam, didn't order yet. I notice these folks have eggs. Don't find 'em in many towns out here. Reckon I'll have 'bout a half dozen of 'em, biscuits, venison, fried potatoes, an' I'll pay."

Slagle nodded. "Sounds good to me. Go ahead an' order for the both of us."

After their breakfast came, Sam chewed, swallowed, and pinned Lingo with a questioning gaze. "Know what, Barnes? After I left you last night I got to thinkin'. Miles Colter ain't the kind o' man to stay to himself for this long at a time; he's a right friendly sort. 'Sides that, seems like he'd'a come in town for a drink. He likes his evenin' toddy.

An' he sure would need supplies." He took a forkful of potato, swabbed it in the runny egg yolk, put it in his mouth, and chewed. While obviously pondering the problem, he finally nodded. "Yep, he'd need supplies. 'Course he mighta gone over to Durango for 'em."

Lingo shook his head. "Don't know the man, but I can't figure many would go that far to stock up when he can get what he wants this close to home."

Slagle nodded. "Figger you're right. We better nose around up there; see what we can see."

When they finished eating, Sam paid the bill, and to Lingo's disgust, Sam said they'd walk, it was only a little over a mile. Hell, if it had been only across the street, Barnes would have ridden his horse, but he followed Slagle up the hill—afoot.

When they got close, and Sam had pointed out the mine entrance, Lingo held his arm out to stop the miner. "Slagle, let's don't mess up any sign that might tell us somethin'."

Sam's brow wrinkled. "You know anythin' 'bout readin' sign?"

Lingo grinned. "Slagle, I grew up in Comanche country. I wouldn't be part o' this world if I hadn't learned right young to pay attention to what's around me."

Sam's face reddened. "Sorry, young feller, you talk like you done seen the inside o' a schoolhouse. I figgered you wouldn't know nothin' 'bout them other things."

Barnes nodded. "Ma an' Pa both had pretty good book learnin', as they put it, so they insisted that I go to school."

While he talked, Lingo studied the ground. They stood about twenty-five or thirty feet from the mouth of the mine entrance, a heavy, thick-looking pine-slab door. After a few minutes, Lingo took a few steps closer, studied the ground, then closed in on the entrance a few more feet. The ground was soft, but not muddy. All around the area outside of the door footprints sank into the ground.

One set was huge, another small, almost dainty, and another set about the size of his own footprints. Lingo frowned. He'd seen the huge set, and the dainty set before, and had memorized them while tracking them through the forest. They belonged to Shorty Gates and Bull Mayben; the other set he'd never seen before. What were Gates and Mayben doing around Colter's claim? And from the prints, they'd spent quite a lot of time here. That was cause for worry.

The third set was made by a low-quarter town shoe. He knew of no one who wore that kind of foot covering here in this country whether they were miner or cowboy. Of course, it could have been made by one of the townsfolk; some of them wore low-quarter shoes.

"Sam, stay right here. I want a better look at two of those sets o' prints."

Slagle looked from the prints to Lingo. "I know them two varmints who made the big and little tracks. Done had trouble with 'em both. They ain't miners fer sure, an' I reckon none o' you who run cows would claim 'em neither. Don't know who them low-quarter shoeprints b'long to."

Barnes hadn't intended to say anything about recognizing the two sets of prints, but when Sam admitted to knowing the two men who'd made the prints, and not liking them, he relented on that intent a little. He glanced at Slagle, but would still hold back on letting Slagle know why he was here.

5

SLAGLE STEPPED UP beside Lingo. "Let's go rattle the lock on that door. Maybe we can pull it loose."

Barnes had been tempted to do that very thing, then had second thoughts. "Nope. We walk to that door we're gonna let them know somebody's been here. I figure at least one o' those three can read sign well as we can. 'Sides that, I don't know what we could expect to find in there that would help us know where Colter might've gone." He shrugged. "Don't reckon I'm gonna find me a job today."

Slagle looked from Lingo to the door, then again looked at Barnes. "Hell, man, I'm gittin' more'n enough dust outta my diggin's to keep me livin' right good. Why don't you bunk in with me 'til Colter shows up. Know you must a rode the grubline while cowboyin', so figger this here as bein' one o' them ranches you stopped at. Ain't gonna hurt me none to feed 'nother mouth." He grinned. "'Sides that, I like your company."

A rush of warmth flooded Lingo's chest, and with it came trust. He looked Slagle in the eye, and at the same time the warmth pushed up across his face. "Slagle, I've not been perfectly honest with you. If you'll not judge me until I tell you the story I'd be beholden to you."

Slagle eyed him a moment, then motioned down the hill. "C'mon, we'll go sit in my cabin, drink a little o' my whisky, an' you can tell me why you don't trust me."

Lingo shook his head. "Didn't say I don't trust you. What I'm sayin' is, I needed to know more 'bout you 'fore I made up my mind."

Slagle gave a jerky nod. "All right, let's git on down there an' you tell your story."

In Sam's cabin, sitting across the table from each other, Lingo started with the stage holdup and brought Slagle up to where they sat at the table. Lingo spread his hands, palms up. "So you see, Sam, I didn't know who to trust. My ranch is in a hangin' valley not too far on the other side of the mountain. I'm not broke. I know I led you to believe my pockets were empty but I had to have some reason to ask 'bout Colter's mine, an' try to find out somethin' 'bout him."

Sam frowned, pulled Lingo's glass over in front of him, tilted the bottle, and poured them each another drink. He grinned. "Tell you what, young'un; figger I'd' a played the hand much like you done." His brow creased, a deep furrow between his eyes. "Son, I wantta help if we can think o' any way we can work it without messin' up your way o' findin' the man. Little as I knowed 'im, I liked 'im. Hope nothin's done happened to 'im"—he shook his head—"but I ain't holdin' out much faith that hope's gonna pan out."

"For Emily's sake, I hope you're wrong." Barnes knocked back his drink, shook his head when Sam held the bottle to pour him another, and said, "But yeah, let's look at the things I gotta know, an' see if there're any you can help with. Don't want to get you a pack o' trouble though—or stop you from doin' your own work."

Slagle, his face thoughtful, sat a moment, then nodded. "Tell you what, Lingo, I need to take a few days off from that back-breakin' work in the mine, an' trouble here ain't the issue. Me wantin' to help will help all o' us here in Silverton. We don't want that kind o' folks around. We got 'nuff troubles with Saturday night fights, don't need no more."

They studied the problem awhile, then Lingo asked if Sam had any writing paper and a pencil. Sam pulled a tablet from a cabinet drawer, rummaged about in another drawer, and found a pencil. Then they rehashed the things they'd talked about.

As each item for investigation came up, Lingo wrote it down; the first on his list was to find the man who made the low-quarter shoe tracks.

Lingo looked at Slagle. "Neither of those two have the brains to do anything on their own. Maybe this other man doesn't either, but he's our next target. We find him, we may be able to find what they're tryin' to do. Right now, I'm inclined to think they're tryin' to steal Colter's mine, an' findin' out the old man had a daughter threw a rabid skunk into the henhouse."

A frown creased Slagle's red, weathered brow. "We been wonderin' if they wuz anythin' I could do, well, reckon we done found somethin'. Them two dumb ones will know you, but not that you know Emily Lou. You already got trouble with 'em if they see you, so why not let me roam 'round town an' see can I find who their partner—or boss—is. Bet money all three been seen together here in town. Don't figger they spent all their time in Durango."

Pencil point resting on the tablet, Lingo nodded. "You're right. It won't settle anything for me to tangle with 'em here in town. Besides, I figure you being a citizen o' this town, you can get around an' ask questions without arousin' suspicion. Fact is, none o' those three might be pullin' the strings on what's happened. Might even be somebody here in town got wind of Colter's big strike, an' figures to take over his mine."

"Way I got it figgered, too. I gotta be gosh-dinged careful how I ask questions."

Lingo only nodded, then looked around the room. "Reckon I could talk you into lettin' me make a pot o' coffee?"

"Why dadgum it, I wuz jest gonna ask if you wanted a cup. I'll put it on since I know where the makin's are." Sam stood, went to the cupboard, and said over his shoulder, "Once I find them two rascals ain't in town, why don't you move your stuff up here? Ain't no sense in you payin' a hotel bill even if you *can* afford it."

A slight smile crinkled Lingo's lips. "Only if you'll take some money from me an' buy provisions with it. Not gonna mooch offa you."

Sam nodded. "Reckon that'd sortta make us partners in this, but yeah, we'll split the cost o' what I spend." He frowned, obviously pondering the problem further. "Hey, know what? If I go around buyin' stuff, it'll give me a good chance to ask questions in each store I go in. Reckon I can git started now. We'll git you moved down here after dark. You stay here 'til I git back."

Lingo nodded. "I'll be here."

Slagle—already deep into where to get started—left, thinking maybe the general store would be the best place to start.

In the store, he wandered around, looked at items of clothing, went to the grocery shelves, scanned them, and wished he'd made a list of things to buy before leaving his cabin. After his second trip around the store, Ted Murchison, the proprietor, walked over to him, grinning. "Damn, Slagle, you've been around the store twice, still lookin' like you don't know what you wantta buy. Can I help you?"

Sam shrugged. "You right. I left the cabin without makin' a list." He grinned. "Always hate pickin' up a pencil 'cause I know writin's a hard chore fer me. Thought if I walked around an' saw anythin' I wanted it might let me know what I need."

"Tell you what, I just got a shipment of them airtights, vegetables, fruits, stuff like that. Why don't you go in the back and look the boxes over, pick what you want, an' I'll sack it up for you. Ain't had time to put 'em on the shelves yet."

Sam nodded and grinned. "Bet they's stuff there I ain't tasted since last spring when some o' them farmers outside Durango brought in some. I'll go back there an' see what you got."

He headed for the back of the store. In the musty, dusty, dark confines of stacked boxes he read the labels on each box, made a mental note of what he wanted—cans of beans, peaches, greens, cherries, dried apples—and then came to a box without a label defining what was inside. It had a name on it he didn't recognize: Randall Bartow. He scratched his head. He'd heard the name somewhere but couldn't place it. He knew the man wasn't a mine owner, and wondered what was in the box. He checked it further; the box came from a company in Baltimore, Maryland. Slagle knew every miner in the area by name, and by sight. Several of them were Easterners, but none was named Bartow. He went out to the front of the store again, and selected pipe and cigarette tobacco, coffee, cornmeal, flour, and other items until Murchison, after taking care of a customer, walked to his side. "Find anythin' back yonder you want?"

Sam nodded, called out a list while the proprietor wrote it down, then said, "Seen a box for a man named Bartow. Don't recollect makin' 'is acquaintance. He a miner?"

Murchison shook his head. "Don't know. He ain't very friendly. He come in here with a woman by the name o'

Maddie Brice. They got a cabin up a draw somewhere outta here. Don't make no pretense as to bein' married, but they're livin' together, which ain't none o' my business. She comes in here to buy groceries an' other things once in a while. She ain't talkative neither. Ain't seen neither one of 'em in a week or more."

Still holding the pad of paper on which he'd written what Sam wanted, he nodded toward the pad. "You want anythin' else, or you want me to sack this stuff up?"

Figuring he'd gotten all that he could out of Murchison without arousing suspicion, he thought a few moments, frowning. "Don't know, Ted. Why don't you put it all in a gunnysack an' hang on to it while I roam around town awhile. If I think o' anythin' else while I'm gone, I'll get it when I git back. Tally up what I owe you an' I'll pay when I git back."

While walking about the town, he went in stores and bought things he really didn't need, but wanted an excuse to talk. He bought a belt, Sunday-go-to-meeting shirt, and trousers, didn't get anything out of talking to those storekeepers, then thought of boots—or shoes. Maybe the bootmaker would know something. He looked down at his boots, grimaced, and reckoned he could use a new pair; the ones he wore were cracked out at the sides.

When he walked through the door of the bootmaker's shop he was butted head-on with the greeting, "Hey, Sam, I figured you'd damn near be barefooted by now. Reckon you need a new pair of boots?"

Slagle grinned. "Never mind givin' me your special brand o' horse hockey. Yeah, figger these ain't gonna last much longer, an' ain't got nobody to leave them nuggets an' dust to, so I'll git me a new pair." While removing both boots for the bootmaker to measure his feet, he looked up. "You ever make low-quarter shoes fer anybody?"

The bootmaker, who went by the name of Stanton Levell, frowned. "Funny you should ask." He nodded. "I just a couple weeks ago wuz asked to make a pair of those kind o' shoes for a man. Told 'im, yeah I could make 'em, fact is that's all I ever made in Boston 'fore comin' to this here country." He scratched his head. "Cain't remember his name, let's see." He turned to pick up a scratch pad from his workbench. "Yeah, here's his name. Man by the name of Bartow, Randall Bartow. Said he'd come by an' pick 'em up when I got 'em made." Levell grinned. "Told 'im to give me three weeks." His grin widened. "Didn't tell 'im we'd most likely have snow butt-deep to a Texas longhorn by then. Those shoes ain't gonna give 'im much comfort with snow piled over the tops of 'em."

"You got an idea when he'll pick 'em up?"

Levell checked his pad again. "Yep. Told 'im November tenth. He said he'd be here."

The bootmaker noted the measurements of Slagle's feet, then Sam put his worn-out boots back on and left to check out the saloons. He'd not asked about Gates and Mayben in the places he'd been.

In the fifth saloon he went in, the bartender remembered the brawny troublemaker and his short sidekick. "Yeah, they come in here 'bout every night, 'cept they ain't been in here in some sort of time." He frowned. "Hell yes, I remember 'em. You friends o' theirs?"

Slagle shook his head. "Ain't no way. I got a friend who's had trouble with 'em. Wanted to tell 'im to stay clear o' where them two hang out. Ain't no point in borrowin' trouble."

The bartender nodded. "An' I guaran-damn-tee you I 'preciate him stayin' away. Don't need my place wrecked agin."

"Figger to keep 'im outta here 'til we're sure they ain't gonna be here. He got the hell beat outta him last time they tangled over in Durango, an' he's still hurtin'." Sam dug in his vest pocket and pulled out a small leather bag, obviously containing heavy nuggets. "Want a couple bottles o' the best whisky you got." He raised his eyebrows and smiled. "Gonna sample a shot outta both them bottles 'fore I take 'em." His smile widened. "Whisky, even the same brand, out here, can taste one helluva lot different from bottle to bottle."

"Don't blame you, but my *good* whisky comes straight outta Kentucky. Seal ain't broke 'tween here an' there." He hesitated. "Tell you what I'm gonna do; you keep your friend outta here, an' I'll sell you two bottles o' my *good* stuff for what it cost me. Okay?"

Sam nodded. "Reckon I'd keep 'im outta here forever for that kind o' deal." He picked up the two bottles the bartender pushed across the bar, checked the seal around the cork, paid the saloon keeper, and left.

Outside, he leaned against the wall, frowned, and wondered where the bully and the gunslinger were. His guess was that they had gone to Durango. If he could have looked in a cabin up Catamount Draw, he'd have known better.

Randall Bartow, Bull Mayben, and Shorty Gates stared across the table at each other. Maddie Brice stood by the stove listening to what they had to say.

Bartow, knowing the two were afraid of him—and his sleeve gun—enjoyed browbeating them. "Since you two stupid bastards can't seem to do anything right, I think I'll keep you close to me for a while. Maybe you won't mess anything else up that way."

Gates squirmed, stared into his empty glass, then looked at Bartow. "Boss, wasn't nobody could've got that girl here. We had too many men to fight."

Bartow stared at Shorty for several long moments. "You just shut the hell up." He twisted to look at Maddie. "Don't stand there like a dumb cow. Our glasses're empty. Fill 'em."

He raked Bull and Shorty with a look he tried to make contemptuous. "Tell you what I want you to do. I'm gonna be gone for a couple of days. This hick town doesn't have an apothecary shop, but I know of one in Durango. I need to get some medicines." He picked up the fresh drink Maddie poured, knocked it back, coughed, then gave the two men a hard look.

"While I'm gone, Maddie's gonna fix up some good food. Want one o' you to scout out the mine each mealtime, be sure there isn't anybody can see you go to it, then I want you to take the old man a good supper, or breakfast, or dinner, or whatever the hell meal it is. I want him fed three times a day. I'm gonna bring back medicine to doctor the burns and cuts we've given him."

"What you gonna do that fer, boss? We damned near got 'im where he'll talk."

Bartow pinned Bull with a look that yelled, Dumb, dumb, dumb. "It ever enter your thick skull that rather than talk, he's 'bout dead, an' if he ups an' dies we won't get a thing outta him? He's the only one who knows where that rich vein is. We've looked for it in the shaft, and in the area outside. We haven't come close to finding it." He didn't say that none of the three would know the vein if they bumped head-on into it. Their knowledge of geology was absolutely nil.

He looked at Maddie. She poured him another drink. He shivered and swept Bull and Shorty with another look. "While I'm gone, I don't want either of you in town at the saloons or whorehouses. You stay right here, an' I'm tellin' you both, keep your eyes and hands to yourself. You bother my woman, even a little bit, an' I'll kill you. Understand?" They both nodded. "All right. Get outta here. Go to your cabin. Being it's only 'bout fifty feet from here, shouldn't anyone see you. Stay there except to take meals to the mine."

As soon as they cleared the door, Maddie shook her head. "Randall"—she never called him Randy; it made him angry—"Randall, you ever think that one day they might shoot you?"

He nodded. "Yeah, but I'd have to turn my back to them—an' run outta money. Long's I have gold to pay 'em, an' they don't know where I'm gettin' it, they won't shoot me."

"How'd you find out 'bout Colter's strike?"

He stared at her a moment, long enough for her to shrink back into the corner. "First place, woman, that's not any o' your damned business, but I'll tell you this much: There was a pretty reliable rumor goin' 'round the saloons in Durango that he'd made a good strike. I decided I'd take over his claim; didn't know he had a daughter, but I'll get rid o' her."

"Yeah, if you can find 'er."

"Don't smart mouth me, woman. Now get my clothes packed; gonna leave early in the mornin'." Maddie's shoulders slumped. She reminded him of a dog that just got kicked. He liked to keep her like that.

Emily Lou finished setting the table while Kelly dished up the food. When she'd placed the silverware beside the plates to her liking, taking more care than usual, she continued staring at the table. Kelly shook her head. "Em, that big man's all right. He ain't gonna get into nothin' he cain't get outta all by hisself." She put a bowl of mashed potatoes in the middle of the other dishes. "An' I know you're worried 'bout your papa somethin' awful. Don't be. Lingo'll find 'im, an' get 'im outta whatever mess he's in."

Emily looked up. "There isn't anything you can think of that you don't believe Lingo can't take care of, is there?"

Kelly smiled. "Nope. An' I'll tell you like it is; ask Wes, he'll tell you the same thing. There ain't any ten men in this country can stop Lingo Barnes when he sets his mind to somethin'."

Wesley sniffed. "Reckon we could talk while we eat. All the smells o' that food mixed together's got me 'bout starvin'."

"Oh, Wes, you say the same thing ever' time supper's almost on the table. I ain't never seen you when you wasn't starvin'. Sit. We'll eat an' talk."

For a few minutes, the only sound was that of flatware against bowls, then Emily finished chewing a hot buttered biscuit and looked at Wes. "That fire didn't come across the mountain, although the smoke's still layin' thick here in the valley. You reckon Lingo got caught in the fire?"

Wes shook his head. "I figger he was high enough on the mountain to be above it."

"Do you know the way he took outta here?" Then not waiting for him to answer, Emily fired off another question. "Reason I ask, suppose those outlaws decide to dynamite the pass; if they did, we'd be trapped in here."

Wes shook his head. "Nope. First place, I know the way out. Second place, they gotta figger there must be another way outta here, an' they cain't count on you not gettin' out an' tellin the law what they done. No, I don't think they're dumb enough to seal off the pass." He grinned. " 'Sides that, I figger to spend enough time up there to stop anybody what'd try to bottle us up."

Kelly stood, filled their coffee cups, pulled her chair out, and sat. "They could be up there right now."

"Yeah, but I scouted the other side 'bout six miles 'fore I come down for supper. They wasn't nobody even close to the valley. Soon's I finish eatin' I'm goin' back up there an' keep watch."

When he finished supper, Wes brought in a couple armsful of firewood, shrugged into his sheepskin, and left to the tune of two voices telling him to be careful. Kelly watched from the doorway while he rode away.

"If I felt about a man the way you do, Kelly, I think I'd take the bull by the horns and just flat out tell 'im."

Kelly looked from the disappearing rider to Em. "Even if I did have feelin's for him, I'd be fearful of scarin' 'im off. Ain't sayin I got them kind o' feelin's, but if I did, don't reckon I'd be tellin' 'im."

Emily put her arms around Kelly's shoulders. "Oh, honey, every time Wes is close to you, I can see how you want to be even closer. One of these days you'll face up to how you feel. 'Til then you'll yearn for him, but you'll kid yourself that you're happy with the way things are. C'mon, let's get the dishes washed."

Kelly grinned. "Yeah, an' how long're you gonna think 'bout Lingo 'fore you get to thinkin' 'bout him like I do Wes?"

"Oh, pshaw, I just admire him for bein' a whole lot of man."

Kelly's grin widened.

Bartow rode from his cabin before daylight the next morning. He wanted to get salves and any medicines the pharmacist might have in his shop to take care of Colter. Certain the apothecary shop would not be as well-stocked as those where he came from, he decided he'd make do with what the man had.

If he could find Colter's rich vein, he wouldn't wait to do away with Emily Lou. He'd take over the mine, and have a friend of his forge the old man's signature on a phony deed—then he'd wait for Colter's daughter to show up.

He'd rig an accident to eliminate her, as well as any hint that she'd ever been in these parts. Maybe he could fix it such that the men who had rescued her would be blamed for her disappearance. The farther he rode, the more self-satisfied he became.

By the time he walked into the apothecary shop shortly before sundown, he felt that the sun had only then risen on his dream. He would be rich before long.

He bought the latest in salves for burns and cuts, and at the pharmacist's suggestion that he must have had someone hurt badly, he told him that he only wanted to be prepared in the event one of his miners got hurt. Then when the proprietor asked where his mine was located, he gave a vague answer that it was between Silverton and Ouray.

He left the shop, went to the hotel, rented a room, then washed trail dust from his face and hands and went to find a place to eat.

In the cafe, with its tables of rough-hewn boards with benches on each side, only one seat stood empty. He sat, and found that his supper partner was a man wearing a badge. After introducing himself, he glanced at the marshal's badge. "See you're the law in these parts."

"Just in this town. I'm a marshal, not a sheriff," Nolan said. He glanced at Bartow's clothing. "You new around here? We don't see many city folks here abouts."

Bartow chuckled. Then trying to sound as though he was from this part of the country, said, "Naw, I'm a miner, that is, I own a mine. I like to clean up an' dress up when I come to town."

Nolan glanced at Bartow's hands. Not a callous. The marshal knew a phony when he saw one, and this man was phony as a three-dollar bill. He wondered why the man lied about what he was.

Nolan dawdled over the rest of his supper. He wanted to watch the man walk from the cafe. Finally, after more coffee than he wanted, the marshal studied Bartow when he stood and walked away. The man wore run-over-at-the-heels, low-quarter shoes, a suit with an Eastern cut that had seen better days, and no hat—rather odd for a Rocky Mountain miner. He'd have to think about what he'd seen for a while. He'd been a lawman too long to dismiss small things like he'd just observed. Too, he thought he'd met or seen the man before. He thought about that a few moments, then shrugged mentally. He'd think of where he'd come across the man.

His thoughts shifted to the tall rancher. Why? Was there some tie-in with the rancher and the miner? Nolan shook his head. The rancher was a straight-forward, honest-as-a man-would-want-to-meet sort of man. The miner would bear watching. Nolan chuckled. He'd been a lawman so long it had gotten to the point where he found shadows and suspicions everywhere he looked. He groaned, pushed back from the table, and set out to make the earliest of his nightly rounds—saloons and brothels.

Lingo cocked his head. Someone was trudging up the path to the cabin. Sounded like a big man carrying a load. He grinned, and wondered if Slagle had found out anything. He went to the door, and then rushed out to help the brawny miner with his load. "Damn, man, looks like you bought out the stores."

Slagle grinned. "Bought a bunch o' stuff I shoulda bought a long time ago." His grin widened. "Hell, I even ordered myself a new pair o' boots." He looked down at his feet. "Not that I needed 'em. Could a worn these 'til they sifted snow onto my toes." He went through the doorway and swung the gunnysacks to the tabletop. "Brung us a couple o' jugs o' *good* whisky, too."

Lingo crinkled his brow. "Reckon you can figure those jugs o' whisky are on my part o' this bill. Never figured on gettin' another partner in this problem I got."

"You got 'nother partner?"

Lingo studied the big man. He actually looked disappointed to find that Barnes had another partner. Lingo nodded. "I was talkin' 'bout this problem I got with those two varmints who took Em offa that stage, but yeah, I got another partner, in this problem, as well as in my ranch.

"He don't know it. Figure to let 'im know that half the ranch is his when he grows up."

Slagle eyed him with the most solemn look Lingo had seen in a long time. "Figgered on you bein' my partner, after we got through catchin' them varmints what's givin' you a bad time. Figgered we might do some prospectin' together."

Lingo studied the big man a few moments. "Tell you what, big'un, let's wait 'til you meet Wesley Higgins, then if it's all right with the both of you, we'll partner up the three of us." He grinned. "An' to my way o' thinkin', it's gonna be all right."

Like a slow rising sun, a smile started at the corners of Slagle's lips and spread until it covered his face. "Well I'll be damned. I got myself a partner." He cocked his head and squinted at Lingo. "Tell you right sudden though, I ain't no cowboy, fact is, I don't know nothin' 'bout cows, but I got a right good payin' mine here. We could lump 'em together an' maybe have a business that would keep us outta the poor house in bad years. Know sometimes them gold-bearin' rocks get skimpy, an' I figger the cow business has slim times, too."

While he talked, Lingo worried the cork from one of the bottles the big miner had brought home, then he tilted it over a couple of glasses. "Big'un, we won't worry 'bout paperwork right yet. Don't want people here 'bouts knowin' we know each other, but soon's we find Emily Lou's pa, an' those men who took 'er off the stage, we'll get papers drawn up to make us real partners. Too, it'll give us both time to think 'bout it, an' if we decide partnerin' up won't work, then we can simply say so an' nothin'll be hurt."

Sam shook his head. "Don't need no paperwork. We drink that whisky you done poured in that glass to seal the deal, then far's I'm concerned we're partners."

Lingo nodded, held up his glass, touched the glass Slagle held, and knocked his drink back. "Wait'll I tell Wes."

Lingo stayed in Sam's cabin, took exercises for hours each day, and finally pronounced he felt good as he ever had. His rib had healed slower than the wound that broke it, but now he thought he could fight a grizzly.

Slagle had looked at him every day, but never questioned why Barnes felt the need to stay strong. Now he frowned and looked at Lingo, who dripped sweat. "Why you always doin' them exercises?"

Lingo let the corners of his mouth break in a smile, but knew his eyes remained cold as a glacier. "Remember I told you Mayben wanted to fight me in that Durango saloon, an' I held 'im off at pistol point? Well, I figured he might kill me if he hit me in the side, splintered that rib, an' drove it into my lungs.

"I no longer have that worry, an' I promised 'im that one day we'd get it on. I figure I owe 'im a good lickin'. He don't know I saw 'im take Em off o' that stage. Not gonna tell 'im either, 'til I find her pa, then I'm gonna tell 'im just before I put a bullet 'tween his eyes."

Sam stared at Lingo a moment, then blew a silent whistle through pursed lips. "Young'un, if that man could look in your eyes right now he'd pack 'is gear an' make tracks outta here." He threw a towel to Lingo. "Here, dry off, then tell me when an' where you figger to tangle with 'im."

Barnes toweled the sweat from his brow, face, and shoulders, went to the water bucket, drank a dipperful, then glanced at Slagle. "Only thing we've seen of either of 'em 'round here since we started lookin' is their footprints. Since you couldn't find 'em here, I figure they must be in Durango." He drank another dipper of water, wiped his mouth, and nodded. "Yep, an' if they're not there when I get there, I'll wait for 'em. They'll be there sooner or later."

"When you leavin'?"

"Come daylight I'll be headin' out."

Sam grinned. "Ain't gonna ride with you 'cause it'd let folks know we know each other, but I'm tellin' you right now, young'un, I ain't gonna miss watchin' that fight. I won't be more'n an hour behind you—an' if you find 'em 'fore I git there, hold off 'til you see me in the saloon."

Lingo shook his head, and his face solemn, said, "Damn, Sam, you're a blood-thirsty old devil, aren't you?"

Slagle's grin broadened. "Lingo, I done watched you all this time. You ain't jest got muscles; you got muscles on top o' them what most men's got. If I hadn't seen you with your shirt off, I'da figgered you for almost slim. An' to top that off, ever'thing you do is quick, like a cat. That there man's gonna get mighty surprised."

The morning after sitting at supper with Marshal Nolan, Bartow packaged the medicines he'd bought and headed back to Silverton. While riding, he mulled over what to do about Mayben and Gates. He never had a thought but that he'd get rid of them when they ceased to be useful. He wondered if that time had come. Could they still be of use to him? Too, he didn't need Maddie Brice for anything except to cook and clean house for him. He could take care of his woman needs in town. He shrugged mentally. He'd worry about when and how to rid himself of all three after he got Colter well enough to talk.

He blamed Mayben and Gates for not doing the job right when they took Emily Lou from the stage. Thinking about it caused blood to flood his brain, bile to choke him, his fists to clench. Hereafter, if he wanted something done right, he'd do it himself; but there might still be a few things they could do for him.

Tired of seeing the two louts hanging around, and not being able to help him get the information he wanted, he decided to send them to Durango for a few days. If Emily Lou showed up there he told them to think of some way to get rid of her. At any rate, he wanted them away from his cabin for a while; he'd take over feeding and caring for Colter until he got what he wanted from him.

The next morning, long before sunup, Barnes and Slagle readied themselves for a few days in Durango. After putting all in their bedrolls they'd need away from home, Slagle busied himself with setting the table, placing stove wood handy, and putting cooking pots and pans by the stove.

Sitting at the table, watching his friend, Lingo smiled. They'd done the same thing down Texas way. If travelers passed by, they could come in, prepare a meal, clean things up, and leave them as they'd found them. He felt good to know Sam observed the same trust and courtesy that he'd known at home. When Slagle looked to be satisfied that his unknown visitors could make do, they picked up their bedrolls and went to saddle their horses.

Slagle pulled the cinch tight, then looked across his saddle at Lingo. "You go on ahead. I'll sit here, smoke my pipe, then follow you in 'bout an hour. Now you remember; Don't you tangle with that there Bull Mayben 'til you see me."

Barnes nodded. "Been thinkin' 'bout that. I'll make sure you're there 'cause I want you to cover my back. That worm of a Shorty Gates is the kind who'd shoot me in the back, especially if I'm gettin' the best of his partner." He held up his hand in a casual wave. "See ya in Durango."

6

ANXIOUS TO GET to the saloons and brothels of Durango, Gates and Mayben rode at a fast pace, and if either of them had looked behind during the straight stretches in the trail they might have caught a glimpse of Lingo Barnes only a few minutes behind. Bull glanced across his shoulder at Shorty. "Wonder why the boss give us a few days off. Reckon he really thinks that there girl's gonna show up in Durango or Animas City?"

Shorty squinted, and looked down the trail between his horse's ears. He nodded. "Yeah, he might think such, but I been givin' it some thought. I figger he wants us outta the way while he works on that Colter feller. Figger if Colter tells 'im anything, Bartow don't want neither o' us to hear what he says."

Bull shook his head. "Why you think he don't want us to hear? Hell, we're his partners. He done said we gonna split the takin's from that vein—a half to us, an' a half to him. You an' me, we figgered that wuz fair since he thought up the deal."

Shorty rolled a cigarette before he answered. He took a long drag, let the smoke curl out of his mouth, and inhaled it up his nose. "Bull, if they wuz a whole pile o' gold a'layin' on the table an' you could have it all by gittin' rid o' your partners, what would you do? Or, if like in this case you found out where it was an' the other two didn't know what you'd found out, would you tell 'em?" He shook his head. "Nope, don't figger we ever gonna git none o' that gold if he finds where the old man struck the vein."

"What we gonna do then?"

Shorty took a last drag off his cigarette, pinched the fire out between his thumb and forefinger, then grinned. "Tell you what I figger we gonna do. If we find the girl, we gonna git rid o' her, then watch that slick willy we done tied up with 'til we know what he knows, then we kill 'im, an' if Colter's still alive we get rid o' him, too, an' keep it all."

Bull bit off a huge chew of tobacco, settled it in his jaw, and frowned. "I ain't gonna take a chance o' drawin' against that sleeve gun Bartow's so smooth with."

"Don't neither o' us have to buck that kind o' odds. We'll nail 'im from the trees, or brush, or along the trail somewhere when he don't know we're around."

"Think it'll work, Shorty? You notice he don't ever let neither o' us git behind 'im."

Gates nodded. "It'll work. Now let's git on down to town, have a few drinks, see if that girl's done showed up, an' if that gutless bastard who wouldn't fight you last time we wuz here is in town you can whip his butt." He grinned. "Then we gonna git rompin', stompin' drunk."

"Whoooee, you make it sound mighty good." They urged their horses to a faster gait.

Lingo kept his horse to little more than a walk. He'd seen the two horsemen ahead of him, didn't recognize them, but didn't want company, so he rode slowly. He thought about the upcoming fight, if Mayben was in Durango.

He didn't want to fight Bull, but figured he'd rather do that than have to shoot him. He'd rather see him and his partner hang for what they did to Emily Lou. The more he thought about seeing the slip of a girl pulled off the stage and flung onto a horse, the more his mind settled on giving Bull a good whipping. Then if he and his partner, Shorty Gates, wanted to make it a gunfight fine, but he wanted to know who they worked for before he allowed guns to be the solution.

Thinking back on his confrontation with Mayben, he couldn't remember what started it, except that Bull wanted to fight simply because he didn't dress like a miner. He shrugged mentally. To hell with them both—fists, guns, or knives—but now that his rib had healed he wanted to settle with Bull with his fists first, then he wanted to find out who this guy Randall Bartow was, and why he'd been snooping around Colter's mine.

Sam had told him about Bartow ordering the low-quarter shoes, and they'd agreed it was probably his footprints they found outside the mine. The only problem they had with the knowledge was: Who was he and what did he have to do with Em's father?

He'd been riding deep in thought, not noticing anything about his surroundings until his horse walked through the door of the livery, stopped, and swung his head to look at his master as if to say, "This is where I want to go, you pick your own place."

Lingo chuckled, closed his eyes, and inhaled. "Hell, old hoss, I'll get you fed and watered, then I'm gonna take care o' my thirst and hunger." He swung his leg over his horse's rump, stepped to the ground, and told the livery man to take care of the gelding.

He left the livery and walked down the street to the cafe

on the opposite side, across from the saloon where he'd had trouble with Mayben. People stood against the wall waiting for a seat to open up. Lingo took his place at the end of the line. He stood there about twenty minutes, watching a few people leave, and those at the head of the line take their place at one of the tables. Then a short, wiry man alongside a huge, beefy man stood and came toward Barnes. They had come abreast of him, and were about to pass, when Mayben's head snapped to the side to peer at Barnes. "Well I'll be damned, jest the yellow bastard we come to town to see."

"Not in here, Mayben. Soon's I get somethin' to eat, I'll meet you in the saloon across the street. We're not gonna wreck this man's place o' business."

Bull lowered his head like one of his namesakes might do before charging. "Still scared, huh? You wantta put off gittin' your butt kicked for now, give you a chance to run. Well, I ain't gonna give ya that chance."

Lingo's neck muscles tightened, blood rushed to his head, and his hand flicked his .44 from the holster. He pushed the barrel into Mayben's gut. "Yeah, you gonna wait 'til I eat, then we'll get it on. Now, 'fore I splatter your guts all over this cafe, turn around and walk out that door. Take that little worm you got with you or I might change my mind 'bout where I take care o' you."

Gates, eyes slitted, hand clawed above his holster, pulled Bull to the side, then stared into Lingo's eyes. "This's the second time you made a sneak draw on us. After Bull breaks ever' bone in that yellow body o' yours, you an' me's gonna see who can shoot fastest an' straightest."

Lingo stared into the worm's eyes. "Get outta here 'fore I change my mind. I'll meet you in the saloon in 'bout an hour. Be there."

Shorty glanced at Barnes's gun, shifted his gaze to his face, nodded, and said, "We'll be there, just make damned sure you show up." They spun on their heels and walked out.

Barnes glanced at the line and saw that everyone had been seated except him. No one seemed to have been aware that there had been a shooting situation very close to happening. Lingo slipped into a seat against the wall. He thought to have a few cups of coffee, steak, potatoes, and any kind of vegetable they might have, then changed his mind. To fight on a full stomach would not be the smartest thing he'd ever done. He shoved back from the table and went outside. He'd wait until he saw Slagle ride in. He wanted the big miner in the saloon—at Shorty's back before he tangled with Bull.

He slouched against the wall for several minutes before Sam rounded a curve in the street, rode to the hitch rack, and tied his horse. Lingo had crossed the street as soon as Slagle reined in to hitch his horse. He came abreast of him, and said out of the side of his mouth, "Get in behind the short one. Don't do anything unless he looks like he's gonna take a hand in the fight." He walked on past, flicked the thong off his Colt's hammer, and pushed through the batwing doors.

Mayben stood, his back to the bar, telling all who would listen how he figured to stomp hell out of a yellow-livered coward who he figured would come through the door at any minute.

Before Bull had time to note that the man he talked about had entered the saloon, Barnes pulled his .44, and held it pointed toward the two outlaws. "You two droppings from a cur don't make a move toward your holsters." The two of them simultaneously swung their heads to look toward the door.

Shorty's hand clawed above his holster. "This's the third time you done drawed a gun on me without givin' me a chance."

"Just wanted to make sure I had an even chance with your white trash partner. Now both o' you shuck your hardware an' lay it on the bar behind you."

Slagle had taken his position alongside Gates. Lingo looked at him. "You, mister, pat 'em down. Make sure neither of them have any weapons left on 'em." Sam did as Barnes directed, then pushed holstered guns and sheath knives across the bar to the bartender.

It was then the man behind the bar swung a double-barreled Greener to the top of the polished surface. "All right. I got their weapons, now you put yours right here alongside of 'em."

While Lingo walked to the bar, unbuckling his gunbelt, the bartender kept all three under the business end of his shotgun, then waved it toward the door. "None o' you are gonna wreck my place of business. You gonna have a fight, take it outside."

Barnes spun on his heel and headed for the door. Off to the side, one of the miners yelled, "You make damned sure ever' fight you have that you outweigh the man you gonna fight by 'bout fifty pounds, don't you, Bull?" That started the betting.

Sam was the first to pull his money belt from his waist. "Anybody gonna give me three to one odds? I figure the slim cowboy'll win this." Instantly, a surge of miners surrounded Slagle covering his bets. When Sam had emptied his money belt, another miner stepped to his side.

"I ain't never seed Sam Slagle back a loser. I'll take some more o' that three-to-one money he's been coverin'."

Finally, the bartender taking care of the bets waved his Greener toward the middle of the street. "Now, git out there an' get at it."

Bull ran to the middle of the dusty trail and turned—in time to catch a right to the ribs that Barnes brought straight out from his belt, then followed with a left to the gut. His fist sank into Bull's gut a good couple of inches. Mayben stopped, sucked air, and swung his huge fist at Lingo.

Barnes moved to the side in time to catch the blow on his shoulder. Despite the flab Lingo detected with his punch to the gut, Mayben's punch showed he was something other than fat. His blow hurt.

Barnes slipped to the side, then closed under a roundhouse swing Bull made with his right. Lingo pumped a right, a left, and a right to Mayben's gut. Bull's eyes bulged. He stumbled backward a couple of steps, caught his balance, and stepped toward Barnes. A roundhouse swing grazed Lingo's head. Lights exploded behind his eyes. Blindly, he moved back, caught his heel on his boot toe and fell. As soon as he felt the ground at his back he rolled to the side. The kick Mayben swung toward Lingo's head caught only air.

Barnes grabbed Mayben's foot and twisted. The big man rolled with the twist, fell, and in one fluid move Lingo gained his feet. He waited for Bull to climb back out of the dirt, then clubbed him with another right to the ribs. Bull's eyes widened. He stepped back out of Lingo's reach, pursed his lips, and sucked air. Barnes hit him again, working on the big man's body, this time an inch or two below Mayben's rib cage. Bull moved beyond Lingo's reach.

Barnes bored in, swinging with each step—every punch going to Mayben's soft body. Each punch drew a ragged, sobbing breath from the big man.

Lingo, at the fringe of his awareness, heard the crowd going wild. He shifted his blows to the heart. Bull's face purpled. Lingo wanted to give the woman-stealing bastard something to remember. He shifted his punches to Mayben's face.

Mayben now gasped for breath, his arms hanging at his sides, barely leaving his body for a weak punch. This opened up what Barnes wanted. He meant for his punches to cut, to maim.

A sharp punch to Mayben's left eye opened a cut that gushed blood, spilling it into his eye. Knowing he was blinded in that eye, Lingo hooked a left to Bull's right eye. It opened a long bloody gash. That punch flowed blood into that eye. The big miner stood, his head swung from side to side. Lingo had seen desperately wounded buffalo do the same. He wasn't through.

Thoughts of Emily Lou being pulled from the stagecoach clouded any thought of knocking the big man out. He'd make this last as long as he could swing a fist.

He swung a right to Mayben's mouth. The miner gagged, spit teeth, and tried to swing his hamlike fists at Lingo. They made only a slow arc in the thin air. Lingo went to work on the man's cheekbones, opened cuts in both of them, then delivered a hard right that flattened the miner's nose. When he saw no more places to cut the man, he dropped his right to his waist and swung, hoping it was hard enough to break his jaw—or his neck. The big man stood there, stared vacantly, stupidly at nothing, then took a staggering step toward Lingo, and fell. His face plowed dust and dirt in the street. He didn't move.

Noise erupted around Barnes. Every man on the street—bet winner or loser—yelled and pummeled each other on the back. One miner yelled, "Don't give a damn if I did lose my poke, it wuz worth it. I been wantin' that bastard to git his comeuppance fer a long time."

Lingo glanced around the crowd. Slagle stood in back of Shorty Gates, one arm wrapped around the little worm's neck. "You ain't gonna go to your partner. We gonna let 'im lie there awhile so's the whole town kin see 'im, an' most who look on 'im gonna be glad he got what wuz comin' to 'im." He continued to hold the short man.

Barnes, his arms feeling like they were made of lead, walked through the batwings and to the bartender who still held his Greener, only now pointed at the ground. "Bartender, don't know how you feel 'bout it, but I figure I earned wearin' my Colt."

The barman grinned. "Reckon there ain't a man here who don't figger it that way. Go on, buckle your belt on, pour yourself a drink from that bottle under the bar while you're at it."

Lingo nodded, staggered a step to the side. He was so tired he could hardly stand. "I figure on shuckin' the shells from Gates's *an'* Mayben's guns while I'm at it. Don't want to kill 'em this time, but I'm gonna do just that next time we tangle."

A look around the crowd showed Sam Slagle pouring nuggets, minted money, and bills into his money belt, and pockets. Barnes smiled. He wished he'd had a few bucks of his own to bet. He shrugged. He'd gotten his satisfaction and pay from doing what he'd waited to do.

Inside the saloon, he first poured himself a liberal drink into a water glass, tasted it, and felt it burn the inside of his cheek. He ran his tongue around his teeth, found them all there, and took another swallow. He'd taken more punishment at Bull's fists than he remembered. Now, it seemed he had sore spots all over his body. He sighed. That rib had taken a few punches and had stood up under the punishment.

After knocking back the rest of his drink, he pushed cartridges from the loops in Bull's and Shorty's gunbelts, emptied the cylinders of each gun, shoved them back in their holsters, walked to the nearest table, and slumped in a chair.

Outside, Slagle glanced at the big miner, Whitey he was called, who had shared his faith in Barnes. "What say we buy these guys a drink? Reckon we done won enough to do that without makin' a dent in what we won."

Whitey held his hands over his head and waved for the crowd to go inside. "C'mon, me an' Sam's gonna buy y'all a drink."

They ran for the batwings. The bartender, already inside, tossed Slagle a clean towel, handed him a bucket of water, and flicked his thumb toward Lingo. "Clean up the man's face. I ain't pourin' nobody nothin' 'til that man's feelin' better."

When Sam took the towel and bucket from him, Shorty Gates came to the bar. "Want me an' my partner's gunbelts and six-shooters."

The bartender handed them across the bar. "Tell you somethin', Gates. Don't want you or your partner in this saloon anymore. You come in, I'm gonna have you throwed out."

Without a word, but with a look that promised he and Mayben would be back, Shorty took the belts and guns from the bartender's hands and walked out. Without saying any more, the barman picked up a bottle and poured drinks. Through all this, Sam gave no hint that he and Lingo were friends. The fact was, he asked Barnes what name he went by and made sure there were men standing close who would hear.

Outside, Gates looked toward where Mayben had fallen. Bull apparently hadn't moved. There were a few men who hadn't gone in the saloon with the rest. They stood, staring at the man who most would have bet nobody could whip. Shorty handed one of them his and Mayben's weapons, went to his partner, and squatted at his side. The big man didn't stir.

Gates stared at where Mayben's eyes should be, but couldn't tell whether he tried to open them. They were both swollen shut behind mangled, purple flesh. "Can you hear me? You can, jest nod your head; gonna see can I get you to a doctor. That scrawny cowboy worked you over somethin' awful." He shook his head. "Never figgered nobody could do that."

Mayben's mouth opened, closed. He pushed a clot of blood and teeth between his cut and swollen lips, then mumbled, "He hit me 'fore I wuz ready. He cain't do it agin in no fair fight."

Gates put his hands under Mayben's shoulders and tried to pull him to a sitting position. "He ain't gonna git no chance to do it agin, partner. I'm gonna fill 'im so full o' lead he ain't gonna be able to do nothin'. Gonna kill 'im, Bull. We ain't gonna argue 'bout that. Next time I see 'im I'm jest gonna start shootin'." He pulled on Bull's shoulders again. "See can you stand an' we'll find a doctor. Then we gonna git a hotel room 'til you heal. Then we gonna go cowboy huntin'." He helped Mayben stand, pulled his arm across his shoulders. "Don't know where he'll be, but we'll find 'im." A few staggering steps farther, Gates stopped, gasped under the heavy load, then said, "We wuz gonna keep that cowboy from drinkin' in a miner's waterin' hole; now damned if that bartender ain't said we wuzn't to come in there no more."

Wes spent most of his time guarding the pass. Kelly brought him his meals, even brought him water, razor, and changes of clothing. Each time she came, she wore clean clothing, and smelled like she'd only moments before gotten out of the big tin tub they kept hanging on the wall outside of the kitchen door.

He'd taken to looking at her—really looking at her. That poor little thing he'd kept out of the reaches of ne'er-do-wells down Taos way had grown up while he wasn't looking. To his way of thinking, he'd never seen a prettier woman anywhere. Of course, that Emily Lou that Lingo had brought home was right pretty, too—but to his thinking, not as pretty as Kelly.

The afternoon of the same day Lingo whipped Bull Mayben, Kelly harnessed the team and drove the buckboard to the pass with food for Wes.

She jumped from the boot, spread a blanket, and set out plates for the two of them. She glanced over her shoulder at him. "Me an' Em figgered you needed some company, so we packed a picnic dinner for you an' me." She then went about taking several pots and pans of food from the wagonbed.

The smells of hot vegetables, baked venison, biscuits, even coffee, caused saliva to flow under Wes's tongue. "Aw, hell, Kelly, you shouldn't oughtta done that. It makes more work for you an' Em. Beans an' bacon woulda been good 'nuff fer me."

Kelly looked at him a full moment. "Wes, you been makin' do with almost nothin' good to eat ever since Lingo left you to do all the watchin'. 'Course I know he didn't have no choice, but you cain't stay healthy eatin' the way you been doin', so me an' Em decided we gonna feed you right from now on." She sat and patted the blanket next to her. "Now come on. Set an' I'll fix a plate fer you."

While they ate, he kept glancing at her, finally she pinned him with a no-nonsense look. "Wes Higgins, why you lookin' at me that way? It's—it's . . . well, it's almost like you ain't never seen me before."

He finished chewing a bite of venison, then nodded. "Ain't 'til just recent. Aw, I been lookin', but I ain't never really seen what wuz happenin' right before my eyes."

A rosy glow flushed Kelly's face. Her eyes opened wide. "What wuz happenin' right 'fore your eyes, Wesley Higgins?"

It was *his* turn to blush now, and he did. He felt like his face was on fire. "Kelly, while I wuzn't lookin' real hard, you done turned to a growed-up woman—a danged pretty growed-up woman."

She lowered long lashes over her eyes, then looked at him straight on. "You know what, cowboy?" He shook his head. "I wuz beginnin' to think you wasn't ever gonna notice I wasn't the same scrawny little thing you brought to yours and Lingo's camp. You ain't the same hell-raisin' cowboy you wuz back then neither. You done growed up some yourself." Her face turned pink again. "But you know what? You ain't a danged bit better-lookin' now than you wuz then."

She took a swallow of coffee. "Know why I don't think you're any better-lookin'?" She lowered her lashes, hid her eyes from him. "You ain't no better-lookin' now 'cause you wuz so pretty back then I knowed you couldn't git no better-lookin'."

"Aw hell, Kelly, a man ain't never pretty. He might be right good to look at, but he ain't never pretty."

Kelly took another swallow of coffee, looked him in the eye, and nodded. "You are."

They ate in silence. Then, their meal finished, Kelly covered the pans, gathered the dishes, and placed them in the buckboard. She looked over her shoulder at him. "Wes, I wuz gonna offer to stay up here tonight, keep you company. Don't reckon that'd be a good idea now." She said it, but Wes detected a tone of hope that he'd ask her to stay.

He wouldn't do that. He wasn't going to spoil something he'd only now realized that he'd had before his eyes for a long time. He shook his head. "Naw, now Kelly. Don't reckon you an' me better push our luck any more'n we already have. We got a long time in this life, an' I want it to be somethin' we'll look back on an' be right proud of someday."

Kelly pinned him with a look that entered his very soul. "Knowed you wuz gonna say that. Sorta hoped you would—an' sorta hoped you wouldn't; but you're right. We ain't gonna push our luck. 'Sides that, we gotta talk to Lingo 'bout what we done found out."

"Why we gotta talk to Lingo?"

She grinned. " 'Cause you an' me always talk to him 'bout ever'thin' important. An', cowboy, I don't reckon neither one o' us ever gonna have nothin' more important than what we jest now been talkin' 'bout." She put the rest of the gear she'd brought with her in the buckboard, climbed to the seat, slapped the reins against the horse's rumps, and drove down the trail.

Wes watched her ride off. He frowned. Somehow they'd said a lot without saying much. Neither of them had talked of love, wanting, hurting for each other, but somehow, it had all been said. Wes smiled. He'd wait, and yeah, they'd talk to Lingo about what they'd discovered.

When Kelly walked into the cabin with a load of pots and pans, Emily Lou rushed to the buckboard to finish getting the gear Kelly had taken with her. When she came in, Kelly sat at the table staring at the wall; her expression was one that said, "Everything's right with the world." Emily took a chair across the table from her newfound friend.

"I don't have to ask. I think Wes has finally seen that you're a woman, a woman with the feelings, emotions, and needs of a grown woman."

Kelly continued to stare at the wall. She nodded. "Yep. An he's got them same needs an' all you said, but even if he's been a hell-raiser most o' his life, he's a gentleman. We never said nothin' 'bout love—but it wuz there." She smiled. "I told 'im I wanted to stay on the mountain with 'im tonight." She turned her look on Emily Lou. "Know what he said? He turned me down, said as how we wuzn't thinkin' straight, said we'd talk to Lingo 'bout it." Her eyes swimming, she shook her head. "Reckon we gonna have to get Lingo's sayin' it's all right even when we decide we gonna do what all men an' women do." She sniffled, blew her nose, and grinned. "Know what? I figger it's what we oughtta do. Even though that big man ain't much older'n me an' Wes, he's been almost a daddy to us." She nodded. "Yep. We gonna talk to Lingo 'bout it."

Emily pulled Kelly to her breast and hugged her, and while holding her close, a knot formed in her throat; she couldn't swallow, tears flooded her eyes, and the pride she felt for the big man who had so recently come into her life swelled her chest. Why should she feel this way?

She was beholden to him—even more than that, it was such a weak word for saving her from the most degrading experience a woman could suffer. Gratitude—yes, and many other words that would say "thank you." But at the ground roots she had *faith* that he would make the right decision. Was her faith justified? She would not try to answer that question . . . yet.

Lingo went from the saloon, got himself a room, and ordered hot, not warm, but hot bathwater. He waited. About a half hour after sitting in the only chair in the room, a light tap on his door sounded. He slipped his Colt from its holster and turned to the door. "It's unlocked."

Sam pushed through the door, a lopsided smile sliding his lips to the side, and a jug of whisky in each hand. "Jest wanted to tell you, ain't a miner in town what wouldn't buy you a drink, an' welcome you into bein' a miner."

Lingo stared at his friend. "You're drunk."

Slagle opened his eyes wide, stared at Barnes, and walked to sit on the bed. He nodded. "Yep. Figger I'm a *leettle* less than sober, an' ain't said a word to no one 'bout us bein' partners, but this here's a day to celebrate. You done whipped the worst bully in the state, I done won more gold than I can take outta our mine in a month, an' you done made more friends than either one o' us can count. Danged right I'm just a leetle drunk."

Barnes stared at his friend a moment. A warm feeling flooded his chest. He knew then that he'd made a real friend, a friend he could ride the river with. He smiled, and his insides smiled with him. He was the luckiest man in the world. The kid he'd taken under his wing had grown to be a man to be proud of, he'd found a new friend to partner up with, and he'd met the most beautiful woman he ever hoped to meet but—why had he included Emily Lou in the avalanche of good luck he was having? He frowned. He didn't want to think about that yet.

He looked at his partner, then grinned. "Well, partner, I reckon we'll know whether it's a day to celebrate when I have to meet that short little bastard with a gun in my hand, an' I figure he's not all talk. He may be right handy with that six-shooter tied to his side. Every time I pulled a gun on 'im, I did it before he had an idea I intended to make a draw."

"Aw hell, Lingo, I figger ain't any two men in Colorado can beat you to the draw. I seen the slick way your gun comes to hand. You're fast, man. I ain't never seen nobody who could beat you." He popped the cork on one of the bottles he'd brought into the room, poured a glassful, looked for another glass, and not seeing one, handed the glass to Lingo who took only a sip and handed it back.

Sam grinned, took a swallow, and shook his head. "Ain't told you yet, but I seen you in a gunfight in Abilene. You took on two o' Kansas's fastest gunfighters and beat 'em seven ways from Sunday." His grin widened. "Hell, you gonna beat that there runt, an' give 'im time to git 'is .44 clear of his hoster 'fore you even start your draw." He opened his eyes wide. "Ain't gonna tell nobody I seen you draw, an' damned sure ain't gonna tell nobody we're partners." He toppled back on the bed. Out cold.

7

SHORTY GATES LED his partner to the cheapest hotel in Durango. The fact was, it was a one-story building, half of it with rental rooms, and the other half reserved for soiled doves and their friends for the night. When the proprietor got enough women of that bent, he had less rooms to rent to tired customers.

Shorty told the man when he checked in that he wanted a pan of warm water. The proprietor told him to get his own water, cold or hot—he didn't give a damn.

Gates steered his partner to the bed, pushed him back, gently, to lie on the bed, then went to warm a pan of water. He wanted to bathe the blood from Bull's face, then see if he could open his eyes enough to see. He'd never seen a man take such a beating. He fingered the grip of his Colt .44. He'd even the score when he and Mayben could work together again.

While water warmed, he glanced at the shell loops on his gunbelt. Empty. That cowboy had not taken any chances. He'd buy a box of cartridges come morning. He didn't think Bull would be able to get out and around this night.

When the water heated to Shorty's satisfaction, he gently sponged dried blood from each of Bull's eyes. They were swollen closed. "You see anythin' outta either eye, partner?"

Bull shook his head. Gates grimaced, then sponged around Mayben's blood-encrusted lips. "What the hell you tryin' to do, start them to bleedin' all over agin?"

"Jest tryin' to git your mouth so's you can open it 'nuff to git some whisky in to gargle with. You gotta git the blood out, along with them loose teeth, them you ain't already spit out."

Bull moaned, winced, and opened his mouth enough for Shorty to pour some of the rot-gut whisky in. Before more than a dribble could touch his raw and bleeding gums, he spewed the whisky out between his lips. "Damn! You tryin' to torture me? Ever'thin' in my mouth hurts." He brought his right hand to touch his cheekbones. "He cut my face up some, too, didn't he?"

"Bull, I had a gun in my back the whole time, or I woulda stopped it. That cowboy wouldn't knock you out. He done that on purpose. He kept on hittin' every place on your face what wasn't already cut an' bleedin'." And, although Bull couldn't see him, he shook his head. "He kept on hittin' you like he had a score to settle more'n jest from us tryin' to keep 'im from drinkin' in that there saloon. Ain't nobody gonna git as mad as he wuz jest from us pickin' a fight with 'im."

Through his bruised and lacerated lips, Bull grunted, "Don't know what he coulda had agin' us other than that. We ain't never seen 'im 'fore, less'n o' course we had trouble with 'im on our back-trail somewhere."

Shorty nodded. "That might be it, but seems like we'd a remembered him."

"Well, we don't, so git on with gittin' my face cleaned

up, then I'm gonna sleep 'til I cain't sleep no more, then we gotta talk 'bout how we gonna git even. I'm gonna put a bullet in that bastard's back, but we cain't do it here in town."

Barnes let Sam sleep off his unaccustomed drunk before waking him for breakfast. Slagle groaned, pulled the covers up around his chin, cracked one eye, and peered at Lingo. "Let me sleep awhile. Gotta git them whisky fumes outta my head so's they won't blow the whole top o' my skull off."

Lingo grinned. "Sleep long's you want. We aren't gonna be seen together anyway. I'm goin' to the cafe across the street an' eat breakfast, if my sore bones an' muscles'll get me there."

The big miner nodded, grimaced, and said, "You sore all over, huh?"

"Sore? Man, I'm not just sore: I hurt, really hurt, but I'm gonna eat, then move around town, see if Emily Lou minded what I told 'er to do. 'Course, as worried about her pa as she is, she mighta kicked over the traces and come in town to see if she could find 'im." Lingo walked stiffly to the white porcelain water pitcher on the nightstand and poured himself a cup of water. He drank it, then checked to make certain his holster was tied tight to his thigh, settled his Colt in it, and looked at Sam. "If Em's not in town, think I'll ride out to the ranch an' see how things're goin'. Wantta come?"

"Yeah, I'll meet you outside o' town on the Chama trail in a couple o' hours. Gonna sleep a little more first." With those words, Slagle pushed his head deeper into the pillow, and snored before Lingo pulled the door shut behind him.

Barnes didn't expect trouble out of Gates this morning; and certainly not Mayben, but he flicked the thong off the hammer of his Colt before walking from the hotel. He searched every place a man could hide to take a shot at him before he stepped onto the street to angle across to the cafe.

It seemed that every miner he met had something friendly to say to him. One said, "Hey, young'un, I bet agin' you last night; cost me ever' danged dime I had—but it wuz sure worth every penny o' it."

Lingo stopped, came back to the man, reached in his pocket, and pulled out four or five cartwheels. "Bet you haven't eaten breakfast if you're broke." He held out the silver dollars. "Here take this to eat on 'til you get back to your mine."

"Naw now, hell, I ain't takin' your money, 'sides it wuz worth walkin' 'bout with an empty stomach."

Lingo pocketed the money, flicked a thumb toward the cafe. "C'mon, I'll buy you breakfast; an' you damned well aren't gonna say no. Fact is, I'll take it as unfriendly if you do."

The miner grinned. "Since you put it that way, reckon I cain't refuse. 'Sides that, my stomach would raise all sorts o' hell if I did."

After eating, Lingo walked about town, looked in every store to see if Emily might be in it, and moved on to the next one. Finally satisfied that the petite girl had done as he'd told her, he went to the livery, saddled his horse, and rode about a quarter of a mile toward Chama, then pulled his horse under some trees, packed his pipe, lighted it, and settled back in the saddle to wait for Slagle.

Sitting there, alone, smelling the pure clean air, scented with pine and spruce, he mulled the few things over that he knew to be fact. Despite Slagle finding the name of the person who wore the low-quarter shoes, Lingo finally cast that name, Randall Bartow, aside. He had nothing—except the shoe prints at Colter's mine site, along with Mayben's and Gates's—to tie them together. Besides, Bartow and Colter might be friends.

His thoughts went to Emily Lou. He was accustomed to stepping in and assuming leadership in situations, so it didn't seem strange that she and most of those he knew accepted his role as leader and willingly followed. What did seem out of the ordinary was how calm she remained when her entire world fell apart around her. Calmly, she accepted that he knew what to do—and could do it. That thought caused him a twinge of discomfort. But, it didn't make him uncomfortable enough that he could push aside how much beauty she had packaged in that petite body of hers; beauty that came from the very core of her being. He took a drag on his pipe, exhaled, and shook his head. He had to stop thinking of her that way, or he'd convince himself that they meant more to each other than was possible with what little they knew of each other.

Then his thinking centered on Wesley and Kelly. He smiled to himself; they were no more than children in the ways of the world. He wondered how long it would take Wes to realize that Kelly had grown up and that she was as pretty a woman as he would probably ever look on; *and* that with growing up she had cast aside thoughts of any other man.

He chuckled at the thought that they both, yeah, even Wesley, thought of him more as a father than a friend. Hell, he wasn't much older than Wes.

The slow plodding of a horse broke into his thoughts. He looked down the trail. Sam rode toward him. He sat the saddle like it was an enemy. He sat stiffly, not allowing his head to bounce or move from side to side; he sat as though he'd come apart at the seams if he moved an unnecessary part of his body, and his expression was that of a man being submitted to extreme torture, Apachelike torture.

Lingo kneed his horse into the trail. "Howdy, partner. Looks like you've got some rough times behind you."

Sam moved only his eyes to look at Barnes. "Ain't got nothin' 'hind me that's as bad as I got ahead o' me." He squinted a bloodshot eye at Lingo. "You ever gonna have 'nother fight, or you see me ever take 'nother drink o' that there pop-skull whisky jest go on an' shoot me right where I stand. Be a helluva lot more con-considerate o' my feelin's that way."

Barnes stifled a laugh, swallowed, and trying to make his voice sympathetic, shook his head. "Aw hell, Sam, reckon I've done the same thing before. After deliverin' a herd o' longhorns to trail's end I've been known to drink too much o' that cheap whisky. We all been guilty o' that." He chuckled. "But I'll tell you somethin'; I won't hold you to havin' me shoot you if you take another drink. Fact is, I figure when we get to my valley, I'll take one o' these bottles outta my saddlebag an' we'll have a drink of *good* whisky. It'll sit right on top of that bad stuff an' make you feel better right off."

A quick pull to the side of the trail, a lean to the side of his horse, and emptying his breakfast onto the dusty soil was Sam's only response. He brightened up after that. "Let's git on up to your valley; figger I'll live 'til then."

Lingo chuckled, kneed his horse ahead, and led the way toward—Emily Lou? Why did he think of going home in that manner?

He led them across meadows speckled with late-blooming flowers, down into narrow valleys, and then up a steep, climbing rocky trail.

Ahead of them the trail pinched off to not more than wagon width. The metallic sound of a rifle lever pushing a shell into the chamber caused Barnes to halt his horse, hold his arm out in front of Slagle, then look toward the fold in the rocks where Wes should be. "Wes? That you?"

"What's the matter with you, Lingo, don't you never trust me to do the job you done give me?"

Barnes chuckled. "Only wanted to make sure they hadn't sent an army against you, an' taken the pass. Come meet my new friend, Sam Slagle."

When Wes came around the fold of rock, Sam extended his hand. "Well, damned if you ain't a full-growed man.

Way Lingo's been talkin' 'bout you I figgered you might be not more'n knee-high to a tall Indian."

The poisonous look Wes cast at Barnes brought a deep chuckle to Lingo's throat. "Don't let 'im kid you, young'un. I been tellin' 'im 'bout you growin' to be a man along those cattle drives we made together."

Eyes cast heavenward, Wes shook his head. "Lord, seems like I ain't suffered enough what with havin' to put up with Lingo. Now you done sent another varmint to give me a bad time." He lowered his eyes to look at Sam, grinned, and grasped the big man's hand. "Howdy, Sam, don't know how you put up with bein' round my boss, but I reckon we all got to make mistakes so's we learn the hard way."

After they'd gotten off on the right foot, the way many men do who turn out to be fast friends, Barnes led them around the fold in the rocks. He swept the area with a glance, and grunted with satisfaction. "See Kelly's been up here takin' care o' you, an' cleanin' up the area fast as you mess it up."

A huge grin split Higgins's lips. He nodded. "Yep. You ain't gonna pull my rope on that one, Lingo. That girl's done took care o' me like she wuz my ma. She's fed me, brought firewood up so's I could stay warm at night, took my dirty clothes back down the mountain and washed 'em, why gosh darn it, she's been all a man could ask for."

Lingo studied his young friend a moment, then nodded to himself. It looked like Kelly and Wes had discovered each other at last. A warm feeling flooded his chest. He looked at Slagle. "Kelly's the young'un I been tellin' you 'bout. To be so young, she sure takes hold o' things, gets 'em done right good."

Wes took the bait. "She ain't as young as Lingo lets on, Sam. Fact is, she's danged near as full-growed as me."

"Wondered when you were gonna notice that. She's as

much woman as you are a man." Lingo reined his horse down the mountain. "C'mon. Ain't nobody followin' us. We'll get Sam acquainted with the womenfolk."

Wes frowned. "How you know they ain't nobody on your back-trail?"

Slagle chuckled. "Barnes took care o' that right handy. Tell you 'bout it when we get to your cabin."

When still about fifty yards from the cabin, Lingo yelled, "Hello the cabin. We're ridin' in."

He urged his horse toward the cabin, only to see Emily Lou and Kelly open the door and walk out, both holding rifles.

Kelly smiled. "You gotta git used to givin' a yell a little sooner, Lingo. Close as you got, we mighta shot you."

Em shook her head. "Knew it was you a pretty good way up the trail, but didn't think you'd be bringin' anyone with you. We made sure there wasn't someone holdin' a gun on you."

She turned toward the door. "C'mon in. We were about to put victuals on the table." She cast a look at Slagle. "We get inside an' hang these rifles on the wall, maybe Lingo'll introduce us."

Over supper, Lingo and Sam told the two girls and Wes all that had happened since he left the cabin, while the girls made the two men aware of how things had gone for them.

After eating, and sitting around the table drinking coffee, Emily studied Lingo's face. "Knew you had a fight. A man can't get those face bruises from shaving. Does Mayben or Gates know that you know they helped take me off that stage?"

"Nope. The fight wasn't about anything like that. And far as I know, they don't know Sam an' I are workin' on this together." He frowned. "Em, we aren't any closer to findin' your pa than when I left here. We've both watched his mine. Haven't seen 'im around there." He shrugged. "The only solid thing we've got is that Mayben and Gates are part of it. We don't know whether your pa took a trip somewhere, whether he's come to harm in some way. Don't know why your brother hasn't gotten here yet—or if he has, maybe he's met with harm, too." He shook his head. "We just don't have a thing to get our teeth into."

Emily frowned and stared straight ahead. "I think if I go back with you, I might see something, or hear something that might help." She stood, went to the stove, and picked up the coffeepot. After filling each of their cups, she again sat. "If I go back with you, they might try to take me outta town again. You men could watch and trail them then."

Barnes stared at her a long moment. "Em, have you forgotten the things they said they had in mind to do to you?" Her face flushed a bright red. Lingo shook his head. "There's no way I'm gonna allow you to put yourself in that position again."

She pinned him with a look that would penetrate a granite bluff. Then she surprised him with using language much like what he would expect from Kelly. "Gonna tell you somethin', Lingo Barnes. That's my pa out there somewhere, who may be hurtin', may be mistreated, may need me. What you will allow is not exactly the way I figure to act."

Blood rushed to Lingo's face. Embarrassed, he stared into his cup a moment, then looked at her. "Em, reckon I get a mite bossy at times. The way I shoulda said it is: I heard the terrible things they said. I saw the way you reacted to their words, I know what kind o' men had you, and even as spunky as you are, you couldn't defend yourself. I'm much more experienced at fighting men of that stripe than most men, not to mention women."

Emily stared at him a long moment. "Why're you doing this, Lingo Barnes? You don't know my father. You don't owe me anything. The fact is, you hardly know me."

He shook his head. "No, ma'am, don't reckon I owe you anythin'. No, ma'am, don't know your father, an' no ma'am, I don't know you near as well as I figure on knowin' you someday."

Then never taking his eyes off hers, he took a swallow of coffee, clamped his teeth together until his jaws knotted, then nodded. "Gonna tell you somethin' you wouldn't know, comin' from the East. Out here, we take care o' our women. Don't nobody mess with 'em or we get right upset; an' when we get upset we raise more hell than you'd believe a man can raise." He wagged his head from side to side, slowly. "You can do what you feel like you gotta, but what it'll do is maybe get me, Sam, or Wes killed. Don't b'lieve that's anythin' you want—despite not knowin' me very well."

Emily blushed, lowered her eyelids to hide her eyes a moment, then looked at him straight on. "Oh, Lingo, I'm sorry. Of course we know each other, of course I'll listen to you, and heed everything you said; the thing that's most true is, I don't want you, Wes, or Sam getting hurt on account of some dumb thing I did. Fact is, I don't want *you* getting hurt for any reason." Somehow, that last sentence brought another blush to her face and caused her to lower her lids again.

Her words flooded his chest with warmth, his throat muscles swelled until he found it hard to swallow, but he tried anyway. He hoped that in a heated discussion like this it would cause a person to say things that in a more guarded moment they would never say.

"Tell you what, if Sam an' I get to the point where we figure we're not getting anywhere, I'll come back up here and take you to Durango with me; force 'em to make a move. Whoever is at the bottom of this is gonna pay; an' those two who took you? Well I don't figure to kill 'em. I want the law to take care of 'em all—at the end of a shiny new rope. I want to see their faces turn purple, see 'em twist an' turn at the end of that rope, see 'em kick 'til their last breath was the one they took 'fore their necks got stretched.

But, I'm not gonna do anything to 'em for now with the hope they'll lead us to whoever's givin' 'em orders."

Sam, now apparently fully recovered from his bout with John Barleycorn the night before, glanced around the table. "Know what? Lingo promised me a drink when we got here, so now if everybody agrees on how we gonna take care o' this here problem, reckon I'm gonna hold 'im to that promise."

Lingo stood, went to his saddlebags, and pulled both bottles from deep in one pocket. Straight-faced, he looked at Slagle. "Soon's you drink this, reckon I'm gonna have to shoot you. I never go back on what I promise a friend."

Sam's face reddened. "Aw hell, Lingo, I wuz feelin' sorta like death would put me outta my misery back then. Let's drink to the new friends we done made."

After their coffee and drink, the men readied the dishes for washing, despite Emily's and Kelly's protesting that the chore was women's work. Then, Lingo took Emily's arm, said he had something to talk to her about, and asked her to go for a walk. She studied the solemn look on his face a moment, then nodded. "Let me get my coat."

He held her coat while she slipped her arms into it, then walked out ahead of him. "This must be something you don't want to discuss before your friends."

He nodded. "Well, one of the subjects is right private, an' the other might embarrass Wes and Kelly."

Now out about a hundred yards from the cabin, she turned to face him. "All right, first tell me the private thing." For some reason her breathing came in shallow gasps. He wondered why.

He looked at her straight on. "Em, I don't want to scare you, but you're gonna have to be ready to accept that whatever has caused your pa to disappear, or wherever he is may not be good. Like I said before, he mighta just taken a trip. Maybe he didn't get your letter before he left."

He shrugged and held his hands out from his side.

"Reckon I want you to face up to whatever. I've seen you in some pretty bad situations an' you took them better'n I figure most would. That's why I'm tellin' you this now."

Eyes wide, and showing fear she obviously tried to hide, she stared at him. "You're telling me this because you have reason to believe he's met harm?"

"No, little one. I told you before: I don't know a thing. I only want you to be ready for anything."

She nodded. "I have already told myself these things, Lingo." She took a deep, tremulous breath. "I think I'm as ready as one can get. Now, tell me the other thing you brought me out here for."

He grinned, kicked a clod of dirt around, then shook his head. "You gonna think I'm a meddlin', mother hen sort o' man, but I like to be ready for anything." He took a deep breath. "You notice while I was gone that maybe Wes an' Kelly finally figured out they're both grown, an' have grown-up wants, feelin's, desires?"

Em chuckled deep in her throat. "Wondered if you would notice that." She nodded. "Yes, Mr. Mother Hen, they've come to that conclusion." She placed her hand on his forearm. "But, I have to tell you, you did a mighty good job raising them both. Nothing's happened." She stammered, obviously embarrassed. "Well, you—you know what I mean—don't you?"

"Yes, Em. I know what you mean. Have either of them said anything 'bout gettin' married?"

Em shook her head. "All I know is, Kelly's waitin', an' there is no doubt she's gonna say yes after Wes has a chance to talk to you." She laughed outright then. "Lingo, despite you not being blood kin to them, they both feel they need your approval."

"You reckon Sam, Wes, and I could build another cabin closeby without them knowin' it was for them?

Emily shook her head. "Don't do it, Lingo. It'd make

them feel that you were pushing them into something. Wait'll they talk to you."

He nodded, took her elbow, and steered her farther from the cabin. "Mind takin' a walk with me now we got business out o' the way?"

"If you hadn't asked, I think I might have brazenly done so." She breathed a great breath of the sweet, pine-scented air. "Suddenly I feel that all is gonna work itself out to a happy ending."

She had placed her hand in the crook of his elbow. They walked like that for several minutes when she asked, "Lingo, why did you come home? Was there a reason? Did you want us to do anything?"

He smiled into the dark knowing she couldn't see his face. "No, little one, I didn't have a special reason other than wanting y'all to meet Sam." Abruptly, a knot formed in his throat, and trying to talk around it his voice came out deeper than usual. "An' to tell you the truth, I didn't think of it as comin' home." He pushed his hat to the back of his head. "Reckon I thought of it as comin' to see you. That seemed important to me."

Her hand tightened on his arm. Neither said anything, and after another several yards they turned and retraced their steps toward the cabin. "Reckon Sam an' I'll head back to Silverton tomorrow. Somethin' might happen to let us know where your pa and brother are."

"Please be careful. And I repeat what I said earlier, I don't want *you* getting hurt."

Without words, he tightened his elbow to his side, her hand holding to it. Somehow, to Lingo's thinking, they'd said a whole lot without uttering a word. He wanted to think so anyway.

The next morning before daylight, Emily, Kelly, and Wes stood outside the cabin and waved until darkness swallowed the two riders. Kelly looked at Wes. "Reckon we gonna pack your gear, an' ride with you to the pass. You gonna stay out there like you been doin, ain't ya?"

Wes nodded, still looking toward where the night had swallowed his friend. "Kelly, reckon Lingo said it all when he said as how a Western man takes care o' all women, but somehow I figger Em's more'n all women to 'im. Yep, I ain't lettin' nothin' happen to either one o' you." Somewhere in the middle of his sentence, Emily turned and hurried into the cabin, leaving only Kelly standing next to him. Wes smiled toward the door she had hurried through.

"Wes Higgins," Kelly slapped his arm—gently. "You done made that poor little thing 'barrassed when you said them words."

While Kelly and Emily packed what Wes needed to settle in at the pass, Lingo and Sam rode toward Silverton. "What you gonna do if we meet Mayben an' Gates when we get to Silverton?"

"If I see 'em first, reckon I'll ride a wide circle 'round 'em. Don't wantta have to shoot neither one. They gonna slip one o' these days, an' we gonna know who they work for." The sun now pushing its light in between the mountain peaks showed the desolation the fire had left; blackened earth, and sad black spikes reaching toward the heavens, all that only a few days ago had been beautiful forest.

Lingo tamped tobacco into his pipe, lighted it, and looked squint-eyed between his horse's ears. "Sure would like to know where that Easterner Randall Bartow fits into the picture. One thing for sure, he doesn't fit into the West. He just flat isn't our kind o' people." He took a deep drag on his pipe, blew the smoke out in a cloud, and looked at Slagle. "Was Miles Colter sorta like Bartow, or did he fit in with this country, these people, this kind o' livin'?"

Sam shook his head. "Don't know Bartow at all, but gonna tell you, Colter would fit in with any bunch. He wuz a real gentleman, but could git down in the muck an' grime with the best o' us." He nodded. "I done told ya, I liked 'im."

Barnes flicked a thumb toward Silverton. "We better split now. Think I'll stop in the saloon, have a drink an' keep my ears peeled for anything I might hear."

Sam nodded. "I'll have supper ready when you git to the cabin." He grinned. "Ain't gonna be near as good as those two young women done fixed us yestiddy."

"I get so's I can't stand it, I'll cook a few meals."

"Ain't no damned way, Lingo. I done et what you cowboys call trail food; ever'thing fried in deep grease, same thing all the time: bacon, beans, fried hardtack." Sam shook his head.

Barnes chuckled. "All right, I'll see you in a couple o' hours. I'll chop some stove wood then; don't reckon the wood I chop'll mess up the food." He reined his horse toward town, while Sam continued down the hill toward his cabin.

A couple of hundred yards from the edge of town, a rifle shot sounded, then the whine of a bullet passed his ear, and Lingo left the saddle dragging his rifle from its scabbard. He hit the dirt, and rolled toward the bole of a large pine.

BARNES CAME UP hard against the tree, stetched out behind it, and peered around the trunk. Another shot chipped bark off just above his head. He jerked his head back. Who the hell would be shooting at him? He didn't think Gates and Mayben would be back so soon, and he could think of no one else who'd take a shot at him. Besides, who would know he would be on this particular trail at this time?

He eased his rifle around the tree and blindly pointed it toward the area from which the shots had come. He fired and pulled back behind the trunk. Immediatly, another shot followed his own. This time bark chips flew into his eyes. He dropped his rifle and wiped, forcing tears to flow. Now, still half-blinded, the tears washed some of the small chips away and he could see large objects up close.

He'd made up his mind to stay where he was, keep his head down, and wait the man out. His resolve was needless. The sounds of a horse ridden away at a dead run broke the silence.

In case the horse had bolted and left the dry gulcher behind, Lingo lay perfectly still, but at the same time hoped the horse had a rider. He had been pinned down, no chance to get away, and no chance to take a bearing on where the shooter hid. He stayed where he was for a good thirty minutes, and gradually his nerves relaxed. Finally, he edged his head around the bole of the tree.

He swept the area with a searching look, decided he was alone, and stood. His horse had moved off only a hundred or so yards. He'd stand there until Barnes came for him.

Lingo walked to the jumble of rocks and brush from where he estimated the shots came and studied the ground.

Brush, already beginning to stand back up from being pressed against the earth, told him the man had not been there long or the growth would have remained flat for a much longer time. But again he wondered how anyone would know he rode the trail he had followed. A glance toward town showed that anyone on the single street could see the area in which he'd gone to ground. He turned his glance up the mountainside. The winding path on which he'd ridden wound in and out of trees, angled down almost in front of Miles Colter's mine, and on down the hill. Some of the spots bereft of trees stretched as much as a quarter of a mile. He nodded. His attacker had decided on the spur of the moment to try to get rid of him, and had plenty of time to get from town to the spot from which he'd selected to set up the ambush.

He turned his attention back to the ground upon which the dry gulcher had lain. Something shiny caught his eye. He picked it up. A rifle casing. There had been three shots. In only a few seconds he found the other two casings. He rolled them around on the palm of his hand. They were standard .44-caliber shell casings. They didn't tell him anything.

He frowned. Someone, and maybe it *was* Mayben or Gates, wanted him dead. Maybe they'd come back to Silverton. He'd have to look the town over more carefully than he'd at first intended.

The creases in his forehead deepened. Shorty and Bull were always together, yet he'd been attacked by a lone gunman. That conclusion was the result of hearing only one horse ride away. He shrugged. Maybe on seeing him from town, and not having time to get his partner, one of them decided to try to take him out single-handedly. He walked to his horse, toed the stirrup, and rode toward the cluster of buildings down on the flat. He resisted wiping at his eyes, which only made them feel more scratchy.

Wanting a cup of coffee and something to eat, he decided against giving in to his wants. He reined in at the general store, and went to sit on the smooth bench polished by many pairs of jeans. If Mayben and Gates were in town, he thought to see them, and he could avoid being seen by standing and slipping into the store.

In the two hours he sat there, he figured he saw everyone who had come to town on this crisp autumn day. Finally, the sun slipped behind the Uncompahgre Peak. Darkness forced the long shadows to blend and fade with the coming of night. Lingo stood, walked to his horse, and rode a wide circle around the stores. Then he straightened his course toward the gulch where Sam had his cabin.

Sam met him at the door. "Where the hell you been, boy? I wuz gittin' some worried 'bout ya."

Lamplight bathed them both standing in the doorway. Lingo pushed Sam back into the room. He grinned. "Reckon I been some worried 'bout me, too. Been dodgin' bullets."

Sam stepped back and swept him with a searching look. "Don't look like they done you no harm."

"Nope, but I got some tree bark in my eyes that scratches like hell."

Slagle guided Lingo to a chair by the table. "Here, sit an' let me take a look. Supper's ready to dish up, but it can wait."

Sam took a dish towel, wetted the tip of it, and carefully picked the remaining bark from Lingo's eyes. Finally, Barnes pushed his hand away. "That's good, Sam. Reckon my stomach's hurtin' more'n my eyes. Let's eat."

While eating, Lingo told Slagle what had happened. When Lingo finished, Sam pinned him with a look. "Tellin' you right now, boy, we ain't lettin' you outta this here cabin 'til I can find out if them two varmints done come back to Silverton. If they have, reckon we gonna know who tried to kill ya."

Barnes shook his head. "No way, Sam. I never hid from trouble in my life. Not gonna start now."

Slagle stared at him a long moment. "Well, damn me, I'm gonna lose a partner almost 'fore I got 'im."

Lingo chuckled, then laughed outright. "Hell, partner, don't get me buried 'fore I'm dead." He sobered. "Tell you somethin', I'm a right hard hombre to kill, so don't give up on me yet."

They talked on into the night, drank three pots of coffee, then a half bottle of Sam's whisky. They decided to operate the same way they had been, definitely not letting on that they knew each other. The result was that Lingo *would* stay in the cabin the next day until Slagle could find out for certain whether Mayben and Gates were back in town.

"If'n they're here, Lingo, you figger to go out an' brace the both o' 'em?"

Barnes shook his head. "That's what I'm most tempted to do, but findin' Emily's pa is more important than me gettin' even with those two." He took a swallow of his drink. "But I'm tellin' you one thing, partner, when we know where and how Miles Colter is, *then*, you can bet everything you own that I'm gonna get even. An' whoever is givin' em' orders is gonna get it first, or last, if I gotta track 'im to hell an' gone."

Sam gave him a sly grin. "You gonna let me get in on the act?"

Lingo took another swallow, eyed Sam, wondered if he wanted to take a chance on the big man getting hurt, and decided he didn't. "Reckon I dragged you into this, Sam. It's none of your fight." He shook his head. "Nope, want you to stay clear."

The next morning Slagle ate Barnes's cooking, after allowing that there weren't many men who could mess up eggs and bacon. Slagle made the biscuits.

Most stores opened early, about six o'clock. Sam sat outside the general store when the sun inched above the eastern peaks. He spoke to most who walked past. One miner stopped, then studied Slagle a moment. "You sick, Sam? Ain't never seen you sittin' 'round when there wuz work to do."

Slagle chuckled. "Naw, ain't sick. Jest figgered a man should oughtta take a day off once in a while. Thought I'd sit here an' speak to all my friends; then I'm gonna go back to the cabin an' read a paper Slim Goodrich give me a little while back." All the while he talked, he glanced at every passerby, spoke to them whether he knew them or not, and moved his eyes to the next person.

The saloons never closed their doors. Miners worked in different shifts around the clock, and the watering holes sat there ready to take the hard-earned dust or nuggets they'd torn from the hard earth. Sam showed special interest toward every person who pushed through the batwing doors. About eleven-thirty, he straightened from his slouch, closed his eyelids to slits, and studied the two men who'd only then stepped to the boardwalk in front of the Hole-in-the-Wall. He nodded to himself, figuring that now he knew who'd taken those shots at Barnes.

Mayben looked like he'd been late getting out of a mining shaft when a dynamite charge went off. He peered through purple, swollen eyelids while Gates steered him toward the doors still flapping from the last person to enter.

Slagle stood. He'd forfeit making another strike in order

to hear the story the two would tell as to how Bull got in the shape he was in. He angled across the street in ankle-deep dust to the saloon.

He wanted to set the record straight for all to hear as to the way Mayben came by his condition. No one that he knew liked the Bull, or the worm he'd partnered up with.

He found a chair at a table close to the bar so he could hear what they said. Gates was talking when he sat. ". . . you shoulda seed Bull, fightin' three men, an' wuz doin' right good for hisself, even though he don't look like it right now. Fight lasted almost an hour when Bull knocked the last one out with a roundhouse right he brought from behind his back."

Sam stood. Then raising his voice so any in the room could hear, he walked to the bar, and turned his back to it. "Now I'm gonna tell y'all what really happened. First off, they wuz only one man, a cowboy, what whipped Mayben." He shook his head. "Don't know who he wuz, but I danged sure know who won, an' how many they wuz fightin'.

"I know. I wuz there an' won a chunk o' dust, double eagles, an' paper money on that fight. That cowboy wuz maybe forty or fifty pounds lighter'n Bull, but he took it to that there big man like he weighed a hundred pounds more'n him. He . . ."

Shorty Gates pulled his side gun and stepped toward Slagle. "You callin' the way I done told it a lie?"

Brassy fear bubbled to the back of Sam's throat. Abruptly, the sour smell of yesterday's whisky, and tobacco smoke caused his stomach to roil—and those smells really had little to do with his stomach turning over.

He looked at the gun in Gates's hand, and held his hands wide of his sides. "I ain't packin' no gun, Gates. You shoot me, an' these here people gonna hang you higher'n an eagle can fly."

Then despite looking down the barrel of Gates's handgun, he nodded. "Either you seen a different fight than I did, or you're tellin' the biggest lie in history." He stared into Shorty's eyes. "Yep, that cowboy done whipped the hell outta your partner."

Every miner in the room moved closer to Gates. His eyes swept the room, sweat stood in huge beads on his forehead, his face paled—and his hand moved to his holster. His .44 slipped into leather. His stare moved from all in the room to pinpoint Slagle. "Gonna git you, you dirt-grubbin' bastard, gonna git you good. You ain't always gonna be standin' in the middle o' your friends."

When Shorty's gun slipped into its holster, Slagle slowly blew his breath out between stiff lips. He'd never come as close to meeting his maker as he'd only seconds ago come. And from the speed of Gates's draw, he figured Lingo might have a hard time beating him. He'd have to warn his friend. Every time Lingo had pulled a gun on the thin, ugly partner of Bull's, he'd never had to face the chance Shorty could beat him. And with all the faith Slagle had in Barnes, the speed with which the little wormy partner of Bull's got his handgun out of its holster gave Sam a huge dose of fear.

Gates took his partner's arm and guided him from the saloon. As soon as they cleared the batwing doors, questions came at Slagle from every angle. He took time to tell about the fight, and that there had been several miners from here in Silverton who witnessed it. "Most o' 'em lost their poke bettin' on Bull Mayben, not 'cause they liked 'im, but 'cause he wuz so much bigger'n that there cowboy; but I'm here to tell you, that cowpoke took it to 'im from the start."

He told the story two or three times, then wanting to get back to his cabin, grinned, although he didn't feel much like a grin, and said, "Reckon the holiday I took for myself didn't pan out so hot." He pushed his hat to the back and scratched his head. "Reckon I'll have to be careful not to get so lazy in the middle of the week after this."

He left in the middle of warnings to watch out that he

didn't get back-shot. He didn't expect trouble in the middle of town, in full daylight. He headed for his cabin, took a roundabout trail to it, and looked to his backside every step of the way.

Back in his cabin, he walked past Lingo, reached in the cupboard, pulled out a bottle, and poured himself a hefty drink. Barnes frowned. His friend did not usually have nothing to say, and he seldom had a serious expression. "All right, tell me what happened. You're not your usual self."

"Almost wuzn't any kind o' self. Danged near got my fool head blowed off."

Lingo studied Slagle a moment. "Tell me about it."

Sam started at the beginning and told Barnes what happened, leaving out no detail. When he finished, he knocked back his drink and poured another, then, with a sheepish look, held the bottle out to Lingo. "Pour yourself one. Reckon I ain't very polite right now."

Barnes took the bottle from Slagle, knocked the cork back in the neck, put it on the table, and shook his head. "So Mayben an' Gates are back in town. Didn't figure they'd come back 'til Bull lost all sign from his appearance that he'd had a fight and lost."

"Wouldn't of made no difference if'n I hadn't been there to call Gates a liar. The story they told might've been believed." Sam pinned Barnes with a questioning look. "You figger it like I do? You figger one o' them varmints took those shots at you?"

Barnes frowned, causing a deep furrow to crease his forehead. After several long moments, he shook his head. "Might believe it happened that way, Sam, but if they had been the ones who shot at me they'd have known I was in town. If they'd known that, I figure they'd a stayed outta sight 'til they could get another chance at me."

He took a glass and poured himself a drink. "Don't think they'd have showed themselves in town 'til they were sure they had me outta the way." He stared into the amber fluid that filled his glass. "Way I figure it, somebody else took that shot at me." He shrugged. "Wish to hell it had been one of those two. The way I got it in my head is that somebody else has me pegged for interfering in their game." He knocked back his drink, shook his head, then packed his pipe and lit it. "Wish to hell I knew who it was, an' why they figure I'm interested in what they do." He shrugged. "I haven't any interest in anything around here."

"Yeah, you do, Lingo. Stop an' think, what wuz it brought you to this here town in the first place?"

Barnes raised his eyes from staring at the table to look into Slagle's eyes. "You think those shots had anything to do with Colter's mine?"

Sam squinted his eyes to stare at the wall, obviously mulling the puzzle around in his head. Finally, he nodded. "Only thing I kin think. But we gotta figger out why they think you got any interest in that there mine."

Lingo shook his head. "Don't know, but what you say makes sense. Let's think 'bout it awhile."

A couple miles away, in another gulch, Randall Bartow sat at the table next to the stove cleaning his rifle. It was the third time he'd cleaned it since the night before.

Maddie turned from the stove and looked from the rifle to Bartow. "That gun ain't got a speck o' dirt, dust, or nothin' else on it, or in it. Why don't you hang it on its peg an' forget it?"

Bartow glanced at her. "Instead of messin' in my business, why don't you pour me a drink, then get busy an' start cookin' supper? I'm tired of bein' around damned fools who don't know how to do anything right."

She smirked. "Seems to me *you* didn't do it right yesterday or you wouldn't be sittin' here stewin' 'bout missin' them shots. 'Sides that, you don't even know that man was doin' anythin' 'cept ridin' his horse past the mine."

She was right. Bartow knew it, and that stirred his anger even deeper. He had overreacted to seeing a horseman coming from the direction of Colter's mine, and had exposed himself to having whoever that was he'd fired at getting curious as to why anyone would take shots at him. Too, he'd not gotten a clear look at the man, and wouldn't recognize him if he met him face-to-face.

His anger boiled over. He cast her a poisonous look. "No one asked you your damned opinion. Now, pour me that drink I told you to pour an hour ago, then get the hell busy with supper."

She poured a glass almost full. He snatched the glass from her, and when she shrank from him, he slapped at her, his hand passing only a breath away from her face. He uttered a raspy laugh. "Scared I might give you what you deserve? Better be, or I'll forget supper 'til after I beat the hell outta you." Maddie turned her back to him to busy herself at the stove, but not before he saw pure hate fill her eyes. To hell with her.

He turned his thoughts to the old man lying at the back of the living quarters in the mine. He'd fed Colter a few solid meals, and doctored the open sores on his feet and legs. He'd soon have him well enough that he could start the torture process over again. He had to know where to look for the rich vein the old man had found—and he had to get rid of the daughter. Knowing Colter held a full house to his busted flush only infuriated him more. He didn't dare kill the old man, and he knew that Colter knew he wouldn't, couldn't. He stood and poured himself another drink. Maddie glanced toward him, stark fear showing in her face.

Over in Lingo's hanging valley, Emily Lou listened to the wagon's sound disappearing toward the pass. She stared at the wall. Why would Wes say what he did about Lingo caring about her? And then, clear as this mountain air, she'd reacted in a way to tell the world she felt more for the tall man than gratitude for him rescuing her from those sent to abduct and kill her.

Then, despite her worry for her father—she had all the faith in the world that Lingo would find him—her thoughts centered on the cowboy. She trusted him to do anything he said he would do—only now it was the things he hadn't said that occupied her thoughts. Did their unspoken words mean anything? Why had she chosen to construe them as meaning more than trust, meaning more than friendship, meaning, perhaps—caring? And why should it make a difference whether caring made a difference? She'd never seen a man who could stir her emotions, who could make her question the importance of caring. She smiled. Maybe she'd met a man who would make caring a part of her life. She nodded. Maybe!

She busied herself cleaning the mess from supper, then sweeping the puncheon floor, then waiting to hear the wagon return from the pass. She'd never met two men who she put her total trust in . . . until now.

A glance at the windows showed that the sun had long ago sunk behind the western peaks. She stood, and not wanting to waste a lucifer, took the tongs from beside the fireplace, plucked a coal from the fire, and put it to the lantern. Not long after lantern light pushed evening shadows to the far corners of the room, the rattle of the wagon told her Kelly had returned, had left her man up there alone to keep them safe. She sighed. Would this threat never end? At the same time, she was reluctant to admit it had to end. It might mean she'd no longer see her newfound friends. She clamped her jaws tight. She'd not let that happen.

Kelly came through the doorway, her face glowing. "Oh, Em, life is so wonderful. For the first time I figger I ain't gonna have to worry 'bout anybody ever tryin' to do me harm agin."

Emily stood in the middle of the floor, stared at Kelly,

then smiled. "What happened that's so wonderful, Kelly? You look like the sun could rise right in the middle of your face." Abruptly fear squelched her happiness for her friend. "You didn't, well, you didn't let him . . . ?"

"Aw now, you know I didn't—at least he didn't try. But I'da let 'im if he did try. Em, he kissed me." She spun around the middle of the room, almost as though she danced on air, her arms outstretched. "Oh, Em, it was wonderful. I always thought a man's kiss would be somethin' dirty, somethin' slabbery, somethin' with his paws all over me." She sat at the table and stared starry-eyed at Emily. "Wa'nt nothing like that at all. It wuz probably the next thing to heaven with his arms around me."

Emily's throat tightened against the knot that formed there. Her eyes flooded with tears she had seldom shed. She couldn't see much in the room except for Kelly sitting at the table glowing brighter than any sunrise she'd seen. She went to the table, put her arms around Kelly's shoulders and hugged her tightly. "Oh, I'm so happy for you. He say anything about getting married?"

Kelly shook her head. "Don't reckon neither one o' us is ready to look at that happenin' 'til we talk with Lingo." She looked at Emily. "What you reckon Lingo's gonna say 'bout us carin' for each other?"

Emily smiled. "Why my newfound friend, almost a sister, I'd say the first thing you gotta get ready for is that Lingo Barnes is going to kiss you, tell you how happy he is that you've found your man, then he'll give Wes a punch on the shoulder, grin, an' ask 'im when the preacher's gonna come visiting." Her smile turned pensive, and under her breath she muttered, "Wish I had to worry about getting someone's approval to love a man."

"What'd you say, Em? I couldn't hear you."

Emily shook her head, wondering where the thought had come from, or why she'd wished such. Was she wishing she could find her father and get his permission—or was she wishing Lingo would ask her? "Didn't say anything, Kelly. Must've been talkin' to myself."

While Emily's thoughts centered on Barnes, his thoughts went from her, to her father, back to her, and returned to Colter. Where could he have gone? Where would he have gone? Of course maybe he didn't know that his daughter had pulled stakes in Baltimore and headed west. If he had known, he would have been in Durango to meet her.

According to Em, she had written her pa. Had the letter gotten lost? Or had someone intercepted it so they'd know when she arrived, and had that person posted an outlaw gang to take her off the stage before she could get to the town and be met by her father? Who picked up his mail in Silverton? He'd have to check on that. But how could he check on it? The postmaster in Silverton didn't know him, didn't know why he'd have any interest in Miles Colter.

Her brother had left Baltimore to come out here, but apparently had never arrived. What had happened to him? Had the same gang taken him off the stage upon which he was to arrive? The more Lingo mulled the problems over the more confused he became.

He looked at the drink Sam had poured him, left it on the table, and decided if he was to think clearly, he'd better not have another drink until he solved the puzzle. He told Slagle his decision.

"Aw hell, Lingo, a leeetle old drink ain't gonna hurt. You get all tangled up, I'll hep ya git untangled."

Barnes chuckled. He nodded, then grinned. "You know what that'd do, partner? Well the way I got it figured, it'd be *two* confused, *two* half-drunk neophytes trying to solve a pretty complicated puzzle." He shook his head. "Neither o' us has ever run up against a problem like this."

Sam looked as though he'd lost his last friend. "Don't reckon I got anybody to drink with no more." His face brightened. "But gonna tell ya one thing, I ain't never gonna be one o' them neo-neo . . . whatever the hell you called us."

Lingo couldn't hold back the deep-chested, rumbling laugh. "Sam, soon's we got a sensible answer to some o' the questions we ask ourselves, I promise you we're gonna get downright hootin'-owl drunk. Then we gonna go outta here an' corner the stinkin' trash that'd do somethin' like this to a pretty"—he shook his head—"nope, more'n pretty, just downright beautiful little woman, then we gonna kick the livin' hell outta him 'fore we get 'im hanged." He looked slit-eyed at Sam. "An' I'm here to tell ya, I'm gonna be the one to put the rope 'round his stinkin' neck." He stood, left his full glass of whisky on the table and headed for his bunk. If he'd turned to look at the table, he'd have seen Sam stare at the drink a moment, shake his head, pick the drink up, knock it back, then follow him toward their bunks.

Although getting late, Randall Bartow took another swallow from the cup of coffee in front of him, glanced at Maddie lying in bed, her mouth open, uttering small snores. He looked at her a few moments, stood, and walked out the door. He'd see how Colter was doing, see if he was able to withstand another series of punishing, torturous treatments.

He studied the surrounding area, then satisfied there was no one close, he headed for The Emily Lou Mine, about a half-mile away.

When about twenty yards from the door, he again checked to see if there might be anyone close by. Satisfied he was alone, he unlocked the door, went in, and pulled the door closed behind him. Only then did he light a lantern and carry it to the back room where he kept Colter, stretched out, arms and legs tied to the bedposts.

He stood looking at the old man. Colter stared back, no fear, no pain in his eyes, only muscles at the back of his jaw showing knots formed by tightly clamped teeth. "You're still convinced you can withhold the information I want, aren't you?"

Colter only stared, and gritted his teeth.

"I'll tell you something, Colter, I'm getting damned tired of this, so tired that I'm thinking of doing away with you whether you tell me or not. After you're outta the way, I'll hire someone, a geologist, to find that vein for me."

He pulled a chair to the bedside, sat and looked at his prisoner. "Gonna tell you, too, your daughter came out here. We took 'er off the stagecoach, but she got away. When we find 'er, I intend to kill 'er an' hide her remains. That'll clear the way for me to get a good forger to fix me up a deed to this mine." He twisted his mouth into a smirk. "You see, I don't really need to keep you alive. I can do it all without you."

Colter's face hardened. "You hurt Em, an' this country won't be big enough to hold you. Every man able to carry a weapon'll be on your trail." He nodded. "An' they'll know. Somehow the word always gets out, an' when it does, you'd better be runnin' like the slimy coyote you are."

Bartow grinned down at his captive, then shrugged. "You might be right if I was the one who got rid of her." His grin widened. "But I'm not as stupid as you seem to think. You see, when she's done away with I intend to be miles from where it happens—with witnesses to prove it." He shook his head. "I have a couple of men who are about as dumb as you think me to be who'll do the job. The law will home in on them. The fact is, I intend to make sure there's evidence pointing to them." His face hardened. He checked the bindings on Colter's arms and legs, turned toward the door, and left.

Colter listened for the scrape of the padlock against the stout oaken door. He knew how stout it was because he'd built it with his own hands. Even if he got his legs and hands free, he'd have to stumble around in the dark to find an ax, or a pick to attack the door. Bartow, when he'd let his true colors show, had taken matches, tobacco, everything from him. But that didn't stop him from struggling with his bindings.

He already knew how brutal Bartow could be. His entire being shrank from the thought of what had been done to him, and would be done again as soon as the smooth Easterner thought he could withstand another bout of torture.

Colter pondered all his captor had told him. Only as a last resort would the greedy bastard hire someone to forge a deed; and only if Emily Lou was dead. Too, as long as she was out there, there was a chance someone would befriend her, help her. Bartow had made the mistake of his life telling him about her escape. That gave him hope, determination, to do whatever he had to to brace himself against the pain he knew only too well. He again struggled with his bindings.

Lingo awoke the next morning determined to attack his problem with his head rather than his gun and muscle. He had an idea that Mayben's and Gates's trail would be easy to trace, but they were only hirelings. The man who had hired them was the one he wanted—but who the hell was he?

Before throwing his covers off, he stared at the ceiling for several minutes. Was the man he wanted new to the area? If so, how had he found out about Colter's new strike? Or maybe the man he wanted had been here all the time, and heard Em's father brag about finding a rich vein. He mentally shook his head. He believed, only from knowing Emily, that her father would have been too cagey to mention a rich vein unless he already had control of the vein with his existing claim.

After pondering the puzzle another few minutes, he decided to try to find the names of any who'd shown up in the area in the last few months, then he'd try to backtrack and find out where they'd come from. He studied on that approach another few minutes, then smelling bacon frying, and knowing Sam was already up and about, he threw the covers back and crawled from his bunk.

He first poured himself a cup of coffee, then sat at the table and stared into his cup, not taking a swallow of it.

Slagle put a plate of bacon, eggs, and fried potatoes in front of him. Lingo didn't reach for his fork. "What you thinkin' 'bout, partner? Somethin' I can hep you with?"

Barnes thoughts came back to where he was. He looked at Sam and nodded. "B'lieve so, Sam. If you'll tell me what you take outta your mine every day, an' let me pay you that amount for each day you miss workin' cuz I need you to do the things I can't do bein' a stranger here in Silverton."

"Wh-why hell, Lingo, what kind o' friend you think I am? You want help, you got help, an' I ain't gonna listen to no more talk 'bout payin' me. You listenin' to what I'm sayin'?"

Barnes, a huge lump in his throat threatening to choke him, studied the big, brawny, red-faced man. How did anyone luck into making friends with a person like Sam? Most people went through life and made a lot of acquaintances, but if they made one true friend they were among the luckiest people in the world. And he counted himself extra lucky: He had Wes, Kelly, Em, and now Sam Slagle. He shook his head. He wouldn't count Em among them; she was extra-special. He nodded. "I'm listenin', Sam. All right, I'll tell you what I have planned."

Sam finished fixing his own breakfast and sat across the table from Lingo. "Let's hear it."

Barnes queried Slagle as to how well he knew the postmaster, and found they frequently met for a couple of drinks after the general store closed. The post office, located in the back of the store, was run by the owner, Ted Murchison.

"You figure Murchison will keep his mouth shut 'bout us checkin' on people 'round here?"

"Lingo, that man's as tight with a word as he is with a dollar. Sometimes I wake up in the middle of the night an' figger I can hear old George Washington's picture on one o' them dollar bills squallin' for hep 'cause Ted's squeezin' it so tight." He nodded. "Yeah, he'll keep 'is mouth shut."

"All right. Here's what I want you to do." Lingo spelled out in detail what he wanted to know from Murchison, then took a bite of eggs, chewed, swallowed, and stood to pour them each a cup of coffee. "While you work on it from here, I'm gonna go to Durango, an' work on the same thing from there. They know me down there, an' I don't figure on havin' problems finding out answers to some of the questions we been kickin' 'round." He stood, and took his plates to the pump to wash them, then looked over his shoulder. "Not gonna leave 'til after dark. Don't want anyone to see me leave your place."

When Bartow walked away from the locked mine door, he thought on what he'd said to Colter. He realized he'd made a mistake in telling Colter about Emily Lou. That knowledge alone would give the old man hope—and the strength to continue withholding the information he sought. At the same time he decided he needed help, more help than those two stupid bastards Gates and Mayben had enough sense to give.

He pondered that problem a few moments and came up dry. He just flat didn't know people in this area. He walked to a large spruce, raked needles into a pile and sat. Where could he get the kind of help he needed? Two or three men would be enough, men like he'd traveled with back East.

Back East. Maybe that was the answer. But bringing in more men would complicate his scheme. He thought on that a few moments, then decided they didn't have to be a problem. He'd get rid of them, too, one at a time, and create a situation that would make it look like friends of Colter's had somehow figured out their part in trying to get the mine—or maybe he could make it seem that Mayben and Gates had decided to take the mine for themselves.

Finally, he stood, and leaned against the tree. He'd send a telegram to Vic D'Amato, a man he wouldn't trust as far as he could throw one of these mountains; but he needed him. He'd have him contact two more of his friends and come west. He'd tell him when and where to come. He'd meet them in Chama.

He thought on that a moment. Why Chama? He thought about that a few minutes and decided to keep any activity away from Durango or Silverton. The fact was, he'd ride to Chama to mail the letter. No one here knew where he was from, and he didn't want them to. Some of these hicks might be intelligent enough to backtrack and find what his past had been. He didn't want that. And, if his plans worked out, he wanted no one to tie him in with the three men he'd send for—or with Mayben and Gates for that matter.

9

LINGO ARRIVED IN Durango slightly before six the next morning, registered for a room at the hotel, and went to bed. His stomach growling for food wakened him at four o'clock. He packaged a change of clothing, went to the barbershop, got a shave, took a bath, dressed, and went to the same saloon in which he'd whipped Bull Mayben.

Inside, contrary to the way he was greeted by Mayben and Gates, the miners all wanted to buy him a drink. After all the backslapping and refusing one drink after the other, he stood at the bar drinking a beer. The man next to him was a talkative sort so Barnes listened.

The miner, Bob Single, had come to Durango from Virginia City, Montana, and had known a Bull Madden in the gold fields there. "Tell you, Mr. Barnes, that Madden wuzn't the same man as this'n, but they wuz cut from the same bolt o' cloth. The Bull Madden I knowed up yonder wuz part o' the Henry Plummer gang what wuz robbin' the miners o' their poke."

Lingo smiled. "Sounds like you have Mayben figured

for that kind o' man—one who'd not be too careful how he made a livin'?"

Single nodded. "That's 'zackly how I got 'im figgered. I hear he lives up yonder in Silverton, but don't do no minin'; fact is, he don't do no work at all." He shook his head. "Never seed a man what did no work an' wuz still able to eat, 'less'n o' course he wuz gittin' money some other way."

Lingo raised his eyebrows. "He doesn't work for any miner or have a claim of his own?"

Single shook his head. "Nope. He don't do nothin'."

Lingo bought the miner a drink, talked to the man a few more minutes, and said he had to see another man on business—cow business—and left.

The conversation, mostly one-sided, had told him what he suspected. Mayben and Gates had some other way of earning a living. But someone was paying them, and that was where Lingo hit a stone wall. Who was their boss?

He glanced at his watch: after six. He thought to wait until the next morning to talk to the postmaster, then figured with the post office being located in the Wells Fargo office, maybe, if they expected a stage, the postmaster/station agent would be there. He angled across the street, then walked toward the livery. He lucked out—the glow of a lantern lit the window of the stage office.

"Howdy, Barnes, what you need? You figgerin' on takin' a trip?"

Lingo grinned. "Nope. Still got my horse. He's not fast as one o' your stages, but he don't bounce me or my rear end around as much. I'll keep on ridin' 'im 'cept on long trips."

He pushed his hat to the back of his head. "Tell you what I need. You had many Easterners come to this town lately, or any newcomers who didn't look like they belonged in a minin' town?"

The agent pulled his mouth to the side in a grimace. He

nodded. "Hell yes, I see folks come in every time a stage comes in who look like they don't b'long nowhere 'cept in a city. Ever' one I look at I wonder how long it'll be 'fore I see 'em catchin' another stage outta here, most o' them headin' back East, an' for most I hope it'll be right soon. They's some right slick willies amongst 'em."

Lingo stared at the wall a moment, then looked at the agent. "If I brought you a list o' names, any way you could find out where they come from?"

"Nope, most of 'em come into St. Louis, or other towns by rail, then switch to stagecoaches or another train, an' they don't have to give a name when they buy a ticket." He shook his head. "Ain't no way I got o' findin' out where they come from." He frowned, and looked squinty-eyed at Barnes. "Why you want to know all this?"

Barnes shrugged. "I just wanted an answer about a man I met the other day. Nothin' important." He stepped toward the door. "Thanks anyway."

After leaving the stage station, Lingo wandered down the street, went to the Animas River, listened to the water flow across the rocks, then went back into the middle of town.

Not getting any answers from Wells Fargo meant only a minor setback. He really hadn't expected too much, but had hoped.

He glanced down the street and saw Marshal Nolan come out of one of the many watering holes. Wanting company, he hurried to catch him. "Howdy, Marshal, you 'bout through with your rounds?"

Nolan smiled. "Howdy, Barnes." He nodded. "Yeah I'm through with this round. I'll make a couple more 'fore the night's over. Come on over to the office. We'll have a cup o' coffee."

Lingo didn't want coffee, especially that mud that Nolan let simmer from day to day on his stove, but thought he might ask how a lawman went about finding where people came from, and if they had anything on their backtrail to hide. Too, he wondered if the old timer had seen anything of Colter.

The visit was a bust. Nolan had little more than Wanted notices he could check, and no, he'd not seen hide nor hair of Em's father. He didn't bother to ask the marshal about Mayben and Gates, although certain they had Wanted notices out on them. He'd made up his mind to take care of them in his own way when the time came, but the person he wanted to find was their boss, and he was no closer to getting that answer now than when he'd first encountered the two men.

From the marshal's office, he went to The Golden Eagle, had a nightcap, and went to the hotel and to bed. He thought, when he got back to Silverton, to watch The Emily Lou Mine and see who might be interested in it. He shrugged mentally. Hell, he could do that anytime. Nope, he'd check out his other options first, although he felt like he walked in a fog where they were concerned.

He kept thinking he'd forgotten to ask the station agent something, then nodded, remembering the station agent was also the postmaster. He figured if he gave the agent a name, the agent could watch for mail to that person, see where it was from, and feed that information to him. Then he could backtrack and try to find out things that might impact his finding Colter; and perhaps find out who had taken Em off the stage—or paid to have it done. But he wasn't ready with names yet. To say he suspected anyone was way ahead of where he would admit to being. He had more checking to do.

He stared into the dark, his mind spinning from one option to another. If he was to check people out, he needed names, and right now he had only one name he wanted checked. He raised up, pushed the covers back, and lit the lamp.

A piece of paper was what he needed. He looked at the

bedside table, saw no paper, looked around the room, still no paper, shook his head, and reached for his shirt. He had a scrap of paper and a stub of a pencil in one of the pockets. He wrote one name on the slip of paper; the Easterner Randall Bartow. Then he shook his head. He would make a helluva detective. He didn't even have reason to suspect Bartow. He stuck the slip of paper in his shirt pocket, turned the lamp down, and crawled back under the covers.

The darkness, velvety black, shrouded Bartow. His mind had been on finding men to do the things he needed done. He'd forgotten for a few moments that these mountains were heavily populated with grizzlies and cougars. Now he pushed away from the tree against which he'd been leaning; his head swivelled from side to side as his eyes tried to penetrate the darkness. He shivered. The only weapon he had with him was the sleeve gun. It would not slow a bear or a mountain cat enough to keep them off him. He headed toward his cabin, his pace between a fast walk and a run.

When he pulled the door open, he sucked in large gulps of air—some from fear, some from exertion. Maddie looked up from mending one of his socks. "Gracious goodness, Randall, what's got into you? Someone after you?"

He stared at her a moment, still panting. "No, there's nothin' or nobody after me. Pour me a drink, then find me a sheet of paper an' an envelope. I got a letter to write."

She gave him a knowing look, a look that said she knew he'd been afraid of the dark. Then with a smug smile she poured him a drink.

While he knocked it back, she rummaged through a drawer and found pencil, paper, and an envelope. When she handed the material to him, she asked, "Who you gonna write, Randall? Where they live? You ain't never told me where you come from."

He slanted her a look, his eyes flat, his brow furrowed,

and his lips curled in contempt. "Not a damned thing you asked me is any o' your business. Now shut the hell up an' pour me another drink."

She shrank from him and picked up the bottle. She wondered why she stayed with him. He treated her like a dog. Her questions had only been an attempt to start a conversation—something they never had.

At the same time, she questioned what she'd seen in him. She thought perhaps his smooth manner, his Eastern dress, and the way he treated her, at first, gave promise of a better life than the one she'd known. She made up her mind then: When she saw an escape, she'd take it. Whatever it promised could not be as bad as this.

She watched his glass and as soon as he emptied it, she poured another. Maybe if he got drunk enough, he'd pass out. That would give her the rest of the night to herself. She'd not have to listen to words that took away any vestige of self-respect. She'd not have to put up with his pawing her body, and her having to fake a response to his animal-like advances. He knocked back the drink she'd poured, smoothed the sheet of paper on the tabletop, and proceeded to write whoever it was he was writing. She poured him another drink.

He knocked back that drink, finished his letter, put it in the envelope, wiped some glue on the flap, and sealed it. She watched the envelope being sealed, sighed, and poured him another drink. She'd not be able to read the letter and maybe find out where he came from, but from experience, she knew with the drink she'd only that moment poured, he'd lie back and wouldn't waken until morning. Maybe, like in the past, he'd go someplace else to mail it; not Silverton, not Durango, probably Chama. She sighed, hoped she was right; that would give her about a week to herself—a week of peace.

The next morning Bartow wakened, raised hell because

breakfast wasn't on the table, and told her in the same breath to pack him enough clothes for a week.

When she'd finished both tasks, she fidgeted, then looked at him. "Randall, you gonna be gone a week I need a little money to buy food with; ain't enough here to last that long."

He stuck his hand in a pocket almost devoid of coins. He had to find money somewhere, and fast. He'd spent most of what he'd had been able to locate—money that Colter kept for living purposes. He decided to take Gates and Mayben with him. Although not good for much else, they'd be of help if he ran into easy pickings.

Early that morning, while Bartow rounded up his two henchmen, Barnes sat in the cafe. He'd finished breakfast, took the last swallow of his coffee, decided he didn't want more, tossed the proprietor a two-bit piece, and went to the stage station.

"Howdy, need to bother you again." He pinned the postmaster with a questioning look. "Would it be illegal for you to watch the mail an' tell me where mail came from when mailed to a certain person here?"

The man frowned, obviously thinking about what Lingo asked. Finally, he shook his head. "Cain't think o' no regulations I've read that says I cain't do that. What you want to know?"

Lingo grinned. "You reckon you could keep it under your hat that I asked you to do this?"

The postmaster, whose name was Braun, shrugged. "Don't see as I would have reason to tell no one. All I do when they ask for their mail is look through the stack, an' if they got any I give it to 'em. Don't usually have no more conversation with 'em than that." He nodded. "Yep, I got a pretty big hat. Ain't gonna let slip you been doin' anythin' 'bout checkin' on anybody."

Barnes smiled. "Thanks, *amigo*. The name I want you to keep tabs on is Randall Bartow." He stuck his hand across the counter, shook Braun's, and when leaving, said, "Next time I see you in The Golden Eagle I'll buy you a drink."

Braun nodded. "Gonna hold you to that."

When Lingo left the stage station, he thought to collect his horse and go to his ranch. He wanted to make sure Wes, Kelly, and Em were all right. Then he decided to stay around town, see if Gates or Mayben were around, maybe find what they were up to, maybe something that would lead him to their boss.

He loafed most of the day, shopped for a few things he didn't need, then seeing women's things—dresses, jewelry, cosmetics—made a decision to start thinking about Christmas presents. He shrugged mentally. It was too early to buy anything yet; he had plenty of time. He smiled to himself. He'd heard somewhere that most men put off doing things, especially shopping, until the last minute. He shrugged, and reckoned there was no reason for him to be different.

About midafternoon, he sat in front of the mercantile store, watching wagons, surreys, buggies, men on horseback, and pedestrians clog the street and boardwalks on each side. His gaze shifted to the end of the street toward Animas City and Silverton. Three riders. He studied them a moment, then nodded. A surge of energy pumped through him. Mayben, Gates, and a man he'd not seen before, but one dressed in Eastern fashion. He would bet he looked on Randall Bartow. If true, he believed he'd made a good step toward identifying the man Gates and Mayben took orders from. But he needed much more to make certain. He'd keep a close watch on the Easterner.

He thought they would pull rein in front of the Big Gulp saloon. They didn't. They rode straight through town. He made sure which trail they took. Chama. He'd not follow them this time, but would later. If they headed for Chama, they'd be gone a few days. He'd take those days to go to the ranch.

He stood. It was too late to make it all the way to the ranch, so he changed his mind about following the three men. He'd follow them only far enough to ensure they were not headed for the pass going into his hanging valley.

By the time he'd saddled his horse and gotten on the trail to Chama, the three were only specks in the distance. He stayed behind them until certain they didn't head up into the mountains toward his ranch, then reined his horse back toward Durango. On the way he had an idea, and wondered if he'd put himself outside the law if he did it. He stopped by the marshal's office.

Sitting with a cup of Nolan's coffee—almost thick as paste—in front of him, he eyed the marshal. "Nolan, I'm not askin' you to approve what I'm gonna suggest. I just want to know what you think 'bout it."

Nolan's eyes crinkled at the corners, about as close as Lingo had seen him come to a smile. "Ain't gonna know what I think 'til you tell me what you got on your mind."

Lingo took a sip of Nolan's mud, grimaced, then leaned across the desk. "I got an idea that if I got inside Colter's mine there'd be somethin' in there to tell me what's happened to the old man." He sat back, spread his hands palms up, and hunched his shoulders. "The hell of it is, that mine's got a door looks like Colter mighta sawed trees 'bout six-inches thick to make it out of, an' it's got a padlock on it. I have it in mind to break that lock, go in an' see what I can find. How much trouble will I be in if I do that?"

"You askin' me to approve what you jest told me?"

Lingo shook his head. "Not askin' that at all. Know you don't have jurisdiction outside o' town. I just want to know if I'll be in any trouble with the law?"

The marshal toyed with his cup, picked up Barnes's cup, stood, went to the door, and tossed the dregs of each cup into the street. He came back, reached in his bottom right-hand drawer, and pulled a bottle from it; he then poured them each a cup full of whisky.

He closed his eyelids down to a squint. "You ain't got no right to go in that mine, 'less you find somethin' in it to indicate somebody's done harmed the old man"—he gave a jerky nod—"then, young'un, you gonna be in a heap o' trouble."

Silence fell between them thick enough to cut with a knife. Lingo watched Nolan's throat bob with a swallow of the drink he'd poured them, then he took a swallow. "Nolan, there's a way I could do it an' make it legal, but I'm not ready to go to those lengths yet."

A hard smile broke the corners of Nolan's lips. "You thinkin' 'bout gettin' Colter's daughter involved?"

Barnes's neck muscles tightened. He should know by now the salty old marshal would be way ahead of him when it came to plotting. He nodded. "That's what I was thinkin'; but like I said, I'm not ready to go to those lengths yet."

"Jest be damned sure if you do have to rely on her you can keep her safe."

Lingo sighed. "That's one thing you can bet your best saddle on. She's one helluva beautiful an' spunky woman. I like 'er—a lot. There's no way I'm gonna jeopardize her." He shrugged, gave Nolan a chagrined smile, and shook his head. "If I give any hint to her what I have in mind there'll be no way I can keep her from goin' ahead with bustin' in the door."

"You got any idea yet who ramrodded them men takin' 'er off'n that stage?"

Barnes nodded. "Got a pretty good one, but I can't prove a damn thing. I'm gonna work on that next."

"You ready to tell me what you done come up with?"

"Nope. Soon's I have somethin' with absolute proof, I'll let you know, then I'm gonna lure them to town an' get you to arrest 'em."

" 'Fraid you wuz gonna say that."

Lingo grinned. "Marshal, I'll tell you what's a fact. You won't be standin' alone. There'll be a whole bunch o' us to help you. I'll make sure of that."

He knocked back his drink, stood, shook the marshal's hand, and left. He went to the hotel, packed his gear, and made ready to get on the trail for the ranch the next morning.

After letting Wes know it was him coming up the pass, Lingo rode up to the cabin with him. Emily was first out of the door. She stopped short of throwing herself at Lingo when he stepped from the saddle. She stood, her face red, a huge lump in her throat, then he held out his arms to her. "Aw hell, little girl, c'mon, give me a hug; I need one, especially from you."

She launched herself into his arms. If he said he needed a hug "especially from her," she'd surely give him one.

"Oh, Lingo, I've been so worried about you." She stood back and raked his tall frame with a searching look. She smiled. "Don't see a sign that anybody's been shootin' at, or pounding on you in any way."

A slow shake of his head told her he was all right. "Nope. Reckon I've been real careful to keep my pretty pink body outta harm's way. I'm right sensitive to pain."

She pulled her mouth to the side. "If I hadn't seen you in action, I might believe that. Come on in. Tell us why you think it's all right for Wes to be down here with you. You have it all settled?"

He snorted. "Wish I could say 'yes' to that question, but I'll tell you this much: I believe I'm a lot closer to findin' answers to a lot o' things now than the last time I saw you."

"You gonna tell us what those answers are?"

He shook his head. "Not yet—but soon, I hope."

She noticed that Wes had his arm around Kelly's shoulders, and wondered if they'd decided to tell Lingo how they felt about each other; Lingo, too, glanced at them and a slight smile broke the corners of his mouth. She knew then what his reaction would be.

"Well, for goodness sakes, we gonna stand out here an' talk, or we gonna take this big man inside and feed 'im." She looked at Lingo. "I know you must be about starved."

"Just about, little girl."

After supper, drinking coffee, Wes and Kelly squirmed, took a swallow or two of their drink, looked at each other, then looked away. Finally, Emily shook her head and pinned Wes with a no-nonsense look. "All right, you gonna tell 'im, or you want me to?"

Wes gave her a hard look. "Ain't never asked nobody to ride broncs what I done cut out for myself." He looked at Kelly; she gave him a slight nod. He turned his head to look into Lingo's eyes. "What I wantta know, boss, is how you gonna feel if I tell you I wantta court Kelly."

Emily choked back a laugh when Lingo put on a severe, chastising look. He pinned Wes with a hard look. "You said anythin' 'bout all this to Kelly yet?"

Wes shook his head. "No, sir. Reckon we both knew what I wanted to do, but figgered we better ask you first."

"You both figured it that way?"

"Yes, sir."

"Well, damnit, don't reckon I'm the one you oughtta be talkin' to. Turn around, look into her eyes, an' tell 'er you love 'er—or don't you feel that way?"

His face red as a Texas dust-laden sunset, eyes hard as granite, Wes gazed at Lingo. "They ain't no other reason a man would want to court a woman far's I can figger; less'n o' course he's a piece o' slime, an' I don't figger you put in all that time raisin' me for me to be that way." He took Kelly's hand in his. "C'mon, girl, ain't gonna do like he said; gonna tell you in private. Ain't none o' Lingo's damned business what I say to you."

A laugh rumbled up from the bottom of Lingo's chest. When he could get his breath, he nodded. "Get on outta here, tell 'er what you figger you haven't said yet, then come back an' we'll talk 'bout findin' a preacher."

Wes stared at the floor a moment, then raised his eyes to Lingo's. "Damn you, boss, I reckon you knowed all along 'bout us."

"Yep, just wondered how long it was gonna take y'all to notice you were grown, an' had the right to figure things out for yourselves." He turned his eyes on Kelly. "Figure you got your feelin's sorted out long before Wes did. I was 'bout ready to give 'im a shove in your direction if he hadn't waked up soon."

Kelly grabbed him about the shoulders, stood on tiptoe, kissed his cheek, layed her head against his chest, and looked at Wes. He stood there grinning like a mule eating briars.

For the first time since coming to Lingo's valley, Emily felt left out—not part of this close-knit family. She twisted to pick up the coffeepot.

Lingo's brawny arm shot out, encircled her shoulders and pulled her to him. "You're as much a part o' this as you want to be, little girl." His eyes twinkled, his brow furrowed, and he smiled into her eyes. "An' the way I have it figured you want to be part o' our carin' for each other as much as we want you to."

She stared at him, and never breaking her gaze, nodded. "In some ways, mostly in different ways. They look on you like a big brother—almost as a father." She shook her head. "I don't look on you as either."

"An' how do you look on me, little girl?"

Her face flamed, but she still held his gaze. How had she let their conversation take this twist? "Lingo Barnes, a lot has to take place before I answer that question. Suffice it to say, I want to be a part of the caring I see between all of you." She stepped out of his arm and picked up the coffeepot. Where his arm had held her shoulders was almost as warm as the coffeepot, and they tingled as though in anticipation of feeling his arm holding her close again. She swallowed against the tightening in her throat. What was the matter with her? She'd never felt this way before, never thought she *could* feel this way.

She poured them each a cup of coffee. While they were drinking, Lingo told them about the men he suspected were working together. Then he looked at Emily. "Now I'm not gonna tell you who I think they are, other than the two who're left of those who took you off the stage, but I b'lieve I'm right close to figuring out who the boss is.

"When I'm sure, real sure, I'll come up with a plan. I'll need your help then." He frowned and shook his head. "I want to keep you out of it long's I can, keep you safe as I can, but there's gonna come a time when I'll need you to step up an' identify them."

Emily's stomach knotted, her supper sat uneasily in its pit. "You're gonna be out there alone fighting my fight? I'll not stand for that. You need help now and I'm the one to do the helping."

Lingo smiled and shook his head. "Nope, you're not gonna do one thing 'til I know the time's right." He leaned toward her. "An' I'm tellin' you right now's not the time. 'Sides that, Sam's gonna do all the helpin' I need for now." He swallowed the last of his coffee and pushed away from the table.

"Wes, I think Gates an' Mayben's gonna be gone a few days. We need to take that time to get as many of the fall calf crop branded as time'll allow. Let's hit the hay. We got a whole bunch o' work to do tomorrow."

Lingo and Wes helped clean up the kitchen. Emily dried the last dish, and knowing it would do her no good to argue with Lingo about any help she could give, told the men good-night and climbed to the attic.

After getting ready for the night, Kelly pulled her bed alongside of Emily's. Her voice, little above a whisper, broke into Emily's thoughts. "Em, you beginnin' to think 'bout Lingo like maybe he's your man?"

Emily's eyes snapped open, widened. "Why, Kelly, what in the world are you talking about? I've never given such a thing even one thought." Kelly chuckled into the dark attic.

"Reckon you kin tell yourself such, but you gotta remember I'm a woman. Seems to me y'all done said a lot to each other without sayin' one word." She turned on her side. " 'Night, Em. If them men gonna brand calves tomorrow, you an' me's got a lot o' work to do."

Emily lay there staring at the rafters not far above her head. What caused Kelly to ask her about her feelings? Had she done something that would indicate she had feelings for Lingo? She sighed. *Did she have feelings for the big man?* She tried to push those thoughts from her mind, but she spent long hours staring into the dark.

10

BARTOW LED HIS two henchmen toward Chama. Out here on the flats a slight breeze stirred the cured-on-the-stem grass, and wafted the scents from the mountain slopes to the three men. Bartow explained what he wanted them to do. "See you brought your sawed-off Greeners like I told you. After I take care of my business in Chama, we're gonna relieve the stage driver of whatever shipment he's hauling outta Durango to the railhead.

"We need money. I've not found where Colter keeps his stash, an' I've just about spent all I could find of his every-day expense money." He reined in his horse and faced them. "I don't think that stage's gonna slow down when we try to stop it. It might if you damn fools hadn't killed that one who drove the stage Colter's daughter was on." He shook his head. "Gonna make it a little harder. In case it doesn't stop when we hail, it, I want the two of you to have your horses close by." He shook his head. "No, I want you to stay on 'em an' if he whips that team into a run, you'll be able to chase 'im without losin' any time." He searched their faces. "If you have to, shoot the guy riding shotgun first, then take care of the driver. Got it?"

Bull pushed his hat to the back of his head. "What you gonna be doin' while we put our butts in front o' the scattergun that guard's gonna be carryin'?"

Hot blood pushed to Bartow's head. Who was this big dumb bastard to question *him*? He swallowed his anger and forced a cold smile. "Well, I'll tell you, Mayben: I'm gonna be sittin' behind a big rock with my Winchester trained on the two o' you in case you mess this job up."

Gates's right hand eased along his thigh, then caressed the smooth leather of his holster.

Bartow's eyes squinted. He pinned Shorty with eyes that felt like they were on fire. "Go ahead, Gates, make a grab for that gun an' Mayben and I'll have to do this job alone."

Fear washed across the little bandit's face. His hand moved away from his thigh. Bartow's lips curled in contempt. He chuckled. "Afraid, Shorty?" He cut the chuckle short. "Tell you, when you decide you can beat this sleeve gun I carry, go ahead an' try me. There's nothing I'd like better than to put lead into that scrawny body o' yours." He reined his horse to the side. "You two get on toward Chama—I'll ride behind."

The rest of the way to town, Bartow made certain neither of the two got to his side, or behind; pure hatred had dripped from the eyes of each when he'd threatened Gates. He shrugged mentally. He'd never seen the day two dumb, Western hicks could take him, whether with guns or brains.

"Pull up in front of the saloon. I have enough to pay for a couple drinks apiece. I'll meet you there in a few minutes. Right now I have business to take care of." He reined his horse to the hitching rack in front of the general store. He'd been here before. The post office was in the rear.

After checking to see if he had mail, posting the letter he'd written before leaving the cabin, and ensuring he had the right information as to when the stagecoach from Durango would arrive, he headed for the saloon.

Lingo rousted Wes from his bunk before daylight the next morning. Trying not to disturb the girls asleep in the attic, Barnes stoked the fire in the stove while Wes brought in more wood, then readied the coffeepot so they could have a cup before leaving for the far end of the valley.

Then they went to the barn. There, they checked their lariats and saddles, took branding irons from the nails on the wall, saddled up, and rode to the hitching rack only a few feet in front of the porch. The smell of bacon frying stopped them in their tracks. Lingo grinned, then shrugged. "Well, we tried to let them sleep."

Wes raised his eyebrows. "Sure glad they woke up though. My stomach was already growlin', an' givin' me hell for not puttin' some food down there."

Lingo shot the kid a disgusted grin. "Wes, I don't remember ever seein' you when your stomach wasn't growling."

When they walked into the warm main room, the table was set, and Emily had only then put a platter of bacon, eggs, and a huge bowl of country-fried potatoes on the table. Kelly opened the oven door and took a tin of hot biscuits from it. She looked over her shoulder. "Emily ain't never seen no branding done. Figgered you men needed help out yonder, so I told 'er we could keep the fire goin', an' the brandin' irons hot for y'all."

Lingo shook his head. "Tried to be quiet so's not to waken you." He smiled. "Gotta admit, we can use the help."

While eating, Kelly suggested that Lingo and Wes go ahead and get the fire started while she and Emily cleaned up the kitchen, got out of their robes, and into work clothes. They'd be to the branding site before the irons got hot.

Lingo shook his head. "No, y'all hold up 'til in the

mornin'. I figure we'll ride to the end of the valley and haze all the young stuff back to this end. That way we'll have plenty to keep us busy for a few days."

The second day, late in the afternoon Emily's stomach roiled at the sight and smell of burned hair and flesh, and while not about to get used to that, she marveled at the way the men worked together, one roping and holding the young calves down while the other applied the iron. Their horses also seemed to know what to do and when to do it. It was almost as if they and their horses had practiced working together all their lives; she said so.

Wes grinned. "Em, you go to any brandin', you gonna see the same thing. Ain't no cowboy what don't know how to do his job, whether it's ropin', brandin', keepin' the irons hot"—he shrugged—"or whatever. Reckon any top hand can do it all."

"Is that what you and Lingo'd be called?"

Wes looked at Lingo, then back to Emily. "Top hand?" He nodded. "I figger me an' Lingo'd be able to hire out as top hands on any ranch in the country."

Emily shook her head. "Well I declare, I b'lieve I learn more about you two men every day."

They worked from sunup to sundown for five days, came in every night, tired, dirty, took turns bathing in the wash-tub, ate, and turned into their bunks about midnight, and got up the next day to do it all over again.

The night of the fifth man-killing day, at the supper table, Lingo told them he would go back to Silverton the next morning. Emily stared at him straight on. "You're going to try to do this alone aren't you?"

He shook his head. "Only 'til I know for sure what I'm doing, an' who I'm fightin', then I'll yell for help."

She didn't break her gaze. "I noticed you and Wes

worked together, you didn't have to yell for help then. Help was already there." She pulled her shoulders up, then lowered them. "Why not now?"

" 'Cause when Wes and I work together, we don't figure it to be dangerous work. This is."

Kelly snorted. "Dangerous? Em, there ain't no work more dangerous than cowboyin'. I've seed a many a cowboy git hurt, killed, doin' the things they do every day, an' they don't think nothin' of it. Why heck, a horse can throw 'em, a bull can stick a horn in 'em, a rattler can bite 'em, a horse can stumble, fall, an' the saddlehorn can stick into their stomach." She shrugged and spread her hands palms up. "They's so many things a cowboy does that get 'em crippled or killed don't nobody think on it much."

Emily turned her eyes on Lingo, and very un-Emily-like, said, "Damn you, Lingo Barnes, *you'd better* think something of it. Anything happen to you I'd die." She didn't blush. She didn't hedge on what she said. Her only reaction to her own words was to stare directly into his eyes, her look daring him to say something trite. He didn't.

On the way to Silverton, and even after he got there, Lingo mulled over Emily's words. Had they come from her because of friendship, a feeling of debt for what he was doing for her . . . or had she a deeper feeling for him? He hoped for the latter.

Sam had been watching for the reappearance of Bartow and his henchmen; they'd not been back to town. Barnes studied on what Slagle told him, frowned, then looked at him. "Sam, I'm gonna go back up to Colter's mine, take a harder look at it, see if there's been anybody around there. If there has, there should be footprints, or something to tell me how many men we're dealin' with."

Sam shook his head. "You ain't gonna find no footprints up yonder. We had a gully-washer of a rain two days ago; figger it washed out any sign what mighta been left."

Lingo shrugged. "That don't make it much harder, I figure to have a closer look at it anyway." He smiled. "An' I guarantee you I'm gonna wipe out any sign *I* been pokin' around there."

The next day, to have an excuse for being in town, he went to the cafe and the general store and left an order for some merchandise to be delivered in a couple of weeks. The cafe owner had told him his patrons were beginning to growl about eating venison three meals a day. Then, about three hours until sundown, he left town at the opposite end from where he'd leave if going to Slagle's cabin.

He circled, pulled up in back of Sam's cabin, took care of his horse, put on moccasins, and headed into the woods. Again, he took a circuitous route to Colter's mine, squatted in the trees long enough to make certain there was no one around, then went to the mine entrance.

Before stepping toward the massive wooden door, he studied the ground for tracks, but true to Slagle's supposition, the rain had washed out any sign that anyone had ever been there, although there were some small indentations in the soft soil, as though someone with small feet, wearing mocassins, had been there. He shook his head. He could think of no reason why someone, maybe a woman, would be nosing around the mine. He shrugged off the only clue he'd found.

He stared at the door. What did he expect to find? He didn't know what he looked for. The heavy door showed no sign that it had been opened. He looked at the hinges. They were well oiled and showed no sign of rust, but he figured they wouldn't have, in that they were mounted such that the hinge-pins and the hinges themselves couldn't be removed from the outside. Then he looked at the lock, frowned, and turned the lock such that it hung in its hasp on the side from which the door would open. Again, he studied the door, the area around it, frowned, shook his head, and backed toward the woods, carefully wiping out his track as he left.

Back at the cabin, he told Sam what he'd seen, shrugged, and admitted he found nothing to arouse his suspicions. "The way I rehung the lock might give me a hint that someone has been there, but hell, if anyone has been there the lock might just naturally fall back the way I placed it." He slammed his fist against the table. "Dammit, Sam, I reckon I'm stumblin' 'round in the dark. Don't know what to look for; don't even know if I see anything that I'll recognize it of importance."

"Settle down, young'un, we'll find somethin' soon. I figger if they is any chance Colter's been harmed, that is, if he ain't on a trip somewhere, we gonna find somethin' what'll send us off in the right direction."

Barnes grimaced. "Hope so, Sam, I sure do want to be able to give that little girl some good news 'bout her pa."

Slagle took a sip of coffee then looked at Lingo from lowered brows. "Reckon you think a mighty lot o' that little woman, don't you, son?" Then without waiting for a reply, he said, "You keep callin' 'er 'little girl;' you better take a mighty close look at 'er, partner. She ain't no little girl. She's a full-grown, beautiful woman what any man would be mighty proud to call his'n."

Lingo swallowed a knot in his throat, frowned into the bottom of his cup, then nodded. "Yeah, Sam. I know she's full-grown. I know she's beautiful. I know most any man would be mighty proud to call 'er his woman. An' yeah, I think an awful lot of her. Suppose I'm beginnin' to realize how much, an' admit it to myself. Didn't ever think there'd be anythin' I thought as much of as Wes, Kelly, an' the ranch." He stood, poured their cups full, then sat. "B'lieve she sits right up yonder at the top of what I think most of."

"You sayin' you in love with 'er?"

Lingo shook his head. "Don't even know what love is; wouldn't know how to describe it, but all I can say is I have a mighty strong feelin' for her. I feel mighty good when I can look across the room or the table an' see her smile at me." He shook his head. "Reckon what I miss most is the sharing. I enjoy sharin' things with her."

A laugh rumbled up from the bottom of Slagle's chest. "Son, you mighta jest described what love really is. Think on it awhile."

Lingo snorted to himself. Think on it awhile? Hell, that's all he'd been thinking about—when he should have been concentrating on the problem of her father.

Bartow had been concentrating on an entirely different problem—the stagecoach. What would be the safest way to hold up the damned thing? He wanted what it carried, but he didn't plan to stick his neck out very far. Finally, he nodded to himself. They'd do it the way he'd first thought. He never wanted to let either Gates or Mayben anywhere close to his back.

He wished he'd had time to ride to the end of track and send a telegram to D'Amato, but he didn't want to stay away from the mine too long; Colter might die of thirst if Maddie failed to take care of him as he'd instructed her to do, even though he'd regained much of his health. He'd have to wait for his letter to get the results he desired.

The three had been riding toward Durango through most of the day. Now, a little after noon, he thought they'd better find a place to stop the stagecoach. He studied the trail ahead. After about another thirty minutes, he noticed two piles of boulders. The road ran between the two, then curved sharply to the right on the other side. He couldn't have asked for a better place. The driver would have to slow the horses to make the curve without taking a chance on overturning.

He'd been riding behind Gates and Mayben; now he talked to their backs. "Those rocks up ahead. Stop this side of them, stay on your horses, and when the driver slows to come between them I want you, Mayben, to grab the reins and stop the team. You, Gates, drop the guy riding shotgun.

I'll shoot the driver. If they're carryin' passengers, kill 'em when the stage stops."

Gates reined in and faced Bartow. "Reckon you gonna stay in them rocks where they ain't gonna be no chance o' catchin' lead. Right?"

Bartow allowed a slow, cold smile to break the corners of his lips. "Damn, Gates, didn't think you had enough sense to figure that out." He wiped the smile away, squinted his eyes, and curled his lips. "An' like you figured before, I'll be where I can see that you carry it out the way I say." He patted the stock of his rifle. "This baby'll shoot a lot farther than my sleeve gun, an' it'll be pointed straight at you."

They came up on the boulders. Bartow took his station close to the top of the pile where he could see in both directions. Gates and Mayben took station on the Chama side. Bartow thought they'd have close to an hour's wait before the stage came into sight. He was right.

Just as Bartow thought, the driver slowed the horses to a walk before entering the narrow passage between the boulders. Mayben reined his horse alongside the lead horse. He made his move too quick.

Gates hadn't time to bring his Greener to bear on the guy riding shotgun. A double-barreled roar from the shotgun in the stage's boot, only a split second before Shorty fired, told him he didn't have to look to know he no longer had a partner. The sounds of Bull's horse bolting pushed into the back of Gates's hearing. The shotgun guard lay sprawled across the seat. The charge in Gates's Greener had done its job.

The driver grabbed for his handgun. He never got it out. He slumped into the bottom of the boot with Bartow's rifle slug through his head. Now the frightened team took the bit in their teeth. From a slow walk, they went into an all-out run. Gates spurred his horse to catch them.

Two men hung outside the windows of the coach firing

six-shooters. Shorty slowed his horse to stay out of six-gun range. He waited until their guns went silent, then spurred his horse alongside. They frenziedly pushed shells into the cylinder of their six-shooters. Gates, his horse at a dead run, thumbed off shots into the stage's interior. The passengers would never finish loading their handguns.

He dug heels into his horse. The animal sprang ahead. Shorty came abreast the lead horse, leaned from his saddle, caught the reins in his right hand, and slowed his horse. The team slowed, then stopped.

Gates warily moved back to look in the coach. The two passengers lay slumped onto the floorboards, one lying half on the body of the other. He glanced toward the boulders. Bartow was only then climbing aboard his horse to come to him. The Easterner never glanced at the body of Bull Mayben lying in the dust at the foot of the boulders.

Blood rushed to Gates's head; angry bile bubbled at the back of his throat. That bastard didn't care that his partner was dead. Shorty swung his Colt in the direction of Bartow—but the Easterner's rifle pointed directly at him, and even from the distance he sat his horse Gates could see Bartow's smug smile. He didn't know how he'd accomplish it, but he'd kill that slimy bastard someway, somehow, somewhere.

Bartow reined in his horse in front of Gates. "Climb to the boot and throw down the chest."

Gates thought to tell him to go to hell, if he wanted the chest to climb up and throw it down himself, but with Bartow's rifle still pointed at him, he climbed to the driver's seat, pushed the bodies aside, looked under the seat—and there was no chest. "Ain't no chest up here, Bartow. Looks like we done come up empty."

Bartow's face reddened, veins stood out on his forehead, then his face purpled. "What the hell you mean, there's no chest up there? By God there'd better be. I'll kill you right here if there isn't. I need that money."

Gates went dead calm inside. He figured he'd be dead in the next second, and again thought to try his luck at outshooting the Easterner—but couldn't remember whether he'd emptied his revolver. He decided not to take a chance. "Tellin' you right now, Bartow, there ain't no chest up here." His every muscle tightened, braced for the expected slam of a bullet. It didn't come.

Bartow still held his rifle on the skinny gunman. He grabbed the handle of the coach's door, threw it open, and stepped from his horse. "Climb down and stand out here where I can see you." Gates did as directed.

Bartow went inside the coach, felt for money belts on both men, pulled them free, then went through their pockets. The money belts felt heavy, and their pockets yielded several hundred dollars in double eagles. He grunted. It wasn't as much of a dry run as he'd first thought.

And along with that thought had been the one in which he would get rid of Shorty Gates. The skinny bastard could take the hot ride to hell with his partner. Then he decided he would let the little outlaw live. He might need him later. He climbed from the coach and, careful to keep his horse between him and Gates, toed the stirrup. "Let's get back to Silverton."

Gates swallowed a huge lump in his throat. "What we gonna do 'bout Bull? Cain't jest leave 'im lie there in the dirt."

Bartow looked at him straight on. "The hell we can't."

Shorty came close to letting anger override caution. His fingers twitched ready to make a sweep for his six-shooter. Again he didn't know whether he still had any live loads in the cylinder. He took a deep breath, pushed his anger deep into his chest. "Gonna tell you, Bartow, them who finds Bull gonna know right away I wuz in the holdup with 'im, 'cause ain't nobody never seen one o' us 'less'n the other wuz there." He threw a sly smile at Bartow. "There's them 'round Silverton who've seen you with us, too. You want 'em to start lookin' into what you doin' out here? 'Sides that, they wuz a whole bunch of people seen us ride through Durango together."

The Easterner sat there a moment, not taking his eyes off of Gates. He obviously thought about Shorty's words. He nodded. "Load 'im on your horse, you can walk to where we get rid of him. We'll dump 'im into a ravine somewhere."

"Gotta have help gittin' 'im across my saddle. I cain't handle 'im alone; he's too big." Then hope swelled his chest. Maybe he could get his .44 out while they struggled with Mayben. Bartow squelched that thought as soon as it entered Gates's head.

He nodded. "All right, drop your gunbelt, keep your hands where I can see 'em, then I'll help."

Hope left Shorty. He felt as though he'd been punched in the stomach. His hands went to the buckle on his gunbelt, loosened it, and his gun and gunbelt slipped to the ground. "All right, let's get 'im across the saddle."

They rode well off the trail until they found a deep slash in the earth where snowmelt runoff had cut into the hard ground. With Bartow's help Shorty pushed his partner down the side. He then slipped down the embankment alone and piled stones over his body.

When convinced animals couldn't paw the stones aside to get to Bull's body, and despite Bartow cursing and telling him to get the hell back to his horse, he removed his hat, stood there a moment and asked God to be kind to Bull Mayben, the only partner he'd ever had.

All the while he stood there, he expected to feel one of Bartow's rifle bullets cut through him. Right then he didn't give a damn.

When he again climbed aboard his horse they circled around Durango to keep anyone from remembering they'd seen them in the area, then they headed for Silverton. He hoped Mayben's horse found a place to stay in one of the mountain meadows, hoped the horse wouldn't make it back to Durango or Silverton. People knew the horse and who he belonged to.

After going to bed that night, Emily pulled the covers up under her chin and stared into the darkness. She should feel shame—but she didn't. She had practically told Lingo how she felt about him. *Weeell*, not practically; She'd just flat stopped short of saying she loved him, and everyone in the room knew it. Should she feel unlady-like? Should she be ashamed of violating everything her father had taught her about behavior in both speech and actions when talking with a man? She mentally shook her head. She wasn't ashamed, she admitted that to herself, but she wouldn't admit to loving him. She thought an awful lot of him, cared whether he put himself in danger for her, cared that he wanted to keep her out of harm's way, and yes, she thought it would kill her if anything happened to him.

Then out of the dark came Kelly's voice. "You don't need to lie there fightin' the bed, wondering why you said them things to Lingo. If you won't admit it, I'm gonna tell you flat out: You're in love with the big man." Then from her bed, Kelly took her hand. "Em, me an' Wes love Lingo, too, but our love ain't the same as your'n. We got family love for 'im. You got man-woman love for 'im." She chuckled deep in her throat. "Now, woman, admit it to yourself. Lie there an' wish he wuz next to you an' don't feel no shame for the wish. There ain't a woman alive who don't have the same feelin's 'bout her man. An' after you do them things, Em, turn over an' go to sleep." She chuckled again. "Bet you have sweet dreams."

Emily didn't answer Kelly. If she had, she would have to face up to something she wasn't ready to face—yet. Despite not wanting to face up to it, she lay there until daylight pushed its way into the cabin.

Despite being tired, sleepy, and wanting to snuggle into

the covers and go to sleep, she wouldn't think of letting Kelly shoulder the load of keeping things going. They had to eat, wash clothes, clean the cabin, feed the stock, even chop stove wood. She threw the covers back and dressed.

From the moment Maddie Brice watched Bartow ride from the cabin to be gone about a week, she struggled with whether to pack her few belongings, catch a stage to anywhere, and see if she could find work—but she had no money to pay her fare. She didn't have enough to even get out of Silverton.

When Bartow had taken her out of the saloon in which she worked, her self-respect was dragging the bottom of the barrel, she thought. But now, after a few months with Bartow and being worse than his slave and personal whore, she realized there were not many things worse than what she had let herself in for. If she could get a few dollars, she'd made up her mind to leave. But where could she get even a few cents? The only things she knew were cooking, house cleaning, washing clothes—and warming a man's bed. She had dealt the last thing out. She'd done all of that she intended to do—unless a man showed he cared for her . . . and she didn't know where she'd find a man like that. She held the two dollars Bartow had left her to buy food. She took one of the cartwheels and stuck it in her shoe. She'd not eat but one meal every other day. She did the shopping, so she decided that when she went to the store, she'd keep some of the money for herself. Maybe by the time Bartow got back and left again she'd have stage fare. For the first time since she'd left home three years ago she felt like she might end up worth something.

Barnes and Slagle decided that the only sensible thing was for one of them to keep track of things in Silverton, and the other in Durango. And in talking they thought it wouldn't hurt to keep a closer eye on the Easterner. Slagle said the only reason he had to suspect the man was that he didn't seem to have any kind of job. To Slagle's thinking, every man needed a way to earn money to live on. Lingo agreed.

The morning after they made their decision the two men sat in the cafe finishing breakfast. Lingo sat by the window. About to take a swallow of coffee before climbing on his horse and heading for Durango, he stiffened, and nodded to the hitch rack. Shorty Gates was looping the reins of his horse over the rail. "Never seen 'im without havin' Mayben taggin' along at his side."

Sam shook his head. "Me neither, but it looks like he's gonna come in here. You better cut out. Don't wantta let 'im see you an' me together."

Lingo stood, tossed a two-bit piece on the table to pay for his meal, and pushed out the door, brushing by the skinny gunman. He felt Gates's eyes boring into his back until he'd toed the stirrup and pointed his horse toward Durango.

Two days later, Barnes sat outside Durango's general store. He'd already been to see the marshal and brought him up to date on the Emily Lou Colter situation. And after telling him that he had nothing new to report other than that Gates and Mayben had been gone for over a week, and that Gates had showed up in Silverton alone. Lingo thought it strange his partner hadn't been with him, nor had the man the two left Durango with.

Nolan told him about the Chama-bound stagecoach returning to Durango with two passengers, the shotgun guard, and the driver all dead. And that the passengers, well known, and known to travel with heavy money belts had no money belts strapped around their waists, and no money in their pockets when the stage brought them back. Nolan figured it as clearly being the result of a holdup.

Now, a couple of hours later, Lingo sat on the smooth wooden bench, hunched down in his sheepskin, smoking his pipe and studying the people streaming along the street. Durango was a busy town.

A man walked from the land office: Bartow, the Easterner. The first thing Lingo's eyes honed in on were the man's shoes. Yep, they were low-quarter. Barnes shrugged. Hell, that didn't prove anything. He'd never seen a city man in boots.

He squinted, looked at the man closer. He'd seen the same man in Silverton, so he wasn't new to the territory. He glanced at the door from which the Easterner had come, nodded to himself, and stood. Maybe he'd find out what the man had been doing in there.

The agent smiled and asked why Lingo wanted to know about the man. "Well, gonna tell ya, that man didn't look like any miner I've ever seen. Just thought it odd he'd have business in your office."

The agent studied Barnes a moment, then nodded. "Reckon I had the same idea." He pulled a map over in front of him. "This's the area he asked about." He pointed a pencil toward where Lingo knew Colter's claim to be. "Strange, too, he wanted to know the names of the people who already had mines there. Don't seem to me a man'd give a damn who owned the mines around him long's he got the claim he wanted."

Barnes leaned in to see the map better. "He seem interested in any particular spot for his claim?"

"Yep, he chose a spot right up the mountain above Miles Colter's claim. I asked 'im if he knew Colter or much about mining." The agent grinned. "He told me it wasn't any of my damned business." He shrugged. "If he'd been more polite, don't think I'da told you what he was doin'."

Lingo smiled, thanked the agent, and offered to buy him a drink if he saw him in The Golden Eagle. He left.

Why would anyone want to know the names of mine owners before selecting a claim? He pondered that question a few moments, shrugged, and chalked it up to people having strange quirks. But before casting the question aside, he thought it strange that the man's claim was right close to Colter's.

He walked down the boardwalk toward the end of town, having it in mind to walk along the river and sort out his thoughts. He'd gone only two store-lengths when yelling and people running past him caused him to stop and look in the direction they ran.

He frowned. People gathered around a riderless horse. He turned in that direction, stopped, and crossed the street to Nolan's office. "Looks like there might be somethin' out here that's your business, Marshal. A horse just came into town with no rider, but still saddled."

Nolan stood, picked up his hat, and followed Barnes.

They pushed through the crowd together. Lingo recognized the horse as soon as people opened a lane for him. It had the same markings as the bay Bull Mayben rode. As soon as he got close enough, he studied the black, dried buildup of something all over the pommel and down the fender. From experience, he knew dried blood when he saw it. He looked at the marshal. "Reckon I know why Shorty Gates wasn't with 'is partner. That's Mayben's horse."

Under his breath Nolan muttered, "Reckon that's one we won't hang." Barnes picked up the marshal's words.

"Nolan, I reckon it's sort of a shame, Bull was just a big dumb animal who could be led by anyone with one brain cell more than he had—an' he wasn't overloaded with 'em."

Nolan took the reins of the horse, and led him toward the livery. The animal looked as though he'd not had food or water in days. When they reached the front of his office Nolan told Lingo to strip the gear from Mayben's horse and take it into his office. He wanted to take a closer look at it.

When Nolan got back to his office, he glanced at the saddle that Barnes had dropped to the floor at the side of his old scarred desk. He nodded toward the gear Lingo had dropped there. "Reckon we know at least one o' them who robbed the stage."

Barnes stared at the saddle. "Nolan, there's no way in hell you gonna prove that, an' even less likely that you'll be able to prove Gates had anything to do with it."

A jerky nod told Lingo that Nolan agreed. "Didn't figger on tryin' to prove they had anything to do with it. We find out who's callin' the shots in whatever game they're playin', an' we hang that jasper an' Gates, then I reckon I'd have to say justice has been served."

Lingo stared at his friend a long moment, then nodded. "Marshal, I reckon if we had more law officers like you, an' less lawyers, we'd serve justice a helluva lot more often."

Nolan stared at Barnes a moment. "Son, gonna tell you right now, we gonna see the day when justice ain't the issue. We gonna see slick-willy shysters take advantage of the law an' git them who breaks the law off scot-free." His face, to Lingo's thinking, crumpled a little. "Son, when that day comes, an' it's almost here, a law officer's job's gonna be only for the most dedicated men around; men who'll do their jobs against almost impossible odds." He nodded. "Yeah, they'll be a few officers who'll git in this business for what they kin git outta it, we got some o' that kind now, but for the most part they's gonna be law officers who'll make livin' tol'able for honest folk."

11

SAM SAT IN front of Murchison's general store on the sunny side of the street. This crisp autumn day, he soaked up the warmth, nodded, then nodded again. Damn, he could get used to loafing right sudden. He nodded again, then jerked upright, all thought of sleep gone.

His look held on the trail leading into town. The Easterner rode in alone.

Sam thought about that for a moment. Who the hell did they think they were fooling? Gates, Bull, and Bartow had all disappeared from town about the same time, then when one showed up, not too long after another of the three made an appearance. He nodded to himself. Yep, he couldn't imagine them fooling anyone. They been out of town together. He wished Barnes could know what he'd just seen.

The Easterner, Randall Bartow. He'd seen, or heard the man's name before—but where? Bartow tied up at the saloon and went in. Slagle stood and walked to the watering hole.

Inside, at the bar, he ordered a whisky, straight, and when it came, picked it up and turned his back to the rough puncheon boards. Bartow sat at a table against the back wall. Gates stayed at the bar. Neither of them acted as though they'd ever seen the other. Sam knocked back his drink, made sure the two men had only then gotten a drink in front of them, then he pushed through the batwing doors.

He walked directly to the hitching rack and studied the imprint of the horses' hooves both Bartow and Gates had ridden into town on. He nodded, and walked to the edge of town. There, he singled out the tracks he'd only a few moments ago identified as those belonging to the horses Bartow and Gates had ridden. Here the tracks were separate. He turned his steps out of town. He'd followed the trail less than a quarter of a mile when the separate tracks fell in side by side. To make certain one had not simply ridden past the other, he walked another half mile or so to prove to himself that they'd ridden together from wherever they'd been. Sam had proven that to his own satisfaction.

He went back to sit outside of Murchison's store. Many of his friends had stopped to ask if he wasn't feeling well. His response had been, "Naw, I ain't sick. Jest got a hitch in my back an' figgered to give it a few days to get well—but I'm sure enjoyin' jest sittin' aroun' doin' nothin'." His words seemed to satisfy them.

He sat there a couple of hours and mulled over what he'd discovered. He was certain that Gates and the Easterner were tied in together, but couldn't figure what their game might be. Too, he wondered where Mayben was. He sat there hoping to see the two leave, but on into late sundown they still hadn't left the saloon. He wondered at people who could hang over a bar that long.

He stood, stretched, and headed home—toward his empty cabin. He smiled into the night, wondering at how quickly he'd gotten used to having a friend close by. He'd not had anyone to share with since his wife had passed away eight years before from pneumonia.

Slagle thought to find where Bartow's and Gates's cabin was—squat in the woods close by and see what they did, and where they did it. He quickly vetoed that idea. He wasn't a woodsman, never had been. Lingo was the one to do the thing he thought to do. Lingo was an outdoorsman, a woodsman, an Indian fighter; hell, he could do things that Sam Slagle had never been able to do. Sam picked up an armload of stove wood when he got to his cabin, sighed, and went inside to fix himself something to eat.

Wes shrugged into his sheepskin. The night air had the feel of snow in it, and up here on the mountain it pushed into his bones. He figured he'd stay at the pass until it began to snow, then he'd go down to the cabin, get warm, eat a good supper, and go to bed. He'd come back up here before daylight. What was he thinking? Eat a good supper? Long before he left the pass, the girls would probably be asleep. He shrugged to himself. He'd fix his own supper.

Unconsciously he glanced at the sky to see what time it might be. The sky had a heavy overcast. He sat there another hour or so, to make sure he waited long enough, then stood, unwrapped his blanket from about his shoulders, tied it behind the cantle, and rode down the mountain.

He'd gotten within only a couple of hundred yards of the cabin when Kelly's voice reached him. "Yell out if'n you're friendly. If you ain't, sit right there, cross your hands on your saddlehorn, an' sit still while I decide where to put my lead."

Wes chuckled. "It's me, Kelly. Don't drop that hammer or you ain't gonna have no future husband. Wantta come in, warm up, an' fix myself somethin' to eat. You go on now, climb back under them covers, an' git warm. I'm gonna take care o' my horse 'fore I come in."

By the time Wes had his horse taken care of,

woodsmoke boiled from the chimney, and the scent of cooking food came to him. He shook his head. He had no idea what he'd done to deserve a woman like Kelly. Just pure dumb luck—he figured.

While eating, he told the two girls that he figured the pass would be sealed off with deep snow come morning. "Ain't gonna be a chance for nobody to git in here, so I figger we can relax, git some rest, an' don't worry 'bout gittin' surprised. I'll check the pass ever' day to make sure it's still closed off. We git a thaw an' it'll open for traffic agin."

Emily sighed. "That means Lingo's not gonna get in to see us, doesn't it?"

A momentary stare from Wes said he wished he could tell her the big man would get in to see them, but he shook his head. "Em, if anybody could git in here, it'd be Lingo, but you're right; he won't git in here neither."

Kelly, who had stood to pour coffee, placed her hand on Emily's shoulder and gave it a gentle squeeze. "You quit worryin' 'bout Lingo, Em. He ain't gonna git into nothin' he cain't git outta. An' when he said he wanted to handle things alone until he knew more 'bout what's goin' on, he wuz tellin' us he didn't want to have to worry 'bout us while he tried to unravel the problem." She squeezed Em's shoulder again and poured the coffee.

Emily twisted to look at Kelly. "Don't you suppose if I were over there in Durango I might be able to help him—in some way?"

Although she had asked the question of Kelly, Wes answered. "Gonna tell you for a fact, little lady, I've knowed Lingo longer than either o' you; been in a bunch o' scrapes with 'im, an' been kept outta just as many as I been in." He shrugged. "When he says he don't need or want any help 'til he hollers fer it, he sure as hell means it. He knows how much he can handle, an' when others are gonna mess up his fight." He took a swallow of coffee, then gave her a no-

nonsense look. "We gonna stay outta his way 'til he tells us he needs help."

The way Emily's shoulders slumped would have told the world how disappointed she was. She worried about her father, worried about Lingo, worried that he was doing something for her that might get him killed, and each time the load on her shoulders and heart grew heavier. Wes misunderstood her signs, judging from his response. "Em, I know you got worries 'bout your pa, brother, an' Lingo, but let that man handle things—he knows what he's doin'."

Emily opened her mouth to tell him she wasn't worried about her brother, Rush, but clamped her mouth shut. Rush was her father's and her problem; and they'd worry about that problem when she knew her father was all right. But where *was* Rush?

Lingo sat across from Nolan, thought about his words as to where shyster lawyers were steering the law, and shook his head. Then his thoughts went back to the Easterner who had only an hour or two ago filed on a claim above Colter's claim. He thought on that a few moments, then thought about Gates's and Mayben's disappearance from Silverton. He wished he had some way of finding out if the Easterner and the two were tied in together. He'd seen them ride out of Durango together, but that didn't mean anything. They might have met up along the trail and decided they needed company. There was no way he could get an answer to that.

The coffeepot stood empty, and Lingo couldn't help a feeling of satisfaction. If he had occasion to drink another cup of Nolan's coffee between now and bedtime, it would have to be fairly fresh. He sat frowning into his empty coffee cup.

"What you got on your mind, young'un?"

Lingo looked up. "Thinkin' the Easterner's gotta be involved in this. Know I don't have a damned bit o' proof, but wonderin' if I stick as close to him as a cocklebur in a horse's tail if maybe I wouldn't come up with somethin'."

Nolan frowned and leaned across his desk. "What's got you so all fired stuck on tryin' to find somethin' to tie the Easterner to Gates an' Mayben?"

"Well, there's the shoeprint I saw outside of Colter's mine, along with Gates's an' Mayben's; too, most of the time he seems to always be close by wherever they are. An' thinkin' back on it, I don't remember seein' 'im around after they got gone for a while." He grimaced. "Hell, Nolan, I don't know. Maybe I'm just grabbin' at straws, but I'm gonna shadow that slick sonofagun 'til I'm convinced I'm either right or wrong, one way or the other." He stood. "I'll keep you aware of what I'm doin', an' what I find out." He put his hat back on and stepped toward the door. "Gonna eat supper, then go to The Golden Eagle and have a couple o' drinks. You feel like it, come have a couple with me."

Nolan grinned, making him look a lot younger than his early forty years. "Jest might do that, young'un. Jest gittin' to look at Miss Faye will sure make it worth it without havin' to look at you all the time."

"Nolan, she isn't much younger than you, an' she's a mighty handsome woman. You oughtta spark her."

"Aw pshaw, young'un, you're jest joshin' an old man, now ain't ya?"

Lingo, knowing how solemn his expression could be, pinned the "old" lawman with a look that said it all. "Nolan, if I didn't suspect I'd found my woman, I sure as hell wouldn't overlook Faye Barret. She's quite a woman."

When he pushed out the door, Nolan sat there, his expression saying he took Lingo's words at face value. The marshal sat there for quite a spell, first thinking about Faye, then his thoughts switched back to Barnes thinking the Easterner might have something to do with Gates's and Mayben's lawlessness.

He pondered all that Lingo had told him about Colter's daughter's abduction. Having studied every aspect of the case, he had to admit to himself that he'd set out to solve many a crime with less to go on. He stood, put on his hat, and went out the door to make another round of the saloons and bordellos. He wished Barnes would break the lock on Colter's mine, and not tell him about it. If he knew, he'd be honorbound to tell the sheriff. He wasn't ready to bring him into the puzzle.

The cafe stood only a couple of doors from Nolan's office. Lingo had already ordered and sat drinking a cup of coffee when the marshal went out to start his rounds. Barnes, sitting at a table by the window, watched him walk past and smiled.

He'd put the idea in the marshal's head, now he'd see if he had a different attitude when around Faye. It was obvious the man was lonely, and he was a good man, a man The Golden Eagle owner could trust as being a one-woman man.

When he finished supper, Lingo walked down the street, slanted across, and went in the Eagle. Faye washed a glass, dried it, and without asking, poured Barnes a drink of her "good" whisky. She smiled at him and put it on the bar in the space next to the man standing there.

Lingo picked up his drink, then glanced at the man next to him—the Easterner. He nodded a greeting, picked up his drink, and knocked it back. Faye tilted the bottle to pour him another, and spilled a small amount on the Easterner's sleeve. Her lips pursed into an "O," she shook her head. "I'm so sorry, that was terribly clumsy of me." She quickly pulled a towel from under the bar and brushed at the man's arm.

The Easterner jerked his arm from under her hand, moved down the bar a few feet, and nodded. "Yes, you're damned right it was clumsy." He brushed at his coat sleeve, reached for his drink, knocked it back, and held his glass for another. "See if you can hit the glass when you pour mine."

Lingo twisted to face the man. "Mister, the lady apologized. A gentleman would accept her apology and disregard something as small as a wet sleeve."

The Easterner swept Lingo's tall frame with a look that said he didn't discuss gentlemanly qualities with a cowboy. "Sir, I seriously doubt you would know how a gentleman would react under *any* circumstance." He pinned Faye with a contemptuous look, his upper lip curled to the side, his eyes closed to slits. "And as for a *lady* apologizing? I didn't know *ladies* ran saloons."

Hot blood rushed to Lingo's head, his throat closed down to almost choke him, and he stepped closer to the Easterner, his fist clenched. Before he could swing, Faye's hand shot out to rest on his arm. "Don't, Lingo. Please don't. He's not worth it."

A deep breath to soothe his anger didn't work. His breath came in short gulps. "Mister, get the hell outta this saloon. You gonna drink, find some hog trough, but you aren't gonna ever be served another drink in here."

Bartow stepped away from the bar, facing Lingo square on. "You sound like you think you can put me out of here."

From the corner of his eye, Lingo saw Faye give her huge bouncer a signal. He waited. Gunplay in here might get Faye a chunk of lead, and she'd already experienced getting shot when Quint Cantrell had his legendary gunfight in here. He didn't see a gun on the Easterner, but he might be wearing a shoulder holster under his coat. The bouncer stepped between them.

"Either o' you slap leather, I'll break your arm." He looked at Faye. "You want me to throw 'em both out, or can one o' 'em stay?"

"Mr. Barnes can stay. He was only taking up for me. I want that man outta here." She pointed to Bartow. "And I never want him to come in here again."

The bouncer looked at the Easterner. "You heard the lady, an' don't you never butt your way through them swingin' batwings agin."

Bartow, his right arm hanging stiff at his side, moved from the bar. The bouncer followed him to the door, then turned back. "Ma'am, why didn't you let Mr. Barnes take care o' him? Fast as he is that trash woulda been long gone into Hades by now."

Faye pulled in a deep breath, obviously to calm her nerves. "Because Mr. Barnes would have had at least two slugs in him by now. That man was wearing a sleeve gun. I felt it when I tried to wipe his sleeve dry."

Lingo, still trying to swallow his anger, calmed when he heard her words. "Faye, reckon I owe you my life. I was lookin' for a draw from under his coat. I'd never have beat a sleeve gun as close as we were standin'." His smile was tight. "But I'm gonna tell you somethin'. If we meet again, an' I figure we will, I won't let him get close enough to hit me with one o' those little pepperboxes."

Faye nodded. "A pepperbox will still throw a .44 slug pretty accurate up to ten feet." She smiled, a rather sad smile to Lingo's thinking, and said, "Thanks for defending me as a lady, Lingo. I try to earn those words every day of my life."

He shrugged. "Ma'am, those who know you already know you've earned them." He grinned. "Then there's those who don't know you, an' I figure they don't count for much anyway." His grin widened. "Who the hell cares what they think?"

Faye smiled, then laughed deep in her chest. "Reckon you're right, cowboy. As long as my friends know me for what I am, then nothing else matters." She reached for the bottle under the bar and poured him another drink. "On the house—all three of them."

Lingo slowly shook his head. "Not in a million years,

pretty lady." He picked up his drink, and this time only sipped it.

He considered going to a table and relaxing, then changed his mind. Nolan should be here soon and he wanted to give the marshal a chance to talk with Faye.

When Nolan came in, he looked around and walked to Barnes's side. Before either of them said anything, a miner by his dress said, "You shoulda been here a few minutes ago, Marshal. You almost had a shootin' to take a look at."

Lingo nodded. "Reckon I come right close to killin'—or gettin' killed. That Easterner had some mighty bad things to say to Miss Faye."

Nolan looked at Faye. She shrugged, then told him what happened. While she talked, Lingo studied the marshal for his reaction. He'd never seen Nolan let his personal feelings show; this time was different. At first his face reddened and his eyes shut down to slits, then he swallowed twice. His Adam's apple bobbed with each swallow. He swung his look to Barnes. "Why didn't you kill 'im?"

Lingo grimaced. "Reckon Miss Faye saw it differently." He grinned. "She sicked her bouncer on us." He gave a jerky nod. "Glad she did, too. When she wiped his sleeve, she felt a sleeve gun; I was standing too close to beat 'im." He shrugged. "I mighta got lead in 'im, but he'd sure as hell put a couple o' .44 slugs in me."

The reddened face slowly subsided and Nolan knocked back the drink Faye had poured him. "Ma'am, you let me know next time anythin' like this happens. In my reckonin' I got you figgered for one o' the finest ladies I ever come acrost."

Despite having run a saloon for a number of years, and having seen it all, Faye's face turned a delightful pink. She placed her hand on Nolan's forearm. "Why thank you, Marshal; true or not, I treasure your opinion."

Lingo thought this would be a good time to hunt for

another watering hole; leave Nolan and Faye a chance to discover what they'd missed during the few years they'd known each other. But he couldn't just walk out—it might be too obvious. He stayed long enough to buy the marshal a couple of drinks, then told them he thought to go to the hotel and get a good night's sleep.

About the time Lingo finished his daily bath and crawled under the covers, Bartow, in the Sundowner Saloon, poured himself another drink from the bottle he'd bought as soon as he entered after the confrontation with Barnes. The bottle was more than half empty.

He stared into the full water glass of whisky. He'd been told that the cowboy who'd braced him about his judgment of the saloon keeper was the one who had beat the hell out of that dumb gunny he'd hired to take Emily Lou off the stage and get rid of her.

That dumb hick cowboy had gotten in his way, although probably not knowing it. He didn't give a damn if the cowboy had beat Bull Mayben *to death*—but he *did* give a damn about the yokel making him seem like something less than a gentleman in front of the customers of The Golden Eagle.

Being seen as a gentleman in this area was part of his plan and he didn't want it disrupted. When D'Amato got here he'd have him take care of the cowboy.

Satisfied he'd be able to take care of that problem, his thoughts went to Colter. The old bastard had shown far more guts than he'd anticipated. The old man had withstood everything he could throw at him short of dying. And then there was Emily Lou. Where the hell was she? Who had taken her away from the bunch he'd sent with Gates? Why had they saved her from his men? And how did they know she was on that stage? And, if she showed up in the wrong place, at the wrong time, she would mess up his plan to become a rich man, a respected man, a man who would lead this new Western town the way he wanted it to go—his way. And when he'd milked it dry, he'd go back East and live the life he thought he deserved.

He mentally shrugged off the thought of Gates. He'd have D'Amato and whoever he brought with him get rid of the stupid Westerner. To his thinking, there wasn't one Westerner who had enough sense to challenge a man from the East. He poured himself another drink.

Then, he centered on The Golden Eagle: He'd put it out of business. The marshal didn't know him, had no reason to know he had a bone to pick with its owner, and would probably side with law and order. He nodded, although it was a sloppy, drunken, sidewise nod, yep, that's what he'd do—he'd own The Golden Eagle before he got through, and Miss Faye Barret Hardester—the *lady*—would be out of business. He emptied the bottle into his glass, slammed the bottle to the table, knocked his drink back, and at a very unsteady pace headed for his hotel room.

Lingo shadowed Bartow for two weeks. In that time he'd made two trips back to Silverton. There, at night, when he watched him go into his cabin he ended his vigil and went back to Sam's cabin. He stared at Slagle across the supper table. "Sam, I know that slime is involved in Colter's disappearance in some way, an' I figure he's responsible for Emily's being taken off that stage; but I've not seen one thing to substantiate my suspicions. I've watched 'im from the time he's left his cabin in the mornin' 'til he gets back at night. He's not met with Gates, which I was hopin' for so I could tie 'im to Emily's abduction." He shook his head. "That's not happened." He shrugged. "I don't know what the hell to do next."

Slagle stared into his empty coffee cup, then raised his eyes to look at Barnes. "Maybe you ain't watchin' 'im close enough. Maybe you ain't watchin' 'im long enough. Maybe what he's doin' is after you turn 'im loose at night."

Lingo shook his head. "Sam, I can't watch 'im twenty-four hours a day, and I can't believe he does his plottin', plannin', an' carryin' out those plans all day an' all night." He held out his hands, palms up. "What the hell else can I do?"

Sam stared at the table a moment, then looked at Lingo. "Tell you one thing you can do—let me watch Bartow from night 'til mornin'. I figger 'tween us we'll find more than you been able to do alone."

Lingo stared into his empty cup a long moment, then nodded. "All right. When I'm not able to watch, you do it. An' if he leaves town, I'll follow him—you watch Colter's mine. Remember, he's got a woman who'll do as he says—an' then, there's Gates."

"You still gonna get 'im hung 'stead o' shootin' 'im."

Lingo nodded. "Yeah, if I can make it happen that way." He sighed. "When we can we have to let the law handle things."

The next morning, Barnes sat huddled in his sheepskin on a blanket of pine straw about fifty yards from Colter's mine. From where he sat, he had a clear view of the mine entrance, and could look down on the main street of Silverton. He'd eaten breakfast before daylight, before taking his station for the day. Abruptly, he straightened. The man he looked for came into sight, but not outside the mine. Bartow rode along Silverton's main street in the direction of Durango. He had a bedroll tied behind the cantle, and a rifle in his saddle scabbard. Lingo watched him out of sight, stood, and headed for Slagle's cabin.

After pouring himself a cup of steaming coffee, and holding the cup with both hands to warm them, he looked across the room at his friend. "No need to watch the mine. Bartow just rode outta town, bedroll an' all. I figure he's gonna be gone awhile. When I get back we'll take up watchin' the mine again."

"You figger to follow 'im?"

Lingo nodded. "Gotta see what he goes outta town so

much for; might find out if he has any more henchmen to do his biddin'."

"Wuz Gates with 'im?"

"Nope, just Bartow." He shrugged. "Which means we still don't have anything to tie the two together as operating with the same goal in mind." He pressed his lips tightly together and clenched his fists. "But, Sam, I know damned well we're not barkin' up the wrong tree."

While Barnes busied himself packing for the trail, Sam packed provisions. Then finished with that task, he flipped his thumb toward the mine. "You reckon Gates might be nosin' 'round the mine?"

"No. I figure any interest the Easterner has in that mine, he's keepin' for himself." He frowned. "But I do wish you'd keep track o' Gates, see what he might be up to while Bartow's gone."

Lingo picked up his bedroll and the gunnysack of provisions Sam had packed and opened the door. "See you when I get back."

He rode at a trot, a pace that would shake the guts out of a man unless his horse was smoothly gaited. It still wasn't a comfortable ride, but he figured to bring Bartow into sight quicker. He was right.

Before noon, he had the Easterner in sight. He held back far enough so as not to be recognized if Bartow looked to his backtrail. When they got to Durango, the Easterner took his horse to the livery and headed for the hotel. Barnes frowned. Why the bedroll if the man was going to stay in the hotel? He thought on that a moment and decided this wasn't the end of the trail; Bartow would leave town again the next morning.

Damn! He didn't dare go to the hotel, the slippery Easterner might leave and he'd miss finding where he went. Lingo sighed and told the liveryman he'd sleep in the loft. It would be a cold night, but he wouldn't take the chance on getting left behind.

Sure enough, about four o'clock the next morning Barnes was wakened by the rustling of leather being dragged off a stall wall, then the sounds of a man grunting to throw the saddle across a horse's back. He moved softly to the ladder and peered below. It was too dark to see, then the person below growled, "Stand still, you bastard, or I'll kick your ribs in." Lingo nodded. That was Bartow's voice.

He waited until Bartow rode from the stable, then saddled and followed. Again Barnes held a good distance between them. Bartow headed toward Chama. Lingo wondered what Chama held for Bartow that he couldn't find in Durango. He shrugged mentally. Hell, finding the answer to that question was why he followed the man.

Maddie Brice, after preparing breakfast for Bartow, and watching him ride off, sighed. She'd have a few days of peace. She fingered the double eagle Randall Bartow had tossed on the table before leaving, telling her to buy provisions, enough to last awhile, enough for more than the two of them. She stared at the money. He'd never let her have more than two or three dollars at a time. To leave her this much money he must have three or four people coming. She shuddered. He'd most likely pass her around to be used by them any way they saw fit. She stood, went to the area behind the curtain, and pulled a carpetbag from a pile of junk on the floor. She'd never have a better chance to be shed of Bartow than now.

She'd no more than put her only spare dress in the bag when a light tap on the door sounded. She frowned, hid the carpetbag behind the curtain, then opened the door a crack. Shorty Gates.

"What you want, Shorty?"

"Need to see the boss. He here?"

Maddie shook her head. "Gone, be gone a few days."

Shorty pushed his way past her into the cabin. "Let me

in, cold out here." He looked around, apparently noticed that food for breakfast was still on the cabinet, and said, "Fix me some breakfast; ain't et yet."

"You want breakfast go back to your cabin. Maybe Bull Mayben'll fix you some."

Shorty stared at her a long moment. "Ain't Bartow told you?" He shook his head, and his face almost crumpled. "Bull's dead; been dead a couple weeks or more."

Her heart softened. She had seen how close Shorty and Bull had been, and despite not liking either of them, knew how much it must hurt to lose a partner. "I'm sorry, Shorty. Wantta tell me what happened?"

He shook his head.

Despite her telling him to have Bull fix his breakfast, she went to the cabinet and broke a couple of eggs into the skillet, then placed some thick-sliced bacon, the rind still on, in the same skillet. "Set. I'll feed you, then you gotta git gone."

"Why? Ain't nobody here but you an' me. I been thinkin' 'bout you all the time Bartow's been beddin' you. He ain't got a damn thing 'cept them pretty little shoes he wears what I ain't got."

Maddie had been through situations like this many times since she was fourteen years old. At first she'd been terrified, then resigned to what befell her—now she was determined it wouldn't happen again. She looked at him and smiled, knowing he probably wouldn't even take his boots off.

She pulled a chair over close to the bed. "Here hang your clothes on this here chair." While talking, she unbuttoned her blouse. The firm swell of her breasts pushed above her shift. Shorty's gaze locked on her bosom. He unbuckled his gunbelt and slung it over the back of the chair, pulled his belt loose, unbuttoned his trousers, and pushed them down to his boottops. She was right: He didn't figure to pull his boots off.

She unbuttoned the top two buttons of her shift, and looked him in the eye. "Git on over in the middle o' the bed, I gotta have room to show you what I really can do for a man."

Shorty, his breath now coming in short gasps, his eyes glazed, jumped onto the bed, scooted to its middle, and drooling from the corners of his mouth, swung his eyes to look at her.

As soon as his back hit the mattress, she reached for the chair, and pulled his .44 from its holster. It was heavy, so very heavy. She pulled at the hammer with her thumb, tried again, and it came back to full cock. Then, making certain she wouldn't miss, leaned over the bed and pulled the trigger. Shorty bounced on the bed when the slug hit his gut. He reached for her, and the second slug went inside his reaching hands. It hit him dead center in the chest.

"Y-you damned animal—trash, didn't even figger to take your boots off. Now whoever finds you can bury you with your boots on." She emptied the Colt's cylinders into him, then her hand still holding the smoking .44 dropped to her side. She felt like she'd been beaten with a bullwhip, and at the same time a sense of freedom flooded her chest such as she'd never known.

She didn't know when the next stage to Grand Junction would run, or whether they could get over the pass. It might be choked with snow by now; but one thing she was sure of—she wasn't going to be in Silverton. She threw her few belongings into the carpetbag, made sure she had every dime she'd managed to hold out of what Bartow had given her to buy groceries, took a last look at Shorty lying on the blood-soaked bed, and left the cabin. She kept Shorty's Colt .44.

At the edge of town, walking at a frantic pace, she stopped, almost skidding on the slippery, mud-laden path—that poor man locked in the mine, the man Bartow had told her to be sure to feed and give water at least every other day. What would happen to him if she left now?

She couldn't—wouldn't, go back to the cabin, but she had to make sure the old man didn't die of thirst, or starvation. She *did* go back to the cabin. She needed the key Bartow had left with her. The key to the lock on the mine shaft door.

As soon as she could get the heavy lock open and free of its hasp, she swung back the door, and left it swinging on its hinges. She went inside, groped her way around the wall until she found a lantern on a shelf about head-high, then struck a lucifer and lighted it.

Unlike most mines, she stood in a living quarters. Shorty had been feeding Colter during Bartow's other trips, but she'd heard them talk. She went to the back, pushed the curtain aside, and saw a frail old man strapped to a bunk.

She fingered the knots on his bonds, failed to get them loose, then tried until the ends of her fingers were bleeding and so sore the pain brought tears to her eyes. Then aware that he stared at her, his eyes never leaving her, and that he seemed to be lucid, she thought to remove the gag he had around his head. "Cain't git these knots untied. You got a knife anywhere 'round here?"

Colter's eyes slanted to the side. He opened his mouth to talk, but only a rasping, choking sound came. Maddie rushed to a water bucket and took a dipper of water to him. She let a few trickles flow into his mouth, then a couple more. She brought the dipper to his mouth again, but he pushed it aside with his tongue. "Knife in bottom drawer over yonder."

Maddie rushed to the cabinet, pulled the bottom drawer out, and pulled a heavy kitchen knife from it. Only a couple of slashes with the sharp blade had Colter's bonds severed. "Oh, you poor man, let me help you." She reached for his shoulders, tried to lift him, but even in his half-starved, skeletal state she couldn't handle him—and he couldn't move enough to help her.

"More water. I'll help all I can. Been lying here so long, don't know how long, but I can't seem to move."

Now afraid that someone would come and blame her for his condition, and with strength gained from terror, she shoved her arms under his legs and swung them to the side. It was then that she heard footsteps come through the entrance. "Hello in there. Who's there?"

Every nerve in her body tightened into knots. A knot formed in her throat such that she couldn't answer. She pulled her carpetbag close and pulled out Shorty's .44. Her throat opened enough that she got a few words out. "Come. Let me see who you are."

A big man, brawny and middle-aged, came into the room. He had a handgun in his huge fist. "Who're you, ma'am? What you doin' in here?"

She pointed the Colt at him. "You put that there gun back in its holster; then we'll talk."

The big man slipped his handgun back in its holster. "All right, let's talk, but first let's get that man outta here, an' made comfortable." Ignoring the gun she held on him, the big man went tò Colter's bunk, lifted him as though he was no more than a small child, and headed for the door. He looked over his shoulder. "You comin' with me, git after it. Lock the door when you leave."

Maddie, Shorty's gun hanging at her side followed the big man down the hill, around a ridge, and into a gulch. He walked to a cabin, snug by anyone's standards, opened the door, walked in, and placed Colter on a neatly made bunk. He turned to her. "Ma'am, I'm Sam Slagle, been wonderin' why that there mine door wuz always locked, then when I seen it open like it wuz, figgered I'd take a look."

Maddie stared at Sam a moment, put the Colt back into her bag, and shook her head. "Glad you did, Mr. Slagle. I couldn't handle 'im. 'Fraid I wuz gonna have to leave 'im there without your help." She went to Colter's side. " 'Fore we do anythin', let's git some victuals an' water into this here man. He's been sadly mistreated."

Sam showed her where he kept food, where the water bucket stood, and asked her for the key to the mine. He wanted to get Colter some clothes. He needed a bath, clean clothes, and a good night's sleep. He'd take any weapons he found also.

While Sam was gone, Maddie cooked, fed the old man, and despite his protests, stripped him, bathed him, and waited for Sam to bring clean clothes.

When Sam returned with clothing and weapons, they dressed Colter for the night, put him into Lingo's bunk, made sure he was comfortable, and only then did Sam tell him about the attempt to kidnap Emily, first assuring him that she was all right, but that they wouldn't be able to get to her until they had a thaw. "You git a good night's sleep now. Ever'thing's all right. When you git up in the mornin' gonna tell you all 'bout it, then I want you to tell us what happened."

"Reckon I kin tell you most o' that side o' the story." Maddie blushed. "I ain't proud o' my part in it, but reckon I *did* have a part in it. I'll tell you 'bout it an' hope you'll forgive me. I ain't much of a woman, but I sure ain't bad as I wuz bein' forced to be."

She looked at her carpetbag. "I wuz 'bout ready to catch the next stagecoach to Grand Junction, hopin' I could git away 'fore he, Bartow, caught me—then I thought 'bout that poor man there, all locked up in that mine without no water or food." She shrugged. "I jest flat couldn't leave no human bein' like that."

Sam stood, pulled a Winchester off a peg on the wall, loaded it, checked his handgun, cleaned and loaded the weapons he'd found at the mine, then thinking he'd done all he could to make certain they could defend themselves, he shook his head, and shrugged. He looked over his shoulder. "They ain't no stages leavin' for Grand Junction. Pass is closed." He hefted his Winchester and grimaced. "Wish we had more shootin' irons, but these're all we got. Glad I found them in the mine, but we gonna need more shells fer these guns we got." He shook his head. "Hope we don't have to do no shootin' at all, but just in case, I better git shells."

"I got one gun here." Maddie handed him Shorty's Colt. Sam swung the cylinder out. The gun she'd held on him was empty, every cartridge had been fired. He chuckled. "Ma'am, this here gun ain't got a live load in it. You been shootin' it?"

She looked from the six-shooter back to Slagle, then slowly nodded. "Mr. Slagle, I shot a man." She shook her head. "Nope, not a man, a flat out animal. He wuz gonna use me like I reckon I got to figgerin' all men would. I shot 'im, killed 'im, an' I ain't sorry one bit fer doin' it." She then told him about Gates, Bull Mayben, and their being Bartow's henchmen. "They wuz sent out to take Mr. Colter's little girl off'n a stage, do what they wanted to with 'er, then kill 'er. Them two are dead, but Bartow's still alive an' he's done gone fer a few days. We gotta keep 'im from findin' Mr. Colter when he gits back."

Sam took some cleaning patches from a drawer and proceeded to clean Shorty's .44. Then he loaded it and set it alongside the other weapons. He looked from Colter to Maddie. "We'll keep 'im right here. Git 'im fed, put a little meat on 'is bones, get a little strength in 'im, an' set tight. We'll see what Bartow does when he gits back. He ain't got no reason to figger I had anything to do with settin' his prisoner free." He shrugged. "Hell, he don't even know me, or nothin' 'bout my cabin."

"Gotta tell ya, sir, I figger Bartow's gone after more men. We ain't gonna jest have him to deal with."

Sam glanced at the weapons again. His face hardened. "We'll deal with 'em, Maddie. We cain't git Colter to

Barnes's ranch by then. The pass into Lingo's valley is snowed closed. We gotta wait fer a thaw, so I figger he can help us fight Bartow an' whoever he brings with 'im."

For the first time, Colter entered the conversation. "I want Bartow, he's mine. After what he did to me I'd like to return the favor, but I think we'll not have a chance for that sort of thing. If he comes here, I think we'll have a fight on our hands."

Sam shook his head. "No. If possible, I want to turn 'im over to Lingo. Lingo Barnes figgers to hang 'im—an' I got it set in my mind that if the law don't do it, he'll do it all by hisself."

Colter frowned. "He doesn't sound like a much better man than Bartow."

"Aw now, I didn't mean to make Lingo Barnes out as that sort o' man. He's a good man, soft as a kitten when he's dealin' with them he likes." He shook his head. "But you do those he likes wrong, an' he's 'bout the hardest man you gonna ever meet." He smiled. "You gonna like 'im. I guaran-damn-tee you gonna like 'im." Then to himself he added that he hoped so, because he thought maybe Emily Lou and Barnes had ideas of their own about what her father would mean to them, although neither had said anything to each other about their feelings.

He glanced toward the shelf he kept foodstuffs on. It was almost empty. He turned his eyes on Maddie. "You mind stayin' here 'til this here business is all over?"

She shrugged. "Ain't got much choice." She glanced at Colter, then back to look Sam in the eye. "But I'm here to tell you, Mr. Slagle, even if I had a choice, I'd stay to take care o' Mr. Colter. I feel like I been partly at fault for 'im bein' in the shape he's in." She nodded. "Yep, I'll be here 'til you want me to go."

"Good. Now I gotta git myself down to the general store an' stock up on provisions since we got more mouths to feed than jest me." He went to a chest of drawers, picked up a pencil, found a blank sheet of paper, and handed them to Maddie. "See what I got an' what I ain't got to feed us pretty good. Make a list an' I'll go git what you done writ. Now don't you try to save on the supplies, we gotta feed that there man good. Get 'im strong."

Maddie checked the shelf, then laboriously tackled writing a list.

12

BARNES RODE TO the back of the livery, and took his horse inside. Bartow had hitched his horse at the front of Chama's only cafe.

After Lingo told the hostler to grain feed his horse and give him a good brushing, he stood in the door of the stable and watched the cafe. After about thirty minutes Bartow came out and went directly to the stagecoach office, stayed there only a few minutes, then went in the saloon next door.

Barnes waited a few moments, long enough for the Easterner to get to the bar, or a table, then went to the stage station. The agent looked up from shuffling a stack of papers. "Help you, sir?"

Lingo nodded. "Maybe. There was a city man in here a little while ago; you mind tellin' me what he was lookin' for?"

The agent studied him a moment, then nodded. "Yep. Reckon I do mind. Don't see as how his business is any o' your'n."

Barnes sighed, then smiled. "Yep, you're right." He turned as though to leave, then thought that maybe Cantrell's name might make a difference. Quint Cantrell had married the daughter of the biggest rancher in the country. Ian McCord owned the Bar I-M, the BIM. McCord was the father of Elena, the girl Cantrell had married. He turned back, then frowned. "Told Mr. Cantrell I'd find out if the man had any money comin' in on the stage. He's been talkin' 'bout buyin' some o' McCord's cows. Quint wanted me to find out if he's wastin' 'is time talkin' to the man."

The agent's attitude changed. From semibelligerent, he was all smiles. He cleared his throat. "Sorry I was so short with you, cowboy. I get a lot o' questions that don't seem to be nobody's business." He shook his head. "Naw, he wasn't askin' 'bout money comin' in. He said as how he's got some friends he figgers to be on the next stage. He wanted to know when I'd guess it'd be here." He shrugged. "Told 'im it wuz gonna be sometime tomorrow. Couldn't say 'zackly what time."

Lingo frowned. "Wasn't looking for money, huh?" He shook his head. "Reckon I'll have to tell Quint I don't know what kind o' game the man's playin', but he ain't got no money to buy cows."

The agent smiled, a sort of fawning, weak thing to Lingo's thinking. "Hope you'll tell Mr. Cantrell I hep'ed you some."

Barnes gave him a jerky nod. "You can bet on it."

He left the stage office feeling a little guilty, then mentally shrugged. Hell, Quint wouldn't mind him using his name to get information, especially when he told him his reason for asking.

When he left the stage office, his mouth set for a drink, even if it was rotgut whisky, he shook his head. If he faced the Easterner again, and he would if he went in the small saloon, it would result in a shoot-out. He had a lot more unanswered questions he intended to get answered before he wanted to face the sleeve gun.

Feeling comfortable that Bartow would stay in town overnight, Lingo rented a room in the hotel. He wanted a good hot meal, but figured he'd be too easy to spot if he went to the cafe. His saddlebags, slung across his shoulder, had jerky in them. That would have to be his meal.

The next morning, not worried that he'd miss hearing the stage come in with all the yelling, rattle of trace chains, and whip popping that always went on with a stagecoach arrival, Barnes sat inside the window of his room looking down on the street. He wanted a cup of coffee more than anything he could think of.

Sitting there, half dozing, his mind flitted from his ranch, to Marshal Nolan, Faye Barret, then back to his ranch. He wanted to be there with Wes, Kelly, and that small bundle of womanhood, Emily Lou. Damn, he missed her.

He shook his head. If he was at the mouth of the pass he'd never be able to get to the cabin. He had no doubt but that they were snowed in. Then he thought of Shorty Gates. It would have given him a lot of answers if the skinny gunman had been with Bartow. Where was Gates? After thinking, and worrying about Gates's whereabouts, he figured if the pass was snow-blocked, then the little worm couldn't get in any easier than he could.

He dozed awhile, then abruptly jerked awake. The sounds of the stage's arrival jarred the quiet from the small town.

The bouncing, bumping vehicle pulled to a stop in front of the station. Bartow stood at its side. A man, and apparently his wife, were first off, then three men, all dressed much alike: dark suits, white shirts, black ties, black bowlers—and low-quarter shoes. They stepped from the stage, swatting dust from their coats and trousers. Lingo studied each of them closely. As far as he could tell, none of them were packing side arms—but then, looking at Bartow he couldn't tell he packed a gun either.

The men the Easterner met waited for the driver to throw their luggage to the ground, then Bartow, not bothering to shake hands with but one of them, motioned toward the livery. The man he'd shaken hands with shook his head and motioned toward the sign that said SALOON.

Lingo rolled his eyes upward. He'd hoped they'd go to the livery, rent some horses, and leave town. He wanted a good hot meal. He'd have to wait awhile.

After they disappeared through the saloon's doorway, he frowned. It looked like Bartow had recruited help. Help for what? Maybe he figured to have Gates show them where he and Mayben lost track of or had been driven from finding, Emily Lou. Too, since Mayben had been killed, and realizing that he needed more help than Gates, he'd had plenty of time to write to his peers back East to get help.

Barnes's chest felt like one big hollow. He'd never been so convinced of anything with less to go on. Maybe his attitude stemmed from a total dislike of Bartow. Maybe he just flat out didn't like cityfolk. No, that idea was not very smart; he'd had many friends back East when he was in college—all city boys. And, there was the matter of the sleeve gun. Now that was sneaky. It was like drawing your weapon, taking aim, and not allowing your opponent a chance to draw.

He shook his head. He admitted to himself that he just didn't like the man. He'd try not to let his opinion color whatever action he had to take.

While Lingo sat at the window of his hotel room pondering reasons for his suspicions, Bartow brought his henchmen up to date, as far as he figured was necessary, on what was happening, and why he needed them. "There's a woman in hiding around Durango or Silverton that I have to find. If she gets out of wherever she is, an' talks, my whole operation will be in the sewer. If that happens, every damned one o' us'll be runnin' from the law."

D'Amato sliced him with a gaze. "You didn't say there was any chance the law would close in on us."

Bartow waved his hand as though to brush the idea aside. "The law out here is usually some yokel who got tired of lookin' at the hind end of a bunch of cattle, or tired of swingin' a single jack."

"Don't know what a single jack is, and don't know why a man'd be lookin' at the butt end of a bunch of cows, but I'm tellin' you right now, if the law comes after us, this's gonna cost you a bunch more money than you an' me talked about."

Bartow swallowed a couple of times to squelch his anger. He hadn't expected to be braced by a man he'd considered a friend. He forced a smile. "Like I told you, the law isn't much out here. Durango's got one lawman, a marshal who keeps the peace in the saloons, an' there's a sheriff who patrols more territory than the whole state we come from." He shrugged and spread his hands, palms up. "Hell, man, we don't have anything to worry about. If either of them get in our way a rifle bullet will end that problem."

D'Amato stared at Bartow a moment, his eyes black, flat, no expression in them, then he turned his eyes on the two men he'd brought with him: one squat and swarthy, the other pale, blond, and thin. "We play his game long's it looks like we gonna make money outta it. If that ends—he ends. Got it?"

Bartow's guts tightened. His chest felt hollow. A chill ran up his spine. D'Amato had changed. When he was about seventeen and still learning the ropes, he'd followed every suggestion Bartow made. He looked closer at the man he'd taught every crooked game he knew, then he looked at the two men D'Amato brought with him. The squat, swarthy one was called Rick Sinatra, and the other man—pale, blond—was Bob Clinton. Each of them was a seasoned thug. With D'Amato's words, Bartow knew he'd lost control of his own game, and he'd better take it back right sudden. And the weapon he packed had only two bullets; he'd better get another soon, very soon.

He stared at the man he'd thought of as his friend. "D'Amato, don't you ever threaten me again. You do an' I'll kill you quick as I would a rattlesnake." He made his promise knowing the thug wouldn't force the issue at this time. Greed controlled all of them, and as long as there was a chance to make a bundle, they'd follow, but as soon as they thought they knew how to win the game alone, and didn't need him, he'd better have more up his sleeve than that pepperbox.

They knocked back their drinks, had one more each, then left the saloon. He led them to the livery. "I rented horses for you. Put your bags on that packhorse and let's get outta here. We'll sleep somewhere along the trail tonight an' get on to Durango tomorrow."

"Whatcha mean, sleep along the trail? We ain't gonna have a hotel room tonight?" the pale one, Clinton, asked.

Bartow shook his head. "That's somethin' else you're gonna have to get used to. Out here, when you can't reach a town, you make camp and ride on the next day. Many times, you might have to camp out a week or more before reachin' a town that might have a hotel."

All three of his henchmen cursed, growled, and stared at him as though they'd like to spill his guts into the manure of the livery floor, but when he toed the stirrup to ride out, they did also.

They'd gone only a few feet out the door when Bartow reined in. "Any of you bring a rifle?"

As one, the three shook their heads.

Bartow reined toward the general store. "We'll get each of you one. We'll need them tomorrow afternoon. I have it in mind to hold up that stage you rode in on. It'll be on its way back from Durango—an' usually carries a shipment of gold when coming this way. We might as well take what it's carryin'."

"I like that idea, Bartow. We can always use extra money; but I'm telling you right now, there'd better be more to your game than holdin' up stagecoaches." If the other two were going to say anything, D'Amato's words killed their opposition.

When they came out of the store, they each carried a new rifle, a saddle scabbard, and two boxes of shells. Bob Clinton glanced at Bartow. "Don't know what the hell we're gonna do with rifles, I don't believe there's a one of us ever fired one."

"Well, if you can't do anything else with them, you can scare the hell outta the shotgun guard."

When they rode out, Lingo watched them go with a deep furrow between his brows. Another stage holdup? It sure looked like it. He let them get clear of town, then ran to the livery, saddled his horse, and followed.

He let the trail dictate how close he could ride to Bartow and his bunch without being seen. As soon as they rounded a bend, he'd ride to it and watch until they rode around another, then he'd follow the same routine.

When the sun dipped below the western mountains, he sat his horse within a quarter of a mile of a jumble of boulders, about halfway to Durango. When Bartow came abreast of the rocks, he led his men off the trail into a copse of pines, and there they made camp.

After taking care of their horses, Bartow led the three men to the rocks, and pointed at a man, then to a place among the rocks. After doing this with each of them they went back to camp.

Barnes, sitting out of sight, frowned. What was the Easterner doing? It looked like his guess had been right—they were setting up to make a holdup. Then he thought of the stage and nodded to himself. Yep, the stage would be due to come back this way tomorrow. He wondered what he could do. But first he wanted to make sure he was barking up the right tree. He'd have to snake his way up close to their camp before they crawled into their blankets and listen to what they talked about.

A ridge separated him from them. He looked up the slope, saw a place to make camp, shook his canteen to see if he had enough water for coffee, and kneed his horse to the spot he'd selected to make camp. Once he found out if he was right about their intending to hold up the stage he'd figure some way to stop them without killing Bartow. He had to keep the Easterner alive until he found Emily Lou's father.

He built a small fire, cooked supper, ate, and checked his surroundings. He might be able to use the trees for cover to the edge of Bartow's camp. A glance at his rifle and he shook his head. If they discovered him, he thought the gunplay would all be in close enough for a six-gun.

He then removed his spurs, checked his clothing and everything about him to make certain he had nothing on him that would rattle or make a noise. Then he put out his fire with what remained of his coffee and slipped into the darkness.

He moved through the trees, placing his feet softly to the ground, testing it for small branches that, if stepped on, would snap and cause a noise that might alert Bartow and his bunch. Small stones he pushed aside with the edge of his boot. The pine straw made noise no louder than a whisper. He moved slowly, his nerves loose, not tight like he'd experienced in the past. He wondered at that, then decided it was because the men he worked his way toward were not woodsmen. His study of them in Chama marked them as probably never having been off the streets of a city.

When still a hundred or so yards out, their fire, a large one, lit the surrounding woods like a beacon. He nodded to himself. He'd been right; only a tenderfoot would have a fire that large in these woods. His nerves tightened, pulling at his neck muscles. Maybe they'd go to sleep and let the fire burn to embers before they could ignite this entire side of Colorado. Too, the light thrown out by the fire made getting as close as he wanted more hazardous. Despite that danger he closed in on their camp.

Still fifty or more yards out, he relaxed a bit. Bartow and his imported thugs sat around the fire sharing a bottle—more than one. Lingo squinted to make sure, then he knew he was right. Each man had a bottle clutched in his fist; and none of them seemed to care a damn about who, or what, crept close to them from the woods. He moved in closer.

He slipped in behind the bole of a large tree and then tuned his ears to pick up their voices. Long before getting this close, he'd checked the wind direction—it blew toward him. The horses couldn't give him away. Smoke smell permeated the air about him, and best of all, the breeze carried their voices as though he sat close to their fire.

Bartow, his speech slurred, was talking. "Don't want any o' you to get too nervous 'bout holdin' up that stage tomorrow. Hell, you fire a couple o' shots at it an' the guard'll throw down his shotgun, the driver's gonna be mighty busy with the team of horses he's gotta control, an' any passengers aboard are gonna be too busy savin' their own skin to give us any trouble." He tilted his bottle and drank, pulled it down, shivered, coughed, cleared his throat, and let his eyes move over the huddled bunch. "Know none o' you ever fired a rifle, but bein' accurate with it isn't the idea. The idea is to scare the hell outta them aboard that stage, an' cause 'em to hold up their hands. Once they get their hands in the air, an' away from their weapons, we can take care of them easy."

From where Lingo stood, he could see Bartow's grin slide off to the side. The man was drunk—down right drunk—but so were the rest of the imported thugs. They were believing what the Easterner told them. He grinned to himself. He knew how he could spoil their game, and hopefully keep the driver, guard, and passengers from harm. His grin faded. He didn't know how much he might put his own skin in danger. He stepped back. He'd found what he came for.

He eased away from where he'd watched them, as careful leaving as he'd been coming. He never turned his back to their fire, and soon, considering their drunken condition, got far enough away that he turned and walked toward his own camp.

Now he had to figure a way to spoil their holdup attempt. He didn't give a damn if he had to kill all of Bartow's men, but he was determined not to fire a shot at Bartow.

He sat by the coals of his long-dead fire and thought about what he'd do on the morrow. Thinking back to the scene he'd witnessed when Bartow apparently assigned his henchmen their positions for the next day, he decided how he'd mess up their game. Finally he crawled between his blankets and went to sleep.

The next morning, a light rain moistened the dusty trail. Barnes fixed a breakfast of beans and bacon. He had no water for coffee. By the time he'd eaten, the trees dripped steadily onto his small fire, sending out sizzling sounds with each drop. He cast a sour glance at the poor excuse for a fire, and no coffee, then he walked to the edge of the trees and studied the pile of rocks from which he now knew Bartow intended to stage his holdup.

He checked the area around the site and could find no truly safe place to hide. He'd hoped for another pile of boulders well within rifle range of the rocks, but there was none. His next choice was a ridge or ravine—still nothing. He settled for a tree trunk, hoping that none of the Eastern thugs got lucky with a shot. He wasn't sure the tree would stop a rifle bullet.

Although he figured the stage wouldn't be along until after noon, he took up his station midmorning. His slicker had long since started leaking around the seams. His shoulders and back, wet, chilled him such that he shuddered. And while waiting it occurred to him that this was probably where Bull Mayben got his comeuppance, and he would have bet Bartow had a hand in that holdup also. If he had been involved in it, it would tie him into the abduction of Emily Lou. Still he waited.

He watched while Bartow made sure his men were where he wanted them to be. They hunkered down in the boulders. None of them had rain gear. Lingo smiled to himself. If he was chilled and wet, they had to be near frozen and miserable. He waited.

True to his estimate, about one-thirty the sounds of the driver yelling and the stage slowing to pass between the boulders broke the stillness and the dripping of the raindrops. The bandits, clearly in his sight, all straightened and flattened against the rocks, their rifles pointed in the direction of the oncoming stage. Barnes hoped his first shot would warn the stage driver and cause him to stop the stage out of rifle range. He thought to fire only to warn the driver, then figured to hell with it—that trash was intent on breaking the law, and probably killing all on the stage. He decided he'd eliminate any of Bartow's bunch he could.

Making certain he knew which one was Bartow, Lingo took careful aim between the shoulders of the man nearest to him. He squeezed off a shot, watched the man's body jerk and go limp, then moved his sights to the next man.

But now, the three remaining outlaws jumped to their feet, looked frantically around, and ran for their horses. Barnes squeezed off his next shot. The second man stumbled, took a couple of drunkenlike steps, and Lingo's third shot took him through the head. He fell and didn't quiver.

Barnes jacked another shell into the chamber and sighted on the one Easterner left besides Bartow. He was already in the saddle. Lingo fired. Missed. Jacked another shell into the chamber—but too late. Bartow and his henchman were already out of range headed up the side of the mountain. Someone from the stage was firing and missing with every shot.

Lingo sat still a few moments waiting for those on the stage to cease fire. When all went silent, still using the tree trunk as cover, he yelled, "Don't shoot! It was me who fired on them to warn you. I'm comin' out with my hands in the air." He moved from behind the tree's bole, and still out of sight of the stage walked around the pile of boulders. They came into his line of vision. He walked slowly, carefully, hoping none on, or in, the stage would fire on him.

When sure they could see him plainly, he looked at the shotgun guard. "Any o' you hit?"

The guard, a young, slim, hard-eyed man, kept his shotgun pointed at Barnes. The driver reached across his chest, and with his right hand pushed the shotgun's barrels up toward the sky. "Take it easy, young'un. That there man's the one what saved our bacon. I know 'im." He spat a stream of tobacco juice off to the side, grinned, and pinned Lingo with his gray-blue eyes. "Howdy, Barnes. How'd you know this's gonna be a holdup?"

Lingo let his arms drop to shoulder height. "Howdy, old timer. 'Fore I begin to explain, you care if I lower my hands all the way?"

"Aw hell, Lingo, course I don't care. Drop 'em an' come up to this here bumpy bit o' hell."

Barnes walked to the side of the stage, looked in, saw no passengers, and looked up at the driver and guard. "I followed 'em outta Chama yesterday, saw 'em buy rifles an' ammo in Chama. They didn't look like hunters, an' knowin' one of 'em I figured they were up to no good. So after they made camp last night I eased up to where I could hear 'em talkin'. Their words told me I'd figured right, so I set up to spoil their game."

The rawhide, tough-looking old man chuckled. "Reckon

you done a mighty fine job o' doin' that. You know any o' that bunch 'sides that one you spoke of?"

Lingo shook his head. "Only one of 'em who got away. Didn't want to kill 'im. He's a special one to me. I want to get 'im hung." He nodded. "Gonna do it, too."

The driver's face lost any semblance of a grin. "Lookin' at your eyes right now, if I wuz that there man I'd keep right on ridin' slam outta the country. What you got agin' 'im?"

"Marshal Nolan knows what I got against him, an' he'll let me handle it my own way 'til time to put a rope 'round his neck." He frowned. "You carryin' anything of value this trip?"

The driver nodded.

Barnes thought about the time it would take, but offered anyway. "You want me to sit up there with you and the guard?"

The old man shook his head. "Naw. 'Preciate the offer, but this here's 'bout the only place what ain't very safe headin' on the rest o' the way." He took the huge chew of tobacco from his mouth, threw it aside, and bit off another chew, but only after he'd offered the guard and Barnes a bite. "You git on back to Durango—or go after them what figgered to take what we're carryin'." He grinned. "If they knowed Lingo Barnes wuz on their tails, reckon they'd build a fire under the tails o' them jugheads they're ridin'."

Barnes gave him a jerky nod, held up his hand in farewell, and turned toward his camp. "Probably see ya next trip."

The driver chuckled and popped his whip over the backs of his team. "Hope we don't meet under these same conditions." Before Lingo could think of anything else to say the stage disappeared through the pile of boulders.

While he rolled his bedroll and tied it behind his saddle, Barnes wondered what he should do next. He was sure, in his own mind, that Bartow, Mayben, and Gates were tied into the abduction of Emily Lou, and of course that other holdup, but he had nothing to prove it to others, others like those who would sit on a jury. Of course, Mayben was out of the picture, but there was still Gates and Bartow. He wanted indisputable proof, proof that would put a rope around their necks. He'd better talk to Nolan.

He rode toward Durango, and while riding pondered the problem. He'd ridden only a couple of miles when a rider came around a curve in the trail, his horse in an all-out run.

The Outlaw Trail crossed this part of the Bar I-M range. Playing it safe, Barnes flipped the thong off the hammer of his Colt. When only about a quarter of a mile separated them, he smiled to himself and thumbed the thong back over the hammer. Quint Cantrell.

Cantrell hailed him first. "Hey, *amigo*, what the hell you doin' out here all by your lonesome?"

Barnes had been riding on BIM range for the last twenty or thirty miles, long before he interrupted the stage holdup. He wasn't surprised to see a BIM rider, but pleased to see his friend. "Howdy, Cantrell. Good to see you. What the hell you runnin' your horse like that for?"

"Heard rifle fire out yonder behind you. Somebody out to get you?"

Lingo shook his head. "Other way 'round. Four men were gonna hold up the stage. I stopped 'em—got two of 'em. Two got away."

Cantrell's face hardened into flat planes. "Well c'mon; I'll hep you git them other two."

"No, not now. I know who they are. I'll get 'em later." Then trusting Quint's judgment, he nodded. "Even better'n chasin' 'em all over hell, I got somethin' I wantta talk to you 'bout."

Quint slanted him a crooked grin. "Somethin' tells me I ain't gonna like hearin' this. Ever' time you talk to me like that it's gun trouble."

Barnes grimaced. "Yeah, Quint, reckon it is." He shook his head. "But I'm tellin' you right now, I'm not askin' you to step in, I just want some advice."

Cantrell frowned. "Too far back to the ranch to ask you to come on over an' spend the night. Elena ain't 'spectin' me home fer a couple o' days, she figgers I'm headin' fer the north line shack." He shrugged. "So why don't we make camp, an' you tell me what's botherin' you?"

They set up camp in a place much like the one Barnes had chosen the night before. They fixed supper, and after eating, Cantrell broke out a bottle of whisky he'd been taking to his saddle partner, Art King. They spiked their coffee, and sat back to enjoy the hot liquid, as much as the dripping, constant rain would let them.

While they drank, Barnes told Cantrell the story of Emily Lou's getting taken off the stage, and all that he knew that had happened since then. When finished, he spread his hands palms up. "Quint, Marshal Nolan's a friend to both o' us. Somehow I feel like he's stickin' 'is neck out for me." He gave Cantrell a straight-on look. "Gonna tell you, cowboy, there's nothin' I wouldn't do for that old man." He shook his head. "Don't want 'im gettin' in trouble of any kind 'cause of me."

Quint slanted him a thin-lipped smile. "You know Nolan, I know Nolan, an' I guaran-damn-tee you, even though we're his friends, he ain't gonna break no damned laws to protect nobody." His smile widened into a grin. "I figger he'd uphold the law even if we wuz his brothers." He shook his head. "Don't worry 'bout it. You ain't gitten' 'im into no trouble."

Even though Cantrell had said exactly the words he thought he would, Lingo breathed a sigh of relief.

Quint pulled the cork from the bottle and freshened their drinks. With a smug smile, he pushed the cork back. "Art King's gonna be mighty proud we drank his whisky. He likes to feel like he's been right hospitable."

Barnes chuckled. "Quint, that's the damnedest outright lie I ever heard you tell. Art's gonna be mad 'nuff to spit nails when he figures we sat here an' drank his whisky."

"Naw, don't reckon he will when I give 'im his pay Lion sent out with me, an' tell 'im to take off for Durango a couple o' days." He slanted Lingo that hard, thin-lipped smile again. "But I'm here to tell you, I'd a drank ever' drop o' it jest to see 'im raise hell 'bout it."

Barnes wagged his head slowly from side to side. "No, you wouldn't, Quint. That man's close enough to you to be your brother."

Cantrell's face sobered. "Reckon you're right—same as you an' that kid, Wes. You took 'im to raise, an' you got the best friend you'll ever have." He stared into his now empty cup, apparently thinking hard, then he raised his eyes to pin Barnes with a no-argument look. "Gonna give King a few days off, then I'm gonna take them same few days off, go by the ranch, tell Elena I'm headin' fer Durango, then I'm gonna side you in whatever trouble you got. A sleeve gun, huh? Know you're fast, but not fast as a sneak shot with one o' them little pepperboxes. Me an' Art's gonna be there to see you git a fair shake."

"Aw hell, Quint, didn't tell you all this to get your help. I saddled this bronc; I'm gonna ride 'im. Just wanted to know what you thought 'bout me gettin' Nolan in trouble."

Quint grinned. "Nope. What you're tryin' to do is hawg all the fun to yourself." He nodded. " 'Nuff said. Me an' Art's gonna be there."

Lingo knew there was no sense in arguing. Cantrell had the bit in his teeth.

13

BARTOW DUG SPURS into his horse. He'd never felt fear like now. He'd not caught lead, but rock fragments had dusted his face and arms. His gut muscles pulled tight, his stomach churned, making him think he would lose his breakfast; every muscle in his body pulled tighter. He spurred again. "Let's get outta here," he yelled across his shoulder. "We're not goin' to Durango. We'll ride around it, make camp on the other side."

D'Amato only cast him a look filled with blame and hate. They rode their horses hard for about thirty or forty-five minutes. Bartow looked behind every few seconds of that time, then reined his horse to a walk. "No need to kill our horses; there's no one following."

"Damn you, Bartow, what you get me into? Those two men back there were friends of mine. We left 'em for some lawman to pick up. Left 'em for evidence to tie 'em to us."

Bartow stared at his "friend." He shook his head. "No. They weren't yours or anybody's friends. They came out here to make a killin' off of these hicks; same as you did."

He pulled a cigar from his shirt pocket, bit the end from it, lit it, and slanted D'Amato a cold look. "We can still get outta this game what I figured, if we can establish we were in Silverton while all this was going on. Don't think whoever was shooting at us back there can identify either of us." He shrugged. "That bein' the case, we'll go ahead an' play the hand out like it was dealt."

D'Amato only stared at him. The look was enough to put the fear of the Almighty into Bartow. He'd known D'Amato since they swiped tobacco and candy from the corner store. The Italian had been ruthless even in those days; now it was obvious the man had only grown colder and harder. A chill ran up Bartow's spine.

They rode in silence for at least a half an hour, then D'Amato, his words falling between them like shards of a broken mirror, said, "So we're gonna play the hand that was dealt, huh? Well I'm tellin' you right now, Bartow, you better hope you got dealt a pat hand." He slanted a look across his shoulder. "Any more shootin' at me when I don't know who's shootin', or when I got no chance to shoot back, I'm gonna be aimin' my gun toward you. Know what I mean?"

Bartow shrank into his saddle until he felt no more than a foot high. "Hell, Vic, I had no reason to think there'd be someone in those rocks who knew, or thought they knew there was gonna be a holdup." He shook his head. "This deal I asked you to come out here for is a sure thing. Don't worry 'bout it."

A thin smile broke the corners of D'Amato's lips. "If either of us has a reason to worry, Bartow, I think you've about decided you're the one." His smile disappeared. "You'd better give it a lot o' worry, 'cause you got two sides to think about—those you're thinkin' to take to the cleaners . . . an' me." His smile came back. He slowly shook his head. "Way I've got it figured, you've bit off more'n you can chew either way."

Bartow stared straight ahead. Fear wouldn't allow him to look at his henchman. He knew his eyes would show that fear had him in a death grip. Still east of Durango, they rode on and all the while Bartow thought of ways to rid himself of the trap he'd gotten himself into.

He'd thought at first he could take over Colter's mine with having to kill only one person. Of course he'd thought Mayben and Gates would get rid of Emily Lou and that would only leave him her father to take care of. Then he'd decided he'd have to kill the two hick cowboys after he gained ownership of the mine. Then, when he'd had to call in friends from back East, he thought that eventually he'd have to get rid of them. Now there was only one left—Shorty Gates. Too, he would probably have to kill D'Amato as soon as he had a chance—in the back, or however. He had to eliminate him. That made two left he had to get rid of. He thought he'd take Maddie with him until he had no more need for her; she was good for taking care of his physical needs, as well as cooking and keeping his clothes clean.

Then he noticed, as though his "friend" read his mind, he rode slightly behind, and when Bartow would slow his horse, so would D'Amato. Adding ice to his bones, D'Amato knew he carried a sleeve gun. He shivered.

Barnes and Cantrell sat across the desk from Marshal Nolan, a full cup of coffee in front of them, the three slowly puffing clouds from their pipes, all obviously in deep thought. Lingo had already told the marshal about the holdup, and that he knew it was Bartow who pulled the strings on it. He'd asked Nolan to hold off on the holdup arrests until he took another shot at tying Bartow into the taking of Emily Lou.

"Son, we got 'nuff to hang the Easterner without gittin' him tied into snatching the girl offa that stage. Hell, let's take 'im in, try 'im, hang 'im, an' be done with it."

Lingo shook his head. "Nolan, we leave it like that an' I won't know who bossed snatchin' Em offa that stage, or that she's outta danger. There might be somebody else out there who wants her dead." He sucked on his now cold pipe. "Gonna ask you, give me time to prove it one way or the other."

"You know where Bartow is now?"

"Not for sure, but if he figures whoever attacked him at the stage couldn't recognize 'im, he probably headed for Silverton, at least he was headed in this direction after I spoiled their game. Silverton's where I think I'll find 'im." Lingo struck a lucifer and held the fire to his pipe. When he'd puffed life into it, he said through the cloud of smoke, "Quint an' I've spent a day of searching through this town for the Easterner, he's not been here, so I figure he circled the town an' headed straight to Silverton. That's where we'll find 'im if he's dumb enough not to keep goin'." He took another drag on his pipe, then frowned. "If he figures nobody recognized him at the stage holdup, he just might stay in Silverton an' try to bluff it out."

Nolan switched his gaze to Cantrell. "What's your interest in this, Quint? Seems to me you find enough trouble to keep Elena worried all the time without you huntin' up things what ain't none o' your business."

Cantrell grinned. "Hell, Nolan, I'm 'bout to go crazy as a rabid skunk out yonder since we cleaned up that bunch from the owl hoot, along with what was left o' the Hardester brothers. Lingo come along an' give me a chance to have a little fun. Less'n you tell me flat out to leave it alone, I'd kinda like to cover his backside."

A hard, thin smile broke the corners of Nolan's lips. "Know what, Cantrell? I shoulda not ever told you you wasn't wanted by the law, then maybe you'da kept on ridin' slam outta my life. All you ever brought me wuz a whole bunch o' misery."

A belly laugh rumbled up from Cantrell's stomach.

"Hell, Nolan, you'da died from boredom a long time ago if people like Lingo an' me didn't come along to put a little Mexican spice into your days."

Nolan growled. "Like hell." But his eyes twinkled, and the corners of his lips crinkled.

He looked at Lingo. "All right. You go ahead an' do it your way, but I'm tellin' you right now, don't you let that varmint git away. He needs to git hung."

Lingo looked at the old marshal. His face felt stiff and cold. "Nolan, that man won't stand a chance o' gettin' anywhere without me ridin' right close to his coattails." He closed his eyelids to slits. "I have a special reason for wantin' 'im to hang, an' I damn well figure on seein' 'im swing an' jerk at the end of a rope." He cocked his head to listen, and looked toward the window. "You reckon it's rainin'? Water's drippin' off the roof and I didn't figure it to rain when we came in here."

Cantrell shook his head. "Naw, ain't rainin', but I been expectin' a thaw, early as it is in the fall." He put a lucifer to his pipe, puffed until he had a cloud of smoke that engulfed the three of them, then finished his thought. "Reckon we gittin' what I been expectin'."

Lingo shook his head. "I been wantin' to get up to the ranch for a week now but couldn't 'cause of the pass bein' choked up with snow. Now it's thawin' I can't go. 'Fore I do that I gotta find that miserable skunk that brought all this on us."

Nolan nodded. "Better git after it, son. You don't an' he might git long gone toward Grand Junction."

Quint shook his head. "That pass 'tween here an' Grand Junction might git open, but I figger high as it is it's gonna take a lot longer to open up than that pass into Lingo's valley. It's maybe thirteen-thousand-foot high." He shook his head. "That pass ain't gonna open up 'til late spring."

Barnes took a swallow of his coffee. "Quint's right. I

think I'll head for Silverton, see if he's there, then head for Red Mountain Pass."

"I'll trail along."

Lingo looked at Quint. "Why? You think I can't handle it?"

"Nope. Jest figger I'd sit here an' eat my guts out knowin' you wuz up yonder havin' a whole bunch o' fun an' me sittin' down here gittin' stiff in the joints doin' nothin'." He chuckled. "Fact is, Art King damned near had a conniption fit when I told 'im me an' Lingo wuz gonna go after that Easterner, an' I wanted 'im to stay at the line shack a few more days. Lingo made 'im feel better though, when he dug out a full bottle from his saddlebags he'd been hidin' from me."

Nolan chuckled. " 'Stead o' gittin' stiff from doin' nothin' you gonna git stiff from the butt freezin' cold up yonder." His chuckle turned to an outright laugh. "I'd sure like to see you shiverin', shakin', an' wantin' to cuss at Lingo fer gittin' you into a pickle like that, but then you'd remember you had only your own rear end to kick." He took a swallow of coffee and shook his head. "Sure is hard on a man when he has only his own self to blame fer his predicament." He turned his look on Barnes. "Go on, Lingo, take 'im with you."

Barnes knew Nolan wanted the two of them to tackle the problem together, knowing they'd be safer that way, but he also knew the marshal would never let on that he gave a damn one way or the other. He nodded. "All right, Cantrell, reckon you've bought into this game. Let's head for Silverton."

When they walked from Nolan's office, Cantrell hesitated, looked squint-eyed at Lingo, then glanced toward the general store.

Barnes's look followed Quint's. "What you thinkin'?"

Cantrell slanted him a questioning look. "When you left your ranch, you bring 'nuff warm clothes with you? We have to head for Red Mountain Pass we gonna git almighty froze up if we ain't fixed for what we gonna face up yonder."

Lingo studied on Cantrell's words a moment. He shook his head. "Don't have anything that'll protect me from what I know is waitin' for us up yonder. Let's go to the store an' get outfitted."

"We better git provisions, too. Don't like sittin' round a fire without a cup o' hot coffee." He grinned. "'Course I reckon a cup o' coffee without a healthy slug o' whisky in it ain't gonna make me a whole lot happier."

Barnes nodded. "I'll pay for what we need—whisky included, but first let's get the clothing we gonna need."

Quint nodded. "Better add some .44 cartridges to the list—we gonna need 'em.

Bartow and D'Amato camped east of Durango, with the Italian complaining that he had thought to sleep in hotels and eat in restaurants, not sleep on the cold ground or eat poorly prepared food. Bartow tried to quiet his complaints with the promise that they'd both sleep and eat in the finest places in the East as soon as they got control of the mine, and knowledge of the whereabouts of the new vein.

He shook his head, mentally. He'd had enough of Colter's stubborness. He'd give it one more try, and if the old man didn't tell him where his new strike was, he'd kill him anyway. He'd already filed on the claim above his, and he'd start looking for the vein.

The next morning they broke camp, with Bartow first doing the cooking, and most of the other work.

Riding toward Silverton, Bartow told D'Amato about Maddie, and that they'd keep her as long as she was useful. "She's a good-lookin' woman, damn good-looking—but dumb. She does whatever I tell 'er to do, doesn't ever complain, an' is a good bed partner. She knows what I'm after, an' thinks she's gonna share in it." He chuckled. "You think anybody could be that dumb?" Then assuming D'Amato agreed with him, he added, "Yeah, she's gonna share in it long's she keeps us warm, fed, and comfortable." He glanced at the Italian and felt icicles crawl up his spine.

The Italian looked at him, his eyes flat, dead, and deadly. "My *friend*, I keep *myself* warm, fed, and comfortable. The only one I figure as being dumb is you. If this whole plan of yours doesn't pan out, an' I mean right down to a fifty-fifty split of some pretty hefty profits, you won't be needing her to keep you warm, or fed, or comfortable." D'Amato's lids closed down over his eyes until they were only slits. "Know what I mean?"

"Aw hell, Vic, let's don't get to threatening each other. You know you can trust me." He knew immediately he shouldn't have mentioned trust, and D'Amato's chuckle put the emphasis to his thought.

"Trust you, Barlow, or whatever you're callin' yourself? Hell no. I don't trust you far's I can throw this horse I'm riding. You forget I knew you back East. I didn't trust you then, don't trust you now, and never will. Why you think I ride behind you all the time?" He nodded. "Yep, you got that right. You an' that sleeve gun you wear won't be enough to take me, mostly 'cause I won't give you a chance to use it." He sucked in a breath of the clean, pine-scented air. "Now that I believe we understand each other we better get on toward this town you call Silverton."

They rode in silence until Silverton spread below them. Bartow led a few paces ahead all the way. His mind worked frantically for a way to get out of the mess he'd gotten himself into. He didn't worry that D'Amato would shoot him in the back on the way to town. The Italian would want him alive until he knew enough of the facts to make a profit for himself—then he'd have to make certain D'Amato never got behind him again. Or, if it worked out, he'd have Shorty Gates shoot him from ambush.

• • •

Sam Slagle looked across the table at Miles Colter. He marvelled at the progress the old man had made in the few days Maddie had been taking care of him.

She had hovered over him like he was her own child, even though she was the one young enough to be *his* child. When it looked like he might need something, she stood and asked him what he needed. Or before he got back on his feet, she put salve on his feet and legs where Bartow had burned them. She'd look at his thin arms and legs and go to the stove to dish up more food for him, and if he'd profess to not be able to hold another bite, she'd scold him, and tell him he had to put on weight.

Sam stood, went to the stove, picked up the coffeepot, and poured the three of them a cup of coffee. "Miles, if I hadn'ta seed it with my own eyes, I wouldn't believe how much you done got better."

Colter smiled. "Sam, there's not a person in this world who wouldn't have improved, what with the way you an' Maddie have taken care of me." He nodded. "I owe you both my life and I'll not forget it." He took a swallow of coffee, then looked at Maddie. "How much longer you think Bartow'll be gone?"

She studied the tabletop a few moments, then shook her head. "Don't know where he went, but if he went to the same place he always seems to go when he leaves like he did I'd say he'll be gone another two days."

Sam nodded, then cocked his head to listen.

"You hear somebody, Sam?" Colter and Maddie asked at the same time.

Slagle nodded. "Not somebody—somethin'." He grinned. "You reckon you can sit a horse for a couple o' days, Miles?"

"Yes. Where're we goin'?"

Sam's grin widened. "Like I jest told ya, I ain't hearin' *somebody*, I'm hearin' water drippin' off'n the roof. We got us a thaw. The pass over into Lingo's valley'll be open by tomorrow." He took another swallow of coffee. "I figger we'll pack up an' head outta here in the mornin'."

He noticed when he made that announcement that Maddie's face crumpled a bit. He frowned. "What's the matter, Maddie? You don't seem excited 'bout gettin' outta here."

"Aw, pshaw, I reckon I jest done got used to takin' care o' Mister Colter. Now I gotta see if a stage'll be leavin' for Grand Junction."

Before she finished, Sam's head wagged back and forth. "Maddie, I reckon that pass over Red Mountain ain't gonna open up 'til late spring. I wuz hopin' you'd go with us."

Sam reckoned until that moment that he'd seen beautiful sunrises, but not one of them compared with the light that brightened Maddie's face. "Wh-why I ain't got nothin' else to do, so if you're sayin' 'come on along' that's eggzactly what I'll do." She stood. "Well gosh-ding it, what're we all sittin' here for? We got packin' to do." Tears—Sam figured them as tears of happiness—streamed down her cheeks.

Sam and Colter chuckled, then laughed right out loud. It was then Slagle began to ponder the idea that Miles, after all this was over, might need someone to care for him, with the proper pay, of course. He figured Emily Lou would be all tied up with caring for Lingo Barnes. Of course he might be wrong.

While Colter and Maddie finished packing, Sam saddled and rode into town to rent a packhorse from the livery stable. He didn't figure to come back to Silverton until Bartow and his bunch were taken care of. He left word at the general store that he'd be out of town for a while, and that he didn't expect to have to run a claim jumper out of his mine or cabin.

When he got back with the packhorse, Colter sat at the table, a sheet of paper in front of him. "Whatcha writin', Miles?"

Colter looked up from the paper. "You think it'd be safe

to go to Bartow's cabin an' pin this note to the door, or maybe leave it on the table so it'll be seen right away?"

Sam frowned, thought for a moment on what Miles had asked, then nodded. "I'd have to be the one to take it there. With this thaw takin' place I'd leave tracks, an' I don't want them tracks to lead back here—or in the direction we take outta here, but yeah, I'll take it over yonder."

"Don't do it, Sam, if there's any chance it'll lead to more trouble."

Slagle glanced at the note. "What you tellin' 'im?"

Colter picked up the paper and handed it to Sam. He walked over to the lamp and held the note so he could read it. It read,

> *You unappreciative bastard. I've managed to get away. Now I intend to spread the word all over this territory about what you did to me physically, and that you have tried to steal my mine. If you're smart, you'll get clear out of this country. I want you to know, though, I'll have the law looking for you here, all over the West, and on the East Coast.*
>
> *Something else you'd better be aware of is that when you tried to have Emily Lou raped and killed you set yourself up for every man in the West to kill you on sight—now run like hell, you bastard. Miles Colter.*

Slagle frowned. "Why for you warnin' 'im, Miles?"

Colter smiled—and there was no humor in it. "Way I have it figured is, he's yellow, an' to top that off, he doesn't know this country very well. He doesn't dare go into Silverton, or to Durango. His only option is Grand Junction. He'll try the pass, and he'll never make it. Somebody'll find his body up there in the spring."

Sam shook his head. "You don't know Lingo Barnes, but I'm here to tell you he's gonna be right down disappointed he ain't gonna be the one to hang Bartow." He folded the note, stuck it in his pocket, and said, "Be back soon's I kin git this taken to Bartow's place."

When he reached to open the door he stopped, frowned, and shook his head. "Nope, reckon I ain't gonna leave tracks direct from here to Bartow's cabin. Think I'll saddle up, ride back to town, an' go to his cabin from there, then back to town, an' in a round about way work my way back here." He nodded. "Yep I figger that'd work. If I left tracks back to this cabin, Bartow'd burn it down out o' pure dee-cussedness." He grinned at them and went into the warming air.

His horse slopped through the muddy ground already thawed an inch deep. He rode straight through town, circled, rode under trees where a thick matting of pine needles blanketed the ground, found smooth rocks to ride across, and in every way he could think to leave as few tracks as possible.

With every step he worried that he left a clear path behind, then thought of the kind of man he knew Bartow to be—a city man, a man who knew nothing about the woods, or tracking, a man who had only walked sidewalks and cobblestone streets. Finally, he nodded, then forced the worry from his mind. Hell, if the Easterner did find his tracks and managed to track him toward Lingo's hanging valley, Bartow would be out of his element; he'd either get lost, or a bear or cougar would get him—and if neither one happened, Wes would take care of him.

Slagle, honest with himself, admitted he couldn't under any circumstances be considered a woodsman, but even at that he'd be a lot better than Bartow.

He wasn't the best rifle shot in the world, but if Bartow followed, he'd take care of him. He'd take his shotgun and rifle with him. Too, maybe Colter knew a little something about shooting.

When he got within fifty yards of Bartow's cabin, the

smell of death assailed his nostrils. He squinted at the still locked door and nodded. Looked like Maddie was right so far. Looked like the Easterner hadn't gotten home yet.

The closer he got, the worse the stench. Freezing weather hadn't done anything to keep Shorty's dead body from rotting and stinking.

He held his hand over his nose, and with his right hand reached into his coat pocket for the two small nails he'd brought with which to nail the note to the door. Not wanting to dismount and leave footprints, he pulled his handgun, leaned from the saddle, and nailed the note to the door. He studied the note and nails a moment, figured unless the wind picked up considerably the paper would stay in place. He reined his horse back toward town.

He looked back the way he'd come. His horse's tracks left a trail a child could follow, but on second thought, once back in town he could lose the tracks his horse made in those left by the hundreds of other animal tracks in the muddy street. He doubted that any animal track would be discernible in the quagmire the street would be after only a little traffic. He nodded. Hell, even Lingo couldn't track him in that mess.

Maddie had guessed Bartow would be back within two days. Slagle figured he'd need both of those days to get Maddie and Colter to Trap Valley, as Lingo insisted on calling it, and from what Sam had seen, it would have been, had it not been for this back door Barnes had shown him when he'd been there. The hell of it was that if Bartow knew anything about tracking, a talent Sam didn't give him credit for, this thaw left ground that gathered tracks like ticks to a hound dog. Anybody could follow them.

Back at his cabin, Sam, with Colter's and Maddie's help, went about setting the cabin up for any visitors. With the task finished except for bringing in a couple armloads of firewood, Sam told them to finish up, that he would go load the packhorse, and saddle the three they would ride.

Finally, ready to leave, Sam took a last look at his cabin, the only home he'd had in many years. He didn't know whether the next time he saw it it might be a pile of ashes—if Bartow managed to find where Colter and Maddie had gone. He sighed. He could always rebuild.

He led them toward Silverton, reached the south edge of town, then cut toward Durango. He'd be taking a chance on the well-travelled road if Bartow came back earlier than Maddie had figured, but he only planned to stay on the road long enough to mask from which direction they'd come.

They came to the place he wanted to angle off the trail and head to the southeast. He glanced across his shoulder at the other two. "We gonna ride on down the road a piece, then come back an' head off yonder toward Barnes's ranch." He pushed his cap off his forehead, rolled a cigarette in brown corn shuck, and nodded. "Figger that way won't nobody know we just come outta Silverton."

Colter chuckled. "Slagle, I doubt that anybody traveling this trail would be interested in who turned off." He frowned. "As a matter of fact, with all the holes we been punching in these mountains it could be anybody looking to strike it rich."

Sam grinned, then nodded. "Sort o' the way I seen it. Let's ride on apiece, then we'll backtrack."

They rode toward Durango only about another quarter of a mile when Slagle reined his horse around. "This's far as we go in this direction. Now we go back to that stand o' trees what was growin' right down to the edge o' the trail, then we cut off toward Lingo's valley."

Another fifteen or twenty minutes and they sat at the edge of a copse of pines a little above the one from which they'd turned off the trail. Sam looked down on the muddy road, stiffened, and looked at Maddie. "Your guess as to when Bartow would be back wuz 'bout one day too long, an' only a few minutes from gittin' us in a heap o' shootin' trouble." He squinted and nodded toward the road they'd left only minutes before. Bartow and another Easterner rode where Sam and his small party had ridden only moments before.

He glanced at Colter. Emily's father, jaw knotted, eyes slitted and cold, tugged at the rifle in his saddle scabbard. Sam clamped his hand over the old man's fist. "Don't. We gonna let Lingo take care o' that garbage."

Colter turned his look on the big miner. "What makes you think Barnes is anywhere around, and why are you so all fired sure he is capable of handling those two? That trash needs taking care of now."

"I know how you feel, Miles, but knowin' Lingo I'd bet all the gold I'll take outta my mine in the next year he's not far behind, an' what he's got planned for Bartow is a lot worse than a bullet. Hell, a bullet would end it too quick, too sudden. Let's let the big man take care of it. And believe me, he is capable of taking care of a half-dozen like those two."

The fire left Colter's eyes and his shoulders slumped. "Slagle, I surely hope you're right. I never wanted to see a man die before, but I tell you right now, that man we're looking at is one I want to see suffer—slowly, after all he put me through."

Sam, feeling the stiffness go out of the hand he grasped, nodded, and his voice soft, said, "I know. I unnerstan', an' I'll tell you right now, Lingo's got a mighty powerful reason to see 'im hang. I got an idear we ain't got too long 'fore we see that man down yonder jerkin' at the end o' a rope. C'mon, let's head for the valley."

D'Amato, riding behind and a yard or so to the right of Bartow, reined in his horse, looked at the ground, then glanced at Bartow. He flicked his thumb to the side of the trail, then up the side of the mountain. "What's up there? These tracks lead off the trail."

Bartow shook his head. "You might see tracks leading off into the mountains anywhere along here. There're mines all over the sides of these hills. Let's get on down to my cabin. I need a drink." He urged his horse toward town, then thought they'd have time for several drinks. Maddie probably wouldn't be expecting him back this soon, and wouldn't have cooked for anyone but herself.

He led them straight toward his cabin. When he again showed himself in town he wanted to be noticed coming from the direction of where he lived.

Still several yards from his cabin, D'Amato rode to his side. "What's that stink in the air?"

Bartow reined his horse to a stop, sniffed, shook his head, and glanced around. "Don't know. Somebody must have killed an animal of some kind and left it lay." Then his gaze centered on his cabin. He stared at the door, and from the distance he sat his horse, a piece of paper looked to be tacked to its surface. His breath came in short gulps, his gut tightened, and his scalp tingled as though his hair stood on end. Something bad wrong must have happened. Maddie might have run away, or maybe she was dead—that smell could be the stink of a dead body, a human body. He hoped it was an animal, but either one was not anything he was prepared to find. He kicked his horse into a run, sprinted to the door, and tore the note from it. While he read, his world shattered. The old man had escaped. And where the hell was Maddie?

He frantically pulled the door toward him and ran inside. He gagged. Stink invaded his every sense, rotted flesh, long dead. Maybe it was Maddie. He covered his mouth and nose, glanced around the room, and saw Gates lying on the bed he usually used when not using Maddie to satisfy his needs. Gates lay in a black pool that could only be old dried blood. He stumbled to the bed and looked down at the short, bloated figure. The body had six holes in it, all in the chest. He turned toward the door, tripped, almost fell, caught his balance, and staggered out the door. D'Amato had not left his saddle.

The Italian stared at him a long moment while Bartow felt himself shrivel, shrink into himself. This might be the last straw his henchman would stand for, but a lie would not fix things now—only the truth and what it meant they must do.

Where was Maddie? He was certain she must be the one who'd killed Gates and then gone to the mine to free Colter. Then, without telling D'Amato what he'd discovered, he spun, and again entered his cabin.

He ran to the pegs on which Maddie's clothes usually hung. Only bare wood showed. He looked for the food he'd left her money to buy. Nothing. His eyes flicked to the gun rack seeking the shotgun he'd left behind when he headed for Chama. Those pegs were empty also.

He stepped toward the door. He had to tell D'Amato what had happened and that they had to try to cross Red Mountain Pass. He stopped. D'Amato would kill him. He had not the slightest doubt the cold, ruthless Italian would wait until they got on the trail, slow his horse to drop behind so Bartow's sleeve gun would be ahead of him, then he'd kill him and calmly turn his horse back toward Durango. D'Amato had no reason to think anyone would tie him to the mistreatment of Colter—or the muffed stage holdup.

If he was going to get rid of the Italian he had to do it before they left the cabin, *and* he had to get him close enough so the short-range gun would drop him without a chance.

"What're you doing in there, Bartow? Come out here where I can see you, and don't tell me something else has gone wrong."

Bartow sprung the sleeve gun into his hand, then went to the center of the room so his voice wouldn't come from close to the door. "Nothin's wrong except Maddie's gone and left a haunch of venison in here to rot. That's what we smelled while riding in. C'mon in, I'll cook us some dinner." As soon as the words left his mouth, he ran to stand behind the door.

D'Amato cursed, then Bartow heard the sound of his horse plodding to the hitching post outside the steps, then the sloppy squishing of his shoes when he stepped to the thawing ground. The footsteps stopped. Bartow's breath caught in his throat. What was the bastard doing? Then the stomping, scraping of the Italian's feet while he obviously tried to rid his shoes of mud, another curse, then steps bringing him inside the cabin.

The footsteps stopped. "Where are you, you sneaking bastard?" D'Amato's voice came out ragged, as though he knew he'd stepped into a trap.

A feeling of power came over Bartow. His chest felt as though it swelled to twice its size. He felt he could outsmart any man alive. His heart felt like it would push its way right through his shirt. "Right behind you. I'm gonna do to you what you planned to do to me. Turn around. Want you to see me when I give it to you."

D'Amato stopped in his tracks, his head tilted back only a hair, but Bartow imagined the proud, cold look on his face. He turned, an inch at a time until he faced dead-on the muzzle of the already drawn sleeve gun, and he was only about six feet from its end. "Shoulda known to not trust you. Shoulda known before I left Baltimore to tell you to go to hell, but a quick, easy buck was more'n I could turn down."

He grinned, and surprised, Bartow held his finger off the trigger until he realized D'Amato's grin had no humor in it. The Italian's lips twisted as though wrapped around ice. "Know what, Bartow? You gonna be the last to die. You won't ever get outta this town. Whoever broke up our stage holdup is gonna be on your tail tighter'n an old maid's corset."

Before he could say more, Bartow's gun belched, then

belched again. The two bullets cut off any other words D'Amato had in his mind. One took him in the chest, the other took out his front teeth on the way through the back of his head.

Bartow, his hand trembling, lowered the pepperbox to his side, then opened the chamber, extracted the spent shells and shoved in two more. All the while, he stared at D'Amato, who seemed to return his stare through sightless eyes.

Bartow choked back bile and hot saliva that abruptly flooded the back of his throat. He gulped, gulped again, then ran to the door and emptied his stomach. He blamed his weakness on the stench that permeated the cabin, but deep in his brain, he knew better.

He wiped his mouth on his sleeve and stood there a moment. He shook his head. He'd not go back in the cabin. After a few moments of standing there he shivered—and only part of it was caused by the cold. He wanted to go back inside and build a warm fire, but that might only magnify the smell, and now there were two bodies to lie there and rot.

He tried to think if there was anything in the cabin he could not do without. After a long moment he shook his head. He'd taken about all he had of worth with him when he went to Chama to meet D'Amato.

Chama, that seemed so long ago, seemed like another world. Before Chama, he had Colter securely in his power, a gold mine with a rich vein almost in his grasp, a sorry woman to take care of him. What had caused his world to unravel?

His thoughts centered on Maddie. Damn her. Where was she? He'd taken good care of the unappreciative bitch. Why would she leave him? Ah. He thought he had it figured. Gates must have come in the cabin and pushed himself on her, then when she shot him she'd been terrified, grabbed her clothes, and run. But where would she run to?

She had little money, didn't know anyone around here, and besides that, she would want to put Silverton as far behind as she could after killing Gates. And where was Colter?

He shook his head, cleared it of thoughts about people who had populated yesterday's world. This was now. Colter had probably gone in town and spread the word about what he'd done to him, told them about Mayben, and what Mayben and Gates had been sent to do with Colter's daughter.

He frowned. There was nowhere in Durango or Silverton that would be safe for him. The only place he could think of as safe lay across the pass, over in Grand Junction, from where he could go in any direction except south to Durango.

He glanced at the cabin, decided there wasn't anything in it he wanted, then took the reins of his packhorse. He wanted to go into Silverton, have a drink, get himself a hotel room, and sleep until he'd had all of that he needed. He shook his head, blew the foul-smelling air from his throat and lungs, and rode to circle Silverton, then head toward Red Mountain Pass. The drink and good night's sleep would have to wait. He had left D'Amato's horse tied to the tie post in front of his cabin. He took his horse and the packhorse he'd taken to Chama with him.

He'd gone about a half-mile when he drew rein, pulled his brow into a deep frown, and glanced back toward his cabin. If those who stopped the stage holdup had followed him and D'Amato they would know there were two men who rode away from the stage—and there were two bodies back there in his cabin. He thought on that a few moments, gave a jerky nod, and headed back to his homestead.

He tied his horse alongside of D'Amato's, stepped from the saddle, and holding his nose went inside.

He thought to swap his shoes for Gates's boots. He tried on the small man's boots, and couldn't pull them past his instep; they were too small. He grunted. Hell, it didn't make any difference. When he got through no one would be able to tell the difference between boots, shoes, Western or Eastern dress.

He twisted to go to the stove. A sloshing sounded outside. His throat tightened and dried, his neck muscles pulled into his shoulders. He'd left his rifle in the saddle scabbard. He thought to try to escape out the side window. He listened again. The sound of feet sucking on the muddy ground sounded again—but seemed farther from the cabin. He went to the window and peered around its edge. A huge bull elk grazed on the few blades of grass, then moved another few feet from the front of his cabin. Bartow's breath escaped as though from a bellows. His hands trembled—he trembled all over.

He turned back into the room, only now he hurried. He looked frenziedly about until he saw that for which he searched—lamp oil.

He pulled a couple of armloads of firewood next to the stove, broke a few sticks of kindling into several lengths, put them into the stove, then threw several sticks of the firewood into the cold maw of the stove on top of the kindling, piled the remaining wood close, then sloshed about a cupful of the lamp oil into the stove, struck a lucifer on the side of the cast-iron firebox, and tossed the flaming stick onto the oil-soaked wood.

Despite the smell of Shorty's rotting body, he stood there soaking up the welcome warmth the stove put out. After a few minutes his sense of smell dimmed. Perhaps he had gotten used to the stench. Every so often, he opened the door to the firebox and peered in.

When finally the fire had burned down to a bed of white-hot coals, he took the can of lamp oil and soaked Shorty's and D'Amato's bodies with all but enough to pour a puddle of it from them to the stove, then he opened the door to the firebox, took a couple of sticks of firewood, and using both hands stood behind the stove and toppled it to the floor. The coals fell onto the puddle of oil. Flames crawled toward Gates's and D'Amato's bodies.

14

BARNES AND CANTRELL got a good night's sleep, and the next morning went to the livery, slung saddles across their horses' backs, loaded the pack saddle, and cinched it down on the horse they'd chosen as a packhorse, then rode from Durango at a leisurely pace.

Cantrell slanted a questioning look across his shoulder at Lingo. "Don't seem like you in any hurry to catch them men we're chasin'."

Barnes grinned, then shook his head. "Quint, I figure we got all the time in the world. They can go only in one direction if they don't figure they're safe in Silverton. Either way we gonna have 'em under our guns 'fore they know it."

After about another half an hour, Lingo frowned and glanced at Cantrell. "Gonna tell you right now, Quint, I want Bartow alive. I don't give a damn what we do with that other Easterner. He didn't have anything to do with takin' Emily Lou offa that stage." He shrugged. "Far's I'm concerned, soon's we come up on 'em we can blow him to hell. It's not like he hasn't done anything, hell, he tried to rob the stage right along with Bartow and the two Easterners I shot."

Cantrell's eyes opened wide. He shook his head. "Ummm-um. You mean you ain't gonna hog all the fun? You mean you gonna let me have one o' 'em? Damn, Lingo, you done got right generous since I last seen you."

Barnes grinned, then nodded. "I don't see how Elena puts up with you. You'll have every beautiful blonde hair in her head a silvery gray in another year."

"Nah, she's too much like her mother, Venetia. Hell, she might even pout when she finds out what you an' me done." He chuckled. "Yep, figger that's jest what she's gonna do 'cause we didn't let her go along an' help."

While they rode, Barnes studied the side of the trail. To his knowledge there were no mines off to the side and off to his left the mountain rose almost vertical to the trail. On the other side the Animas River gouged its way to more level ground beyond Durango. Still about a half an hour from Silverton he pulled in his horse, studied where several horses left the trail and headed for the river.

He twisted to look at Cantrell. "Hold up a few minutes, wantta see how many horses in this bunch. Those Easterners mighta decided to head up into the mountains toward my ranch."

Cantrell hooked a leg around his saddlehorn, pulled out his pipe, and stuffed tobacco into its bowl. He nodded. "Go ahead. I'll wait here."

Lingo followed the tracks as far as the river, only a couple of hundred yards off the road. At water's edge, he swung his leg over his horse's rump, stepped to the ground, and squatted next to the tracks. After studying the signs a few moments he decided there were three ridden horses and one carrying a pack. Obviously, the packhorse was the one being led. It had stayed behind the same horse from the trail to the river. He squinted at the tracks again, climbed back on his horse, and went back to where he'd left Cantrell. He shook his head. "Wasn't what I figured it might be. There were three riders in the bunch and one packhorse. I don't believe those two Easterners will hook up with Shorty Gates, or anybody else until they get to Silverton." He reined his horse toward town, now only around the bend in the trail and about four miles down the slope from there.

As soon as they rounded the bend, Silverton huddled below them. Cantrell gave the town only a glance before he flicked a thumb off to the left of it. "Somebody's cabin's goin' up in smoke down yonder. Lucky they ain't 'nuff trees around it to start a forest fire."

Lingo squinted into the distance. Slagle's cabin was over in that direction. He glanced back to the town, then studied where each ravine or gulch would dig back into the hills. Finally satisfied that the fire burned several hundred yards from where Sam's cabin stood, as well as being in a different gully, he let the pent-up air from his lungs.

He'd hate like hell for Sam to lose that cabin; it was well-built, and Sam took pride in the way he'd put it together. He shook his head. Even though he felt relieved, Slagle's good luck was someone else's bad luck. He kept his horse headed toward Silverton.

He thought to go by Slagle's cabin and bring him up-to-date on all that had happened since he last saw him, and that he was almost certain that Bartow was Gates's and Mayben's boss. Mentally, he shook his head. He wouldn't do that because the big miner would sure as the devil want to join up with him and Cantrell, and Lingo wanted no part of putting Sam in a position to take a bullet. Nope, he and Quint would handle this alone.

He slanted a look across his shoulder at Cantrell. "If we luck out, the Easterner won't figure anybody's on to him. He just might stop in town."

"Don't bet on it, Lingo. You an' me both know not to ever figger a man as bein' dumb." He grinned. "I always try to figger a man as bein' smarter'n he really is, that way I ain't never surprised by lettin' 'im outsmart me."

Barnes nodded. "We'll stop an' check the store an' saloon anyway. We might luck out an' not have to make that ride to the pass."

Cantrell nodded and gave Lingo a thin-lipped smile. "Yeah, I'll check the saloon while you waste time checkin' that there general store."

Lingo couldn't squelch the laugh, it bubbled from between his teeth. "I reckon we'll *both* check the saloon. If you figure to have a couple o' drinks while I'm playin' detective, you've just done what you said you'd never do."

Quint's grin widened. "An' what is it I say I never do?"

"You just now figured me for bein' dumber'n I am. You have a drink I'm gonna be right there beside you."

Cantrell pulled his mouth down into a grimace. "Cain't git away with nothin' no more. 'Tween you an' Elena, I figger I must be as easy to read as a deck o' cards." He kicked his horse into a lope. "Let's git on down there an' warm our insides."

While descending toward the town, they watched the smoke grow, then decrease until it showed only a thin, wispy spiral in the cold air. Cantrell nodded in its direction. "Reckon it's done burned itself out. They's a few riders comin' from that direction, headed back to town."

Lingo squinted toward the trail leading from the ravine, and nodded. "Yeah, reckon that caps it off. We'll go to the saloon first, that's where they'll gather to talk 'bout it. They might even know whose cabin it was."

The two tall men pushed their way from the chill outside air into the warmth of the saloon. Miners stood two deep at the bar, all talking about the fire. Cantrell stood behind a couple of men who'd only then gotten a fresh drink. He asked one of them to yell to the bartender to get him a couple of glasses of straight whisky.

When the man handed him their drinks, he asked whose cabin it was that had burned.

"A Easterner an' his woman lived there." The miner shook his head. "Don't know what happened to her, but they wuz two bodies lyin' in the ashes; both pretty well burned such that nobody could tell who they wuz. Know neither o' them what got burned up in the fire wuz a woman."

"How you figger?"

The miner pushed his cap back on his head. "Well, 'bout the only thing what wuzn't burned to a cinder wuz the boots an' shoes they wuz wearin'. Neither one o' 'em wuz woman's wear."

Quint handed Lingo one of the glasses he held, and nodded. "Let's knock these back, have another, then go see what we figger happened. Maybe both o' them we wuz chasin' burned up 'fore we could catch 'em."

Lingo stared into his glass a moment, knocked it back, and handed the empty glass to Cantrell. "Mighta happened that way, but hope not. I want to make damned sure Bartow was the one causin' Emily Lou all that misery."

The miner standing in front of Cantrell handed him two more glasses filled to the rim. Quint dropped a couple of coins in his hand in payment, handed Lingo his drink, and tossed his down, then tugged on Barnes's coat. "Let's go see what we can find out 'fore they bury them bodies."

In less than half an hour, they stood with a group of miners at the edge of where the cabin once stood. The fire still smoldered, and the smell of burned bodies clung to their noses, and the roofs of their mouths.

The ground, slow to give up its heat, kept them at the periphery of what only a few hours ago had been living quarters. Lingo looked from the ashes to a man standing next to him. "Anybody try to get into the place to see what happened?"

The stranger shook his head. "Ain't nobody figgered to blister their feet in them coals. Them bodies need to be buried, but it's gonna take some time for this ground to cool down enough to let a man walk on it."

Lingo snorted the strong smoke smell from his nostrils, glanced toward the sun, and nodded. "Figure by late afternoon it'll be cool enough to walk on. I'm gonna wait 'til it is."

"You know that Easterner?"

Barnes shook his head. "Nope, but got 'im figured as a man I wouldn't be proud to call a friend."

The man slanted him a questioning look, as if to ask: If Lingo didn't know the Easterner, how did he know he wouldn't call him a friend? But he didn't voice the question, and Barnes moved away from him, not wanting to answer any questions.

He walked to the edge of the clearing and sat. Cantrell grunted and lowered himself to the ground next to him. "What you figger to do now?"

"Well, gonna wait'll I can git close enough to check those bodies out." He pulled his shoulders down into his sheepskin. He snorted. "Damn, never could stand the smell o' burned humans."

"Maybe it'll be gone by the time we can get close enough to take a look."

Lingo shook his head. "You know better'n that. That stink'll still be in our clothes 'til we scrub it out with lye soap."

The two men sat there. Curious onlookers came and went. One man tried to go into the still smoldering coals, but quickly, hopping from one foot to the other, came back to cool ground, glanced sourly at the charred pile of wood, and walked away.

Finally, Lingo stood, walked to the edge of the cabin remains, stooped, and tested the ground with the palm of his hand. He jerked it from the hot soil and looked over his shoulder toward Cantrell. "Still too hot for bare skin, but figure if we get in, see what we wantta see, an' get back to cool soil our boots'll let us stand it a mite."

Quint unfolded himself to stand erect, looked at his boots as if to make sure they weren't a good pair, and stepped toward Barnes. "Let's look, then wait'll we git back here and talk 'bout what we seen."

Lingo answered with a nod.

They stood by the charred bodies, swept the remains from head to toe, then walked around the area, kicked some timbers aside that had not been totally consumed by the flames, and when Barnes feet felt like they had cooked through his bootsoles, he motioned Cantrell he'd seen enough.

Back where they'd left their horses, Cantrell said, "Let's git on back to the saloon, git a water glass full o' good whisky, an' talk 'bout what we seen."

Lingo nodded and toed the stirrup. When they both sat their saddles, one of the onlookers yelled, "Ain't y'all gonna hep us bury 'em?"

Quint gave the miner a long look. "Let 'em rot. They wuzn't worth workin' up a sweat." He reined his horse toward Silverton. Lingo followed.

Again in the saloon, Cantrell bought a bottle of whisky and walked toward an empty table sitting at the back wall. When he had poured them each a glassful, he looked at Barnes. "What you make of what you seen?"

Lingo took a mouthful of whisky, swished it around in his mouth to try and rid himself of the taste that lingered at the back of his throat, swallowed, and gave a jerky nod. "Tell you what, Quint, only one o' those Easterners died in that fire. That other body was Shorty Gates by my figuring. Both of the Easterners that rode away from that stage holdup were tall men. That short body was Gates's sure as I'm sittin' here, and to make me believe it even more, he was wearin' cow boots."

Quint nodded and took a swallow of his drink. "Noticed that, too." He knocked back his drink and poured another. "What else you notice?"

Lingo stared into his glass a moment, then pinned Cantrell with a questioning look. "You see any burnt-out weapons: handguns, rifles, anything like that?" He frowned. "Reckon in addition to that, I figure that fire was set. There was an empty lamp oilcan close to the stove. I figure whoever set that fire got a bunch o' help from a generous splashin' of that oil."

Quint gave him a cold smile. "Nope. An' them two we been chasin' both were carryin' guns accordin' to what you told Marshal Nolan. What you reckon happened to them guns?" He nodded. "I noticed the lamp oilcan, too; an' figgered it the same way you got it figgered."

Barnes took a drink. "I reckon one o' those Easterners is ridin' like his butt's on fire to get to Grand Junction—an' he's carryin' every weapon that was in the cabin."

"Way I got it figgered." Cantrell pushed back from the table. "Let's go check with the storekeeper; see if maybe an Easterner's been in to buy supplies. Cain't b'lieve a man would be dumb enough to head outta here without stockin' up on victuals."

Lingo downed the rest of his drink, stood, and looked at Quint. "All right, we'll check the storekeeper, then go to the cafe, eat, an' then get us a hotel room. We can get an early start in the mornin'."

Cantrell chuckled. "Gonna enjoy sleepin' in a warm bed even more, what with knowin' that bastard's gonna be 'longside that mountain shiverin' an' shakin', an' still not knowin' he ain't got a chance in hell of gittin' over that pass."

Sam led his party ever upward, hoping to cross over into Lingo's valley before night.

Sam's hopes were rewarded. They crossed into the valley that Lingo had watched burn, crossed the acres of blackened trees holding their denuded trunks toward the sky, climbed again, crossed a rocky ridge, and looked down on the hanging valley, appearing even more beautiful after the burned desolation of the one they'd crossed.

Slagle slanted Colter a look. He looked tired, older, his face tinging on gray. The trip so soon, even with the tender care Maddie had given him, had taxed his reserve strength to its limit.

Sam led them downslope until in the trees, then looked for a rock outcropping to shelter them from the wind. He found what he looked for: trees close by, a spring trickling from the rocks, all enclosed on three sides. He reined in. "We'll make camp here and ride on in to Lingo's cabin in the morning." He swung his leg across his horse's rump, stepped from the saddle, and reached up to help Colter down. The old man slumped into his arms.

"Here now, I done wore you out; shouldn't have pushed so hard to git us outta that there burned area." With Miles leaning heavily on him Sam went to the base of a tall spruce, and with one hand raked needles into a pile, then lowered the old man to sit on them. He looked over his shoulder at Maddie. "Ma'am, I'm gonna build a fire, then I'll hep you fix some victuals for supper." He pushed his cap back, massaged his forehead a moment, then grinned. "Reckon we'd all welcome a cup o' hot coffee 'fore we eat. I'll git the water."

"Mister Slagle, you fix the coffee, but you ain't gonna hep me cook nothin'. Cookin's a woman's work when they's a woman around to do it—an' I'm around."

She stood aside a few moments while Sam got the fire going, then got out a blanket and put it around Colter's shoulders. "In your condition you might catch your death o' cold." She glanced at Slagle. "Seen you stash a couple bottles o' whisky in your saddlebags. When that coffee you jest fixed is ready, I figger to pour Mister Colter a jolt in his cup."

To Sam's thinking, her voice meant she was going to give Miles Colter a drink of Sam's whisky come hell or high water. He grinned. "Sorta figgered you an' me might spike our coffee with a little, too."

While waiting for the coffee to brew, Maddie went about getting provisions from the pack saddle while Sam went about unsaddling, spreading groundsheets, blankets, and making their camp as comfortable as possible considering the cold that would penetrate them during the night.

Finally, with the coffee ready, Slagle threw a handful of cold water from the spring into the pot to settle the grounds, then poured them a half a cup. "Figger this first cup oughtta be mostly whisky. Know Miles can stand a heavy shot, 'cause he's done wore out, an' you an' me, Maddie"—he let a sly grin spread his lips and he nodded—"yep, you an' me gonna have a special one to celebrate getting away from Silverton without having to fight, an' along with Miles only a few hours from seein' that there pretty little daughter o' his."

While sitting, letting the fire warm them from the outside, and the whisky burning its way into their stomaches, Slagle felt Colter's eyes studying him. He glanced at the old man and saw that color had come back into his face. "What's botherin' you, Miles? You look like you got somethin' to say; so spit it out."

Colter stared him in the eye a couple of moments, then shifted his gaze to Maddie. He coughed, then glanced at the ground. "There's something I haven't told either of you. I've been making like I knew what you were talking about when you spoke of me having a daughter named Emily Lou, and that she's come out here to see me."

He cleared his throat, took a swallow of coffee, then looked at them straight on. "Tell you what's a fact. I don't remember where I'm from; where Emily Lou has been, or even that I have a daughter—nothing.

"All I can remember is Bartow burning me, starving me, hitting me, an' witholding water from me 'til my tongue swelled up." He took another swallow of coffee. "He kept askin' me where the rich vein was that I'd uncovered—I don't even remember where it is, or even if I have discovered a rich vein; wouldn't have told 'im if I did." He looked at his feet, moved some needles aside with one foot, then looked back at them. "Everything before waking up in my bunk with Bartow bending over me is blank."

Before Sam could soak up what Colter had told them, Maddie dropped to her knees at the old man's side and pulled him to her breast. "Oh, you poor man." Then, as though crooning to an infant, she rocked back and forth, holding him close.

Slagle looked at Colter's face, and despite the seriousness of what they'd only moments before been told, he had to choke back a laugh. Miles Colter was trying to shrink from Maddie's arms, his face now showing more color than a sunburned cowboy.

"Maddie, turn that there man loose. You done embarrassed 'im somethin' awful. Pour us all another coffee an' whisky; then come sit by me. We gotta think on what Miles done told us."

It was her turn to be embarrassed. She dropped her arms to her side, looked to each of them, skittered back on her knees, then quickly did as Slagle told her.

They sat there for several minutes. Sam stared into the fire all the while, then looked from one to the other of them. "Never said nothin' 'bout it 'fore, but I wuz in The War 'Tween the States. Fit fer the North—didn't really give a damn 'bout what they wuz fittin' 'bout but everybody else wuz doin' it so I done it." He shrugged, took a swallow of his coffee; now almost straight whisky since

Maddie apparently thought they needed it after Colter's revelation.

He coughed when the whisky burned down his throat, then shook his head. "I seen cases sorta like this afore. Seen men git their arms or laigs sawed off, an' afterward couldn't remember much, if anything, of what happened before they woke up with part o' themselves missin'."

He took another swallow. "Tell you though, most o' them men started rememberin' a little at a time until after a while they remembered ever'thing. Reckon their mind jest locked ever'thing out 'til they got some healin' done."

He felt Maddie studying him, then after a while she said, "Sam Slagle, you ain't jest sayin' that to make Mister Colter feel better, are you?"

Sam shook his head—slowly. "Maddie, ain't gonna lie to you 'bout somethin' like this. I done seed ever'thin' I said, jest like I said it."

Colter broke into their conversation, and very unlike the gentleman they'd learned to know, pinned Maddie with a hard look. "Maddie, where I come from, wherever that is, we don't put a mister or missus to a body's name if we're friends; and I'd certainly like you to be my friend."

Despite having been kicked around in trail town saloons, and from one man to another, and hard as granite—that is, the part she showed the world—tears streamed down her cheeks. "M-m-Mister Colter, you sayin' I'm your friend . . . that is the kind o' friend what can call you by your first name?"

Miles stared at her a moment. "Maddie, if you're not that kind o' friend, there's not a man in the world who has a friend of that quality." He cleared his throat, obviously trying to rid it of the knot trying to choke him. "You bet you're that kind of friend, and I consider it an honor to call you my friend."

Sam sat there. He didn't say a word. It wasn't often a man could witness the making of a real friend. Money, social status, accomplishments, physical beauty—none of these had anything to do with the making of a friend. It was a feeling, a something he couldn't define—sorta like the way he and Lingo had partnered up. He sat there, but felt so good he thought he'd burst at the seams. Damn! He had to be the luckiest bastard in the world.

After they drank the rest of the heavily spiked coffee Maddie had poured, she cooked supper, threatening to hit Sam with the frying pan if he didn't sit down and let her work without interference.

Before pulling their blankets up under their chins, they talked, and all the while Slagle wished he knew enough about Colter to bring things up that might trigger his memory.

Finally, before closing his eyes, he decided to ride ahead of them in the morning and bring Emily Lou, Kelly, and Wes up to date on what to expect.

The next morning, Sam told them he was going to ride ahead and alert them he was bringing in a couple of friends; told them he figured it would be smart to do so in that Wes Higgins usually fired before asking questions. What he really wanted to do was make them aware of Colter's condition. He gave Maddie directions on which way to ride, saddled up, and left.

It took about three hours of steady riding to get within hailing distance of Lingo's cabin. Then, not chancing getting too close, he yelled, "Hello the cabin. Sam Slagle here. Comin' in."

Wes stepped out of the door, a rifle resting in the crook of his arm. "Come on in, step down an' rest your saddle, Sam. Good to see you; where's Lingo?"

Sam rode on to the cabin, did as Wes had directed, hitched his horse to the post set in the ground for that purpose, and looked at the kid. "Got a lot to tell you soon's my backsides rest a little. Where's Kelly an' Emily?"

"Inside. Come on in. We'll talk."

A few moments later, the four of them sat at the table, a cup of coffee in front of them. Emily, her voice a little breathless, toyed with her cup and stared into the steaming liquid, obviously trying to bolster her courage to ask a question. She looked up into Sam's eyes. "Is Lingo hurt?"

Slagle shook his head. "Naw now, little one, Lingo's all right fer as I know. I figger he's chasin' the varmint what ran the gang that took you off'n that there stage. I got two other people with me. They're 'bout two, maybe three hours behind. I come ahead to let you know what to expect."

He took a sip of his coffee, wondering how to break the news to Emily that one of those he'd left behind was her father, what he'd been through, and that he probably wouldn't remember her.

He decided to put it all on the table in front of them, then let them ask questions.

He looked at Emily straight on. "One o' them folks what's behind me is your pa. He's done been through hell, little girl, an' it's caused 'im to blank out all that happened 'fore this here man tortured 'im."

He lowered his eyes to the table, then again pinned her with a look. "Emily, he might not know you." Then he hastened to add, "But I done seed things like this afore, done seed little things bring it all back into a man's head. I figure that's what's gonna happen here. Figger it might take a little while." He gave a jerky nod. "But by damn, I figger your pa's gonna be good as new soon's we kin give 'im good care." Then despite the seriousness of the subject, he chuckled.

"Gotta tell you, little one, he's already gittin' good care. They's a woman what's been takin' care o' him like he's a little chick an' she's its mother hen. She's back yonder a ways with 'im."

"If she's giving him such good care, why are you bringing them here? Is there still danger for them back there in Silverton?"

Sam stared at her a few moments, wondering how she could appear so calm, wondering whether she loved her father as much as he thought she would, then remembered that Lingo had told him she seemed capable of facing any situation, meeting problems head-on. He knew her stomach must be churning with anxiety, but she put on this icy facade.

"Ma'am, the man what almost done your pa in is back yonder. If he knew where your pa wuz, I figger he'd kill 'im. He'd have to keep 'im from tellin' what he done to him, an' even worse in this here country, he'd have to shut 'is mouth about hirin' them men to take you off'n that there stage, do with you what they wanted, then kill you. Ain't nobody in this country would stand still fer treatin' a woman like such."

Emily sucked in another breath; it caught in her throat. Then she asked the question Sam knew she'd wanted to ask all along, now that she knew she'd see her father in the next few hours. "Where's Lingo? Did he stay back there to fight those men alone? Isn't there any law down there who'll help him?"

"Em, gonna try to answer each one o' your questions. First off, don't reckon I know 'zackly where Lingo is, but, yes'm, he done taken on fightin' them men alone, an' yes'm, they got law down yonder, but the sheriff's got more territory than ten men could take care of. The marshal down at Durango ain't got no authority out in the county." He nodded. "So yeah, Lingo's gonna take 'em on alone."

Slagle drank the rest of his coffee. Kelly stood, poured him another cup, and again sat.

Wes grinned. "Sounds like just the kind o' fight Lingo likes. He don't want nobody messin' round 'im when he's got that kind o' business to take care of."

Emily felt a rush of heat push to her face, tried to push her anger back down inside her, but couldn't hold it back.

She stood, went to the gun rack, and pulled a Winchester .44 from its pegs. She spun toward them. The three stared at her.

"What you figger to do, Em?" Wes stood and walked to her. "Little one, I know how you feel 'bout Lingo even if you ain't let on to us 'bout it, but you got your pa to think of right now."

"Sam just told us Papa's bein' taken care of, an-and there's three of you to help. Lingo has no one to help him. I'm going down there to see if he needs help."

Wes wrapped his fingers around the barrel of the rifle and gently pulled it from her grasp. "Em, if I thought Lingo needed help takin' care o' himself, don't you think I'd be the first to go help 'im?"

She clamped hands to hips, watched him place the Winchester back on its pegs, then, not being able to hold back, and knowing her blue eyes were like a hot flame, she swept the room with a disgusted look. "I've heard you and Kelly practically yell the praises of that man, but even if he's as great as you both say, he's only one man. He-he needs help."

"No, he don't." Sam's voice sliced across the room. "I seen 'im clean 'is guns, then slide that big Colt back in its holster, then draw it faster'n my eye could follow." He shook his head. "No, ma'am, that man don't need no help to fight nobody." He shrugged. " 'Sides that, you git in his way, both o' you might git killed."

Em's shoulders slumped and tears streamed down her cheeks. She wiped angrily at them with the back of her hand, swearing inwardly that they were tears of anger—but she couldn't lie to herself. Her man was in danger, and father, friends . . . nobody was as important to her as the big man she hungered to see.

Wes held his arms out for her. She went into them, sobbing. He patted her back. "There, there, little one. We love 'im, too. If I wuz worried one bit 'bout 'im, I'd already be on my way to help."

"Oh, Wes, can't any man be as invincible as you all believe him to be." She choked back a sob. "Re-re-member, I've seen him take on several men at once, b-b-but it was night, an' he had surprise on his side then."

"Em, they's somethin' you don't know 'bout Lingo." He stood back from her, and using his bandana, dabbed at her tears. "Honey, Lingo don't do nothin' without he first takes a long look at what he's got 'imself into, then he comes up with a plan. He figgers 'zackly how he's gonna take care o' things." He shook his head. "Know it ain't gonna do no good to tell you not to worry—but don't. Ain't nothin' bad gonna happen to 'im."

He cocked his head, then looked at Sam. "Sounds like your friends done got here."

Sam twisted his mouth to the side in chagrin. "Yeah, one bein' an Easterner, an' the other a woman, they don't know to give a yell 'fore ridin' in."

Wes went to the door. "Hitch your hosses an' come on in. We been expectin' you. Sam's in here."

Lingo met Cantrell in the cafe after a good, warm night's sleep. They ate enough that a city man would have wondered that any six men could eat that much. Each had a half-dozen eggs, venison steak, country-fried potatoes, biscuits and gravy, and enough coffee to float a battleship, then topped it off with a half of an apple pie each. When finally Lingo pushed his plate away from in front of him and tamped tobacco into his pipe, Quint grinned. "Don't look like you in no hurry to git on the trail."

Lingo returned his grin and shook his head. "Ain't. I figure there's only one trail outta here, an' one direction Bartow's gonna go." He put a lucifer to his pipe and puffed contentedly. "Reckon we'll let 'im get as cold as a man can get, then he'll stew on the situation he's gotten himself into, then he's gonna begin to wonder if he can make it over the pass. When that happens, I figure we gonna be gettin' pretty close to 'im."

Cantrell packed and lit his pipe, then sat back. "Lingo, I b'lieve you got a little bit o' the devil in you. You gonna make it as hard on that bastard as you can 'fore we end his days on this here Earth."

Lingo nodded. "Finish your pipe; then we'll get on his trail."

15

LINGO AND CANTRELL rode side by side to where the trail tilted upward for the long climb; there, Quint slowed his horse to fall behind. Riding abreast here would not be dangerous, but where the trail narrowed, and where the thaw hadn't set in would be; one or both of them could slip and go over the edge.

Barnes looked over his shoulder. "Looks like five or six folks're ahead of us."

"Don't make no difference, Lingo, them folks prob'ly got a claim somewhere up the mountain." He chuckled. "One o' them though ain't got a claim on nothin' but six foot o' hard frozen ground—six-foot deep an' six-foot long."

Lingo frowned. Cantrell wasn't usually gun-happy, but maybe things had been so boring at the BIM that he was ready for any kind of excitement. "Quint, I've already told you I want that slick willy alive. I wantta see 'im hang."

Cantrell laughed, shook his head, and said, "Don't worry, old friend, I ain't gonna do nothin' less'n things start to happen behind you."

The trail, now a steady climb, showed a set of single tracks leading off to their right. To the left was straight down, a thousand or so feet. Another mile or so and tracks from two horses split off up the mountain. This happened one more time, and then they had only one set to follow.

The trail widened a few feet. Quint eased his horse alongside of Lingo's. "Them others what left the trail prob'ly had a nice cabin not too far ahead of 'em." He tilted his head to nod at the remaining tracks. "That there rider ain't got nowhere to go 'cept to deeper an' deeper snow. He oughtta be gettin' the idea right 'bout now that he's done bit off more'n he can chew."

Lingo gave a jerky nod. "Reckon so. Hope so."

Quint squinted through the bright sunlight reflected off the snow. "Lingo, never seen you hate a man before, but I got the idea you really hate this'n. Why?"

Before answering, Barnes pulled his pipe from under about four layers of clothing, tamped tobacco into its bowl, and lit it. Cantrell had done the same. After taking a long drag, Lingo blew the smoke out and studied his friend. "Tell you for a fact, Quint. 'Sides robbin', or tryin' to rob that stage, I figure he's the one who had Emily Lou taken. Know Bull Mayben an' Shorty Gates was mighty close with 'im." He grinned and shook his head. "Hell I mighta told you all this before, but I'm sayin' it again: I could excuse 'im for robbin' the stage easier'n I can of puttin' that girl in danger."

Quint held him with a long look, then said, "Lingo, I b'lieve you jest 'bout ready to git into double harness. You ever tell that young woman how you feel?"

Barnes dropped his gaze from his friend's all-knowing one. He shook his head. "Not in words, but sorta showed 'er by holdin' her hand." He took a huge drag and blew the smoke out. "Reckon it never seemed the right time to say the words straight out."

Cantrell shook his head, as though wondering how a

man could be so dumb. "Dammit, Barnes, the right time's when you feel it. You gotta git them words said. A woman *needs* to hear 'em said to 'er straight out."

Lingo didn't try to hold in the laugh that pushed past his lips. "Cantrell, Elena told me she dang near had to drag those words outta you, said she and her mother, Venetia, ganged up on you. Hell, Quint, you're not gonna make yourself out to be such a woman's man to me."

"Lingo, I ain't sayin' I knowed all them things 'fore Elena an' me got hitched, but I done learned a whole bunch o' things 'bout women since I got married." He reined his horse back onto the trail, then looked across his shoulder. "Do like I done told you—tell 'er what you ought've done told 'er."

Barnes took a couple more drags on his pipe, then knocked the dottle out against the palm of his hand. Cantrell did the same.

Lingo, from his long friendship with Cantrell, knew that the big gunfighter would usually have taken the leadership role, but this was his show, Quint knew it, so now Cantrell looked to him to make the decisions. Barnes appreciated it.

Quint cut into his thoughts. "How you figger to play this hand?"

Lingo slanted him a grin. "Know you're not gonna like the idea, but I figure to let him suffer a couple o' nights alongside this mountain 'fore we take 'im." He grinned. " 'Course that means we're gonna have to stay up here, too; but we got the clothes for it. Don't think he has."

Quint groaned—an exaggerated one to Lingo's thinking. "Damn! Knowed you wuz gonna say that. We gonna be so froze up we ain't gonna be able to handle our guns."

Barnes pulled his mouth down at the corners. "You're not foolin' me an ounce. If I hadn't said it, you would have. I never knew you to let a man off easy. Easy like takin' 'im when you could make 'im suffer more by waitin'."

Cantrell nodded, then pushed the words through a grin,

said, "You know me too good." He shook his head. "You're right. We gotta make 'im hurt awhile—even after lettin' 'im know we're on his trail."

Now, Lingo smiled, but it showed no humor. "You got it figured right that time."

The mountain cast long shadows across the trail and on into the empty space over the edge of the road. Barnes glanced up the side of the steep slope. Treeline showed a couple of thousand feet above, but the way the trail wound around, it would take several hours of riding to reach the barren rocks. "We better make camp soon's we find a place where our fire won't show from above."

Quint nodded. "Thinkin' the same thing." He stepped from his saddle, stooped, and studied the deep tracks in the snow. There was now no sign of the thaw that took place back down the trail. "Way I got it figured, he ain't much more'n a quarter of a mile ahead of us. Hope he's got 'nuff sense not to try to ride this mountainside in the dark. He does an' he ain't gonna have to worry 'bout gittin' his neck stretched."

They had not ridden more than another hundred yards when Lingo reined into a tumble of boulders. "Think this'll be as good as we're gonna find." He swung his leg across his horse's rump. "Dig some o' those provisions outta the pack saddle. I'll rustle up some firewood."

"Better make it a whole bunch o' firewood. Don't cotton to lyin' on this cold ground an' freezin'."

"Kind o' figured it that way." As soon as Lingo said the words he bent over a windfall and dragged a dead sapling from its pile. Cantrell dug through the pack saddle's contents, took hold of the coffeepot and a package of coffee and put them on the ground at his side. "Now to find them bottles we brung along, and we'll be 'bout as comfortable as we'd be back at the ranch. Tomorrow we'll see where our friend is an' how he spent the night."

Lingo shook his head. "Nope. Soon's we eat I'm gonna slip up on his camp an' see how he's makin' out."

"Want me to do it?"

Barnes shook his head. "Reckon I'm 'bout as good an Indian as you, Cantrell. It's my job to do."

"You figger to warm this here rock we gonna sleep on? If you don't, I do."

"Gonna let you do it while I sneak up on that varmint."

Quint only nodded.

Maddie and Colter went up to the porch, hesitated, and Wes waved them on into the cabin. As soon as they were in and the door shut behind them, Sam introduced them.

Emily stared at her father. He looked much older than when he had left home. She wanted to rush into his arms, but after what Sam had said about his memory, she held back, then stepped toward him. "Papa, Sam told us some of what you've been through and how it's affected you." She tentatively held her arms toward him. "Papa, I'm Emily Lou, your daughter. I won't rush things. We'll let what will happen, happen."

She choked back a catch in her throat. "But, Papa, I've waited so long for a hug. Come here and hug me."

Colter took a shy, hesitant step toward her, then held his arms out. She came into them, and even though he might not remember her, she thought there must be something deep inside of him that responded to her. He hugged her, patted her back, and when she kissed his cheek, tears welled into his eyes and rolled down his face. She stood back, picked up a flour sack, now used as a dish towel, and blotted his tears away. "Know you both must be cold; here, sit down while I get us some coffee." Kelly beat her to it; she was already pouring.

As soon as they were all seated, Em studied Maddie—young, but with the ravages of the life she'd led showing a little hardness on her pretty face. Em, surprised that the woman was little if any older than she herself was, revised her first inclination to think maybe she and her father might have a romantic interest. She'd gotten that idea when Sam said what he did about the care she was giving her father. He'd not said where Maddie fit into the picture. Emily shrugged mentally. She'd get the whole story when they had time to tell it.

While they talked, there was much said about a man named Bartow and his responsibility for what had happened to her father. She wanted to ask if her brother, Rush, had ever showed up, but held back, remembering that nothing of the past remained in her father's mind.

Finally, after visiting more than an hour, Kelly stood. "Goodness gracious, know you folks must be starved. I'll fix supper while y'all visit some more."

Emily pushed back from the table as did Maddie. "Maddie, you sit and entertain Wes and Sam. Kelly and I'll get supper ready." She smiled. "Besides, there's not room for three women to be brushing by each other, all trying to do the same thing."

Maddie pulled up short, a frown creased her forehead, a look of rejection took the glow of newfound friends from her face, then she brightened. "You won't let me hep y'all in here, reckon I could go chop some more wood."

Wes stood, walked to her side, put his arm around her shoulders, and smiled at her. "Maddie, tell you what, you let us treat you like company tonight, then tomorrow you women can figger out what chores each one o' you gonna do." His smile widened to a grin. " 'Sides that, me an' Sam's gonna be fightin' 'bout who's gonna do the wood choppin'. But for now, I reckon I got enough firewood split to last the winter."

When supper was ready, they ate, then Maddie insisted on doing the dishes. When they were all at the table again, with coffee in front of them, Wes poured a belt of whisky in their cups. Even the women nodded when he held the bottle over their coffee to pour them a drink.

During two or three spiked coffees, Maddie told them

her part in Bartow's treatment of Miles, and how ashamed of it she was. Then she got a hard, stubborn look around her eyes and mouth. She gave them a fast nod. "Gonna tell you right now, I done a lot o' things in my life I ain't right proud of, but goin' along with that man's treatment o' Mr. Colter tops the list.

"Now want you to know, I ain't makin' no excuses, ain't no excuse good 'nuff fer what I hepped do to that fine old man asettin' there, but what I'm sayin' right here 'fore all o' you, is that I wuz jest tryin' to stay alive. Lord knows why I wanted to, but I did. Seems like the onliest things I thought 'bout wuz eatin', sleepin', an' doin' what I wuz told."

She glanced around the table. Each of them sat there, their drinks forgotten, all staring at her. But not one of them had a look of blame.

"When I seen a way to git outta the mess I done got myself into, an' took a good look at the kind o' woman I wuz, I decided to try an' make it up to Mr. Colter; know I cain't never undo what I done, but maybe he'll forgive me." She put her cup to her mouth and emptied it, then pinned them all with a hard look. "Ain't askin' forgiveness, jest askin' that y'all know where I'm comin' from." She'd had her hands clenched in front of her on the table. Now she dropped them to her lap. She stared at them, then raised her look to take them all in. Her eyes swam in tears.

"Reckon while ever'body else wuz sleepin' I wuz wonderin' if they wuz any way I could make it up to 'im." She shrugged. "Know now, a body cain't make up fer nothin' like I done been a party to, but I'm offerin' to be a servant to 'im fer the rest o' my life." She looked straight on at Miles. "Don't want no pay; jest a place to sleep, eat, an' stay in outta the cold."

She turned her gaze on Emily. "Know they's some o' that you figger you want to take care of, but, Miss Emily, I'll take care o' you both." Her shoulders slumped. She stared at her hands once again.

The tangy smell of straight whisky in front of her prompted Emily to absentmindedly grip the bottle and pour them all another drink, and she'd never had more than one drink in her life. She stared at it a moment, then looked at Maddie. "Don't know as how I could allow you to do that, Maddie." With her words, Maddie seemed to shrink, become less than a woman, or even a human being.

Emily placed her hand over Maddie's. "Slavery was abolished during The War Between the States. What you're offering is to be Papa's slave. He wouldn't have that, nor would I."

Maddie reached in her reticule to finger the few coins in there. Her eyes swam. "Well, reckon when the stage comes, if y'all will show me the way to git to Durango from here, I'll take it outta there whichever way it's goin'."

Before she could finish, Emily's head moved from side to side. "No. You don't understand, Maddie. You see, I might have things to do in my own life, and Papa's gonna have to have someone to look after him. I'm sayin' you will be that person—but only if we pay you to do it and if you want to do it."

Every person sitting there had tears flowing down their cheeks. Maddie brushed at hers. "Well, dadgum it, don't reckon I'm gonna have to catch that there stage after all. Looks like I got me a job."

Emily shook her head. "No, Maddie, I wouldn't say you have a job, I'd say you found yourself a family." She pushed back from the table, walked around it, and pulled Maddie to her breast. There were a lot of sniffles around the table, then all hoisted their cups and drank of the strong whisky despite the burn it made down their throats.

They talked long into the night, each of them trying to draw Miles Colter into the conversation, each trying to say something that might trigger a small bit of his memory. He seemed to enjoy the family atmosphere, but his eyes still showed a haunted vacancy as though he wanted to be a total part of this gathering, but the parts to make it so were still missing.

Finally, they decided that if they were to get anything done the next day they'd better get to sleep. The cabin barely held all the pallets, but those that slept in them didn't worry about space; somehow they'd all become family. Now all they needed was a big man who was deeply loved by at least four of them.

The next morning, sleepy-eyed, and not moving as briskly as they usually did, they gathered at the breakfast table to sort through chores they would take as their own. There was no bickering; each of them wanted to do more than that spiked out for them.

Colter watched them, feeling a part of them but yet not belonging. He strained to fit the parts together. Sudden flashes showed him a small, young girl in his past, but his mind didn't associate that young'un with Emily. Finally, his mental strain exhausted him. He sat back, relaxed, then made up his mind to let things come to him as they would; all the trying in the world wouldn't help. Too, whether it all came back to him or not, he had friends around him like he'd never had before. Yes, he'd let it come when and if it would.

He cornered Sam. "Slagle, Bartow's reason for torturing me was to find out where a rich vein was that I supposedly had found." He shrugged. "Based on that, I think maybe I did find one." He shook his head. "Can't remember, but when we get back to Silverton, I'm surely going to look."

Sam shuffled his feet, stared at the floor a moment, then looked at Colter. "You trust me, I'll hep you find it. My claim's givin' me more'n a good livin', more'n I ever figgered to have in one lifetime." He nodded. "You think on it awhile. Jest wanted you to know you got hep, if you want it."

Miles looked Sam in the eye. "I don't need to think about it, but I need to see if I can still handle a single jack, see if my old body'll take the punishment." He smiled. "But I'll tell you right now, I appreciate the offer—an' yeah, after what you an' Maddie have done for me, I trust you."

To Colter's thinking, Sam's face took on a new light. He smiled. "Know what, Miles, it ain't been very long ago, the onliest folks I knowed wuz them in Silverton. I couldn't count them as real friends, jest folks I said howdy to when I went to town." He shook his head as though in wonder. "Now, lookin' 'round this here room, I'd say I got me a whole bunch o' real friends."

Colter chuckled. "You and I've been in the same boat, Sam. I suppose, without realizing it, we were both lonely; now I think neither of us'll ever be lonely again."

Sam only shook his head, then swept the room with a look. "Now ain't that somethin'—really somethin'. Hot dang it, I feel so good I could jest 'bout bust."

Colter's chuckle became an outright laugh.

Wes came in from outside, shivered, and shrugged out of his sheepskin. "Thaw didn't last long, it's gittin' colder by the minute. Don't look like it's gonna snow though." He looked at Kelly. "Been thinkin', if we gonna git outta this valley anytime soon, we better make a move fer it right soon."

Emily had been standing by the stove stirring a kettle of soup. She dropped the laddle into the mixture of beef, carrots, potatoes, and beans. "You're thinkin' about goin' to Durango?"

Wes nodded. "Been givin' it some thought. If it's like Sam says that Lingo's tryin' to find the man what took you off'n that stage, I'd bet my saddle he's done figgered out who done it an' is after 'im like a coyote in a henhouse.

"I figger we can head for Durango, stop off at Cantrell's place for a night, let them meet you, Sam, Kelly, Miles, an' Maddie, maybe spend an extra night, then one more night 'longside the trail 'tween there an' Durango, then ride on to town without puttin' you women in any danger." He swept them all with a grin. "Dang! I figgered y'all would be sayin' no by now."

Kelly and Emily engulfed him in the biggest hug he'd had in a long time. His grin widened. "Sonovagun, reckon I got an answer better'n any words." He looked at Colter. "You feel up to climbin' back on a horse another two or three days?"

Colter's face hardened. "I'd *crawl* if it meant seeing that man brought in." He frowned. "I don't know how Barnes is going to tie Bartow in with being responsible for Emily's kidnapping though."

"Miles, Lingo's got a good head on his shoulders. I'm bettin' he's got it figgered right down to a gnat's rear end." As soon as he said it Wes's face felt hot as a poker. He looked at the women. "Aw heck, I didn't mean to say nothin' like that 'fore y'all."

The women, to the last one of them, obviously tried to hold back their laughter. They failed. Every one of them turned red, then guffawed.

"Well, dang it, let's git to packin' fer a visit to town. We'll leave in the mornin'." With those words, Wes, not thinking of anything better to do, started cleaning his rifle and handgun.

After brushing the snow aside, Quint spread a bed of coals on the barren rock where they would sleep, left them there until he thought the ground would be warmed enough such that cold wouldn't seep through their blankets and ground sheets, then raked the coals aside, put the palm of his hand to the rock, grunted with satisfaction, and spread their bedding over it. He poured himself another cup of coffee, spiked it with whisky, then sat by the fire to wait for Lingo's return.

He sat there only a few minutes, sipping his drink, when he felt, rather than heard, Lingo at his back. "C'mon, pour yourself a cup o' coffee. Whisky's over yonder in my saddlebag."

"How the hell you know it was me, Cantrell? It coulda been anybody, maybe even the Easterner."

"Nah, I smelled you, Lingo. You ain't had no bath in two days." He chuckled. "The fact is, they ain't no Easterner as good a Indian as you. I knowed when I felt somebody at my back it had to be you."

"That's gonna get you in a heap o' trouble one o' these days, Cantrell. I ain't the only Indian around."

Quint grunted. "The life Elena's makin' me live these days, I'll be so tamed, ain't no way I kin git into trouble without you bein' 'round. Now with you done found your woman, looks like I'm gonna jest dry up an' blow away. Tell me what you done to that man we been followin'."

Lingo squatted next to the fire, poured himself a cup of coffee, spiked it, then lowered himself to the ground. "Cantrell, I didn't have to be much of an Indian to sneak up on 'im; all he seemed to think about was tryin' to get warm. He built a fire damn near big as the one that burned his cabin to the ground. If there had been more trees around I'da worried 'bout 'im startin' a forest fire."

He wrapped both hands around his cup to warm them, then shook his head. "You know what? He had only one blanket. He wrapped 'imself in it, an' huddled up so close to the fire I figured he was gonna catch on fire. Then finally, even with bein' cold, he lay down an' went to sleep." He took a swallow of coffee, poured more whisky into it, and slanted Quint a disappointed look. "I hunkered there, not ten feet from 'im an' wondered what to do to make him more miserable. Couldn't take 'is rifle without wakin' 'im, so I looked around. Finally I settled on takin' his saddlebags; that's where he had his provisions." Lingo grinned. "That man's gonna get mighty hungry 'fore he has a chance to eat again."

Cantrell opened his mouth to say something and Barnes

cut him off. "What I didn't tell you is, if his rifle ain't loaded to the hilt, he won't be shootin' very much. His bullets are in those bags along with his food."

Cantrell grunted, then cast Lingo a disgusted look. "It ever enter that pea-sized brain o' yours that that Winchester'll have 'nuff bullets in it to blow both you an' me to hell?"

"Nah, we won't give 'im that many shots at us. If this trail don't bend back on itself so he can look back an' see us, he might not get even one shot at us."

Cantrell's look turned sour. "You ever figger that one shot could put one o'us outta business?"

Lingo grinned, then nodded. "Thought 'bout that, then figured if he shot anybody it'd be you so that'd leave me still able to get 'im."

"Hell, let's have 'nother cup o' coffee and get some sleep."

They slept warm, woke up at daybreak, and cooked a good breakfast of beans, bacon, biscuits, coffee, and peaches, which they ate from the can, spearing peach halves with their knives.

Less than a half mile up the trail, Bartow, having slept very little during the night, and still huddled in his blanket, went to a fallen pine tree at the side of the trail, dragged a limb about the size of his wrist to the fire, dumped it on the coals, and went to the edge of camp where he'd picketed his horse. He was sure where he'd left his saddlebags, but they weren't there. A long search around and he still didn't see them. He frenziedly rushed from one side of the fire to the other, looked under the scrub brush close to the tree in case he'd stashed it there, and then saw the footprint. It was a bootprint, unlike what his own shoes would make.

He walked back down the trail until he came to bare rock where the wind had swept it clear of snow. He stood there gazing at the rock. It never entered his mind that the one who had stolen his provisions would be someone who trailed him to take him to the law.

He looked up the mountain. It couldn't be much more than an hour to the top. Then he thought of the twists and turns the road made between here and Silverton, and he studied the upgrade of the narrow trail. That hour he'd figured on might take more than a day.

For the first time, he allowed himself to think of what he could do without provisions and less than a half-magazine of shells in his rifle. His gut tightened, a knot swelled his throat, sweat popped out of his every pore, fear took hold of him and held his chest in a vice. He walked to his fire and sat by its side. He had to think. He'd always been able to think his way out of tight scrapes. Yeah, those times he'd always been in a city, familiar territory. Here, he was at a loss.

He considered going back to Silverton. Yes. That was a good idea. No one there could place him at the site of the stage robbery.

Then his mind centered on Colter, on Maddie. They would certainly have spread the word of what he'd done to the old man, and Maddie knew his entire plan. He shook his head and stared up the barren rock to where the trail curved. He'd have to chance getting to the summit, then on the other side he might find a miner who'd feed him and maybe sell him a blanket or two. If not, he'd kill him, take what he wanted, and move on. Fact was, if he killed him there wouldn't be anyone left behind to tell that they'd seen him. Fear continued to squeeze sweat from him. He rolled his bedroll, saddled his horse, and headed up the mountain.

Bartow had not ridden much more than a hundred yards when he reined his horse to a stop. Those tracks he'd followed until he ran out of snow had come from down the mountain, then gone back down after taking his provisions. He thought on that awhile, wondering if whoever had done it had been going up or down. He finally decided the man had been heading up. If he'd been going down, he'd have been in Silverton in a day, or so, and could have stocked up then.

He mulled that over awhile, then nodded. He'd find a

good place to hide, then hold them up, take everything they owned, including their horses, and leave them to freeze to death without any gear with which to survive. His fear cut back to a small, festering sore in the middle of his gut.

Back down the trail, Cantrell and Barnes were only then breaking camp. They were in no hurry.

While tightening the cinches on his horse, Lingo felt Cantrell studying him. He looked over his shoulder. "What you lookin' at me for?"

"Well it damn sure ain't 'cause I think you're pretty." Cantrell grinned. "Lingo, if somebody done to you what we done to that man, what'd you do?"

Barnes pushed his hat back and stared at Quint a moment, then nodded. "See what you're homin' in on. Reckon both o' us would figure on gettin' even. Right?"

A slow smile spread across Cantrell's cheeks. "You nailed that horseshoe on tight. We better be right careful. Ain't wishin' to make Elena a widow woman right sudden."

Lingo shook his head. "Would agree with you, old friend, but that man's runnin' scared. I don't figure he's gonna slow down enough to try gettin' even."

Quint shook his head. "Damn, don't see how you done stayed alive so long. Think 'bout it. That man's provisions are gone. He ain't got much ammunition left, an' while he's got some left, an' him starin' at starvin' or freezin', I figger he ain't thinkin' 'bout gittin' even—he's thinkin' 'bout stayin' alive."

Lingo slowly nodded. "Reckon you're right. So you think he'll try to hold us up for whatever we're carryin'?"

"That's eggzactly what I'm thinkin'." Cantrell frowned. "How you think we oughta play this hand?"

Lingo shook his head. " 'Fore we go chargin' ahead, we better give it some thought."

Cantrell said, "Way I figger it, maybe we oughtta split up."

16

WES LED HIS party to the hitching rack in front of the huge BIM ranch house. Ian McCord, Elena's father, pushed through the doorway. "Hey, Wes who you got there with you? Step down, rest your saddles." Venetia, his wife, came out and stood at his shoulder.

Wes stepped from the saddle, helped the ladies to the ground, introduced them all around, and Ian hearded them into the front room. "C'mon in. Supper's 'bout ready." Elena came into the room, and after introductions, went to the kitchen to bring in the coffeepot.

While sitting over coffee, Wes told them all that had happened, and that they were headed for Durango to see if Lingo needed help.

Elena smiled. "They won't need help."

Emily frowned. "What makes you say that, and why do you say 'they'?"

Elena studied Emily a moment. "A messenger came out from town a few days ago. Quint had sent him. He said that Quint and Lingo had joined up to chase down a couple of stage holdup gunmen." She shook her head. "As for needing help, I can't think of two more dangerous men than my Quint and Lingo Barnes. No, I don't think they'll need help." Then in a quiet voice, said, "But I still worry. Someday, if he keeps on this way, there'll be a sneak who'll take a backshot at him."

Emily looked at Wes. "There it is again. Everyone I have met seems to think Lingo can handle anything, now I find there is another man who people think of in the same way."

Venetia put her cup on the table beside her. "Honey, if I had a month, I couldn't tell you of all the scrapes those two men have been in; some together, and some all by their lonesome." She glanced at Wes, then back to Emily. "And if he wasn't sitting there next to Kelly, I'd do some bragging about that young man who brought you folks here." She stood, poured coffee, then sat.

Emily stared into her coffee cup a moment, then back to Venetia. "I probably don't have the right or the reason to worry that you all do, but every time I hear of Lingo doing anything like that I'm terrified."

A slight smile broke the corners of Venetia's lips. "Do I detect more than friendly caring in your words—and voice?"

"Mama! How could you ask such a question? Look, you've embarrassed the poor girl to death." Elena turned her look on Emily. "You'll have to excuse Mama, she did the same thing to Quint and me." She grinned. "The fact is, if she hadn't hounded my poor man, I don't know if he'd ever have proposed."

Venetia chuckled. "If he hadn't, you would have. In fact, if you'll think back to that day after the Durango gunfight, I would say that you did propose." Her chuckle grew to a full-blown laugh. "And your father almost had apoplexy."

Elena, used to mimicking Quint, said, "An' I reckon I ain't never been sorry fer it one day." She looked at her father. "And I don't believe Papa has either."

Ian, who was known as Lion to his friends, nodded. "If I'd of chose your mate myself, it would of been Quint."

They talked until called to supper by Rosita, the motherly Mexican woman who had helped Venetia raise Elena. They ate, talked another couple of hours, then Venetia showed them the rooms they were to occupy for that night—and maybe the next one.

The next day Lion took Colter and Slagle around the headquarters to meet Wyatt Mann, his foreman, and Art King, Quint's saddle partner, among others, and by the time he'd taken the time he wanted to make sure the menfolk felt at home, it was too late to leave for town.

At supper that night, Elena told them that she, her mother, and father would ride into Durango with them. It was time for a town visit, and maybe some dinner and dancing. Emily had never thought to wonder if Lingo danced, but she had thought about his arms holding her.

She asked Kelly if Barnes finished his job along with Quint, and if they went dancing, did she suppose the big man would dance with her—if he could dance?

Kelly answered with a sly smile, and a knowing look. "Don't know if he can dance them fancy dances y'all do back yonder in Baltimore. Fact is, don't know if he can dance at all. Reckon you jest gonna have to find that out for yourself."

Emily sighed. She would have to get Lingo's attention all by herself. It wasn't fair. Elena had had Venetia's help—but she stood alone. Well, if she had to, she'd resort to the same methods Elena had used with Quint—if he didn't take notice of her, notice that she was a woman, notice that she maybe wasn't pretty, but she wasn't ugly either. According to Wes and Kelly, the only thing Lingo thought highly of was his ranch and cattle. Well, darn it, she'd make like a cow if she had to.

Lingo looked at Quint a moment. "You sayin' you think we oughtta split up?" He shook his head. "Don't think so. We split, he can pick us off one at a time. Together, if he hits one o' us, the other can get him for sure."

Cantrell frowned, swung his saddle onto his horse, and busied himself tightening cinches. They both rode a Texas rig. Then he looked at Lingo and nodded. "Okay, we ride together, but bein' mighty careful."

They rode up the incline, paying more attention to the few trees ahead and the boulders stacked at trail's edge than they did the trail. The next bend went to their left wrapping itself around the mountain, so they couldn't see around it. If it had gone to the right, they, as well as the Easterner would have been in the open.

Cantrell reached over and took Lingo's reins in his hand. "Hold up. We ain't goin' 'round that bend without scoutin' it. He might be settin' there waitin' fer one o' us to show. Fact is, he might think they's only one o' us. I'll take a look."

He slipped off the side of his horse, handed his reins to Lingo, and eased up to a tree to try to see. He couldn't. He looked up the trail for a pile of rocks, a tree, anything that might hide a man. He saw nothing large enough for a man to conceal himself behind, but the trail continued to bend left.

He slid farther to his left and came up against the steep bluff that edged up the mountain. Despite having done this sort of thing maybe a hundred times, his gut tightened, and his shoulder muscles pulled at his neck. He inched forward, and with each step he searched farther around the trail, and with each step he braced for the feel of a slug tearing through him. He grinned to himself. Despite his fear, this was living, this was what man was made for—without it he became just another dumb animal.

Another step and about fifty or so yards ahead a pile of boulders reared up on the outside of the trail. He ducked back, but not before the whir of a bullet zinged by his head.

A second shot chipped rock off the cliff next to his face. He reached behind and waved Lingo up close to the rock wall.

He searched the pile of rocks for any sign, anything to draw a bead on. Nothing.

He pulled his head back far enough to know that no part of him showed to the rifleman up ahead. He looked at Lingo. "We done found our man. Now we gotta see can we take 'im without killin' 'im."

Lingo nodded. "Damned straight. I wouldn't swap even a little bit of seein' you hurt just to keep him alive." He shrugged. "If we have to, we'll drag his rotten carcass back to Durango for Nolan to bury."

Cantrell sneaked a glance around the edge of the cliff, drew another shot, ducked back, then looked at Lingo. "All right, but just so's you know, I'm takin' a danged strong dislike to that man up yonder. Gonna do all I can to see it like you do. I wantta see a bright shiny rope 'round his stinkin' neck."

Barnes grinned, then tugged on Quint's coat. "C'mon, let's squat here a minute an' see if we can't come up with some way to keep us from gettin' our pretty pink bodies ventilated."

Cantrell swept the area with a glance. "Sure would be nice if there wuz somethin' to make a fire of while we wait." He shrugged. "We passed the last tree 'bout a hour ago."

Barnes wagged his head from side to side, slowly. "Sure is terrible how much a friend can make a man feel deprived of the necessities of life." He grinned. "Now we know we can't have any coffee, let's put our heads together an' see can't we figure how to get him."

They finally decided for one of them to lie flat and fire from a prone position, while the other stood and tried to make Bartow expose himself enough for them to draw a bead on him. Cantrell nodded. "Don't seem they's a better way. You do the standin', fire an' pull back behind the cliff.

I figger he'll show enough o' himself to git off a shot right after you fire, an' when he does, I'll see can I hit him from where I'm lyin' on the ground."

"All right. Let's give it a try."

Barnes eased his head around the cliff's edge, then out of the side of his mouth, said, "Okay, get ready. Next time I take a look, I'm gonna fire." He slowly moved his head out to see. The only thing in sight was the smooth wind- and rain-polished surfaces of the pile of boulders uptrail. He raised his Winchester, aimed at a crack between two of the rocks, and pressed the trigger. As soon as he fired, he pulled his head back to safety.

He'd not gotten his head back and jacked another shell into the chamber when Cantrell's and Bartow's rifles fired, sounding almost as one. "Damn! Fired too fast. Now he know's how we figgered to git 'im, he ain't gonna bite on that one agin."

Barnes frowned. "Reckon we gonna just have to wait 'im out. Bet money he never saw the patience two Apaches can have."

They didn't have to test their own, or Bartow's patience. Steel shoes rang against the smooth, rock trail.

Cantrell ran a patch down the barrel of his Winchester, jacked another shell into the chamber, then looked at Barnes. "Maybe we got lucky. Maybe he'll try to plow through the deep snow up toward the crest an' we can take 'im 'fore he freezes to death."

"Maybe it's a trick, maybe he's not ridin' that horse."

Cantrell shook his head. "Don't think so, Lingo. He ain't gonna put hisself up yonder without nothin' to ride."

While Quint talked, Barnes eased himself farther around the cliff's curve. No shot. "Get the horses. I'll search those rocks, then we'll see how far he can get ahead of us before he hits deep snow."

"Why don't I take a little longer, go back down the trail a ways, an' collect some firewood, maybe even rope one o' them logs an' drag it to a good place to camp." He chuckled. "If he's close enough to see the flicker o' our fire, an' cold as he's gotta be, he might even walk in an give 'imself up."

"Don't bet on it. He knows his sorry butt's gonna hang if he's caught."

Cantrell, holding a sober look, said, "A man gits cold enough, seems like a rope would look mighty good." He walked back a few yards, toed the stirrup, led Lingo's horse to him, and reined his horse back down the road.

Lingo, leading his horse, warily approached the pile of boulders. Although he knew, within reason, that Bartow had vacated the spot from which he'd fired on them, his gut still tightened, but not enough to put the taste of brass at the back of his throat like fear usually did.

In the rocks, Barnes searched for cartridge casings, found three, then looked for signs that the Easterner had firewood. He found no tree bark to indicate Bartow had prepared to stay anywhere until he crossed the crest. Lingo smiled to himself. The man just flat out didn't know this country, didn't know how much snow he'd soon face, didn't know the chances he'd take of sliding over the edge into nothingness on the icy surface. And he sure didn't know the toughness of the two men following him. He gave a jerky nod, even though there was no one there to see it. "Yep, we gonna get you, Bartow. I just wish Em could be there to see you hang."

Cantrell rode to the edge of the rocks, dragging a pine sapling about six inches in diameter behind his horse. In his arms, he had a load of branches. He grinned. "We gonna sleep warm tonight. An' we gonna eat hot victuals. Doubt that man's even got any provisions to fix for 'imself."

Lingo looked at the wood, nodded, and looked at Cantrell. "Good work, *amigo*." Then he glanced up the trail. "Figure he's gonna run into snow pretty quick. It'll take him a little while to get it through his thick city skull that he can't get far before he'll kill 'is horse—maybe himself. Then he's gonna have one choice—come back down the mountain an' take his chances against us."

"Figger you're right." Quint smiled, and to Lingo's thinking, that smile was colder than the snow and ice on which they stood.

Cantrell shrugged. "If I wuz gonna have to face two *hombres* like us, don't know but what I'd try to go on up the mountain and chance the snow."

Barnes laughed, and even to his ears it sounded as cold as Cantrell's smile. "Either way, he's gonna die. But we gotta be mighty careful from here on. If he comes back down, he's gonna be crazy with fear. He'll take chances no sane man would think o' takin'."

While they sat drinking their coffee, Lion suggested they take the big, luxurious coach so the ladies could be more comfortable, since it was a two-day trip from the ranch into town.

Elena shook her head. "Papa, it'd take us another day to make the trip that way. We'll go horseback; in the end it'll be easier on us." Abruptly she frowned and looked at her mother, then at Kelly, Maddie, and Emily. "Oh there I go again. I s'pose I'm so anxious to see my big man I didn't think of anyone else. Why don't y'all have your say in this?"

None of them were anxious to spend more time on the road than they had to, so Elena won out, but not without a guilty feeling that she had unduly influenced them.

Lion sent word to Stick McClure, his wrangler, to have their horses ready soon after sunup—they'd each pack their own blanket roll. They each drank another cup of coffee, while Elena told them of the time she, Quint, and some of the crew shared a cabin, due to an early snowstorm, with several men who rode The Outlaw Trail.

She also told them she'd taken them out of town despite

Cantrell's saying they shouldn't go. She and Quint had not been married then, and being the boss's daughter, she won the argument.

After a few more stories, they went to their rooms. All seemed anxious to get on into town.

The two-day trip into town went without undue incident. They rode directly to the hotel, where Lion insisted on setting them up in rooms of his choice and on his account. He kept rooms there year round.

It was well past suppertime, but the dining room was kept open for them. None of the help seemed to mind, which surprised Emily, and she said so to Elena. In the short time they'd known each other, they had become quite close. Elena smiled. "Emily, Papa will leave them each more money than they make in a week." She shook her head. "He wouldn't—for that matter none of us would—keep these people working late like this if we thought for one minute even one of them minded. They need the money, Mama and Papa have the money, and they like to make sure it goes where it'll do some good."

She smiled. "Many of them knew Papa when he didn't have more than the next payday. Then he met Mama, and she wouldn't let him ride on down the trail. She captured him much like I did Quint." She looked Emily straight in the eye. "Emily, that doesn't sound very ladylike, but when you meet your man, you'll know it." She chuckled. "And I'll say it like Quint would, 'Git your rope round 'im, woman, pull it up tight, an don't let 'im go fer nothin'."

Emily thought how like Lingo Quint sounded, not in grammar, but in the way they thought. She put her head close to Elena's. "He sounds an awful lot like my ma—" She cut herself short, then corrected herself. "That sounds like something Lingo would say."

Elena showed a know-it-all smile. "And that sounds like something a woman in love would say." Then despite Emily's deep blush, she added, "If you need any help,

Venetia and I are experts. We'll capture that big man for you. We won't let 'im get away."

Emily's blush, and her being on the verge of calling Lingo "her man" had shown she cared a great deal about him, and now she told herself the truth. She was in love with him. She looked Elena in the eye. "I guess I'm gonna need all the help I can get. He's not said one word to make me think he cares about me."

Before they could say more, Wes finished the last of his coffee, and pushed back from the table. "Gonna go see Marshal Nolan. Any o' y'all wantta come with me? Gotta find out what Cantrell an' Barnes went outta here for, an' who they're chasin'."

Elena and Emily nodded and stood. "We'll go," they said in unison.

On the way out, Wes paid for their supper, despite Elena protesting that Lion would take care of it. He left a sizable tip also.

In Nolan's office, he made sure the women sat in the only two chairs with which his office was furnished. The grizzled old lawman swept them with a glance. "Know what you're here for, an' I'll tell you right now, Cantrell an' Lingo headed outta here for Silverton. They wuz after an Eastern man by the name o' Bartow."

He looked at Emily. "Reckon you're the young lady Lingo told me about. He finally figured it wuz that man Bartow what had you taken off that stagecoach." He ran his hand through his hair. "Don't reckon he's any closer to findin' your pa. Him an' a feller by the name o' Sam Slagle's been tryin' to find 'im."

"Sam and my father are over at the hotel with Lion and Venetia McCord, along with Kelly and a woman by the name of Maddie who took good care of Papa."

Nolan smiled. "That right? Well, when we get more time I wantta hear how y'all come to git together, but for right now, I'm gonna say how happy I am fer you, young'un.

That's had Lingo some worried. Now all we got to do is wait for your men to bring Bartow back down the mountain." He frowned, then nodded. "Yeah, reckon they had to go on toward the pass chasin' him or they'd a been back by now."

Wes slipped his Colt out of its holster, then settled it back carefully, gently. "How long they been gone?"

Nolan shook his head. "No, no, you don't, you young hellion. You ain't goin' up yonder after 'em. They been gone a couple o' days; don't figger you could catch 'em anyway."

Elena hadn't taken her eyes off of Wes since he'd toyed with his handgun. "Wes, don't you think Lingo and Quint can handle it alone, or are you so much like them you can't stand the thought of them getting into some action and leaving you out of it?"

He grimaced. "Well, hell, Miss Elena, 'scuse me fer cussin', but you know danged well they coulda used me up yonder." He grinned. "An' yes'm, reckon I'm sorta put out that they didn't take me with 'em."

Elena chuckled deep in her throat. She looked at Emily. "See the kind of thing you'll have to put up with?"

Wes stared at the two of them. "What you mean?" He pinned Emily with a know-it-all look. "You done admitted to Elena how you feel 'bout Lingo?"

Emily felt her face turn hot. Right here before a total stranger they'd stripped her bare. Didn't these people think anything was private—sacred? "Mr. Wesley Higgins, I don't see that it's any of your business what Elena and I have discussed."

As soon as she blew up at him, she was sorry. "Oh, Wes, I just can't get used to everyone knowing, or guessing my innermost feelings. I'm sorry."

"*De nada*, reckon I should learn to keep my mouth shut." He gave her a shy grin. "Least ways that's what Kelly tells me." He twisted to look at Nolan.

"Well, Marshal, reckon 'tween you an' Emily you done put me in my place. I'll stay here in town another day, then if they ain't showed up, I'm goin' lookin' fer 'em."

Nolan nodded toward the door. "Now why don't y'all go back to the hotel an' get a good night's sleep. If your men show up, I'll send 'em right over so won't any o' you worry."

When they went out the door, Wes said over his shoulder, "Buy you a drink later. I'll be over at Miss Barret's Golden Eagle."

Cantrell glanced around the boulder-strewn enclosure, then looked questioningly at Barnes. "You figger we gonna find a better place to hole-up than this?"

Lingo shook his head. "Just thinkin' 'bout that. We're sittin' here in the middle of the trail; Bartow can't come down without us seein' 'im. The snow's gonna stop 'im from goin' up. I figure we got 'im trapped."

Cantrell nodded. "We'll camp here. Ain't no trees to make a shelter, but these here rocks are gonna be right good to hold the heat around us."

Lingo frowned. "Trail's a mite wide here, but one o' us can watch where it cuts around the rocks while the other one sleeps." He nodded. "Yep, let's make camp."

Cantrell built the fire while Barnes went to a rocky overhang, scraped snow from under it, and put the coffee on to boil.

They whiled away the hours, waiting until time to fix supper. About midafternoon Lingo stood. "Gonna ease up the trail a ways, see if can I catch sight o' Bartow; see how he's makin' out." Cantrell opened his mouth to say something, but Barnes held up his hand. "No, you're not goin'. It's my job to do." He grinned. " 'Sides that, if I can get close enough, I figure to watch 'im suffer a little."

Cantrell squinted against the snow and rock glare, then nodded. "All right, but you be danged careful. That man's gonna be like a curly wolf. He's gonna be mad, an' he's gonna be scared. I figger he's gonna be dangerous as a trapped mountain cat."

Lingo tied the leather thongs together on his sheepskin, picked up his rifle, looked at Cantrell, and said, "Gonna leave my horse here. Figure it'll be easier goin' on foot." He slipped around the rocks.

He'd not gone a quarter of a mile when he came upon the first patches of snow-covered trail. Wind had swept most of the smooth rock bare, but now it showed signs of packing, signs of sticking. It wouldn't be long before it would cover the road, and from that point it would deepen.

He picked each place he'd stop to get a good look up the incline. He slipped from one to another of these spots, and from each he studied everything above him: rocks, shadowed areas, snowdrifts, and wind- and rain-scoured depressions in the cliffside.

He glanced at the sky. The distant, cold sun stood only about an hour and a half from sunset. Lingo wanted to see what he had to see and get back to camp. He wanted to see how Bartow took the raw country he traversed. He had not long to wait.

Another fifteen minutes and he slogged through deepening snow. It pushed up halfway to his boottops, and the surface had a frozen glaze over it that crackled and crunched when his feet broke the surface. He slowed and tried to move each foot slowly, such that the noise it made didn't crackle. He heard Bartow before he saw him.

Barnes moved over, closer to the cliff. Here he had a double advantage. It gave him shelter from being seen, and the snow depth was less.

Holding his shoulder against the cold, rocky surface, he peered around a bend. There, Bartow led his horse, while he pushed his feet through the crust, taking one weary step at a time. He neither looked back—nor ahead. His head bowed such that his chin rested against his chest.

Lingo felt his lips crinkle at the corners. There was one tired bastard, and he hadn't any idea the kind of trouble he was in. The snow cover would only get heavier. If Bartow was in trouble now, wait. He'd soon decide that neither he nor his horse could make it much farther.

Lingo wondered why he kept going, why hadn't he discovered that each step would cost him more of what little energy he had left?

He followed the Easterner for half an hour. He thought to walk up to his back, stick his rifle hard against him, and drag him back down the slope. He mentally shook his head. He didn't want to end the man's misery yet. The fact was, unless Bartow was a bigger fool than he thought, he'd soon get the idea that the summit wasn't even close, and he'd turn back. But once he turned back, he'd know he faced two men who knew how to survive in this country. He'd be even more dangerous.

Barnes turned back toward camp, stopped, and frowned. Suppose he gave Bartow credit for more sense than he really had? Suppose he continued trying to get to the summit? If he did, Lingo had no doubt the man would freeze to death. From what he had seen, the Easterner had neither the clothes nor the equipment to survive on the mountain—and his horse was played out or he'd have been riding him. He thought about that a few moments, shrugged, and thought to hell with him, if he froze to death it might be almost as bad as hanging. He turned his steps toward camp.

In midstride, he stopped, thought to try to slip up on Cantrell. He smiled to himself. He'd show Quint he was as good an Apache as him. Still smiling, he continued toward the fire and a good cup of coffee.

The closer he got, the easier it got, due to the clean-swept trail. Finally, he ghosted up to the huge boulder that guarded the upslope side of their camp. Quiet as a shadow he eased around the big rock—and bumped into the business end of Cantrell's rifle barrel.

Quint choked, swallowed a laugh, and then guffawed. "Thought you knowed better than that. You ain't gonna take me by surprise—not ever, partner."

Chagrined, Lingo grimaced. "Someday, Cantrell, someday." He smiled. "But I gotta say I still have it to do." He shook his head. "You're just mighty good—a better Injun than me."

Cantrell chuckled and shook his head. "Nope, not really. I just knowed when you left here you wuz gonna try somethin' like that." He shrugged. "So I wuz on the lookout. C'mon, coffee's hot, an' you look like a jolt o' that whisky we brung along would set pretty good on your stomach." He swung his arm around Lingo's shoulders. "We'll have a couple cups, then eat. I already got it fixed."

While they drank their coffee, Lingo told Cantrell what he'd seen, and the shape Bartow and his horse were in. "I figure if he's got a gut in his head he'll be comin' back down this mountain 'fore long." He took a sip of coffee. "Tell you how it is though; if he doesn't head back toward us right soon, we gonna have to go up there an' bring his frozen carcass down." He shrugged. "Reckon I've gotten to the point where I don't give a damn what shape he's in when we get 'im back to Durango."

"Yeah, reckon a man can stand jest so much, an' I reckon that cold an' snow up yonder's 'bout as bad as a new rope." Cantrell took a swallow of coffee, then frowned. "Reckon we better keep a right smart lookout tonight. He comes in this camp while we sleep an' you an' me's gonna have a bunch o' trouble."

Lingo nodded. "Way I got it figured."

While Lingo had been gone, Cantrell had not only cooked supper, he'd spread coals, warmed the places he figured they'd sleep, and spread their groundsheets and blankets.

They ate, and Cantrell suggested that they build the fire up bright enough to lure Bartow to it. "He sees the glow of our fire on them big rocks, he'll come to it like a moth to light."

"Good idea. You take the first watch. Wake me in a couple o' hours." With those words, Lingo stacked more wood on the fire and crawled into his blankets.

Cantrell took up his station between two boulders, pulled his collar up around his ears, and hunkered down to wait. He figured if Bartow was going to backtrack, he'd do it early. If he stayed up there much longer he wouldn't be coming down at all—until he and Lingo brought him down. Even now he could feel the temperature dropping.

17

EMILY SWEPT THE group with a questioning look, her eyes finally falling on Sam. He and Lion were the last to finish breakfast. "Sam, what do you know about this man Bartow, who so sadly mistreated Papa?"

He shook his head. "Don't know nothin', Miss Emily. I seen 'im once or twice around Silverton, but that's all I know. I figger Maddie knows more'n anybody."

Emily looked at her father, wanting to ask him if he had known the man from somewhere before, then switched her question to Maddie. "Did you know him before you met him in Taos?"

Maddie shook her head. "Never seen 'im afore that, an' he never said nothin' 'bout where he come from. He seemed like a nice man, an' he treated me nice—at first. That's why I come with him when he said to." She looked at Miles Colter. "Mr. Colter, I didn't know he figured to steal your mine. He just told me that he knew of a big strike outside o' Silverton. Wanted to know if I wanted to share in it." She shook her head. "'Course I didn't have nothin', an' nothin' else to do that amounted to anything, so I went with him. Don't even know how he knew about the vein you done found."

"Papa wrote me about the vein. I never told anyone, but that doesn't really mean much; he might have told numerous people about it." She twisted to look at Colter. "Papa, can you remember anything before Bartow started mistreating you?"

He shook his head. "As soon as I remember anything, anything at all, I'll tell you. Right now I believe it will all come back to me. I seem to see flashes of things past, and I see you in the things, but I can't yet put you an' me together." He smiled, a rather sad smile to Emily's thinking. "Sitting here looking at you, you can't imagine how much I want to reach out and claim you as my daughter." He shook his head. "But I won't do that 'til I remember all there is to know about our life together."

She placed her hand over his. "It's all right, Papa, I have a hunch we don't have long to wait." And then she surprised herself. "When Lingo gets back, he'll figure it out."

Her face heated and she knew it must be the color of a desert sunset. She swung her glance to Elena, then Kelly. They both sat there with smug smiles, but each obviously trying to wipe their smiles off and look innocent. Then she made it worse. "What I meant was that he always seems to know exactly what to do, and I trust him to do whatever is called for."

Elena chuckled. "I don't believe that for one minute."

Wes sat there looking as though he had no idea what was going on. Venetia had the same kind of smile that Kelly and Elena had.

Lion had experienced this sort of thing with Venetia, and had watched Quint suffer through what Elena and Venetia put *him* through when he didn't know he'd already taken the bait, hook, line, and sinker. "C'mon, y'all leave that poor little girl alone." And then not leaving well enough alone, put his foot right in the middle of a fresh cowpaddy. "Jest 'cause y'all done captured your men you don't have to give that there poor little thing such a terrible time jest 'cause she's still gotta make her man say them nice words all women like to hear."

Emily's face went from hot to cold, to wet with sweat, a cold sweat. She felt the color leave her face. Then in the fashion her father had taught her, she threw her head back and stared at each one of them. Stared until each in turn dropped their eyes from hers. Then slowly, softly, her voice cold as winter winds, she said, "What you have done to me is not only crude, but cruel. I haven't yet had time to evaluate my feelings for Mr. Barnes, but you seem to take great joy in dragging my emotions out and airing them to all within range." She sucked in a tremulous breath, tried to push the anger and embarrassment to the back of her mind. It didn't work. "But I'll tell you this, if I do have feelings for Mr. Barnes, and I do think I have very strong feelings for him, it's nobody's damned business but my own."

She sat back and picked up her coffee cup in hands that trembled. Every woman at the table stood, went to her chair, and apologized.

She was quick to anger, but also quick to forgive. She felt the anger drain from her, and then Lion shook his great white-haired head.

"Ma'am, reckon I done stepped right in the middle o' your heart. Didn't mean to. Reckon I'm just the great big bumbling thing Venetia says I have a talent for. I'm mighty sorry, little one."

By now, Emily felt that she owed them an apology. She felt terrible. She had learned one thing since arriving in the West, and that was if people liked you, they felt free to say what was on their minds. Her temper had always gotten her into trouble, and today it had definitely gotten the better of her. She muddled those thoughts around, and then had a thought that made her feel even worse: These people apparently liked her, and she'd repaid them with a tongue as poisonous as a rattler.

She swung her gaze to them. Tears welled and then spilled down her cheeks. She shook her head. "Oh, I'm so terribly sorry. I've been so mixed up lately. I know it's no excuse, but I've worried about Papa, and I believe I've also been very worried about Lingo, and I took it all out on you when the only thing you tried to do was make me feel better." She dabbed at her eyes, then Kelly and Elena had their arms around her shoulders and all seemed right with the world. It would have been perfect if Lingo were there.

Wes told them he had run out his string. He'd figured to give Lingo and Cantrell another day to get back, and that day had passed. Now it was time he went to see about them. He'd leave in the morning.

Cantrell shivered. He tried to imagine how cold Bartow must be and couldn't. Abruptly his senses sharpened. A soft sound came from only a few feet outside the pile of boulders—the sound of grit, or sand under the sole of a shoe. He brought his rifle up, then lowered it and slipped his .44 from its holster. Lingo had told him about Bartow carrying a sleeve gun. He didn't figure to let this man turn to face him.

He pressed flat against the boulder and waited. There were other sounds: sounds of cloth brushing rock, heavy breathing, sniffling, and more of the grit underfoot. Cantrell smiled into the cold night. The Easterner wouldn't have lasted a week in Comanche country. Then, almost brushing his side, Bartow appeared in the circle of firelight. He carried a rifle. Quint breathed a sigh of relief. Carrying a rifle would render Bartow's sleeve gun useless—he thought.

Then Bartow put the lie to his thought. He gripped the rifle with his left hand and swung his right hand straight out; in it, faster than Cantrell would have believed possible, appeared a snub-nosed little pepperbox. Then even faster, he fired at the curled-up form of Lingo.

Blood rushed to Cantrell's head. Simultaneously he swung his rifle barrel to Bartow's arm. A sharp snap sounded with the contact of his rifle against the arm in which the Easterner held the pepperbox.

Now Bartow's hand no longer held the pepperbox, his arm dangled at right angles halfway between his wrist and elbow—it was broken in half.

He swung toward Cantrell, holding his rifle pistol fashion. He brought it to firing position. Quint swiped the barrel to the side. It spewed flame. A searing pain along his ribs on the right side caused Cantrell to flinch and dodge sharply to the left. At the same time, he grabbed the barrel of Bartow's rifle and jerked it down and to the side.

Bartow, obviously terrified, determined to hang on to his only means of defense, followed the rifle down. He fell to his knees.

Cantrell ignored the Winchester he held in his left hand, holstered his .44 in a lightning quick motion, and followed through with a right to the side of Bartow's head. The Easterner went to the ground—out cold. It wasn't until then that Quint dared look to see if Lingo had taken lead.

Barnes sat, his blankets pushed down to his sock feet, cutting his longjohns away from his thigh—and cursing a blue streak.

Quint grabbed Bartow by the back of his collar, and at the same time sniffed the acrid smell of gunpowder from his nostrils, then dragged the Easterner to the side of Barnes's blanket. "He hit you in the leg?

"Why, hell yes, he hit me. Why you think I'm cuttin' these perfectly good longjohns to rags?"

"Wait'll I git this slime tied good an' tight; then I'll see can I hep you."

"You better take that sleeve gun away from him while you're at it. He might be able to get it in his left hand."

"Figgered to do that."

By the time Cantrell had Bartow tied, Lingo had his thigh bared. It bled in a steady flow. "Lie back now an' I'll take a look."

Barnes grimaced, obviously hurting, but also obviously not wanting Cantrell to see him showing how badly. He eased himself to his back. Quint looked to see where Bartow had been standing when he fired, then gauged where the bullet would have come out. It should have travelled through the top of Barnes's thigh.

He felt around to the other side. No hole. Dammit! He'd have to cut the bullet out; but thank God it hadn't hit an artery or it would have been pumping Lingo's blood out faster than he could staunch its flow.

"You gotta cut the bullet out?"

Cantrell glanced at Lingo's face. "Either that or take you in to Durango an' let the sawbones do it. They ain't got a doctor in Silverton to my knowledge."

"Can you feel where the bullet almost went through?"

Quint shook his head. "Nope, an' I ain't got the right kind o' things to dig down in the hole to find it." He shook his head. "Wuz I you, reckon I'd let me try to git you back to town."

Bartow groaned. Cantrell glanced at him, then again swung his fist against the side of the Easterner's head. He'd be out for some time now.

Cantrell again looked at Lingo. "You reckon you can stand fer me to take you back down the mountain?"

Lingo gave him a weak smile. "Don't reckon I got much choice. I sure as hell don't cotton to you pushin' that bowie knife around in that hole."

"All right. I'll bandage it best I can, stop the bleedin', an' set out."

"You figure to go down this mountain at night?"

"Damned straight I do. Don't figger to let that chunk o' lead git a headstart on poisonin' you."

"Why didn't you kill that rotten bastard?"

"Reckon I done got to wantin' to see 'im stretch a new rope much as you have." Cantrell looked toward the fire, now only a few flickering flames above the glowing bed of coals. "Reckon you'd like a stiff jolt o' whisky in a cup o' coffee 'fore we leave?"

Lingo chuckled. " 'Bout ready to see if you'd fix a pot. Know you're gonna pour a bunch o' that whisky in that hole in my leg; be danged sure you save some for our coffee."

Cantrell let a smile break the corners of his mouth. "Figgered to do just that." He went to his blankets, and using his bowie knife slit strips from one of them, then went to his saddlebags, took a full bottle of whisky from them, poured some into the raw hole in Lingo's thigh, bound his leg tight, watched the bandage a few moments to see if it bled through, then put on the coffee. Lingo had taken the burn of raw whisky in the hole in his leg better than Cantrell thought he himself could have.

While he was busy, he became aware of Lingo watching him. He twisted to look at him. "Whatcha lookin' at me for?"

Lingo flashed him a pain-filled grin. "Just wonderin' how long it was gonna take you before you looked at your own hide. Dang you, Cantrell, why didn't you take care o' yourself 'fore you messed with the coffee?"

Bartow again groaned. Cantrell looked over and found the Easterner staring at him. "What were you two chasing me for? I never did anything to you."

"Weeel, let's just say, we don't like stagecoach robbers; an' even more, we just flat out hate those who figger to mistreat our womenfolk." While he talked, Cantrell poured Lingo a half cup of coffee and filled the rest with whisky. Then he twisted to look at Bartow again. "Figger I'm gonna get a right good feelin' when I see you swingin' at the end o' a rope." He poured himself a cup of coffee and spiked it as strong as he had Lingo's.

"I've not harmed any women, nor have I robbed any stagecoaches."

Cantrell grunted. "Save your breath, you rotten bastard. You ain't gonna have a chance to breathe much longer."

It wasn't until then that Quint answered Lingo. "Hell, Barnes, I knowed when his bullet sliced by me it warn't bad. Figger to git you on down the mountain soon's I can."

Cantrell and Lingo drank the coffeepot dry, along with a goodly part of the whisky; then Quint went up the trail and collected Bartow's horse. Then he wrapped up their bedrolls and packed them on their horses.

Lingo weighed over two hundred pounds, but Cantrell lifted him to the saddle as though he was a young child. When they headed down the mountain, it was still short of midnight.

Riding slowly so as not to give Lingo more pain than he had to, Quint looked across his shoulder at his friend. "Gonna ride 'til you figger you done had all you can take; then we'll rest awhile, then go on. Want to git you to that doc soon's I can."

"You're callin' the shots, *amigo*. I'll let you know when I figure I need to stop."

Bartow, slung across his saddle like a gunnysack full of meal, groaned. Cantrell grinned at Lingo.

Barnes never asked to stop, but Quint stopped anyway, every two hours. When day broke, cold and gray, Cantrell cast a worried look at Lingo, whose entire expression bespoke of having taken about all he could take. He sagged in the saddle, his face had a gray cast to it, and his chin rested on his chest. "You gonna be able to make it, *mi amigo*?"

Without raising his chin from his chest, Lingo looked at Cantrell and in a voice little above a whisper said, "Gonna make it."

They rode all that day, and on into the night, stopping only for Cantrell to fix a meal and coffee. When they got to Silverton, the saloon still showed lantern light. Quint went in, bought another two bottles of whisky, asked if there was a doctor in the town, found there wasn't, and they rode on. Soon after sunup the next morning, a rider came into view from around a bend in the trail. Cantrell, after studying the approaching man for a few moments, figured out that the rider was Wes Higgins.

The closer they got, the faster Higgins rode. Finally, his horse in a dead-out run, he pulled to a stop at Lingo's side. "Where'd he take the bullet, Cantrell?"

"In his laig, 'bout halfway 'tween his knee an' crotch. Didn't go all the way through. He didn't want me diggin' for the slug with my knife, so I'm tryin' to git 'im to the sawbones in Durango."

Wes reined his horse around and rode as close to Barnes as he could without bumping him. "How you feelin', Lingo? You ain't lookin' so good; you want us to stop awhile?"

Barnes shook his head slightly. "Git to the doc. Figure I can take it that long." He twisted his head to the side, only a bit. "Tell Cantrell to give you that bottle, then hold it for me to take a good slug o' it."

By the time they rode into the edge of Durango, Lingo was drunk enough he didn't seem to feel pain—any pain. Wes had fed him the raw whisky every time he looked awake enough to swallow.

Colter sat on the hotel's veranda. He had sat there every daylight hour since Wes had left to go find Lingo. His memory flashed more frequently now. He hadn't said anything to Emily, but he remembered scenes from when she was a small child, scenes from when his wife had run off with the salesman who travelled about the country.

His first wife, Emily's mother, had died when Emily was only two years of age. Then he had married again. That was not a time he wished to remember. Now he studied every person who rode into sight along the dusty street. He hoped they caught Bartow, hoped they didn't kill him. He wanted to see him squirm.

For some reason he knew, without doubt, that Bartow was not only lacking in humanity, but also had no guts when it came to facing adversity. He recognized Wes when he came around the bend in the trail with three men, one of them hurt, and maybe one of them dead in that he lay across the saddle, tied to his horse.

In front of Marshal Nolan's office, Wes peeled off, leading the horse with the man who lay across the saddle. Colter stood and headed toward the four men. When he came abreast Cantrell and Lingo, and not having met either of them, he saw that one of them was hurting badly, and had a blood-soaked bandage on his leg. He pointed toward the hotel. "Just saw the doctor go in the dining room there at the hotel. I'm Miles Colter, Emily's father. I'll see you soon's I see what Wes does with that trash you folks brought to town with you." He headed on to Nolan's office.

While he walked, scenes flicked through his mind faster than he could process them—and Bartow showed in many of them. He stopped, and standing in the middle of the road let his brain run any way it might. Then the scenes slowed and things began to fall into place: Baltimore, the train and wagon trip out here, his mine, and then he knew how Bartow knew about the vein he'd found in his diggings.

Colter now knew it all. Other than a sharp pain in the top of his head, then having it ease off to a dull ache, he abruptly felt good. He stepped toward the marshal's office.

He pushed through the door in time to see Nolan turn the key in the barred door to the front cell and close the door behind him. He headed back into his office. "Got the man what done all them bad things to you, Mr. Colter." Nolan went to the stove, poured a cup of coffee, and held it toward Miles. "Didn't say it like it happened. I didn't get 'im, Cantrell an' Lingo got 'im."

Wes cut in. "Noticed he had a broken arm, broke slam in two for that matter. You want the doc to fix it?"

Before the marshal could answer, Colter said, "No. Let 'im hurt. From the look on one of those riders who brought him in, I'd say he was hurting badly—and the things Bartow, or whatever name he's using, did to me makes me more determined to let 'im hurt."

Wes grinned. "Damn, Mr. Colter, you gonna fit right in out here." His face lost the grin. He turned to Nolan. "First off, the doc's gonna be right busy fixin' Lingo; an' second, I'm with Mr. Colter. Let the bastard hurt all the way 'til they string 'im up."

Nolan nodded, then looked at Colter. "Finish your coffee. Reckon we better go see how Lingo's gittin' along."

Miles Colter didn't let on that his memory had come back; there were things he wanted to tell Emily first, and to get straight in his own mind. They headed for the hotel.

At the desk, they found what room Cantrell had put Lingo in, and the three men climbed the stairs to the second floor and saw Emily, Kelly, Maddie, and Sam standing in the hall outside the room Lingo was in. Wes was the first to speak. "How's he doin'?"

Emily, her face ashen, shook her head. "Don't know, Wes. The doctor wouldn't let us stay in there, said it wouldn't be decent for a woman to see what he had to do, or how he had to undress Lingo to get to his wound." She shuffled her feet a moment, then looked Wes and her father in the eye. "Don't care how decent it is or isn't, I'm going in there if he doesn't hurry up. That's my man in there, an' he's hurting. He needs me with 'im." She shrugged after making that admission. "Besides, he let Quint stay in there with him."

Wes went to her and put his arm around her shoulders. "Honey, gotta tell you, 'sides me, Cantrell's Lingo's best friend, an' 'sides that he's probably fixed 'bout as many gunshot wounds as the doc has." He patted her shoulder.

"Let the doc do 'is work. Quint stayed 'cause he wouldn't of left until he figgered Lingo wuz gonna be all right. He'll be out soon, then you can go in."

He glanced at Kelly. "Where's Lion, Venetia, an' Elena?"

"Venetia an' Elena were shoppin' when all this happened, an' Lion's over at The Golden Eagle at Miss Faye's. I figgered it wasn't any reason to bother 'em 'til we knew how Lingo was doin'."

"Well dadgum it, woman, don't you think Elena's gonna wantta know Quint's back, an' ain't hurt none?"

Kelly gasped. "Oh dear, I hadn't thought 'bout that. All this plumb wiped it outta my mind. I'll go find 'em."

Before she could get to the head of the stairs, the doctor came out, drying his hands on a piece of bedsheet. He smiled tiredly. "He's going to be all right. Got the bullet out, put some salve in the hole, cut into his leg from the other side to keep from having to probe so deep, and found that chunk o' lead only two inches or so from goin' all the way through." He nodded. "He's gonna be as good as new in a few days. Right now he's asleep." He looked at Wes. "Or passed out from all that whisky you fed 'im after you met them. Let 'im sleep."

Emily swept them with a look. "He can sleep. You all can go eat, or whatever you want to do, but I'm goin' in there and sit by his side. He's not going to waken to an empty room. I'll send Cantrell to a room for some sleep. He looked about as worn out as did Lingo when he carried him to that room." She looked at Kelly. "Go find Elena, she's gonna want to know how her man is."

Wes grinned. "Don't know as how Lingo's gonna be safe in there with you all alone. Heck, weak as he is, you might talk 'im into most anything."

Emily gave him a soft punch on his shoulder. "Wes Higgins, there's no way you're gonna get my goat this time." She smiled. "Besides, you just might be right. If I can't get the right words out of him, I might take advantage of his weakened condition—make 'im say what I want to hear."

She turned the doorknob and went into the room. She shooed Cantrell out. Told him to get some sleep, and that she'd meet him, along with the rest of them, in the hotel dining room for breakfast the next morning.

As soon as Emily disappeared into Lingo's room, Nolan announced that he would be back to see about his friend, but for the moment he would look for the judge, try to get Bartow's trial set for the next morning so he could get him hanged by sundown. He looked at Colter. "You gonna testify agin' 'im?"

Colter frowned, studied his boot toe making circles on the floor, then straightened his shoulders and looked at the marshal. "Tell you for a fact, Marshal, I got a reason, a good reason to not want to see 'im hang." He nodded. "But yeah, I'll testify. The world will be better when his kind are all six foot under."

Nolan shot him a grim smile and left.

Knowing that Lingo and Cantrell were both going to be all right after a decent night's sleep, they all went to their rooms to get ready for supper. About a half an hour later, Kelly showed up with Venetia and Elena in tow. They stopped, looked toward Lingo's room, and seeing the hallway empty, Elena asked what room Quint was in. When Kelly pointed to a room across the hall; she said, "Know he's tired, probably asleep, but I'm going in there. I won't waken 'im, but I'm gonna curl up beside him and just know he's all right." She looked at her mother with a mischievous smile. "See you at breakfast in the morning."

Venetia shot her a smile right back. "I'm gonna get Lion out of that saloon, curl up beside *him*—and see you in the morning. Don't know how 'all right' *he'll* be, but I'm gonna be fine." They all chuckled. Poor Lion, but he'd probably show up with a smile, too.

• • •

It was close to midnight when Emily—after feeling Lingo's forehead to check for fever and seeing him still sleeping soundly—went downstairs to find a cup of coffee. She met her father in the lobby. He, too, had been sleepless, so had come downstairs to read *The Durango Herald*. They sat and talked a while, then Emily went back to sit beside Lingo's bed. Colter had still said nothing about regaining his memory.

About four in the morning, Lingo stirred, rolled to his side, and opened his eyes. He groaned. Emily stood and went to him, felt his brow, and sighed. His forehead felt cool and free of fever. "Does it hurt so badly, Lingo?"

He shook his head and winced. "Not the hole in my leg—it's my head. Feels like a double-barreled shotgun went off in it. Wes musta poured a whole bottle o' that crack-skull whisky down me."

Emily wet the only towel in the room from the water pitcher, and placed it on Lingo's brow. "If he hadn't poured that whisky down you, you might have died from pain and shock. Don't hold it against him."

Lingo smiled through the pain of his headache. "Little girl, you should know by now I won't ever hold it against anybody who gives me a drink, an' I'll guaran-damn-tee you I wouldn't hold it against Wes." He closed his eyes a moment, then looked at her. "What time is it?"

"About four o'clock."

"You been sittin' there all night?"

Emily nodded. "Since the doctor came out and said you were going to be all right."

Lingo rolled to his back. "You go to your room and get some sleep." She opened her mouth as though to protest. "Not gonna hear any ifs, an's, or buts 'bout it. After you get some sleep, come back. I got somethin' important to ask you." His face reddened. "What I mean is, I got somethin' that's important to me to say to you. Don't know how you gonna feel 'bout it."

She stared at him a moment. Her heart had quickened with hope. She pushed her greatest desire to the bottom of her emotions. She frowned. "Are you sure you'll be all right? You might need a drink of water, or—or anything, and there won't be anyone to get it for you."

He chuckled. "If that happens, I'll get up and get it for myself." He pinned her with a look. "Em, I been shot before, might even get shot again sometime. This bullet only gonna keep me down 'til breakfast time, then I'm gettin' up, goin' down to the dinin' room, get me 'bout half-dozen eggs, steak, an' potatoes, eat every bite, then drink 'bout a pot o' coffee."

He nodded with a jerky motion, winced, probably from his headache, then said, "If I know the marshal, he'll have already found the judge, and set up the trial for Bartow in the mornin', an' the hangin' for later in the day. I ain't gonna miss either one of 'em."

Emily stared at him a moment, realized it would do no good to argue with him, shook her head, and said, "Lingo Barnes, you're a stubborn, hard-headed man, but do it your way. I'll see you at breakfast." The sound she heard when she went out of the room was a chuckle deep in his chest.

Lingo turned on his side and soon went to sleep. When he wakened, the curtain in his room showed light from outside. He'd slept longer than planned. He was hungry, and intended to do exactly as he'd told Emily he'd do the night before.

Gingerly, he held his leg in both hands and moved it over the bedside. When he lowered his foot to the floor, and the muscles stretched, he thought he'd get sick to his stomach from pain. He choked back a moan, and lowered his other leg. His clothes were stacked neatly on a chair, the same chair on which Em had sat the night before. He knew then that she'd come back in to check on him, and at the same time placed his clothes where he could reach them. He dressed, and favoring his leg with every step managed to get down the stairs. He had to stop about every other step to swallow the pain, and ready himself for the next step. He made it.

In the dining room, the only one he saw of his party was Wes. Nolan sat there with him. Each of them had only a few bites left on their plates. Wes rushed over to help him to the table. Barnes waved him away. "Make it on my own, sit, finish eatin'."

When seated, Lingo looked at the marshal. "You find the judge?" At Nolan's nod, he smiled. "What time's the trial?"

"Judge said as how he'd be there 'bout ten o'clock. Didn't figger it'd take long to reach a verdict. He figgered we'd be outta Miss Faye's saloon in no more'n an hour; she made The Golden Eagle available to us for whatever time it took."

Lingo nodded. "Good. I'll be there. I can testify he tried to rob the stage, an' 'tween Colter, me, an' Maddie, we can put him as torturin' Miles, an' runnin' the gang that took Emily off that stage." He frowned. "Too, reckon if all that isn't enough, we can stick 'im with murderin' that other Easterner."

Nolan glanced toward Lingo's leg. "Me an' Wes'll hep you over to The Eagle."

"No, you won't. I'll get there by myself. Now y'all get on outta here an' do whatever it is you gotta do." He looked at his watch. "Still two hours 'til the trial. I'll eat and be on over. Don't know if the womenfolk'll want to be there, or not."

Wes grinned. "You wouldn't be able to keep 'em away with a team o' mules." He nodded. "They'll be there."

When Nolan and Wes left, Lingo ordered, and while waiting, wondered about Emily. Did she care about him, love him? He thought back over the time they'd spent together. Was that enough time to fall in love? He shrugged mentally. It had been enough for him. Then he thought about the feelings, the unsaid things, the touch of their hands, little things, but enough to convince him that there was more there than just friendship.

He decided that after the trial, he'd talk her into taking a walk down by the Animas River. Then, if he could get up the nerve, he'd tell her he loved her, and ask her to marry him. If he didn't tell her, ask her, he'd never know.

His order came, and before he could begin eating, Emily came into the room. She looked tired—like she'd not slept much, and he knew taking care of him had been the reason.

He asked the waitress to keep his food warm while they fixed Emily's breakfast. When their food came, they ate, lingered over their coffee until he looked at his watch and said it was time for him to get over to The Eagle. He looked at Em. "You goin'?"

She nodded. "After what that man did to my father, and knowing what he told those men to do to me—you bet I'll be there." She stood, and rushed around the table to help Lingo stand.

"Reckon I'll handle this by myself, little girl." He grinned. " 'Sides, if I stumbled, or started to fall, I figure I'd crush you."

On the way to The Eagle, Emily did not hold on to Lingo's arm, but he noticed she stayed mighty close in case he stumbled. When they went in, she sniffed, and looked at him. "How in the world do you men stand the smell of stale whisky and beer in these places?"

He grinned. "We sorta look forward to it." His grin widened. "Besides that, this saloon smells right nice. You shoulda been in some o' the ones I been in. Miss Faye keeps this'n right clean." He looked toward the bar. A few tables in the front row were empty, apparently saved for those involved in the trial. Lingo led her toward one of those tables.

Not long after they were seated, the McCords, Cantrell, and Elena, Wes, Kelly, Sam Slagle, Maddie, and Miles

Colter took seats at tables in the front row. They all took up two tables.

Then, Marshal Nolan brought Bartow in. Emily gasped. Lingo snapped his head to the side to look at her. Her face, ashen, had paled to the color of fresh fallen snow. Lingo feared she would pass out and wondered why she stared at Bartow so intently. He put his hand over hers. It felt cold, as though she'd been on the mountain with him, and had not thawed from it. Her reaction caused a crease to form between his eyebrows. As far as he could figure, she'd never seen the man before—or had she?

18

BARTOW SAT STONY-FACED, and holding his broken right arm with his left and glanced at each front table. His eyes swept past Emily, came back, and stared at her with the deepest look of hatred Lingo thought he'd ever seen. Then his look went to Colter, and his eyes seemed to spit venom, worse than a rattlesnake would eject. Then he turned his eyes toward the wall at the side of the saloon.

The judge, standing behind the bar, rapped the shiny surface with the butt of his six-gun, called for quiet, announced that no whisky would be sold until after the trial, and said the attendees could light up, smoke their pipes, cigars, or the new-fangled roll-your-own cigarettes.

Then he selected twelve men from the audience after determining they didn't know the defendant. He said in that this was an open-and-shut case they didn't need any lawyers to slow the decision down. He'd call the witnesses and turn it over to the jury.

Lingo was the first to testify. He told the court of the stage holdup in which Emily had been taken captive, and his part in freeing her. He told about Bull Mayben and how he figured he'd been killed, then he told about finding Shorty Gates in Bartow's cabin dead, and that he and Mayben had been saddle partners. He looked from the jury to Emily Lou. If anything, her face had paled even more. He marked it as remembering all that had happened to her, and the pain her father had suffered at the hands of Bartow.

He looked back at the jury. "I'm tellin' y'all 'bout the takin' of Miss Colter off that stage because by the time Mr. Colter, Miss Brice, an' Mr. Slagle have their say, you'll see that the prisoner was the boss o' the gang of which Mayben an' Gates were members. The same gang that snatched her off that stagecoach. Tell you also, that Bartow there was the man who tried to hold up the stage for the money chest. I broke up his game that time, too." He looked around the saloon, then to the judge. "Reckon that's all I got to say." He limped back and sat beside Emily.

Maddie was next, and stated the facts as she knew them, and that she had actually witnessed Bartow sticking fire to Colter's feet, body, and hands. Then Sam told of his and Maddie's part in freeing Colter.

After Sam testified, Lingo stood, was recognized by the judge, and told the court that in his opinion Emily Lou Colter should not be called on to testify in that she'd been through enough already. The judge agreed, but stated that if the jury needed more information to hang Bartow, he might call her later.

The judge then called Miles Colter. After being sworn in, Colter glanced about the room, then centered his eyes on Bartow, who sat, now obviously in pain, his right arm dangling. "There are a few things you need to know before I get into what that man has done. Up until yesterday I had shut out the past." He shrugged. "I suppose it was from the pain of what he did to me, but more so because of the pain of knowing the boy I raised could do such a thing. I remember everything now."

He went on to describe the things Bartow had done, all in the interest of greed. Bartow wanted his mine along with the rich vein he'd uncovered.

As soon as Miles said he'd raised Bartow, Lingo heard nothing more—his world fell apart. He'd been steeling himself to tell Emily he loved her, wanted to marry her, but now he was responsible for getting her brother hanged. Now he understood why she had paled after seeing Bartow for the first time.

He'd brought Bartow or, as Colter had identified him, "Rush," Emily's brother, in to be hanged. He'd not only tied him into kidnapping, but also robbery—two robberies—then he'd chased him down.

His shoulders slumped. A man couldn't marry a woman whose brother he'd killed, for kill him he had, as surely as if he himself put the rope around his neck and kicked the horse from under him. Regardless how much they loved each other, the fact that he was the one who brought him in to the law would always stand between them.

He couldn't look at the woman he loved. He dreaded seeing the accusing look he knew she must be sending his way. He fumbled for his pipe, not aware that he did so. He packed it, lit it, pulled the aroma into his lungs, and didn't taste the smell that usually brought him so much comfort. He sat in a daze.

Finally, he became aware that all had testified when Bartow stood and asked the judge if he was going to be permitted to have his say.

"Go ahead, but make it short."

Bartow cast a steady gaze on the jury. "Back East this so-called court would be called a lynch setup. I've had no lawyer, no witnesses called in my defense, and all you have is the words of a saloon woman, a broken-down old man, an ignorant cowboy, and a miner who probably never saw the inside of a schoolhouse. And the old man, by his own admission, couldn't remember anything before a few days ago. How do you know that he remembers anything now? Maybe the rest of that ragtag bunch coached him into saying what he's said. This trial is a farce."

The judge flashed his contempt at Bartow—or Rush, as Colter had named him. He shook his head. "If you have witnesses for your defense, name them and I'll call them." He waited a moment, then said, "All right, I take it you have none." Then the judge addressed the court—and Bartow. "There have been times when I felt bad about sentencing a man to hang—but this is not one of them. I sentence you to hang from the loading arm down at the livery stable at sundown today." He twisted to look at Marshal Nolan. "Take care of it, Marshal." He rapped his six-gun on the bar. "Court's adjourned; bar's open."

Lingo sat there until most had either bellied up to the bar or left. Someone put a drink in front of him, he downed it and didn't taste or feel the raw alcohol go down his throat. He looked to the chair in which Emily had sat. It stood empty.

His pipe had gone out. He again put fire to it, straightened his shoulders, and stood. Emily had every reason to not marry him, every reason to hate him for killing her brother. He'd never dodged facing whatever he must, especially a situation for which he was at fault. He'd find her, and let her accusing looks and words singe him.

He looked at his watch, a heavy, silver railroad watch; it was a little after twelve o'clock. Time to eat. He wasn't hungry, but the dining room was where he'd probably find Emily—if *she* felt like eating.

Before he got to the hotel, he saw her standing on the veranda looking toward him. When he walked up the steps, she never took her eyes off him. He wanted to shrink down in his sheepskin and disappear. He looked her in the eye. "Reckon you hate me; you got every reason to do so. Can't say I'm sorry. Your brother did what he did, an' the judge—all of us did what shoulda been done long ago."

Still without taking her eyes off of him, her face a frozen mask, she said only, "Let's take a walk."

Limping badly, Lingo led her, wending his way toward the river. When standing at its edge, she turned to face him. "Why are you so distant, Lingo? You haven't looked at me, or said anything to me for hours." She blinked, apparently trying to rid her eyes of the moisture that had welled in them.

A huge lump swelled in his throat, then trying to talk past it, his voice little more than a whisper, he put his hands on her shoulders. "Got somethin' to say, an' I figure now is the best time to say it. Even if I'd known, Bartow—or Rush—was your brother, reckon I'd have had to do what I did. Know bein' your brother you can probably excuse him for anything." He shrugged. "But I can't, an' don't think your own pa can." He squeezed her shoulders and stepped back from her. "So there it is, Emily. Like I said, can't blame you for hating me."

"Lingo, you said you had something to say to me and to ask me, when we talked last night. What was it?"

He shook his head. "Lot o' water's gone under the bridge since then, little one. Can't do what I figured on doin', that is, I figured on doin' it 'til I learned Bartow's your brother."

"Lingo, I want you to tell me what you were going to say, then I'll tell you a few things I know you don't know. All right?"

He stared at her a moment, and nodded, his head seeming to be on a tightly wound spring. "All right. First off, reckon I was gonna tell you we needed to go to a lawyer an' get Wes an' Sam made our official partners, split evenly three ways; Sam, Wes an' Kelly, an' you an' me." His face feeling like some of this mountain granite, he forgot his manners, pulled out his pipe, packed, and lit it. He didn't ask her if she would approve of his smoking.

"You notice when I named the partners, you were one of

'em? Well, that's the way I been figurin' things since soon after I met you. Soon's I saw you lyin' there by the bandit's fire, I fell in love with you. Been lovin' you ever since, only now more'n ever." His shoulders slumped. "An' now it's too late. A woman can't marry a man who caused the death o' her brother. We'd be shoved apart by my doin' that for the rest o' time." He took his pipe from his mouth and nodded. "That's what I was gonna say to you. I was gonna say, 'Em, I love you. I'm askin' you to say you'll marry me.' " He shook his head. "Now it's too late."

She stood there, no expression, her face frozen. "Lingo Barnes, I told you there were a few things you didn't know. Now I'm goin' to tell you what they are. When Mama brought me into this world, her labor was so hard it weakened her dreadfully. She lived only a few years after she gave me life.

"Papa was lonely. He married a woman who brought with her a son. She ran off with a salesman who travelled around the country. She left her boy for Papa to raise. He did the best by the boy that he could. Treated him like he was his blood son—but the boy was never any good. He was in one scrape with the law after another. Papa spent most of the few dollars he had saved keeping Rush out of jail. Papa owned a ready-to-wear apparel store back then, and after borrowing on it to keep Rush out of prison, he lost the store. That's why he came West, hoping to find a better life for us.

"Rush apparently read the letter Papa wrote to me, the one telling me where he was, and that he'd made a big strike. He left, telling me he was going to find Papa. Once out here, he probably found out I was coming out and planned then to find the location of the rich vein Papa found, have me killed, kill Papa." She shrugged. "Then he'd have it all."

She stepped back, then obviously still trying to hold back her emotions, but failing to hold back tears, looked at him straight on. "Lingo Barnes, we have a lot of work to do. We have to build Wes and Kelly a cabin, go see that lawyer about making you all partners, an' get everything arranged for Kelly and Wes to get married.

"Now, big man, I want you to say those words to me. You do, and I'm saying 'yes' right now. Then we need to go see that lawyer along with our partners; then we gotta find us a preacher—and arrange for a double wedding."

Her last words came out against his lips. He squeezed her so tightly she couldn't breathe, but to keep the heavenly feeling she experienced, she would have gladly quit breathing.